Praise for *New York Times* bestselling author
NEVADA BARR

THE ROPE

"Terrifying . . . Dark and visceral, the novel is sure to appeal to Barr's legion of fans, especially those who have been clamoring for the author to light the shadows of Anna's past . . . A crisply written and revelatory entry in the Pigeon series." —*Booklist*

"Barr's exciting seventeenth Anna Pigeon thriller takes readers where they've wanted to go for years—to Anna's beginnings as a park ranger. . . . Misdirection and a rising body count ratchet up the tension." —*Publishers Weekly*

"Barr's luxuriant depictions of desert landscapes with its colors and hues and details about Lake Powell's tourist population are interwoven into the narrative as an indispensable element of her popular series. Anna emerges from this canyon escapade as a strong, determined woman . . . Verdict: another awesome winner for Barr." —*Library Journal*

BURN

"This uncharacteristically urban novel may not present Anna with any endangered species to protect or environmental threats to ward off, but it does give her a chance to prove that her outdoor skills are adaptable to city streets. The harrowing plot . . . provides Barr with an opportunity to sharpen her characters . . . [With *Burn*] Barr is writing with the kind of ferocity she usually saves for her backcountry adventures."

—Marilyn Stasio, *The New York Times Book Review*

"Nevada Barr is one of the best." —*Boston Globe*

MORE . . .

THE ROPE

NEVADA BARR

St. Martin's Paperbacks

THE ROPE

Copyright © 2011 by Nevada Barr.

All rights reserved.

For information address St. Martin's Press, 175 Fifth Avenue, New York, NY 10010.

Library of Congress Catalog Card Number: 2011035837

ISBN: 978-1-250-00867-1

Printed in the United States of America

St. Martin's Press hardcover edition / January 2012
St. Martin's Paperbacks edition / September 2012

St. Martin's Paperbacks are published by St. Martin's Press, 175 Fifth Avenue, New York, NY 10010.

10 9 8 7 6 5 4 3 2 1

*This book is dedicated
to the memory of*
LAURIE AXELSEN,
*a good ranger and
a fine woman.*

ACKNOWLEDGMENTS

Thank you, Scott Sticha, not only for making the expanse of Lake Powell accessible but for finding the people who helped me so much. Thank you, Steve Luckesen. You were not only my guide but kept me company during the writing process in the character of Steve Gluck. I hope you enjoy Gluck as much as I enjoyed your intelligence and companionship. Thank you, Valerie Reynolds, for easing me through the technicalities of boating and educating the public on water quality issues. Thank you, Julie Smith, for picking me up and dusting me off every time I threw myself down and wailed, "I can't go on!" Thank you, Nancy Christiansen, for being there when I needed you. Thank you, Mr. Paxton, for being Mr. Paxton.

ONE

Regis Candor took a swig of his beer and watched his neighbor, Jenny Gorman. She was sitting on the other picnic table, her feet on the bench, smoking a cigarette as Gilbert and Dennis swaggered into the square of grass and trees fenced in by seasonal housing. Park employee housing at the Rope was set out in two neat quads, two-bedroom duplexes on each of the sides, surrounding squares of defiantly green grass with four locust trees only slightly taller than Regis and not yet as big around as his wrist.

One square was for NPS seasonals, the other for concessions workers, kids that pumped fuel and sucked crap out of the houseboats and made Dangling Dogs at the Dangling Rope Marina snack bar. The duplexes didn't blend into the red/roan/rust/buff motif of Lake Powell. They were painted the same dead gray as the marina. Regis figured maintenance got a good deal on gray paint.

Gil and Dennis were college boys from Pennsylvania who'd come to Lake Powell to work on their tans and get laid. When they weren't absorbed in one of those pastimes—or both simultaneously, if Dennis was as much of an "outdoorsman" as he claimed—they did maintenance work.

Regis watched them flop bonelessly down, Gilbert next to Jenny, Dennis at her feet, arms thrown along the table. Both were covered in dust and sweat and, no doubt, wouldn't shower until Ms. Gorman had every opportunity to be impressed with their machismo.

"Hey, guys," she said, blowing out a lungful of smoke.

"Hey," they answered in unison. Heckle and Jeckle, clowns.

Jenny Gorman looked like the Girl Next Door every boy wishes lived next door: dark wavy hair, big hazel eyes, a well-cut mouth, and enormous tits. Jenny was used to being ogled, Regis guessed. In high school she must have had to wave "Hi" at breast level when she met guys. That's where they would have been looking. Gil and Dennis still were. Regis didn't think the breasts were implants. Plastic never moved like real flesh and blood.

Gorman didn't flaunt her body, but he'd seen her flash a little cleavage to get some idiot to fall off his water skis or drive his boat into the dock. Served the fools right, he thought, and took another pull on his Dos Equis.

Evenings at Dangling Rope were Regis's favorite part of his job. It was as close to being a kid at camp as a grown man could get and not be arrested. His peers—permanent park employees—whined too much about pay, promotion, retirement. Seasonals, no matter what their age, exuded a sense of childlike freedom, as if they were actors in an old movie and any day now they were going to get their big break. Being around seasonals made him feel like a wise old man, though he'd not yet turned thirty.

Thirty was year after next. He pushed that thought away. Forty wasn't the new thirty, and thirty was the start of forty. Forty was the start of skin sagging, breasts sagging, scrotums sagging, lines and fat and receding hair. Thirty had one upside; at thirty he'd be a rich man. If he fulfilled all the old horror's requirements.

Butt first, Bethy, his wife of at least two more years, came out of their side of the duplex, a casserole dish in her oven-mitted hands. Hash brown casserole, all cheese and butter and potatoes. Four years of marriage and his wife's bottom was spreading big-time. To be fair, the weight gain wasn't entirely her fault, but Regis wasn't in the mood to be fair.

When they met she was a seasonal interpreter at Rainbow Bridge. She'd been thin and athletic in those days, canyoneering on her days off. Regis had loved watching her cute little behind bobbing ahead of him in the slots, and he'd needed a wife, so he'd followed that taut, flexing little gluteus maximus right to the altar.

Bethy's charm—other than the tight ass and the convenience—was the gypsy lifestyle she promoted that summer, the sense of a life full of possibilities. The fantasy Bethy. As soon as she had the ring on her finger she changed back to the real Bethy. Two more years, Regis told himself. Two more years and a lot more drugs.

"Hash brown casserole!" Gil ejaculated. Food excited him almost as much as Jenny's chest.

"Goes right to your hips," Regis said, glancing at his wife's rear end as she bent over to set the hot dish on the table. Gil laughed. Gorman shot him an evil look.

Bethy fled back inside. Regis looked at the screen door and considered going in to make sure she was okay. There was no point. What was "okay" for Bethy?

Jenny stubbed out her smoke and tucked the butt into a ziplock bag she'd taken from the pocket of her shorts. Gil Morraine took the opportunity to inch closer. Regis had read Heckle and Jeckle's personnel files. Ciphers. Dicks for brains and beer for spiritual sustenance.

Both had made a play for Ms. Gorman. Jenny was thirty-three to their twenty-one-going-on-thirteen. Big tits were evidently equalizers on the age issue for these boys. When Jenny blew them off—figuratively, not literally—they'd started a rumor she was gay.

Regis smiled into the neck of his bottle. The fools never did catch on. Jenny *was* gay, queer as a three-dollar bill. She just didn't advertise it. The Park Service was seriously homophobic. Regis had discovered her sexual preferences when he'd gone into her duplex to check on a maintenance report and noticed a letter. "Pornographic" didn't do it justice; it would have won a *Penthouse* Letter of the Week competition.

The letter had been signed "Cindy."

Jenny started rolling another cigarette.

"Oooh, roll your own, tough mama," Dennis said.

"Tougher than you, weenie boy," Gilbert said good-naturedly. Dennis laughed. Regis guessed there was a private joke regarding "weenie boy." He had no desire to be let in on it. Neither, apparently, did Jenny.

She grinned past Gil at Regis, winked, licked the paper, and sealed the tobacco in. The lick was longer than it needed to be and ran lovingly the length of the cigarette. Heckle and Jeckle were entranced.

Dennis took the matches from her hand to light the cigarette. After he'd wasted three without getting a flame he could keep alive in the faint breeze off the lake, Jenny took them back. "Nice try, Casanova." She lit her cigarette.

"I'm off the next two days," Gil said, his tone suggesting this news would be catnip to any kitten. "Got a couple of new videos. How about you bring the popcorn?"

"I thought you'd get enough of this place. I figured you for town on lieu days." Smoke trickled out with the words.

"You call Page, Arizona, a *town*? Come back to civilization with us and we'll show you a *town*." Dennis waggled his eyebrows as if he'd said something wildly suggestive.

"King of the single entendre," Regis said. Jenny laughed. Heckle and Jeckle looked at Regis as if noticing him for the first time. They probably were, hidden as he was behind Jenny's glorious tatas.

"Hey!" Gilbert said. "I almost know what that means. I think you've been insulted, Dennis. You going to take that *lying down*?"

A cue line for the comedy to continue. Tired of the routine, Regis stared coldly at Dennis, finding his eyes in the fading dusk. If Dennis had planned on saying something, he thought better of it. Dennis was a coward. Regis could sniff out cowardice like a truffle hound sniffing out morels.

Dennis changed the subject. "I hear you drove that old black pigeon back to New York's Great White Way," he said to Jenny.

This interested Regis. The "old black pigeon" was Anna Pigeon, Jenny's housemate and assistant pooper-scooper for the water quality program. Anna fascinated him. A woman of dark mystery, he mocked himself.

"Looks that way," Jenny said, sounding a little sad. "By the by, Anna's thirty-five. I asked. I'm thirty-three. If you think that's old, get your sweet cheeks off my picnic table."

"Thirty-five's a lot older than thirty-three," Dennis insisted, affronted that a woman with Jenny's dual charms should put herself in the same boat with a skinny creature who dressed all in black and had eyes that let nothing in and very little out.

In the ten days Anna Pigeon had been at Dangling Rope, Regis had tried to get to know her. He doubted he'd have succeeded if they'd been stranded together on a desert island for twenty years. She didn't join the evening potlucks, hang out on her porch, or do the usual socializing. When she wasn't camped on a beach working with the Fecal Queen, she stayed in her room. With her inky clothes and slender silhouette, Ms. Pigeon was a flicker of darkness glimpsed from the corner of the eye. She scarcely disturbed the air when she moved, barely cast a shadow in the sun. Gone, her presence was greater than it had been when she'd glided soundlessly in and out of the housing compound.

Intrigued by her elusiveness, Regis turned on the charm—and, if he did say so himself, when he wanted to, he could charm the paint off a wall. Flattery bounced off of her. Kindly concern annoyed her. Banter bored her. His best trick, showing deep sincere interest, was met with a level stare that suggested sincerity wasn't his best trick after all. When he'd tried plying Anna Pigeon with treats he told his wife to cook, Bethy decided to rise out of her rabbit skin and get nasty about his attentions to another woman.

"Couldn't take it out here in the wide open and ran back to the city," Gilbert said, stretching his arm along the table, perilously close to Jenny's thigh. Regis watched her look at the large dirty paw, and for a gleeful second he thought she was going to tap her ash there. Evidently she was feeling generous. She tapped it on the grass.

"That woman was freaky. For the first week I thought she was a deaf mute. My folks' Labrador retriever talks more than she did. It's like a hundred and ten degrees and she's dressed for a funeral. And what was with the pasty white face?"

"All New Yorkers wear black and have pasty white faces," Jenny said.

"Not the ones with houses in the Hamptons," Dennis insisted.

"Every summer one or two seasonals go AWOL,"

Regis said. "A bathtub full of Jet Skis doesn't fit a tree hugger's fantasy. They come thinking Ed Abbey and *Desert Solitaire* and find beer cans and party boats."

"Maybe she was kidnapped," Dennis said with a leer. "Kept for a sex slave."

Regis inhaled a sip of beer and went into a fit of coughing. Gil came over to pound him on the back, thought better of it, and sat down again. "That's a thought worthy of your moral rectitude," Regis managed when he got enough air to speak.

"Dennis ain't got no rectitude," Gil said with a laugh.

"If she was kidnapped she took her stuff with her," Jenny said. "One black bag with black clothes, one set of sheets, one towel, and one toothbrush. Ms. Pigeon traveled light."

Kidnapping. Anna Pigeon didn't have much in the way of concerned others, Regis knew. Under "next of kin" on her application form she'd listed a sister in New York. Under "address" she'd written "none." Unless the sister was loaded, the posited kidnap was for something other than money.

Given the choice, Regis wouldn't have hired Anna. A cursory background check showed no wants, no warrants, no living relatives but the sister. It also showed no driver's license, no passport, and way too much education. Before he'd even met her, Regis guessed she was running from something: drug addiction, creditors, an abusive husband—something. Glen Canyon didn't need any more action along those lines.

George Fetterman, Regis's boss, wanted her because

he had some half-baked notion of starting a living history program and wanted a theater type. The park had other plans and assigned her to Jenny to help with the water quality program. Shit detail, literally.

"Kidnapping a seasonal would be the perfect crime," Gil said. "Seasonals are like Kleenex—one gets snotty, toss it out and grab another one. Out here in the boondocks, no phone, no nothing, who'd notice?"

"When the season was over and they didn't show up for school somebody would," Dennis said.

"Yeah, but what if you were too old for school, dickhead? Not everybody still goes to school in the fall."

The perfect crime. Who hadn't thought about that? The way for a crime to be perfect would be if nobody noticed, if nobody bothered to look for the criminal because nobody knew there had been a crime. Maybe Dennis wasn't as stupid as Regis thought. Seasonal employees came from all over the country. Many were young, unattached, seldom called home even when they were stationed near a phone. Nobody but the rangers they worked with would notice they were AWOL for days, weeks, even months.

The perfect victims for the perfect crime. The crime had to be done alone and enjoyed alone, no telling, no boasting, no hinting. Once two people were involved in anything it ceased to be perfect. Two people couldn't keep a secret. Two people would turn against each other.

Regis was willing to bet there wasn't a soul alive who wouldn't steal or rig the lottery, cheat on their taxes, or cheat on their wives if they knew, for a fact, no one would ever suspect. Husbands would kill wives. Kids would off rich parents. Billy the Kid wannabes would pop their neighbors just to see what it felt like. Dear old Dad would run over the family dog so he wouldn't have to pick up its shit.

Mother Teresa would have committed the perfect crime if she'd had a chance.

The catch was, nothing is perfect.

TWO

A wild spin of pain forced the black drowning tide in Anna's mind to recede. Either she was waking up or falling down. She wasn't sure. Hot iron pressed against the soles of her feet, the burn cutting through the crud clogging her brain. The inside of her eyelid turned bleeding red. Shying from the glare, she turned her head, her cheek rasping against whatever she'd passed out on. Movement loosed a vicious wailing inside her skull: an unoiled hinge, nails on a blackboard, a dull Boy Scout knife scraping piano wire.

Blackout; she must have drunk herself into a blackout. Her sister told her every one of them cost her about four IQ points. Anna'd promised there wouldn't be any more. This time she must have wiped out an entire circuit. Knives, drills, awls—anything mean and sharp she could think of—were grinding through bone and stirring gray matter into froth. Each tiny brain cell nailed to its own tiny cross was keening to die.

Molly was going to kill her.

Except Molly couldn't; Anna wasn't in New York City anymore.

Where the fuck was she?

Arizona, she remembered, or maybe Utah.

At the Port Authority she'd gotten on a Trailways bus with a suitcase and three paperback novels. She'd ridden this bus till all the blood in her body had vibrated down into her fanny and feet. A soldier lounging in the seats across the aisle—or a guy in khaki with a webbed belt—had pulled out his dick somewhere in one of those flat rectangular states and waved it at her. She remembered that.

"What am I supposed to do?" she'd asked. "Faint? Scream? What?"

He'd put it back in then. She remembered how sheepish he'd looked.

"Leave it out if it makes you feel better," she'd told him. He'd gotten off the bus a while later, but she'd been asleep when he did.

She'd stayed on the bus until it reached a point a few miles south of the middle of nowhere: Page, Arizona; Lake Powell; Glen Canyon National Recreation Area.

Passed out drunk in Dumb Fuck, Arizona. Or Utah.

"Shit," she muttered. Grit coated her lips and tongue. Sand. She'd passed out facedown in the sand. Through the misery coagulating in her cerebrum she could vaguely see herself camping on a beach, one littered with toilet paper blooms and human feces she had to scoop out as if people were cats and she was the keeper of their litter box. Surely that was nightmare, not memory.

With an effort she raised one eyelid. The other eyelid remained shut, nailed in place by the daggers in her skull or the surface her face was mashed against. Through the slit between her eyelids she could see her left hand, the wedding band Zach had given her glinting dull gold, sparking with a glare so intense it threatened to slam her retina three inches into her brain.

The movie that played every morning when she awoke began unreeling.

The paper bag D'Agostino's had packed her groceries in was limp, wet with drizzle that had been falling since noon, drizzle so stagnant with the heat of July it lost the ability to form real drops. Her hair was damp, braid trailing down her back, heavy as a hangman's rope. The Levi's that had fit when she'd put them on that morning stretched and drooped in the steam till they threatened to fall from her hip bones. Her pants legs trailed on the sidewalk. She was waiting to cross Ninth Avenue at Forty-first; one long block to Tenth and she was almost home.

"Pigeon!" came a shout. Across the avenue, Zach waved both arms over his head, making his six-foot-two scarecrow physique look even taller and narrower. The drizzle and the heat plastered his dark baby-fine hair to his neck and cheeks; his glasses were askew and his clothes loose and ill-fitting. Anna thought he was the most beautiful man in Manhattan. Seven years of marriage had done nothing to dull the thrill she felt when she saw him.

Fire on the soles of her feet banished the dream movie. She must have passed out with her feet in the sun. Sand, sun: outside. Was she a tourist attraction on a dung-infested beach? Turning from the glint of her

wedding band, she tried to push herself up on her elbows. Sharp and grinding pain knifed through her left
shoulder. The arm did not move. Her head threatened
to explode, dimming the vision in her right eye. She fell
to her side. The arm was broken or dislocated or badly
sprained. Her head was broken or dislocated or badly
hungover. Nausea, sudden and violent, spewed the contents of her stomach out. Dizziness, so bad she dug her
fingers into the dirt to keep from being pitched off the
surface of the earth, spun her.

Finally, vomiting stopped. Dizziness abated. Anna
stared at the mess splattered over her bare breasts, the
end of her braid trailing in the muck.

"I'm naked," she whispered.

In front of her was a short stretch of sand, then a
wall. Afraid to move, she rolled her eyes: wall and sand
and sand and wall. She was nowhere. A beach in a box.
She was naked in the bottom of a rock-lined hole and
couldn't remember how she got there. Poison flowed
through her veins, making her eyes blurry and her
thoughts sluggish, but she couldn't remember getting
drunk. She couldn't remember anything. Either this
wasn't a hangover or it was the last hangover, the drunk
that put her down like a sick animal. Or pushed her
back over the edge into crazy. Crazy, she remembered.
Crazy was an empty purgatory ten thousand masses
couldn't free her from.

Panic slammed into her viscera, vision tunneled,
skin prickled.

Squeezing her eyes shut she murmured, "Shh, shh,
shh, you're okay. Naked in a box is better than dead in

a box." The butchered line from *Rosencrantz and Guildenstern Are Dead* brought her back to Zach. He was playing Rosencrantz in an Off-Broadway production she stage-managed. Now she and Guildenstern awaited him in purgatory. Tears of fear seeped from the corners of her eyes. A sane person would know why she was naked and broken, getting stranger and stranger in a strange land.

"No," she whispered. "You're not crazy anymore. This is real. Shh, shh, shh."

Easing to a sitting position, she cradled her left arm across her stomach. Her shoulder was deformed. A rounded lump pushed out in a knob the size of her fist, skin pulled so tight it was shiny. Images of Sigourney Weaver, an alien bursting from her sternum, shot through her mind, making the dislocated shoulder surreal, terrifying.

Closing her eyes against this impossible existence, Anna began the catechism her sister teased her with. Molly was a psychiatrist; she knew crazy when it scratched at her door.

"How many fingers am I holding up?" Molly asked.

That was an easy one. No fingers; Anna was alone with her own ten.

"What is today's date?" Molly demanded.

"July 1995," Anna whispered. "I don't know what day."

"Who is the president of the United States?"

"William Jefferson Clinton," Anna murmured, proud of herself for remembering the Jefferson part. Molly would give her points for that.

"You'll do," Molly said with a wry smile and faded from Anna's internal landscape.

"Don't go," Anna cried, but it was too late, her sister was gone.

Slowing her breathing and relaxing her muscles one by one the way Molly had taught her, Anna felt the panic back off. It wasn't gone, but it was bearable. "This is not purgatory," she assured herself. "They don't let Protestants in."

Encouraged, she opened her eyes again. No longer blind with fear and pain, she saw smooth stone curving up from the cushion of sand where she sat. Streaks of rose and buff and gold whirled upward nearly thirty feet as if sandstone had been twisted, pulled like taffy. The shape was as perfect as an earthenware bottle thrown by a master potter, the upper part flowing gracefully into a narrow throat that curved into a slanting tunnel. At the end of the tunnel an eye of blue was punched out of the sky. A single lozenge of sunshine, scarcely more than a yard across and a foot wide, reached the sand; the source of the sun on her bare feet. Spinning in the petrified tornado, her thoughts were as wild as wind-blown debris.

A solution hole; she was in a solution hole.

That thought was carved out of the chaos between her ears with difficulty. Around Lake Powell were hundreds of solution holes. She'd seen them from the boat. Jenny, her boss, said they were deposits in the sandstone made of softer stuff, and over the millennia they eroded away, leaving smooth, irregular holes. Jenny boasted

Glen Canyon Recreation Area was home to one of the largest of these formations in the world.

Anna was not in the largest, not by a long shot. The bottom of the hole couldn't be more than six or eight yards in diameter. How had a woman who'd never been closer than a boat ride to a solution hole ended up naked in the bottom of one? Had she suffered a psychotic break in the desert sun, thrown off her clothes, and fallen in? Had she gotten drunk and stumbled naked into a pit? Each thought came hard and slow, coated with a residue thicker than booze. Gingerly she touched her head where it hurt the worst. Behind her right ear was a lump radiating heat. The skin was broken; she could feel dried blood in her hair.

If she was sane, if she'd "do," as Molly said, she hadn't suffered a psychotic break. She sniffed her hand, cupped it to smell her breath, sniffed her hair. She stank, but she didn't stink of wine. As crazy as she'd been the last months, she'd never blacked out without benefit of a couple of bottles, yet now she remembered nothing.

Had someone pushed her in? The tumbling fall could account for the knot on her head and her shoulder being out of its socket. Why would anyone steal her clothes and drop her in a pit?

Rape.

"God, God, God," she moaned and spread her legs, pushing her feet back into the searing sunlight. No semen smeared on her thighs, no bruising.

She didn't *feel* raped. A person would feel raped.

"Not raped," she whispered. "Naked in a hole and

not raped." Pushing into the sand with her heels, she backed into the curving wall of her bizarre prison. No exits, no steps cut into the rock face, no rope, no ladder. No way out.

Slapping the stone with the palm of the hand on her uninjured arm, she screamed, "Help! Help me! Somebody help me, God damn it!" Words careened off the wall, echoed feebly, then were gone. She pounded and screamed until it seemed all sound was taken from her, poured out, pooling around her, not a single decibel making it up the sheer walls and out to . . .

To where?

Balling her hand into a fist, she struck the stone hard.

"Stop it!" Molly ordered.

Anna stopped, letting her bruised hand rest palm up on her thigh in an unconscious attitude of supplication.

"Breathe," Molly said from somewhere behind her eyes.

Anna breathed.

Pulling her knees to her chest, she wrapped her good arm around her shins and, rock protecting her back, fought to push through the dense fog clogging her mind.

THREE

Stretches of Anna's mind were blank, black and clean as if wiped with an eraser. The blow to the head, or whatever mind-altering substance she'd consumed, had stolen time from her. For a while she crept across this featureless plane; then, at last, the dim dawning of a memory.

That morning—this morning, a morning, some morning—she'd gotten up early. Before seven, she remembered. Already the day was hot. Summer heat in New York came from milky skies, pouring moist and heavy over the city, flowing down from the buildings and up from the subways until it suffocated. Desert heat came from hard blue sky and weighed nothing. Like a weak acid solution, cleansing and caustic.

Anna remembered that—remembered thinking that on that morning. This morning. Some morning. She reached deeper into her mind and the images scattered, leaves before a thunderstorm, skidding across her brainpan.

Breathe in: one, two, three. Hold, two, three. Out on

a five count. Just breathing, not chasing the memories. Air in, air out.

Tentative, but real, an image drifted back: her, sitting on a rock, looking down at Dangling Rope Marina.

Battleship gray and uniform, the marina was laid out like a kid's game of hopscotch painted on flat, fake, teal green water, a single runway, wider near the shore end where the snack bar and ranger station were, narrowing as the dock thrust into the lake. Blunt rectangular arms stretched to each side, one for boat fuel, one for garbage Dumpsters the size of semis, one for the sewage pumps where houseboats could dump. In between were mooring slots. All gray and square and dull in hot light from a dead blue sky.

"Lake Powell is a hundred and eighty-six miles long and has almost two thousand miles of coastline," she whispered without opening her eyes. That she'd learned during orientation.

Dangling Rope was a third of the way uplake, between Wahweap, which was near Glen Canyon Dam, and Hite Marina to the northeast. Uplake, Glen Canyon National Recreation Area butted into Canyonlands National Park; downlake, into the Grand Canyon. That she'd learned after stepping off a bus in Missouri—or maybe Alabama—and buying a map.

Grand Canyon, Canyonlands—photographs of them were prettier than those of Glen Canyon. Glen Canyon was a warped, half-drowned land. Chameleonlike colors shifted with every change of light. The unnatural lake was not gentle with sand-and-shell beaches and cattails in the shallows, but fever green in a dead world. An inland sea in hell or on Mars under the merciless blue of a hard rock sky. It suited Anna.

Unreal, or surreal, stark and freakish, the landscape could hold no memories. The past was burned to dust by the sun and blown away on winds that were seldom still.

Could hold no memories.

"I hate irony," Anna mumbled. She prodded the image gently, hoping it would metastasize and tell her where she was, how she ended up here, and why her brain no longer functioned properly.

Another image slunk from the shadows at the edges of her mind. A big yellow sun. Eyes lost behind sunglasses, rays spiky, Mr. Sun was smiling down on a powerboat towing a water skier. It was her daypack, bought at Wahweap's gift shop. She remembered opening it, taking out the water bottle the park gave her, uncapping and drinking.

God, but that was a great memory.

My lieu days, Anna thought as the ghost water slid down the throat of her past self.

"It's Tuesday, July 11, 1995, and Bill is still president," she said aloud to her sister.

Molly did not reply. Maybe it was no longer July 11. How long had she been unconscious? Hours? A day? Days? Not days. At orientation they were told nobody could live in the desert for days—plural—without water.

Thirsty, she opened her eyes. No cheery sun in Ray-Bans greeted her. The pack, along with her clothes, had not journeyed with her into this place. No bottle filled with water that, like the rain that often didn't reach the ground in the desert, never seemed to reach her thirst but evaporated in her esophagus.

Did desert peoples cry? she wondered. Or had dehydration reached their Anasazi tear ducts? She no longer cried, and she missed it. Tears were warm and kept her company. When tears were gone, what remained was emptiness the size of a basketball, yet paradoxically as heavy and solid as a chunk of concrete. Inflating her lungs around it was a chore. Swallowing food past it was more work than it was worth. Carrying it from place to place exhausted her.

Out West, where there were wide-open spaces, big skies, where deer and antelope did their thing, she thought breathing might be easier. Out West there was supposed to be more air in the air.

Out West.

Out here.

Outdoors.

Not long ago "outdoors" meant the streets and avenues of Manhattan. "Wilderness" was Central Park after sunset. Robert Rowell, a costume designer she'd been fond of, summed it up nicely. Slamming the window of his ninth-floor apartment, he'd announced, "I love the outdoors! Let's leave it out."

Then Zach left and Anna wanted out: of the city, her skin, her life. Three drinks with a stage manager working at Wolf Trap National Park for the Performing Arts and she'd applied for the first seasonal park job she found.

She'd gotten it.

There was nothing left for her to do but to practice breathing all the air in the wide-open spaces.

Except she was in a hole smaller than the average New York apartment. "Jesus fucking Christ," she muttered and shifted her weight on the sand. A harsh grate of agony shot out from her shoulder to ricochet around her skull.

"Sorry I blasphemed," she managed. Given her situation it was best to stay on the right side of all gods whether they existed or not.

When the worst passed she realized she could keep her eyes open. Pain seemed to be clearing her mind, not enough to produce anything like total recall, but enough that she could open her eyes without the stone tornado spinning her into a vomiting session.

Having her eyes open was not reassuring. From the unsightly alien lump on her shoulder, she could see her arm hanging like dead meat. The tips of her fingers were white, and her hand was numb. The skin was pale and old-looking with papery fine wrinkles. Pain, spread over every square inch, was the only sign of life in the appendage.

In the movies the hero would grasp the hand, give the arm a yank, and, presto, good as new. Tentatively, with the hand of her living arm, she tugged on the cool white fingers. Pain threatened to make her throw up again. She quit, laid her head back against the warm rock. Bone was squashing a blood vessel. That was why her arm and hand were dying. How long before the tissue was so damaged there was no reclaiming it? Gangrene, blood poisoning, necrosis, a litany of ailments of which she was all but ignorant. The classics had been wasting her time. If she'd stage-managed for *General Hospital* or *M*A*S*H* she'd know these things.

No sense worrying about the arm. Thirst would probably kill her first.

Breathe in two three.

Hold two three.

FOUR

Jenny, Jenny Gorman, called the Fecal Queen because she cleaned human waste from the beaches, Anna's boss, Jenny, said there was a trail out of Dangling Rope to the plateau—or mesa or butte or whatever the flat places above the ditch places were called. Anna remembered that.

She remembered shading her eyes and staring up at the sand-colored rock. Never had she seen so much dirt in one place: tan dirt, red dirt, pink dirt, yellow dirt, black dirt. Dirt and rocks. Carved stone heaved up, smooth as polished granite in some places, shattered into avalanches in others, broken rocks flowing down from higher ground, rocks liquid as lava and lumpy as dough. A psychedelic Mt. Rushmore morphing into the Pyramids of Giza, giving way to the craters of the moon, and all of it glazed with white-hot sunlight.

At the skyline, crinkled trees or shrubs showed black rather than green, not exactly poster plants for Mother Nature. One of the few signs of life Anna had seen at Glen Canyon was the fish. Every day, around the dock, the big bums gobbled scraps boaters tossed at them.

They were about as glamorous as rats begging for picnic leavings in Central Park. Bum fish, houseboats loaded with party animals, and a little pink rattlesnake were the sum total of her wildlife experience. This wasn't Bambi and Thumper's kind of neighborhood.

Hand shading her eyes, she'd searched for Jenny's path. To the right of a rubble of rock flowing down a side canyon was a sheer cliff veiled in a skein of black lace—desert varnish, Anna had been told. Even the black gave off a hot shine.

A hat.

Anna remembered Jenny told her to wear a hat. She'd offered to lend her one that looked as if the Yankees had used it for third base for a couple of seasons. Nobody wore hats. Anna hadn't seen a hat in years. The first one she put on that wasn't purely to keep her ears from freezing was the flat-brimmed ranger's hat. Like everybody else, she resembled a hairless, malnourished Smokey Bear when she wore it.

These memories trickled through the toxic sludge in her brain. Like dreams they drifted with color and emotion. Like dreams, they ran together without logic. Rehashing a hike up a pile of rocks wasn't getting her any closer to what mattered. With her good hand, she rubbed the grit from her eyes and tried to fast-forward to the stone pit, the naked, the befogged. Wispy trails of the cliff, the past, the path threatened to dissipate. Anna let go of the effort.

Breathing in: one, two, three.

Hold, two, three.

Exhale on a five count.

Wisps coalesced into memory.

Hatless, Anna was squinting. If she tilted her head to the side she could almost make out a line paler and more contiguous than the rest. It didn't look like a path so much as a scratch on a rock. She could get most of the way up to it via the apron of broken stone. At the top of the pile was the wee scratch that might be Jenny's path, might zigzag up a crack to the ridge. It didn't look far. Anna had walked the length and breadth of Manhattan more times than she could count, hundreds of miles clocked on concrete. The climb looked to be less than a mile. Five crosstown blocks. Piece of cake.

In her pack were most of a liter of water, a map, and a pamphlet identifying area plants. She took out the map. Maybe the black broken lines were trails. None of them came anywhere near Dangling Rope. The pamphlet was even less help. "The Glen Canyon National Recreation Area has highly diverse vegetation typical of the Colorado Plateau."

Humanity's dam and the universe's sun allowed very little to survive. On the flat spots a scanty grass, like the last hurrah on a balding man's pate, grew, but it was so brittle and colorless as to be nearly transparent.

"Hah!"

Anna remembered saying "hah." She repeated it now to break the awful silence of her open-air tomb. The pathetic little gust of noise only made it worse.

Breathe in two three.

Hold two three.

Out on a count of five.

Briefly, she'd considered packing a sandwich, but

she wasn't hungry and figured she would be back long before lunch. Stuffing the papers in the pack's zipper pocket, she headed past the housing area toward the cliff and the thin pale line that disappeared into the scree.

By the time she passed the maintenance barn, with the generators that powered the development, and the sewage treatment area behind it—a total of maybe a hundred yards—she was wishing she'd bought a pair of shorts the last time she was in Page. The straight-legged black jeans and T-shirt, so good in the cool dark of backstage, were hot and constricting in the back of beyond. Black, prevalent in New York because it didn't show every sooty smudge, showcased the beige smudges of what Anna supposed was good clean dirt.

Three hours later she was out of water, sunburned, and three-quarters of the way up the canyon's side. Stopped on a level spot, hands on knees, she gasped for breath. Heat lay like molten lava on the back of her neck and arms. The muscles in her thighs were quaking, and her thin black Reeboks felt as if they were on fire. Not sea level, not flat, not paved, not Manhattan: not a place she could walk a hundred miles.

Slumping to her knees, she stared back the way she had come. Staff housing was tiny with distance, heat making the gray-on-gray shimmer as if the houses were slipping from this dimension into another and, if she watched long enough, would disappear altogether. The trail looked much steeper going down. Climbing, using hands and feet, it hadn't seemed so precipitous. As shaky as her legs were, she doubted she would make it down—

unless she just gave in to gravity and rolled most of the way.

Going down would take too long, and she was too thirsty. After thirty-odd years of drinking various beverages, Anna had assumed she knew what thirst was. She hadn't had a clue. Thirst was not a desire for a beverage; thirst was a screaming need that drowned out all other calls from the body, an obsessive, desperate craving that narrowed vision and channeled the mind to a single topic: finding water.

Old movies, black-and-white, where men were good or bad and never lived with shades of gray, swam through her mind: dying of thirst on deserts with burros or camels or Arabian horses, shaking the canteen, a sip left, sharing it with a buddy. Until this moment she hadn't known what heroism she'd missed in those viewings.

Since Zach was gone and Molly only drank Scotch neat, there was not a buddy dear enough to her heart with whom she'd share her last sip.

She looked up toward the ridge that had appeared so close from the housing area. The black scruff of foliage was made up of actual honest-to-God trees. At this height, they even looked a little green around the edges. Green had to mean water. Didn't green always mean water? If she could make it the rest of the way, she could find a spring or creek or whatever watered the trees. Failing that, she could get to a road or a house or farm or sheep shed or whatever passed for civilization and beg water from them. If she was extra nice and said pretty please, maybe they'd give her a ride down to a marina where she could catch a passing boat with a ranger in it.

If she could get up from her knees, she could make it the rest of the way, she amended as she struggled to arrange burning feet under aching gluteus maximus so she could perform the amazing, showstopping trick of rising from the goddamn rocky red dirt.

The ridge retreated over the next pile of rock, then around the next jagged cut of sandstone. Then it appeared to be just over the next polished haunch of land. Another waterless hour passed before she reached the lip of the canyon. Steep gave way to flat without preamble, and she stood, the canyon at her heels, her hands dangling apelike near her knees from the last bit of the ascent.

Up close the trees weren't much greener than they'd looked from below. They didn't have the decency to form into a proper forest with shady lanes and mossy hollows. They straggled out of soil so arid and stony they were deformed by the effort. Wretched stunted things, they resembled something T. S. Eliot might have run across after the last ding-dong of doom.

Behind her, and to both sides, canyons cut into the mesa. Ahead, another escarpment reared up, crowned with ragged serrated trees cutting into a sky so blue it hurt. There were no roads, no houses, no telephone lines, not an animal pen or a fucking creek or a fucking watercooler in sight.

No water. She wasn't going to find water. The only water in the world was a million miles back down Jenny Gorman's sorry excuse for a trail. The last ding-dong of doom ringing in her ears, Anna limped to the nearest excuse for plant life and thumped down cross-legged in the niggardly shade. Her tongue had grown too big for her mouth. It stuck on her teeth and soft palate. Muscles in her legs were cramping. Skin on her face and the back of her neck stung when she touched it. There was no point in going farther, no point in staying where she was, and she doubted like hell she would be able to make it back down.

Not for the first time, she took the water bottle out of her pack and shook it. Over the months without Zach she'd come to think of the Grim Reaper as a guardian angel, ready to sweep her out of the mortal coils when they cut too deep. Now that He was grinning at her from the dry bottom of a plastic government-issue water bottle, she didn't like him as much as she'd thought she would.

She took out the map and unfolded it—something to pass the time while dying. Subway maps and city maps made sense. Streets had names, they intersected; buildings had numbers. Subways had stops. Wilderness maps had crooked lines going nowhere, and nowhere had horrific names like Dry Fork and Turkey Knob, Panther Canyon and Devil's Garden.

"There is nothing helpful on this fucking map," Anna croaked. She balled the map up and threw the wad of paper over her shoulder.

For a while she sat in defiance, then levered herself to her miserable feet and tottered over to retrieve the litter. Glen Canyon might kill her, but she was damned if it would turn her into a litterbug.

She was picking her trash out of a stubble of desiccated grass when she heard the scream.

The pitiful shriek, scratching through the pitiful trees, lifted Anna's spirits. The cry was too full-throated for a woman dying of thirst. Anna started to run in the direction of the sound. She, the Good Samaritan, would take a thorn out of the screamer's paw, and the grateful thing would give her water.

A lot of water.

FIVE

Running, hoping for water, there memory ended. Between dressed and whole to naked and broken there was nothing but nothing, not even the blank slate. Trying to remember was like trying to see with the tip of her finger.

Hugging her useless arm to her chest and staring up the gullet that had swallowed her whole, Anna wondered: Had she rescued the maiden? Traded places with the maiden? Had the whole thing been the hallucination of a severely dehydrated woman? Was this rock jug she was at the bottom of another hallucination?

Reality, so hard won, began to ebb. "Help! Help me!" she screamed.

Silence slammed down from the buff-and-blue horizon and struck her dumb. Like the silence after prayer, it deafened her; a silence devoid of presence, a wasteland mocking any who dared hope. She didn't yell again. She didn't do anything. She didn't think anything.

Shade swallowed her. The ellipses of light oozed off of the sand and started crawling up the side of the jar.

Where the lozenge of sunlight shone, the stone was burnt orange; behind it the stone was blue; ahead of it, toward the sky where the light was going, the stone was buff, as if the rock that held her prisoner was of living matter, reactive to light and heat.

July in Arizona, the sun set around seven thirty. The girl's scream—and Anna's last memory—must have been around two o'clock. She glanced at her wrist. Her watch was gone. Either she'd been in the bottle five or six hours or a night and a day. Instinct—or body clock—suggested the latter. Fear prickled in her belly. Thirty hours as a prisoner.

Prisoner. The word stuck crosswise in her brain, striking ice crystals from bone. Someone or something had taken her and imprisoned her, stolen her clothes, her watch, her ID, stolen who she was, and hid the leftovers in a pit like garbage.

Or, like leftovers: to be eaten later.

Again Anna started to cry for help. Fear of the answering silence cemented the sound in her lungs.

Soon, somebody—or something—would come. Monsters are a lazy bunch. They don't take all the trouble to catch a thing and put it in a bottle if they don't want it for some reason. They'd want to talk to it or poke it with sticks or make it sing or dance or fuck it. They would do experiments on it at the very least and torture it at the very worst.

Unless they just wanted to watch.

Suddenly Anna could feel hidden eyes leering from behind the rim of her hole, eyes that watched her vomit and scream like a fox in a trap. Watched her naked.

Scanning where cliff met sky, she studied every shadow, rock, and crack.

Nothing.

No one.

The sense of being watched didn't leave her.

Her arm was throbbing, a pulse of all-encompassing pain. The ends of her fingers were numb and turning blue. She eased herself down until she was flat on her back, her bloodless dying limb supported by the sand. Draping her uninjured arm over her breasts to cover her nakedness, she studied the high eye-shaped rim of her world. The sun would come back or the monster would come back or insanity would come back or she would die of thirst. The last option seemed the least nasty.

"You have one job," Molly said, as she had so many times over the past few months. "Staying alive."

"Damn it!" Anna grumbled. "Why do you have to make things so hard?"

With her sister's admonition tolling in her head, Anna realized how desperately she wanted a drink of water. The maiden whose paw she'd intended to de-thorn for a drink must not have come through. Lying in a stupor for—hours? a day?—the lining of her nose had dried to parchment. In place of her tongue was a splin-tery wooden clapper. Thirsting to death lost its place of honor as the least nasty possibility.

Along one curving edge of her prison jar, green plants with wilted white flowers grew. Datura, deadly nightshade; Anna knew that from the pamphlet she'd had in her pack. They needed water to grow. She could dig, then drink from the seep. The optimistic thought was stillborn; desert weeds needed drops, not buckets. If a plant needed serious water to live it would take root in Oregon or Louisiana, not on Mars or the Colorado Plateau.

Galvanized by attention, Anna's thirst became its own entity, a clawed evil, tearing at her throat and shredding her thoughts until she could think of no worse death than death by thirst.

Deadly nightshade.

Did one get the "deadly" if one ate it? It was good to have options. Rising to her feet was too labor intensive, so, shutting out Molly's "staying alive," she held her worthless arm across her belly and knee-walked toward the plants. Chewing on the leaves or the blossoms might produce some moisture or it might kill her. Either way, she figured she was ahead.

Reaching for the juiciest-looking leaf, she noticed a deeper shadow, round and dark, like the back of a turtle—or a land mine—to one side of the scrap of living green. It was half hidden in the sand. Approaching the object with the suspicion of a cat in a new country, she shuffled toward it, each small movement driving knives into her skull and shoulder. Tentatively, she nudged it with her knee. It didn't explode.

It was an old metal canteen, the brown-and-blue fabric cover faded to grays. Folding herself down, she tugged it free of the sand by its army green strap. It was heavy, nearly full. Thirst made unbearable by this promise of water, Anna jammed it between her thighs and awkwardly unscrewed the cap with her right hand. A bit slopped out, and she groaned at the waste and the luxury. Carefully curling it against her chest, lest it be too heavy to hold one-handed, she bent her head, locked her mouth around its metal lips, and drank deeply.

For a moment she felt good, almost giddy with relief. She drank a second time, then screwed the metal cap back on tightly. Her captor had left water for her. That meant he didn't want her to die.

Didn't want her to die *yet*.

If he wanted her alive, that meant he'd be coming back.

Daylight was nearly gone. Night was when predators hunted; at least the cats in New York hunted at night, as did the thugs for the most part. Would her predator make his appearance soon? Hours by herself to look forward to, with only her mind to play with and rocks to keep her company. She was beginning to understand why solitary confinement was such an effective punishment. She wanted her abductor to come even as she feared it. At least, after he came, she would know how frightened to be.

The sky turned from blue to gray to black so absolute the circular walls of her jar seemed to glow in contrast. Stars, bright enough Anna mistook the first for an airplane, pierced the inky eye high above. Clear and sharp, they seemed no more than a hundred feet from the sand and, paradoxically, incomprehensibly far from earth.

Cool air poured into the hole, welcome at first, then chilling. Silence settled like concrete as she strained to hear the approach of a car engine or a footstep, the stealthy scratch of boots on rock.

Lethargy claimed her. Stars became supernovas, then blurred. Her bladder emptied, yet she hadn't the energy to move to clean sand. Fragments of thought bloomed, and in the blooms were serpents of color. Her shoulder no longer hurt, and the pain in her head hid behind a curtain of thick felt. Legs and arms were leaden, too heavy to move.

The water in the canteen was drugged.

When the monster came she would be unconscious, helpless, as she must have been when he'd taken her clothes and pack and wristwatch. She'd been drugged then, too; she should have known it from the hangover, the amnesia, the way her mind wouldn't work, drugged and stripped naked and hurt, smashed on the head, her arm dragged from its socket. Had she fought back?

Pushed by terror, the torpor receded a few inches. It was only a short reprieve. A night blacker than the one above was coming to claim her. She roused herself enough to scream. The breathy *uhhn* didn't get more than a foot from her lips.

She cried, then stopped. Yelled weakly, then quit.

Inner darkness pooled with that outside her skin. Soon she would drown in it.

"What the hell." Her words were slurred and her head heavy with stupidity as she fought to her knees. No light, she found her way by touch. Using her good hand, she laid the knuckles of her useless arm's hand on the sand palm up. "Gravity sucks," she mumbled as her body swayed, threatening to topple her. Inch by inch she eased her left knee sideways until it was in the middle of the palm.

"Shit, shit, shit," she whispered and, with what strength she had left, jerked upward. An agony of pain cut through the drug haze as she heard bones grind and snap and settle. Clutching her arm to her, she fell back moaning. After a minute agony dispersed, leaving behind soreness and a wild itching as blood moved through her veins into her fingers. Either she'd resocketed the bone or the drug was masking the consequences of the attempt. Chemical darkness clogged her eyes. Like a puppy, she curled up. She wanted to pray but wouldn't let herself.

The Bastard didn't exist and didn't deserve to hear from her anytime soon.

SIX

Long after the Candors and Heckle and Jeckle, as Regis dubbed them, had gone to bed, Jenny sat on her porch and smoked. Her erstwhile roommate had been an odd duck, but Jenny had taken to her right off. That was not the usual for the Gorman girls. She and her sisters had to get used to people by degrees, ever wary for signs that they were untrustworthy or cruel or snitched food or lovers. A legacy from their parents.

Jenny didn't often think of her folks. It wasn't that she hated them. Mom and Dad Gorman weren't evil; they'd never yelled or raised a hand to any of their five daughters. They weren't drunks or pedophiles. They were wilting flower children, embracing tune in, turn on, and drop out with the younger generation. They made promises they didn't remember to keep, left bills unpaid, forgot to pick up the children at school, spent birthday money Gramma and Grampa gave their daughters on things for themselves, always with the promise that they'd "pay it back with interest."

Then, when Jenny was twelve, Jodie eleven, Jessie

fourteen, Jean six, and Jenna two and a half, Mummy and Daddy got in the car to go see *Terms of Endearment* and didn't come home for three years. Two weeks before Jenny's fifteenth birthday they'd waltzed into Gramma's kitchen streaming beads and skirts and hair and were hurt to find out nobody much gave a damn. Baby Jenna didn't remember them, and even Jean was a little vague. Jenny and her other sisters remembered too well to believe in them anymore. They remembered too well to believe in anyone who was not yet tested and proven to be reliable.

How had the adorable little Pigeon fluttered so effortlessly through these defenses? Jenny wondered. Lust? As she watched cigarette smoke curling in the still air, drifting in a cloud across the fingernail of moon, she pondered that. What there was of Anna Pigeon was "cherce," as Tracy had said of Hepburn. The long red-brown hair was a definite turn-on, as were the high cheekbones and clear hazel eyes. Her ears were small and neat and close to the head. Her nose was a perfectly respectable nose. If she smiled she might dazzle. A girl could do worse for a bedmate than Anna Pigeon. Customarily Jenny's taste ran to the more lushly upholstered type. Ms. Pigeon's clavicles stood out like a coat hanger, and her scapula could pass for wings when she stretched her arms back. Jenny always joked, to sleep with a skinny woman would be like sleeping in the knife drawer.

The joke was on Jenny this time. Fortunately, Ms. Pigeon had flown the coop before Jenny could get cut too bad.

Anna's darkness had been part of the appeal, she had to admit. The woman walked in a cloud almost as visible as the dust that hung around Pig-Pen in the cartoons. Jenny was a sucker for stray kittens, wounded mongrels, meth-addicted girlfriends, and down-and-out boys. Anna definitely had the wounded bird syndrome going for her. Another lure was her mystery; she never said word one about the gigantic cross nailed to her skinny back.

Jenny ground her cigarette out on the side of the porch, tucked the butt into her plastic bag, said good night to Pinky Winky, the pink pygmy rattlesnake that lived between her duplex and the Candors', and took herself in toward bed. Without Anna to shoulder a share of the work, tomorrow would be a long day in the Fecal Realm. Year eight of her reign as the Fecal Queen.

Her anointing came her third season when there was a most unfortunate spill of some sixty gallons of collected waste she was hauling in her boat.

For the most part houseboats had their own privies. Unfortunately a lot of them filled them up, then dumped them in the lake.

As counterintuitive as it was, Lake Powell, the barren wife of a dam where Gaia never meant a dam to be, needed gray water. Waste put nutrients into the lake, helping an ecosystem that had not had time to evolve. The lake was long and deep, five to six hundred feet in the main channel; she could take a lot of abuse. The problem was the beaches. Any beach where a boat or a Jet Ski could anchor, visitors camped and picnicked and pooped. Some thought they were being ecologically enlightened by cat-holing, but the level of the lake wasn't static. Boats and wind kept it sloshing like a washing machine. Water came up, uncovered the catty little deposits, and dragged them into the reservoir.

Warm-blooded animals, including humans, carried fecal coliform bacteria (FC) in their digestive tracts, along with the pathogens that went with it. Off high-use beaches, where the water was shallow and warm, there were often 400 FC "colonies" per 100 milliliters of water. Anything over 200 FC per million was unsafe for swimming.

Every two weeks for the past seven seasons Jenny had taken water samples from the most popular beaches. Any beach that came up unclean was closed until she had two consecutive samples with an FC below 200. This had worked until visitation reached five million annually. More beaches were closed more often, and visitors howled.

In two years it would be mandatory that all overnighters carry Porta Potties. During those two years of easing from cat box to Nirvana, Jenny would clean the beaches, and gather water samples for the lab. New this season, and most important, it had become her job to educate the visitors in the niceties of proper pooping protocols so that when the rule was enforced the public outcry would be minimized.

Because Jenny didn't have the power to write tickets—or the gun to back it up—she was often teamed with Jim Levitt, a law enforcement seasonal. One wouldn't think discussing toileting practices could get a girl shot or manhandled, but Lake Powell's visitors were rich—many were über rich, the kind that can pay ten thousand a week for a houseboat and another three thousand to put gasoline in it. The kind that don't take kindly to anybody making less than they pay their maids telling them what they can and cannot do on their vacation, in their lake, on their beach, in their world.

Jenny's secret to compliance was pretending she was married to Aristotle Onassis and educating the hoi polloi was simply an obligation of noblesse oblige. When that failed it was good to have a large man with a big gun beside her.

Thinking of guns and bozos, she reminded herself to check the grotto at the tail end of Panther Canyon. A party boat of major übers had camped there, so many college kids per square inch it was a wonder the houseboat was still afloat. Their barge had a bathroom—*a* bathroom, as in one bathroom. With that quantity of booze, bladders, and bowels, they would most definitely be exhibiting poor litter box habits.

There would be many "interpretive moments," educational opportunities.

There would be pounds of human waste.

Lord, but she was going to miss Anna Pigeon.

This was the first season she'd had a full-time seasonal position under her. Anna Pigeon. Mystery woman, wounded bird, waist-length red hair, rich hazel eyes: Jenny went over the litany of attractions as she brushed her teeth. To it she added the one that had first captured her heart, Anna's willingness to do hard dirty work without complaining.

Jenny loved meeting new people, preaching ecological concepts, selling the idea of sustainable wilderness, living out of doors, taking water samples, and sleeping on the beaches. Since the unfortunate incident that had earned her a regal title, she did not love cleaning up human waste. Anna was a gift; she actually preferred shoveling shit to interacting with her fellow men and women.

Though it was clear boats, water, docks, and about anything else in Glen Canyon was alien to Anna, she was quick to learn and a natural at handling lines. She moved with an economy and efficiency so complete it was as graceful as a dance. On the one occasion the weather came up quick and bad, and the lake was set on pounding them into bags of bone and pureed meat, Anna was daring the goddess of the lake to do her worst.

Jenny was convinced a quiet camaraderie had been growing up between them. A respect. Admiration. A deep and abiding affection—

Don't push it, she thought as she spit in the sink.

Anna was gone.

SEVEN

When Anna again awoke—or came to, depending on how she wanted to think of it—she knew where she was before she opened her eyes. In spite of the fact she'd been drugged, sleep had refreshed her and she was able to think with relative clarity. For a time she lay perfectly still, eyes closed, breathing evenly as if she still slept. Before she committed to another day of life in a pit she wanted to be sure she was alone. Light touched her eyelids gently; the sun was up, but not yet in a position to shine into her prison. The sand beneath her body was cool. That would change before long. Thirst was with her, but not with the same screeching, scratching shriek of need as it had been the night before. That, too, would change before long. She would have to decide whether to die of thirst or drug overdose.

She felt queasy—again not as bad as on the first morning—the first awakening? Much of that might have been the head wound. Vaguely, she remembered Molly mentioning that concussions made people sick to their stomachs. Minutely, she twitched the shoulder that had been dislocated. Sore, but better, much better. All in all, it felt as if she would be healthy enough to starve to death or be murdered in a day or two.

It surprised her that she awakened hungry. For the last few months she'd had no appetite and would often forget to eat. Though she was living in New York City within walking distance of the finest restaurants in the world, her weight dropped from a respectable one hundred and eighteen to a boney one hundred and two. Now that she hadn't so much as a stale corn dog in her future, she was ravenous.

The train of thought ran fast; no more than a few seconds elapsed between washing up from the sea of sleep to finding herself aground in consciousness. Stopping her mind before it could clatter down another track, she listened, trying to feel the air around her with invisible antennae. The desert was not silent: A tiny fall of sand whispered; a powerboat buzzed gently, distance muting its roar to a hum that was almost natural; her heart beat, a steady thump in her temples.

Anna didn't think there was a monster leaning over her waiting to strike the moment her eyes opened. Surely in stillness as complete as this bottled quietude, she would be able to hear it breathing, feel the fetid air on her neck, smell the foul stench of its mouth.

Did Jeffrey Dahmer have bad breath? she wondered. Was eating people more unclean than eating cows?

That thought ended the whole exercise of keeping the eyes closed and not moving. Anna's eyes popped open as a jolt of fear electrified her. She was on her back staring up at the all-seeing eye at the top of her world, the clear blue of sky beyond the mouth of her bottle. Absurdly, she wondered if this was the view babies had shortly before they were born. No, they'd see a masked man in scrubs peering back at them. At one time that image would have amused her. Lying naked at the bottom of a dry well, it scared her nearly as much as that of Jeffrey Dahmer picking human flesh from his teeth with his fingernail.

All that kept her from leaping to her feet in terror was the sure knowledge that it would make her arm and head hurt like sons-a-bitches. Carefully, she sat up.

Things had changed.

The night before, when the drug took her, she had been leaning against the side of the jar. She had urinated in the sand where she sat. The canteen was tucked under her arm. Now she was in the center of the arena of sand. The canteen was leaning neatly against the sandstone near the patch of sacred datura, night blooms only now beginning to close with the light. Next to it was a paper sack, the neck rolled down tightly to keep whatever was inside trapped. Around her the sand had been raked into concentric circles as if she sat at the center of a vortex.

Stinging brought her attention back to her body. Her thigh burned. Blood covered the skin, running down and clotting in her pubic hair. Sand stuck between her legs where the blood had pooled and dried.

"Nooooo," she wailed. The monster had come as she slept and raped her bloody. "No!" she screamed as on elbows and heels she tried to escape the red stain. Movement sent more burning from her thigh to her brain. She began to cry. Tears blurred her vision and ran down the side of her nose.

The bleeding, stopped overnight, began again, seeping from the top of her thigh to run in narrow red rivulets down the crease between her leg and her abdomen. Anna sat still. Gathering her courage, she leaned forward to study the bloodied area. Neither the ooze nor the pain emanated from her vagina, but from the flesh near panty-line, had she had panties to boast of. Scooting backward, she moved to where the canteen rested neatly beside the deadly garden. Having unscrewed the cap, she poured a small stream of water onto the wound. The water ran red; then, slowly, cuts began to show, straight, careful lines incised into a strip of skin about two inches wide: W H O R E.

The monster had come and cut his word into her.

She jerked back as if she could escape the message, but it was carved on her flesh. Ignoring the sudden roar of pain in her shoulder and head, she began scooping up sand, burying the horror that had been made of her.

"No!" she said aloud at the same moment Molly said, "Stop it, Anna." Opening her hand, she let the sand trickle out between her fingers, watching it rejoin a million other grains that had been worn from the stone over the last millennium, blown and settled in this trap.

He—the monster—had not made a horror of her. He had made a thing of her, an object, a joke, a notepad, a scrap to scribble on, then throw into the trash. He had made her nothing but his butt, a billboard, garbage.

Trembling took her so hard her teeth rattled and her breath came in short shallow gusts. Folding her legs, she began to rock and moan. The moans turned to anguished sobs, and her lips formed a hard open square as ragged screams were forced through. Far away, in the back of her mind, she could hear Molly shouting something, but the words couldn't penetrate the thick walls of degradation built around her in the night, walls as solid and imprisoning as the stone jar this damaged bit of trash had been dropped into. She rocked and screamed until she didn't even have the will to do that anymore.

Then she was just sitting cross-legged on the sand staring at the desiccated-looking nightshade garden, the canteen of poisoned water, and the paper bag.

Three doors and behind each the tiger. There was no lady for such as Anna. She knew the datura could kill her, but she didn't know if she was supposed to eat it or inject it or smoke it or what. The paper bag held an unknown. The easiest seemed to be the canteen. If she drank all of it, maybe it would be enough.

She waited for her sister to order her to "stay alive."

From a long ways away she could hear her. "So. Fine," her sister called, barely audible in the distance. "A bit of monster garbage. Poor you. The monster wins."

That rather pissed Anna off.

No. That really, really pissed Anna off.

"I will fucking show you," she muttered and thought she heard her sister's fading voice saying, "That's my girl." Fury swept away most of the self-pity. It burned out with the heat and rapidity of a car fire, leaving fatigue, helplessness, and confusion in its wake. How would she *fucking show* anybody? A hundred and two

pounds of naked city girl with a sore shoulder and a broken pate, what could she do? Unless, when the monster
showed up with his number twelve X-Acto knife—or
whatever it was he'd used to carve his judgment—he
was a malnourished pygmy with rickets, she wasn't
likely to overpower him even if she wasn't drugged out
of her mind.

Maybe she'd get lucky, like the girl kept in the stone
pit in the basement in *Silence of the Lambs,* and the
bastard would have a yappy little dog she could hold
hostage. From what she'd seen, Lake Powell wasn't a
hotbed of yappy little dogs, more the big sorts that can
clear a coffee table with one swish of a mighty tail.

Blinking back the last residue of tears with the
thought that she needed all her hydration, she looked
around her sandbox. Not even any rocks for bashing
in the heads of predators. Self-pity was creeping back
when the cat saved her. She remembered Sophie, a five-
pound cat she had when she moved to New York after
college. Sophie was so sweet until someone tried to
make her do something she did not wish to do. Then
she became a five-pound buzz saw, all fangs and claws
and moving at the speed of sound.

Sophie. Gilda Johanson. Gilda was attacked two
floors down in the apartment building where Anna and
Zach lived. She was in her sixties, had emphysema and
high blood pressure. She snarled and snapped at everybody. A burglar had come in and decided to rape Gilda
while he was there. Relating how she had driven the
man off was one of the few times Anna had heard Gilda
laugh—or rather chortle.

"I don't has many things. This *stomme bastaard* he want to take what I got. Then he pull out to *zijn smerige kleine* penis and wave it around," she said when she met Anna and Zach on the landing as they were carting their laundry upstairs.

"Did you knock some manners into him?" Zach asked.

"What I got to knock with?" she demanded indignantly. "I start to piss and do bowels and I spit and act crazy and throw the piss and bowels at him and scream and the piece of *de hond braakt*, he can't get out my house fast enough."

Cat and gross defenses, Anna had those. Though they were ridiculous—maybe because they were ridiculous—she was comforted by remembering them. Her sense of helplessness eased a little. Not trusting her recently dislocated shoulder to take any weight, she struggled up and walked on her knees to the canteen, the paper sack, and the deadly nightshade. Plopping down beside them, she picked up the canteen first. It was full, topped off during the night. She unrolled the crimped neck of the paper bag. Two squares wrapped in waxed paper. To her, the two squares wrapped in waxed paper and stowed in a sack spoke of food. To the monster, it might mean anything, tarantulas in an odd box, rat guts on toast. Who knew what monsters thought was nourishing.

Along with the paper-wrapped squares were two cups of the kind of pudding that comes in little six-packs. No spoon, no napkins. Laying one of the packages on her thigh so it covered WHORE, she carefully folded back the corners of the waxed paper.

It looked to be a regular sandwich, the kind eaten by schoolchildren all over America, peanut butter and jelly oozing out from two slices of bread with the crusts cut carefully off. Molly used to make Anna PB&Js to take to school in her lunch box. The box was black and had Zorro on it sticking his sword into a fat guy in military blue. Anna'd thought it was really keen until she was thirteen and found out both the box and "keen" were suddenly not at all groovy.

Waxed paper, that was odd. Nobody used waxed paper anymore. Only monsters who trimmed the crust away and served massive doses of sugar to their captives to fatten them up for slaughter.

Molly never cut off the crusts. She said they were the best part. Anna wished she had the crusts to this sandwich. Harder to put weird shit in the crusts. Meticulously peeling the top slice of bread back, she looked for anything suspicious, her mind clicking through images from *One Day in the Life of Ivan Denisovich*. No eyeball, no obvious expectoration, dead cockroaches, or rat feces.

Closing the sandwich, her eyes, and her mind, Anna took a bite. Hunger roared, taste buds sang, saliva ran, stomach quivered with anticipation. For that instant Anna was transported from terror and agony to a glorious hedonistic plane. In short, it was the finest bite of food she had ever experienced.

Gourmet gave over to gobbler. She devoured the rest

in three bites and was eyeing the second wax-paper-wrapped square in the bottom of the sack. Was it also a sandwich? The monster was into mind games. Maybe the one on top had been the bait and this second was the switch, the one with the razor blades in it.

She took a pudding instead. It had at least been factory sealed. Running her fingers over the smooth plastic tub and the foil top, she felt for pinpricks. In college, one of her roommates enamored with Psych 101, had used a hypodermic to inject blue food coloring into an unopened milk carton to see if anybody would drink blue milk. Nobody would.

No pinpricks; nothing had been injected into the pudding.

Anna pulled off the foil top. Chocolate. Again saliva flowed from some mysterious moisture source the rest of her body didn't have access to. She licked the underside of the foil, then squeezed the little plastic cup, gushing the pudding into her mouth and over her tongue, and went again to the place where all was good and even better this time because all was chocolate. The last remnants she scraped out with her index finger and sucked into her mouth.

The monster hadn't left her a spoon. Probably afraid she'd tap him to death with it if she got a chance. Which she would. Anna'd never been much on hate, but she hated this guy. Mentally ill or not, she hated him so much that to think of him filled her with an intense anger she could feel to the tip of her braid. Surely this kind of hate would cause one of them to spontaneously combust. Probably her.

Taking deep slow breaths, she blew some of the toxic emotions out of her body and brain. A semblance of calm restored, she folded the lunch sack closed. At the moment she didn't want to know what was in the other package. Supper maybe, should she live that long. The canteen beckoned, and she knew she would have to drink sooner or later. Later was better.

Food had revived her to an extent that surprised her. A sense of optimism came with a full stomach and a shot of sucrose. The downside was now she had to go to the bathroom.

In New York she'd lived in many one-bedroom and studio apartments, some not as spacious as the bottom of her jar. Living small had taught her the necessity of living neat. The thought of fouling where she would be eating, maybe, and sleeping, druggily, was abhorrent, but life apparently was going to go on at least for a while.

Getting awkwardly to her feet, she chose to put her privy to one side of the datura garden. In the old days Chinese farmers used night soil to fertilize their fields. The scraggly plants couldn't be getting much in the way of nutrients from the sand. Hoping the datura would be grateful for her donation, she carefully dug a hole a foot or so deep.

The business of living attended to, she began scooping sand in to cover it up in good cat fashion. Her fingers tangled in a web in the dirt, and hope flickered: Hemp to weave a rope? Old fishing nets to macramé into a ladder? Even if she could have done those things, there was no way to get it hooked to the outside world.

A bit of line with which to garrote a monster?

That was a cheering thought. She tightened her fingers and dragged out the nest of fibers she'd pawed up.

Brown and fine. It looked like human hair. Anna shook her hand free in sudden panic and fell back onto her hind end. The jarring loosed fire-bolts of pain in both arm and head. She almost welcomed them. They made it hard to think.

Nothing much looked like human hair but human hair.

"Help! Help me!" Anna screamed.

EIGHT

Regis was sitting in the bedroom of Jenny's duplex, the one that Anna Pigeon had used for such a short time. It wasn't his lieu day—like a lot of HQ employees, he had Saturdays and Sundays off just like normal people. He had called in sick. The parks frowned on permanents calling in sick or going on vacation at the height of the season, but he'd done it anyway. Seasonals never called in sick. At least he'd never heard of one doing it. They just didn't.

Was it possible they never got sick? he wondered.

He never got sick. There wasn't a day in his childhood he could remember staying home sick. He wasn't sick now. He was—agitated. It wasn't unpleasant. In fact, he liked a change from the neutral nothing he felt most days. A life lived in ecru, he thought wryly. Ecru. That was his mother's favorite color. Half his genes were from a woman whose favorite color wasn't a color at all. "Everything goes with ecru," she liked to say.

She would have approved of the employee housing color scheme at the Rope: outsides gray with no adornment, insides varying shades of ecru. Possibly the original decorators—buyers was probably the more accurate term—who'd chosen the carpets and furnishings had dared a splash of color, but over the years time and use had sucked it out. Dust and the neglect of serial renters had done the rest.

The room Anna Pigeon slept in was no different: a double bed, stripped now, a dresser and bed stand of the processed woodlike substance that looks battered and old a week after it's brought home from the store and limps on in that shabby state for the next hundred years. Opposite the bed were a shallow closet with sliding doors, the wood warping slightly, and a single window, blinds down, three of the bottom slats broken.

Anna Pigeon's things had been taken, but Regis wanted to sit in the room where she'd stayed without people butting in and asking him what he was doing or why he was there. He was in personnel; as far as he was concerned he had a right to be anywhere he wanted. And, in the park, nobody bothered to lock their houses, especially not at Dangling Rope, Bullfrog, Hite, or Halls Crossing. They were too remote by road to attract thieves, and people who came by boat were too rich to covet the trash that could be bought on a government salary.

Regis sat on the bed and listened to his pulse racing in his ears. The emptiness of the shabby space was more than just the lack of a tenant. Too many people who cared too little about the room filled it with ghosts. Not the ectoplasmic phantoms fools pretended to see when they wanted to feel special. Real ghosts, the kind that don't exist, the kind that are made up of dead air, the kind you see in the eyes of an animal when the vet puts it to sleep. The kind that are Not There.

Growing up he hadn't been allowed pets. The first time he'd seen the Not There of death was the previous winter when Kippa died. Kippa was their six-month-old French bulldog. A golden bowling ball of love. Regis smiled, remembering. The image shifted into another, the wide grin red with blood, blood where his ears had flopped, screams that came out through his mashed nose. Regis had been holding him like a baby, looking deep into his brown eyes, when all of a sudden there was no dog, just dog meat, carrion. There, then Not There.

The living are There. Ghosts are the Not There, the blank, the dead, the ecru.

That his mind had come full circle to his mother's favorite color startled Regis out of his self-induced trance.

He'd never seen a human being die. He'd been there when his mother passed, but she was so doped up on morphine it had been a seamless transition. Anyway, her eyes were closed. He imagined it would be the same, though. The person would be There, then simply Not There. The eyes might not be the windows to the soul, but when life left, that was where the falling shutters could be seen.

Anna Pigeon's room felt like that, like the Not There had taken up residence. Regis had wanted to feel the room, and it felt like nothing. Standing, he looked around at the tawdry space. He wouldn't come back. Sooner or later another seasonal There would move in and give it the illusion of life for a few months. Nothing would be different.

Agitation was still making his insides quiver. Being still was impossible. He probably should have gone in to work just to be moving, be distracted by the nonsense of the day-to-day world of the Barely There. Leaving Anna's room, he walked down the hall to the room where Jenny stayed. Jenny Gorman had been an interpretive ranger at the park for nearly a decade, coming back every summer. As he'd anticipated, her room looked and felt as if someone were there. Jenny showed up every season with a huge old hard-sided Samsonite suitcase that she joked was her life in a box.

Regis had never been in her room before, but he expected this was her box-life unfolded. A coverlet with a cabbage rose print, and matching shams, was on the bed; sheets, folded neatly over the bedspread, were printed with sheep in complementary colors. On the bureau a dresser scarf in pale yellows hid the scarred surface. There were two small framed pictures of children—nieces, Regis guessed. Beside them sat an old-fashioned silver-backed brush-and-comb set. He picked up the brush and examined it. Long curling brown hairs were caught in the bristles.

It wasn't just for show, Jenny used it. That made it real. Regis ran the tips of his fingers over the ornate silver casting. Fine things, quality, endurance, he craved those. His boat and his ancient but perfect Super Cub, made life livable. He looked forward to when he could surround himself with tangible proofs human life wasn't all shoddy construction and tedious noise.

An oval mirror, cheap but decorative, was hung over the dresser, one she had bought in Page probably. It didn't look worth enough to haul from wherever she spent her winters. Regis could find out if he wanted. Personnel was where the skeletons of background checks, pay grades, and reviews were buried. Until Anna Pigeon disappeared, Jenny had never interested him enough to bother.

Today Jenny was going up Panther Canyon to check on a party boat full of college kids. Levitt was in court, so she'd be working without law enforcement backup. Regis didn't like it. That might have been part of why he felt shaken, agitated. The party boat had some bad people on it; he knew that for a fact. Dangerously bad people.

Holding the brush, he looked at his reflection in the glass. Bethy told him he was handsome. When he looked at himself, all he saw was that he was There. Replacing the brush precisely where it had been before he disturbed it, he realized calling in sick had been a mistake. Getting caught in the lie was going to count against him, but he had to go out to Panther Canyon and make sure Jenny didn't stir up a hornet's nest.

NINE

Mad as Lady Macbeth, Anna scrubbed her hands together lest any of the long and human hairs buried in the sand should cling to them. Retreating to the far side of the jar, she felt her panic worsening. There was nowhere to be, nowhere to run but in circles like a crazed hamster. Slumping down, she leaned back against the sandstone, hands held before her, too unclean to touch any other part of her body, and stared at the mess of delicate brown strands near her cat hole. "My life is a Stephen King novel," she whispered. "Everything gets worse. And worse. And worse. When it finally can't get any worse, everybody dies."

Everybody dies.

Had she been thrown into a charnel pit?

The monster might have been using this hole for years. Dropping his human garbage into it, playing his games with drugs and cutting and chocolate pudding; watching his victims, sans clothes, sans dignity, sans freedom until, finally, he got tired of them or broke them.

Sans life.

How many women were buried in her sandbox? Into her mind's eye came rotting arms, skeletal fingers, reaching up through the dirt to drag her down.

"Still breathing here," Anna said loudly. "Breathing in. Breathing out."

Bit by bit, a determination that could be mistaken for courage returned.

Gingerly, she made her way across to the tangled strands, aware that she might be treading on the corpses of hastily buried women. A book she'd read came unbidden into her mind, *Chiefs*. The killer had a long and successful career, sowing his land with dozens of his victims before he was caught. Halfway across her prison floor a noise from the other world stopped her.

Something was coming, an engine, tiny and distant. Humming down through the bottle's neck was a comforting burr of sound, a small-engine aircraft, one of the little ones that took sightseers on flights over the lake. The sound grew louder. The little plane was close to the ground, close to Anna. Tilting her head back, she squinted at the impossibly blue eye above. The neck of her jar was canted like the slightly twisted dual necks on the old vinegar-and-oil carafe her mother kept on the kitchen counter. The carafe was for show. The only salad dressing they ate was homemade Thousand Island: ketchup, mayonnaise, and sweet pickle relish.

"Down here!" she yelled. "Help me! I'm down here!"

They were looking for her. They had to be. Over her lieu days Jenny probably thought she'd hitched a ride on a boat headed for Wahweap to spend time in town. By now her lieu days must be over. She'd been in the pit at least a night and a day and a night, thirty-six hours. If her weekend wasn't over now, it would be tomorrow. Without a watch, without knowing how long she had slept or what day it was, time got tricky. Knowing the time kept people from going adrift.

When she didn't show up for work—whenever that was, today, tomorrow—when she didn't show up on her "Monday," Jenny would raise the alarm and the Park Service would come find her. Search and rescue. The rangers were big on that. Visitors, fools like her, were always getting lost, falling into holes, being eaten by wolves, that sort of thing.

Rangers and EMTs. Law enforcement rangers had to be EMTs; she remembered that from the information the NPS sent after she'd gotten the job. They had to take courses every year. Search-and-rescue rangers would search for her and rescue her; EMT rangers would give her aspirin for her head, maybe Valium for her shoulder.

The airplane, it was them.

"Down here!" she yelled again. "Help me!" The plane droned louder. "Down here, goddammit! Help, help!" The engine whined overhead. "Down here, you stupid fucks!" she screamed, leaping to her feet. The plane murmured away. Anna fell to her knees.

The bottom of the jar, down here where the bodies were buried, wasn't visible from airplanes. Nobody would be peeking into the hundreds of holes. First, they'd think of the water. Lake Powell was so deep, in the main channel there was no dragging the bottom. Deep meant cold and dark. Bodies didn't always float up. In the cold and dark, they sank. The rescuers and EMTs, did they think she had gone down to the world of the dead, joined the army of the drowned? Had they stopped looking? Or never started?

She wished she'd told somebody where she was going. Jenny might remember their conversation about the trail out of Dangling Rope.

Not bloody likely. Jenny was all about the fecal materials.

God damn stupid fucking green-and-gray Smokey Bears. Rangers. Telling John Q. Public not to litter and to be sure and hold hands with your buddy on the scary paths.

"Fuck!" she yelled. What she wouldn't give to have the NYPD looking for her, real cops with guns, batons, Mace, handcuffs, bad attitudes, and ambulances that whisked the injured to big shiny hospitals where doctors—"Doctors who've actually gone to medical school," she ranted at the eye—fixed injured arms and broken heads.

Shouting at the fragment of empty sky, Anna realized the jar wasn't as deep as she'd first believed. The way the neck curved and narrowed created a false perspective. The opening wasn't more than twenty feet from where she stood, smooth vertical walls rising for fifteen feet or so, then a steep slope from that to the eye.

Twenty or two hundred, there was no way to climb out.

"I screwed up," Anna croaked, her throat raw and dry from shouting. Her head was aching again and her arm throbbing. "I hoped."

Getting into the solution hole would be easy. A strong person could easily climb down a twenty-foot rope. All he'd have to do was tie it to a big rock and drop it into the throat of the jar. When he left, he could just pull it up after him, no muss no fuss. Unless he drove or walked in from the miles of bleak and rocky desert she'd seen to the north, he'd have to climb up from the lake. That would be hard, harder than the short hop out of this hole. The monster had to be strong.

Strong enough to carry her down into the hole? Maybe not. Her shoulder and head suggested he'd just tossed her over the lip to survive the fall or not.

That was annoying. He wasn't even sure she was a high enough grade of garbage to be monster meat.

"Bite me, you prick!" she yelled at the eye. "I hope you choke to death on my bones."

He would be strong. Strong and young. Movies insisted serial killers were twenty to thirty years old. Anna hoped they were right and he was young; it limited the number of dead people with whom she might be sharing space.

Though the lake was only a small part of Glen Canyon Recreation Area, nobody much hiked. There were a couple of trails used by backpackers, one down from the Navajo Reservation to Rainbow Bridge and another somewhere uplake. A trail led into Bullfrog, but it was long and came from nowhere to dead-end at the lake's edge.

People didn't hike along the shoreline. Lake Powell didn't have shores, not like a real lake. Powell lived in canyon bottoms, cliffs rising vertically two hundred, six hundred, as much as a thousand feet in some places. From what she'd seen of the plateau, there weren't any roads.

Other than on the water, or the few small beaches carved out from the sandstone, there wasn't anywhere to be. Anything farther from the lake than a man could throw a beer can was dry rock and hot dirt, wilderness.

Half a mile as the crow flies from this burial pit, boaters were catching fish, children were splashing in the shallows, and girls in bikinis were flirting with boys in cutoffs. A half mile and a half million light-years.

At least that's what it felt like to anybody but lunatics and coyotes, Anna thought sourly. She would not screw up again. Like praying to a nonexistent god, it was demoralizing to hope for help when none was coming.

No, Anna wouldn't hope.

Turning, she studied her jar looking for anything new, anything she hadn't noticed before—besides the nest of human hair under the sand. Silent walls swirled upward; smooth, beautiful in their way—a perfect palette for an artist.

A perfect lair for a monster; utter privacy within commuting distance of home.

Where was a monster when he was at home?

Houseboats, even those moored in the marinas year-round, were allowed only two weeks on the water. It kept homesteaders from living on the lake full-time. Was the monster a boater who used his two weeks a year to pursue his hobby?

That would work, Anna thought. That would be ideal. Spend two weeks on a houseboat—time enough for a bit of sport—kick sand over the remains, then go home to Oregon or New Hampshire or North Dakota, tanned and rested, plenty of holiday memories to enjoy over the winter, show one's pals slides of the vacation.

Anna swayed, her mind wanting to shut her down in a faint. The possibility that a picture of her misery might live on after she had been murdered to pleasure her killer over and over again was unbearable, worse somehow than death, torture, or rape. To be used after one was dead shouldn't matter. Dead was dead, gone, beyond all pain.

Except it wasn't, not when one was alive to think about it.

"No pictures," Anna shouted. "No fucking pictures!"

For a heartbeat she felt the earth around her as a comfort, clean and honest, a cloak against eyes and lenses. Shaking her head, intentionally eking out the remaining pain from her injury, Anna pushed photographs of her degradation from her reality.

The monster.

Anna had to understand the monster so, like Scheherazade, she could continue to live for a thousand and one nights. Better yet, so she could find his Achilles' heel and escape. Did he brown-bag it, bring his own prey? No. Bringing victims from his habitat would raise too many questions. He took what was offered on the lake, she decided. Safer to have no connection with his victims, and, with a nice boat, it would be easy enough to pick up a party girl—or a seasonal ranger—whom nobody would miss for a while.

If he hunted on the water, why had he found her? Unless she had forgotten climbing down off the Colorado Plateau, she was on the north rim of Glen Canyon, above Dangling Rope, hours from anywhere. Only a crazy person would travel across a zillion miles of desert from Piddlesquat, Utah, on the off chance a woman would be wandering around alone and unprotected. Had it been mere chance? Monster Man is out poaching lizards or snakes or stealing artifacts or engaging in an unrelated monstrous activity and gets lucky? Had she been stumbled upon by a psychopath?

Anna had turned in a full circle. She had searched the smooth circumference of her bottle without seeing anything new or different, anything that could alter her circumstances. Stopping, she lowered her gaze from that single blue glimpse of sky to the hair straggling over the sand.

There was no reason to bother the nest of hairs. A few swipes with the side of her foot and things would be as they were before—nearly unendurable. Digging up whatever it was she'd be digging up might render them completely unendurable. Knowing what was buried beneath her might make her insane. Of course, not knowing would do it quicker. Nothing drove Pigeons crazier than not knowing that which could be known.

That's why Molly went into psychiatry; she wanted to know how people's brains worked. Anna went into theater; she wanted to know how people's hearts worked. Neither she nor her sister was one to let sleeping dogs—or dead girls—lie. Anna assumed it was a girl because of the length and fineness of the hair, and because it was possible she wasn't the first specimen to be bottled up and played with until it wasn't any fun anymore.

Back at the datura, Anna drew a circle in the sand, the strands of hair at the center, and then began gingerly sweeping sand away with the tips of her fingers. The hairs were long, not as long as Anna's, but they would fall to bra-strap level on a woman of average height. As best she could, she combed the hairs from the sand carefully, laying them out to minimize snarling. Partly she did it to show reverence for the dead, and partly because, should she join this woman, she hoped similar respect would be shown her, and partly to put off the moment she would have to look on a lifeless face.

Clearing away the dirt, she watched a well-shaped ear emerge from the earth, two small silver hoops in the pierced lobe. With the ear came the faint odor of decay. Though she hadn't thought it consciously, Anna had been expecting a skeleton: dry, brittle, desiccated scraps of skin peeling away from bone, the way old leather peeled from the bindings of ancient books.

The ear was lifelike, plump and pink, yet there wasn't as much stench as a day-old rat in a subway station. The woman hadn't been in this hole much longer than Anna.

Memory slammed into the back of her eyes, rocking her onto her heels. The scream had come through the tortured piñon trees; hoping for water, she began to run. The clarity was more than remembering, it was reliving. She saw her abandoned pack, the sun appliqué smiling up from the hard ground as she passed the patch of shade where she'd been sitting; she felt the wadded-up map, crunched in her fingers.

Running was hard, as it often is in dreams. Her thighs ached and her feet struck the ground heavily. A stitch was sewing her ribs to her liver. She slowed to a jog, clutching her side and panting. More screams drew her on. Anna became afraid the woman was in deeper trouble than she could handle.

Self-preservation, learned from a lifetime in the city, stopped her headlong dash. Anna remembered trying to suck hot dry air through a throat closed from lack of moisture. She could see herself, dark clothes, pale with dust, hands on knees, gasping and thinking maybe this wasn't something she should get involved with.

Had she not wanted a drink of water so desperately, she might have lost her courage. She straightened up and, still breathing hard, pushed up a small rise of stone. The rise gave way to a round depression half the size of a tennis court.

There were four people in it. A tall boy had a girl with long brown hair, wearing cutoff jeans and a bikini top, in a hammerlock, pressing down on her neck. Her arms were flailing. "Stop it," he was yelling and laughing. "We don't want to have to hurt you." A second boy had his back to Anna. She remembered how his muscles rippled as the sun hit the sweat. His shorts were halfway down his butt as if he'd undone the fly to take them off. He was hopping on one foot, laughing like a hyena, trying to pull off his shorts. He staggered and fell. Drunk, she thought. The fall only made him laugh harder. The third boy, not laughing, not undressing, was a plain-looking kid with ragged brown hair and a fury of pimples across a high forehead. He saw Anna and yelled, "Holy shit!"

The man wrestling with the girl glanced up, locking eyes with Anna. The girl must have hit or clawed him. Letting go of her, he shouted, "Fucking bitch!"

Staggering, the girl fell on her hands and knees. He kicked her. Fighting to get to her feet, she grabbed at his shorts, her fist closing on the front of them. He bent double. For a heartbeat Anna thought he was going to help her to stand. Instead he grabbed up a fist-sized rock and slammed it into her temple.

Anna turned and ran.

The earth lurched and folded beneath her feet, scrub and rock jerking in her peripheral vision. Heat burned up through the soles of her sneakers. A steady strong thud, thud, thud of boots pounded behind her.

Then nothing, then this hole, the dislocated shoulder and a knot the size of a tennis ball behind her right ear.

She hadn't gotten blind drunk and passed out. Bad men had clubbed her from behind. Honor intact, skull not so much. The blow accounted for the patchy memory. "Yay, me," Anna said.

"Blunt trauma to the head is the only cause of amnesia I know of outside paperback novels," Molly once said.

Long brown hair.

The girl Anna was disinterring must have been the focus of Buttboy's attentions. She dug faster. Grit packed the girl's nostrils. Her lips were parted and sand had been shoved into her mouth; that or she'd tried to breathe after she'd been buried. Her eyes were open, scabbed with grains of sand.

"Damn, damn, damn." Curse became mantra and finally made its way from Anna's mouth to her ears. She stopped her frenzied scooping. Clearing the dirt from the girl's nose and mouth was not going to save her.

"Sorry," Anna said to the corpse. Using the end of her long braid as a whisk broom, she gently swept at the dirt sticking to the eyes and teeth. "Were you alive when they buried you?"

Ray Milland, Vincent Price, *Premature Burial, The Pit and the Pendulum;* this girl in the pit—had she awakened to find herself facedown, breathing hard grains of rock into her lungs, sand sandpapering the delicate sclera when she opened her eyes?

Anna had to look away. Her gaze came to rest on the deflated, wrinkled white blossom of the deadly nightshade.

"They hit you in the head," she murmured, unsure whether she spoke to the girl's shade or just to keep herself company. "Then they came after me and threw us both down the garbage disposal." From the wilted flower, her eyes drifted to the walls. With their spin of muted colors spiraling up, she half expected to hear a switch being flipped, a grind begin, and the spiral to move as she and the corpse were ground to mincemeat and sucked into the sewers of hell.

"Young and pretty," she thought half aloud. "It wouldn't matter. Young and pretty or old and scrawny, monsters will be monsters. You were dead when they threw you in, weren't you?" she asked the ghost of the girl. "Otherwise it would be you digging up my grave."

Buttboy with his pants half down, staggering drunk. Hyena Boy, laughing. Gang rape. Anna shows up, hoping for a refreshing beverage, and they kill the girl instead.

The cuts on Anna's thigh stung with sweat and sand. Roughly brushing the grit away, she ran a dirty fingernail along the marks, tracing WHORE in dried blood. There'd been three would-be rapists. There were three. One little, two little, three little monster boys.

Her tongue was dry, big, and thick; her lips stuck to her teeth. The drugged canteen beckoned from the other side of the nightshade. Anna crawled to it, fumbled the cap off, and, in thirst and despair, drank too much, drugging herself more than she had to. Water ran from the corners of her mouth and made mud on her breasts. Instantly, she felt the drug flow into her body, felt her muscles loosening. Her head swam, thoughts sloshing like water in a washtub, slamming against the sides of skull bone and bouncing back on one another.

It came to her then that she had to get the girl out, had to.

Having plowed back though the battered weeds, the pain from her injured shoulder driving her as a whip drives a horse, she clawed wildly at the sand. Scratching and scraping like a maniacal cat in a litter box of burning coals.

The dead woman's head was freed from the dirt.

Sore tendons shoving daggers into her, vision tunneled, Anna scooped and scraped, bulldozed with knees and forearms, kicked and dug with her heels. Sweat poured into her eyes and ran in rivulets between her breasts, leaving trails in the dust and grime. Sand stuck to her skin. Grunts and cries bubbled up the neck of her jar. She scarcely knew if she was standing, kneeling, or lying in the grave with the dead girl. Finally, hips braced against the sandstone, one foot planted on the prone woman's thigh, the other on her shoulder, Anna rolled the body from its grave with an ungentle shove.

Gasping and sweating, she withdrew her toes from the lifeless flesh and surveyed what she had wrought.

A girl—the girl the boys were attacking—lay facing the scrap of sky eyes open and sand-crusted. Denim shorts were twisted around her scissored legs. A pink and yellow Hawaiian print bikini bra had been hiked up over her left breast, showing a white triangle where she wasn't tan and a dark brown nipple. Her right sandal had come un-Velcroed during the one-sided struggle and was smashed beneath her knee. Around one ankle was a thin gold chain, *K* and *A* and *Y* in glittery stones dangling from it, the *K* wedged between chain and skin.

"Kay," Anna whispered. "Welcome to my world."

TEN

Past the no-wake zone of the marina, Jenny opened the throttles. Twin Honda motors lifted the twenty-eight-foot Almar cuddy onto plane and exchanged its blunt-nosed sluggish push for an exhilarating rush. As she had for all the seasons and all the times she had emerged from Dangling Rope into the main body of the lake, Jenny experienced a sense of awe.

Engineers had thrust Lake Powell into this evolving, deformed, magnificent piece of the world. Man still fighting against Nature, and Nature would not lie down and die. She would rage down the Colorado and hurl herself at Man's fabulous wall, scream, retreat, carve out canyons, and return to pile the debris at the foot of his dam.

When the canyons were flooded there had been angry outcries from those who loved the crooked desert channels with their stone arches, rainbow-hued walls, and wealth of history. Jenny would have loved them as well, but not the way she loved the lake, how it met the land, lifted her up, invited her to share secrets hidden for eons.

Uplake, where the water was close to five hundred feet deep, high on a cliff wall was the bottom of a ledge where a slab had fallen away. There, upside down, as if the creature had lived when there was no gravity, was a line of dinosaur prints, three-toed marks, walking into oblivion. Geologists surmised the fossils were hidden when the sediment flipped and heaved, then lay buried for millions of years, to be exposed when the slab fell away. For eons the tracks were lost halfway down a cliff a thousand feet high. With the lake, they could be seen with the naked eye. Backcountry purists suggested that if these sights weren't earned by the labor of hiking in to them, they were undeserved, as if too many eyes sullied them.

That salon-tanned rich women and greedy developers vacationing somewhere they hadn't ruined yet could see the dinosaur prints from the decks of their yachts didn't bother Jenny one whit. Like luck, no matter how many people enjoyed beauty, one's share of it was never diminished.

Of all the wonders the lake made accessible to the fat, the lazy, and the inebriated, Panther Canyon was Jenny's favorite. A conscientious mother, Jenny would never admit as much in front of the other canyons.

Panther was one finger uplake from Dangling Rope. Like the rest of the water-filled crevices, it was a drainage for the Colorado Plateau. It also carried the brunt of the runoff from Fiftymile Mountain. Subsequently it was deeper and longer than most, snaking north and east for eleven miles.

Desert varnish painted the cliffs to either side of the channel, intricate designs in black and red, traceries that looked like the finest lace ever tatted, then slipped into the strong strokes of an irate painter with a burning vision of the universe, only to be offset by a whimsical natural cartoon resembling Snoopy or Betty Boop, or the abstract swish of a soaring bird.

The top of Panther's walls were buff-colored sandstone, the middle red-gold Navajo sandstone, and, near the water, gray Cedar Mesa Sandstone: Cretaceous, Jurassic, and Triassic. Through the windscreen of her boat she could see two hundred and thirty million years into the past.

Jenny cut back the throttle as the channel grew slender, teal water glowing gold where shoulders of stone shrugged toward the surface, light playing from water to walls, sending darting, ephemeral fishes swimming toward the canyon rim. Panther Canyon didn't so much end as unravel in ever smaller side canyons that twisted and shredded into the rock.

There was only one place boats could beach in Panther, and it was Jenny's sacred place. Shortly before one of the unraveling threads thinned to a slot that would wedge a water snake, should it swim far enough, was a clamshell grotto fifty yards long, at least a hundred feet high at the top of the arch, and twenty-six yards deep. Fine white sand, mirroring the crescent shape of the roof, carpeted the floor.

The previous summer it was smooth and flat to

where the wall curved down to meet the sand. Spring of 1995 had been wetter than usual. Flash floods roared down in grinding tides, resculpting the landscape. This summer, halfway between the shore and the back wall was a sandy shelf six feet high.

Sheltered from the elements—and too high for the graffiti vandals to reach—pictographs survived, paintings of strange creatures twice the size of human beings with diamond-shaped torsos, tiny heads, and stunted arms that stalked the imaginations of ancient artists. Three of them kept watch over the grotto.

This sacred grotto was Omaha Beach in Jenny's war—a favorite camp, where people dumped excrement and trash and spray-painted graffiti on the walls. If she could not get visitors to realize that the destruction of this paradise would destroy the soul of humanity, she was doomed to failure in the lesser Edens.

Newer larger houseboats couldn't negotiate Panther's hairpin turns, so most of the traffic was limited to motorboats and Jet Skis. Like drive-by shooters, jet-skiers were hard to catch in the act. Usually she only found the poop they left behind. Chief Ranger Madden laughed when she'd asked if they could send it in for DNA testing and cross-check the results on the various law enforcement sites. She'd argued—futilely—that anyone who would defile the grotto had undoubtedly committed a slew of other crimes.

Motorboaters were not so elusive. Often they camped for several nights. About suppertime, when they would be "at home." Jenny would drop in and educate them. If, when she returned the next morning, they had not learned their lessons, she would come to dinner a second time with Jim Levitt in all his law enforcement regalia and packing ticket book and ballpoint pen.

These were mere skirmishes. Party boats were where the battle line was drawn. Older smaller houseboats could access the grotto. Less expensive barges were often rented by the week by hordes of college kids out of Denver or Boulder, Salt Lake or Phoenix, and loaded with enough beer, drugs, and hormones to compromise the finest minds. These were barbarians sacking the city, infidels razing the mosque, heretics burning statues of Mary, Napoleon's minions blowing the nose off the Sphinx.

Yesterday a party boat had taken over the grotto; a disgruntled boater told Jenny this when she visited his inferior camping spot. She hoped it wasn't the one she'd seen at Dangling Rope. That one had at least forty kids mashed into it. Arms and legs were practically sticking out the windows.

One hairpin turn before the grotto, she throttled down to an idle and checked her watch: 10:00 A.M. Ten was the best time for contacts of this sort. Earlier and the students would be too close to comatose, later and they'd be popping beers. At 10:00 A.M. most of them were sleeping it off but, with the proper encouragement, could regain consciousness in time for a waste management class.

Nosing the throttle open a tad, she eased the boat around the last elbow of sandstone. The party boat was moored at the near end of the beach, two lines running to tie-down bolts pounded deep into the sand. The stern rail was gaudy with beach towels, a Hawaiian shirt, three pairs of swim trunks, and a brassiere that had once been a confection of black lace and satin but now resembled a roadkill crow.

Bodies were everywhere. The top deck of the houseboat was roasting them in the sun. Bare legs, feet, and a tangle of arms and heads were visible through the glass patio doors on the rear deck. Most of the fallen were on the beach. A naked couple lay curled back to back on an old square sleeping bag. A faded motif of cowboys spinning lariats telegraphed the loss of innocence. A boy in a Broncos T-shirt and tennis shoes without socks was spread-eagled on a red-and-white-checked tablecloth, shorts missing, shortcomings visible.

Amid the carnage was a platoon of dead soldiers: beer bottles, wine bottles, and whiskey bottles. Paper cups, bits of cellophane, chip bags, cigarette butts, and other festive effluvia had been strewn across the sand like confetti. A plastic Gatorade bottle, an inch of creepy orange liquid inside, bobbed in the water near the shore.

At the far end of the grotto, near the wall, was an area devoid of bodies or blankets. Wine bottles, shoved neck down several feet apart, marked off a space about twenty feet long and half that wide. Two poles were jabbed upright into the sand with a bedsheet draped over them.

Jenny beached her boat a dozen yards from the barge and got out her anchor. Having heaved anchor and line over the bow, she jumped after, landing lightly on her feet. This far from the washing-machine motion of the main lake the water was calm. Wave action wouldn't lure her boat back into the channel. Barbarians might.

"Uhnnn?"

The bovine grunt alerted her that at least one student body was awake enough to register that an army of one had landed.

"Whathefuh?" came another lowing sound. "Izza fucking ranger."

Taking no notice of these promising signs of intelligent life, Jenny carried on with the task of setting the anchor as deep in the sand as she could manage without a sledgehammer. Rumbles percolated from behind her as she made more work of her anchorage than was needed, giving them time to wake up and pull themselves together. Two bare bottoms and a shriveled male member before lunch had her hoping that they would be not only waking but snatching up wearing apparel and covering the bits of themselves that shouldn't be allowed to flop about in the breeze.

When the stirring became ubiquitous, Jenny dusted the sand from her hands. Mentally girding her loins for battle, she turned to face the unwashed masses yearning to be educated. Hands on hips, she took in the mangy lot of them. Many didn't look to be of drinking age, let alone old enough to be wilderness potty-trained. A few looked properly cowed by, and respectful of, the NPS uniform and gunmetal gray government boat. None seemed overtly hostile. That was a plus. Without the color of law behind her, the only power Jenny had was the power of persuasion.

As she genially surveyed the group, there was one boy who called attention to himself. In this barely undulating sea of lethargy, a kid in iridescent blue swim trunks and a blue T-shirt with the words SHUCK ME, SUCK ME, EAT ME RAW in white under a picture of an oyster was sitting bolt upright on a nest of towels. His sharp quick movements reminded Jenny of a trapped bird flying into windows or the ceiling, looking for a way out. She'd have been hard-pressed to describe this boy as anything but average: average height, weight, eye and hair color. Though, if such averages ever existed, fast food and immigration had altered them in the United States.

Suddenly he met her gaze. Fidgeting stopped; like a rabbit hoping the coyote will mistake him for a rock, he froze.

He was scared, Jenny realized. Drugs were always a good guess—a lid of marijuana? X hidden in his clothes? Heroin, coke? He didn't look like he'd matriculated from misdemeanor to felony yet. Poor lad couldn't know she didn't give a rodent's posterior about drugs.

"Good morning, ladies and gentlemen," she said in her teaching voice, an impressive mix of Miss Jean Brodie and Kathleen Turner. "My name is Jenny Gorman. Welcome to my favorite place in all of Lake Powell."

Red rabbitty eyes blinked blearily at her. The creatures had managed to crawl from the sea onto land but had yet to evolve from dumb beasts to humanoids.

"Last summer you would not have been able to

enjoy this magnificent place. It was closed most of the season because there were three hundred fifty FC colonies—fecal material—per one hundred milliliters of water in the lake. It was too contaminated for our valued visitors to immerse themselves off this beach."

Her students began stretching, rummaging through bags, scratching. One girl, the one who'd been naked on the rope-twirling cowpokes, had wrapped a big towel decorated with a fat striped Kliban cat around her and was heading toward the sheet-draped poles.

"In short," Jenny continued, smiling graciously on her audience, "our visitors would have been swimming in shit. Bathing in crap. Diving into poop. Wallowing in human manure. It was, in a word, caca."

"That's two words," a boy hollered. There was general laughter, low-key, as if real hilarity would jar their hangovers.

"Ah, rapport has been achieved," Jenny said delightedly. She pointed at the heckler. "You, my astute friend, where does a bear shit in the woods?" Jenny was not overfond of the scatological, but she'd found that a good way to bridge the age gap with males was the use of third-grade toilet humor. Girls ceased finding farts and belches humorous before they went to high school. Boys found them hilarious all the way through senile dementia.

"Anywhere he wants." The kid shouted the punch line to the old joke.

"Correct again," Jenny said, looking appropriately impressed. "Now, tell me, do you see any forest around here?" Lifting both hands, she made a sweeping gesture toward the bare bones of Lake Powell's shoreline.

As she opened her mouth to get into the meat of the lesson, the whine of a high-powered engine burned through the still morning air. She turned to see who had the gall to speed in a blind canyon so narrow two boats couldn't pass without fighting each other's wake.

A wave crashed into the outside of the final curve and splintered into wavelets that came begging across the channel to throw themselves at her feet. They were followed by a sleek red cigarette boat Jenny could have identified in a fleet of speedboats.

Regis owned it, and no one but Regis piloted it. Regis was in personnel, an hour away in Page. He'd come to Panther Canyon at breakneck speed. Fear sent cold prickles over Jenny's scalp. One of her sisters had died or been badly injured. No one but her sisters was close enough to merit personal attention from personnel.

Jenna was the youngest but also the most reckless. Car crash?

Jessie was pregnant with her second son. Ectopic pregnancy? Eclampsia?

Jean was a pharmacist in Ann Arbor, Michigan. Surely nothing bad could happen to a pharmacist in Ann Arbor.

Jodie was married to a moron that the other sisters suspected abused her.

Jenny would beat the son-of-a-bitch to death with a tire iron.

Regis beached his precious boat gently, then leaped

gracefully to dry ground. Jenny had frozen her face and body lest the barbarians see weakness. Regis was walking in her direction. She couldn't unfreeze to say, "Hello."

He wasn't smiling.

"Good morning," he said with a curt nod at Jenny's erstwhile students. He turned his back to the now scattering class. "Are you okay, Jenny?" he asked quietly.

"I don't know," she managed. "Am I?"

Regis took her words as either a joke or a brush-off. Aping her arms-akimbo stance, he turned and surveyed the milling kids. "They give you any trouble?"

"No." Jenny waited for Regis to drop the bomb.

"I talked to a few of them the other day. They're an ugly bunch."

They weren't an ugly bunch—or no uglier than any bunch of campers who hadn't been housebroken. They were just younger and running in a pack. Tense, Jenny waited. And waited. Regis had no bomb to drop, she realized. Fear for her family leached away. Anger at Regis flowed in where it had been.

"Thanks for disrupting my class," she said acidly. The teaching moment was gone. She'd be lucky if she could get even a handful to pay attention at this point. "What are you doing out here, anyway? Don't you have important papers to push?" she asked irritably.

Regis stared at her coldly. Jenny didn't apologize. Among themselves, field rangers had a tacit understanding that headquarters brass should not venture out of their cubicles and interfere with the real work of the park. Jenny would never waltz into the personnel office and rearrange Regis's desk. On an irrational level, she expected the same courtesy.

He combed the beach with his eyes, ignoring or, worse, not noticing her ill humor. "That's him, I think. Bastard." With that, he strode across the sand, a man on a mission. Jenny watched him beeline through the groggy campers toward a boy on the upper part of the beach where the cliff of sand bisected the grotto floor, separating those who could still scramble up a soft embankment before they passed out from those who collapsed where they stood, drink in hand.

The "bastard" Regis stalked toward was the antsy kid with the pimples in the oyster shirt. He was drinking from a water bottle when he noticed Regis bearing down on him. His body jerked, seeming to spasm from head to heel. Water spilled over his chin. Then Regis was upon him, hands held in his standard conversational gesture: right hand slightly above shoulder height, index finger pointing heavenward, left cupped near his belt buckle, fingers curved as if holding a tiny world in his palm. It was eerily reminiscent of a whole lot of statues of Jesus Jenny'd seen in the cathedrals of Europe. She hoped the gesture was unconscious. It would be too weird if he'd practiced it in a dusty old mirror in a dank church basement when he was little.

Reading the poor boy the riot act, Jenny guessed, but she hadn't a clue why.

A girl rose from her blanket and headed toward the sheet-draped poles the woman in the Kliban-cat towel had visited. Heaving a sigh, Jenny went to intercept her. The area marked off with upended bottles and furnished with a privacy screen had to be a dedicated privy area. The partiers would undoubtedly be offended that sequestering their fecal deposits was not considered the height of ecological awareness.

Jenny had taken down the sheet and was nudging stragglers toward the houseboat in hopes of forging another interpretive moment from the wreckage. Regis, evidently finished with Joe Average, crossed her path on his way back to his boat. The cigarette boat had acquired a fan club of admiring boys. Fleetingly, Jenny thought of relocating her movable classroom to the beach.

"What was that all about?" she asked as Regis passed her.

He stopped and turned. "What was what about?" he asked blankly.

"Storming the beach, invoking the 'bastard,' cornering the boy in the blue T-shirt: What was that about?"

"I had a bit of a run-in with him and his pals when they were refueling at Dangling Rope. He says he doesn't know where his buddies are."

"Why are you trying to track them down?"

Regis ignored the question.

"What was the run-in about?" she tried when it was clear he wasn't going to volunteer any information.

"It's not something you should have to deal with," he said.

"I deal with shit all day every day," she countered, beginning to go from annoyed to seriously annoyed.

"I'll talk to the chief ranger today. In the meantime, stay as far away from that punk as you can get." Regis started walking.

"What did he do?" Jenny insisted.

Regis raised a hand in dismissal. "I'll get law enforcement on it," he said and strode purposefully toward the throbbing red phallic symbol he loved to ram through the waters of the lake.

Isn't that just the prick calling the bastard rude, Jenny thought and returned to herding hungover visitors in the general direction of the boat, where she might get a hearing. As reigning Fecal Queen, she feared this battle had been lost the moment Regis inserted himself into the equation. But for a horse's ass the battle was lost, she thought. Even butchered, the wisdom of the bard was ageless.

The kid Regis had called "bastard" was on the foredeck laughing and trying to snap another guy's butt with his towel—a hopeless task given that the towel was the size of a volleyball court. Gone were the furtiveness and the twitchy fear. Whatever Regis had hunted him down to impart hadn't cowed him, but had relieved him to the point of goofiness.

The kid caught her studying him. This time he grinned and waved as if she were his dear old auntie come to see him win the three-legged race.

"Stay away from him," Regis had said.

"Law enforcement will deal with it," Regis had said.

The kid struck Jenny as about as scary as a St. Bernard puppy. Still, she decided to do as the personnel officer suggested. Some St. Bernard puppies grew up to be Cujo.

That image in mind, she abandoned the idea of a two-way conversation with her soggy-brained pupils and decided to teach by example. Walking to her boat to gather bucket, rake, shovel, gloves, tongs, and plastic bags, she missed Anna Pigeon dearly. There was, literally and most graphically, a shitload of work to be done.

ELEVEN

Buzzing sounded in Anna's ears. Flies. Kay had been unearthed no more than a quarter of an hour and the flies had arrived. A lousy bug could find a person in the bottom of a solution hole inside of fifteen minutes, and a zillion rangers had let Anna rot for a day and a half.

The smell from the body, faint when it was beneath a foot of bone-dry sand, had increased exponentially since it had been dragged into the light of day.

Anna's arm ached from the tips of her fingers up through her shoulder joint; she was close to exhaustion and had developed a vicious thirst. It didn't matter. After all of the digging up, she was going to have to re-bury the woman. Unsettling as it was, Anna was going to strip her clothes off first. Naked and helpless for however long it had been, Anna craved Kay's clothes, craved being dressed. Even a bathing suit top seemed like a suit of armor. Cutoff jeans promised a return to normalcy, a deformed twisted normalcy certainly, but Anna was quickly learning to take what she could get. The sandals, with their thick rubber soles and sturdy

Velcroed straps, were the very embodiment of hope. If Anna did manage to crawl out of this pustule, she would need shoes to run away. Desert pavement was not as benign as it might sound.

The anklet with the sparkly KAY on it was the first thing she removed from the corpse. Should the murder ever come to light, Kay's mother and dad might recognize it. The second was the bikini bra. It was a string bikini, two triangles of printed fabric to cover the breasts held up with strings tied behind the neck and down with strings tied behind the back. Kay's breasts were considerably the larger, and where it had been revealing on the college girl, it would be almost modest on Anna.

She laid it out on the sand before she realized that she couldn't put it on properly. She didn't trust her arm not to pop out of its socket if she twisted behind her back to tie the strings. Paralyzing disappointment joined fatigue and raging thirst. Anna groaned long and low, sounding like a dungeon door opening into a B-movie chamber of horrors. Then and there she might have given in and given up had not the flies been landing on her, crawling about with their nasty little fly feet, wading through the sweat and the dust.

Flies were said to be subjects of Satan, the Lord of the Flies, but now Anna thought not. Evil, true evil, in her—and, more scientifically, her psychiatrist sister's— belief, fed on despair, the kind that suffocates every glimmer of light and life beneath a cold so intense it becomes darkness. Flies, on the other hand, simply pissed one off. They set about pestering Anna back to life, annoying her back into her body and inspiring her to fight back. "God damn it!" she hissed, swatting at the nearest offenders. For all their apparent loathsome sloth, the flies easily dodged her blows. "Okay, okay, I'm burying her, as soon as she's stripped. For God's sake, buzz off!"

Anger brought energy, and energy focused her mind. With Kay's unwitting contributions, Anna's material estate had been much improved. Despite everything, she experienced a genuine sensation of wealth on becoming the heiress to a pair of old shorts, a bra, and beat-up sandals.

She crawled over to where the corpse lay on its side, rudely booted from its burial trough.

Kay's low-slung cutoff jeans were held up by a worn man's belt, leather, with a simple square brass buckle. Anna unbuckled it, slipped the leather from the belt loops, rebuckled it in the last hole, and put it around her neck. That done, she rested her left arm in the sling. Immobilizing the arm brought instant relief.

Deep in her trap, hungry and thirsty and afraid, Anna actually smiled. She was inordinately pleased with her crude sling. In her thirty-odd years she had had her share of triumphs, but at that moment they all paled in comparison to her satisfaction at having thought to use a belt as a sling, having executed that thought, and having found it worked. A tiny shard of her overweening sense of helplessness fell away.

Much as she might have enjoyed simply sitting in

smug self-satisfaction, the flies again goaded her to action. The constant pain from her shoulder dulled, Anna's mind began to work better.

Work had increased her thirst to the level of incipient madness. She allowed herself one swallow from the poisoned canteen, rinsing her mouth and gargling before she swallowed in the hope of maximizing the wet of the water.

Pretending she was refreshed, she set about unsnapping and unzipping the jeans, then working them off the corpse's hips. As she jerked first one side then the other, lowering them by rude gritty inches, the top of Kay's panties was exposed. They weren't cute or sexy, no black lace, no thong, not even the day of the week embroidered on them.

"Oh jeez," Anna breathed, her eyes filling with sudden tears. "I'm a fucking grave robber. Your last, best ghoulfriend."

It would have been easier had they bespoken some debauchery, a hint of promiscuity. Anna would have settled for an indicator of vanity. There were none of these. Kay wore plain white Hanes underpants. They weren't even bikinis, but the next step up on the modesty scale, hipsters. Simple white cotton panties symbolized innocence and purity. Absurd as that was, Anna felt its truth, and it jarred her humanity.

Still crouched over the corpse as if she might devour it, Anna looked away.

Panties—even used panties—were a terrible temptation. A woman wearing panties was braver than a woman with a bare bottom. Panties would protect vulnerable places from the incursion of grit. All in all, panties would be a fine and wonderful addition to her life.

Anna worked the shorts down to the corpse's knees, then carefully tugged the white cotton Hanes back into place. Kay would meet her maker, if there was such a thing, with at least a semblance of human dignity.

Kay repaid the kindness. As Anna rolled her body onto its hip to make the final adjustment, the outflung arm, half buried during the frenzied excavation, flipped over and exposed itself.

Kay was wearing a watch, a cheap digital Timex, the kind that can be bought at Walmart for less than twenty dollars. It was working just fine. "Takes a licking and keeps on ticking," Anna said. "Hey, Molly," she called up the spout of her bottle, "it's Wednesday, July twelfth, three twenty-six P.M."

With teeth and fingertips, Anna released the watch from Kay's person and buckled the stiff plastic band around her own wrist. Arm bent at the elbow in the standard pose of the time reader, she marveled at the confidence this small machine gave her. She wasn't anywhere or anywhen, lost in a timeless limbo of days and drugs; she was right here on Wednesday at 3:27 P.M. Time mattered, every precious passing minute of it mattered. When all was said and done, time was all anybody really had. X amount of time between cradle and grave. The theft of it was the theft of life; the gift of it, more precious than anything on earth.

Watching the number in the last tiny digital readout window morph from seven to eight, Anna wondered how much time she had left. Allowing herself another swallow of water, she waited to see if she could feel the drug touching her insides. Maybe. Maybe when Monster Man topped it off the previous night he'd forgotten to add more of the knockout drug. Maybe it wasn't as potent as it had been. Maybe it would be safe to drink more of it. Maybe she was just trying to rationalize drinking more. Anna felt as if she could drain the whole of Lake Powell in a couple of gulps and still be thirsty.

Whatever the drug was, it made her groggy. The night before she'd lost control of her bladder and then passed out. Rufies, the date rape drug? Possible. Her memory was compromised, that was for sure. Chloral hydrate? Downers? Sleeping pills? Anna's money, had she had any, would have been on the date rape drug. Not that it mattered. She must drink or die.

She didn't know how long the drugged water had kept her unconscious. Tomorrow, with the fabulous watch, she would know. Then she could imagine all the things that might have been done to her while she was out. More fun to be had with her brain. Unless she didn't have a tomorrow in her future.

How much time did she have?

How should she spend it?

If you were going to die tomorrow—or tonight— what would you do? That question was a fairly standard party icebreaker. Anna had never had an answer for it. Everything and nothing. Now that she was faced with it, without a drink in her hand and a belief she had all the time in the world, she knew what she wanted most right at this minute. She wanted to get dressed.

Awkwardly, but with significantly less discomfort than she'd suffered before she'd fashioned her sling, Anna finished getting Kay's shorts off, dragged up her own legs, and snapped around her middle. The cutoffs were too big. Without the leather belt they hung dangerously low on her narrow hips. Still inspired by success, she laid the bra on the sand and tied the strings in square knots, then eased the loops over her head.

The bikini top hung more like a bib than a bathing suit. Anna didn't care. She had clothes on, just like a real person. It would have been nicer if they hadn't been encrusted with sand and skinned off a dead woman, but being grateful for what she had was getting easier every minute.

The next hour was spent reinterring the corpse. Anna wanted it buried deep enough that the flies and the stink would leave her jar. Every fifteen minutes— Anna knew the time because, in an ecstasy of knowledge, she checked the watch every few minutes—she allowed herself a careful mouthful of water. These dribs and drabs did nothing to quiet the grate of thirst, but she was afraid to take in any more.

At 4:49 P.M. on Wednesday, July 12, 1995, the reburial of the murdered woman known as Kay was successfully completed. The flies left as they had arrived, first a scout or two, then the lot of them. The small part of the day when a globule of sunlight made it down into the bottom of the jar had come and was nearly gone. The golden lozenge was high on the curving wall, below where the neck crooked.

Anna watched it move incrementally up, striking beautiful tones of color from the striated layers. In New York, in the theater, she'd given the natural world little thought beyond the rats in the subway, the fall colors on the trees in Central Park, and the fresh flowers in the corner grocery stores.

The mean streets, she thought idly, feeling the drug in her, strong, but not yet strong enough to take her away. Streets could be mean, cities romantic or dangerous, deadly or ugly. That which people made with their hands absorbed human emotions, radiated them back.

Nature, she realized, was indifferent.

Anna thought of Shakespeare and Johnson, Edna and Emily, Jane and Anne, Ibsen and Albee, Simon and Molière, writers and poets whose winds raged, seas grew sullen, and a thousand other emotions rode in on the tides of their imaginations.

The truth was, humans needed the forces of nature to be invested with emotion because they could not bear the fact that there was something that did not give a flying fuck about them. Anna found this idea comforting. Indifference was clean and honest. Having been begrimed by that which was human, she felt safety in that which was not.

The last sliver of light slipped away, the final beam disappearing over the lip like the tail of a lizard. Anna's thoughts tumbled down into the shadows where her body remained.

Night was coming and, with it, Monster Man with his thigh-carving equipment.

She decided she would take the chance and eat the other sandwich he'd left. If, indeed, the second waxed-paper package was a sandwich and not the fingers of children or dog turds. Keeping up her strength was important.

She would eat, then drink what she had to, but she swore to herself that she would do whatever it took to stay awake.

TWELVE

As Jenny hacked haphazardly through three stalks of celery, it occurred to her that she liked being alone, but only in small increments. Having a house to herself for a few hours was a luxury. Having to rattle around by herself twenty-four hours a day was a drag.

Anna Pigeon couldn't cook, and she wasn't a good trencherman—or was it trencherwoman?—but she was great with a knife, didn't mind dicing and slicing, and, when she could be lured out of her room and into conversation, was good company. Like a soldier in an old movie, Anna wanted to stick with name, rank, and serial number. Jenny'd had to work at it even to get her curriculum vitae.

Anna had a BA in theater arts, did not sing, dance, or act, and had no interest in doing so. After college, she'd started out as a set carpenter. In her late twenties, she moved to assistant stage manager at an Off-Broadway theater she seemed to think Jenny should have heard of. Jenny assumed, but was not sure, this was a promotion. Several years before Anna came to

Lake Powell she'd been promoted to stage manager. The money wasn't bad, she said. That surprised Jenny. She'd been under the impression that everybody in theater who wasn't on Broadway or the West End was starving.

Other than the job litany, Anna didn't open up.

"Open up," Jenny mocked herself. "I am becoming a moron," she announced to the celery as she swept it from the cutting board into a pale green Melmac bowl with a burn trough on the edge where some jerk had used it as an ashtray.

"Open up" was one of a plethora of canned phrases that had flopped into Jenny's vocabulary like a smelly old sardine to keep company with "closure" and "rebirth," getting in touch with inner children, and the rest of the language of self-absorption. Jenny was fluent in psychobabble. Psychologists had made large sums of money trying to help her pin down the precise abuse she had suffered as a very small child—too small to remember it, or so traumatized she blocked it, naturally— that could explain why she didn't like men.

It was all on her own, without a shrink in attendance or a self-help book in sight, that she'd realized she did like men. She just liked women better. Men were best in a bar fight or when heavy objects needed to be moved from point A to point B. Should she ever become a choir director she would want men to sing the bass parts, and maybe the tenor, though she supposed women could be found for that if one looked hard enough.

Men looked better than women in business suits. She'd gotten a lot of argument on that issue but held to her beliefs. Business suits were designed to make the wearer look important, imposing, rather like a powerful block of pin-striped cement with a stick up its ass.

This was not a good look for women.

Men won in contests of strength, in business-suit modeling, and when auditioning for Philip II in Giuseppe Verdi's *Don Carlos*. For nearly everything else, Jenny preferred women.

Women, plural. Sighing, she glopped peanut butter onto the celery, silently declaring it a salad. In her experience lesbians, more than most people, were good and true and honest. They wanted partners, trust, cats, turkey-baster babies, and mortgages.

Grabbing the big spoon from the peanut butter jar, she walked toward the front door and the porch picnic table. Womanizer, Romeo, Casanova, tomcat, playboy, ladies' man, lady-killer, swinging dick—there were a lot of roguish, obliquely charming terms for men who just loved the chase and the sex.

There were only a couple she could think of for women of that ilk. Nymphomaniac, the implied insanity right there in the title. Whore, everything implied in the title and none of it vaguely charming or flattering.

Jenny spooned a crunchy, creamy gob into her mouth and chewed thoughtfully. Maybe not "swinging dick." That was more a military thing and, now that she was considering it, made no sense. It had to be a size thing, she decided. To suggest a pendant was swinging was to suggest it had length and heft. "Bobbing dicks," for instance, would put one in mind of short silly things like Ping-Pong balls bobbing about in a bucket. "Dangling" dicks also lacked the seriousness men felt their penises deserved. Hanging dicks suggested a lack of life or movement.

At one time Dangling Rope was called Hanging Rope because, early on, boaters had seen a rope hanging down a cliff near some possibly prehistoric steps pecked into the rock. The NPS did not have size or heft issues. Hanging Rope was too like a lynching party. They'd changed it to Dangling. Dangling was happy-go-lucky.

Leaning back against the window of her apartment, the table snugged against the wall so a backless bench might be made tolerable, she crunched her dinner and enjoyed the pellucid light sifting from green to gray to blue over the far rim of the canyon. The first star—not the first to show itself, but the first to greet Jenny—did not so much pierce the sky as gently enhance it; no twinkle, all glow.

The second week Anna Pigeon had been in Dangling Rope, Jenny decided to see if she was seducible. She hadn't decided whether she wanted to seduce her or not, but, as a person of gay consequences, she had learned it was politic to test the waters before bringing flowers and candy. Regardless of how lush and tempting the meadow, a girl had to tread carefully. Land mines were everywhere.

Some gay women gave off a vibe. Lots didn't. More "straight" women than anyone not a sexual adventuress would guess wanted to be seduced now and again. Sort of like taking Russian folklore as an elective, Jenny surmised; a breadth class, a taste of another culture.

Jenny had plied Anna with red wine and rapt attention and, at the end of the evening, still hadn't a clue as to which way the woman's gate swung.

The salad was gone. Jenny wriggled from behind the table and, bowl in hand, looked over the edge of the porch and hissed.

"Hey Pinky Winky, I know you're there," she called into the greater darkness between her porch and that of Regis and Bethy. There was no answering stir from their resident rattlesnake.

Anna had been captivated by the snake. At first she'd been taken aback that there were five different species of rattlesnakes in the lake's environs. Pinky was special; she was a midget rattlesnake, her body smaller than that of most rattlesnakes and of a lovely rose pink color, perfect for blending into the desert floor.

"Won't even rattle for me?" Jenny asked. After a breath of silence she took her bowl into the kitchen, exchanged it for a bottle of Buckeye, and returned to the velvet of the night. This time she perched on the table, her feet on the bench.

Days in the desert were grand, but nothing compared to the nights. Had the brass been amenable, and the poop visible, Jenny would have started her day at sunset. Anna Pigeon loved the dark—that, at least, Jenny learned the night of her sexual reconnaissance. Jenny supposed a theater person would have to. After the third glass of wine—and given Anna's size, Jenny half expected her to pass out on the couch at any moment—Anna volunteered that one of the things she loved about theater was that during rehearsal or a performance, she knew precisely where she, and everyone else, belonged, knew what each person's job was and where they would, or should, be at any given moment. Glen Canyon, she said, made her feel like she'd fallen out of bed and woken up on Mars. Evidently finding this a breach of her personal code of nothing personal, Anna had then bowed like an arthritic old earl and took herself off to bed.

"Shoot," Jenny whispered, shaking her head. She was obsessing. Not just *thinking* about another woman, obsessing. Having done both, she knew the difference. A hollow creeping fog of addictive excitement was rising. The Adafaire Mason disaster had been years ago, but Jenny never forgot the symptoms: hyperawareness, overweening curiosity, and constant speculation about anything concerning, or any aspect of, the Subject. That was the court-appointed shrink's list, anyway.

At the time she'd thought it absurd. Maybe these many years later those visits were paying off. Since she recognized the symptoms, theoretically, she could avert the disaster. *Theoretically.* She drained the beer. Anna was gone. Surely obsessing on a missing person couldn't end badly.

"Hsst. Pinky," she tried again, but the snake said nothing.

She managed an entire shower and had nearly completed brushing her teeth without once thinking of the Subject. Mostly, she managed it by worrying obsessively about the possibility her obsessive tendencies had returned, then excusing them due to the Subject's departure for parts unknown.

"Mea culpa, mea culpa, let's blame me, let's blame me," she sang to the tune of "Frère Jacques" as she knelt naked on the rug in front of the cabinet beneath the sink. Singing, she'd discovered, was the only effective measure one could take to shut out unwanted thoughts.

Over the course of the evening she'd swilled sufficient amounts of beer that if she didn't find some aspirin and wash two or three down with a quart of water, she was sure to wake up in the middle of the night with a headache. Her hangovers were precocious things and could seldom wait till morning. She opened the cupboard door and started to reach in.

Anna Pigeon's stuff was still there. Jenny's belongings were neatly arrayed on the top shelf. Anna, as the late arrival, had been relegated to the bottom.

The unhealthy excitement built. This was a treasure trove for a woman who was obsessing. Anna is gone, she told herself. No harm, no foul. Getting comfortable, she crossed her legs, feet soles up on opposite thighs. Full lotus had been easy for her since she was teeny tiny.

The thrill was coursing through her, making her feel half scared, half excited; the way she felt when she met a new woman or nearly got run off the road by a Mack truck. Instead of leaning down and looking into the floor-level shelf, as she'd done when she'd first noticed it wasn't cleared out, Jenny reached in blind, like a child putting its hand into a grab box at a county fair.

She knew it would serve her right if there was a nest of black widow spiders in the cupboard, but she didn't stop. The first prize she grabbed and pulled into the light of the bathroom bulb was a blue plastic Secret solid deodorant dispenser. Jenny set it carefully to the side of the frayed bath mat that served as her bathroom rug. Next was a box of tampons, three-quarters full, then a bottle of Xanax, dental floss, a hairbrush with rubber bands secured around the plastic handle, a tube of ChapStick, a box of Q-tips, toothpaste, hand lotion, shampoo, crème rinse, nail clippers, birth control pills, and an emery board.

Jenny ran her hands over the aged wood of the shelf but found nothing else.

The Subject's items were lined up like soldiers along the edge of the rug.

Tampons.

Xanax.

Hairbrush.

Birth control pills.

These were not things a woman forgot, not things she would leave behind.

Jenny's illicit frisson of excitement took on a sharper edge.

THIRTEEN

The 747 landed without a bump. Anna stood in the aisle with the solid clot of humanity clutching bags to their chests or jostling to drag luggage down from the overhead bins so as not to spend a moment more than necessary on board.

The flight was a blur, as was the Martian landscape of Glen Canyon, and the beautiful deadly jar. All she knew or wanted to know was that she was free and safe and almost home.

The clot began to break up, people bleeding out of the plane's hatch. Anna had no luggage, no purse, no glossy magazine. Her hands were empty, and she felt she flowed rather than shuffled as row after row of blue upholstered seats passed in her peripheral vision. The tube connecting the airplane to the terminal was round, jointed like the hose of a vacuum cleaner, and, like a vacuum, it hoovered Anna up. She was almost flying. Molly would be waiting for her.

The terminal lived up to its name. Anna felt the thud as she slammed into the waiting area and movement stopped. Platinum blond hair, cut fashionably short, jewel-tone suits, posture one salute shy of military, Molly always stood out in a crowd.

Anna's eyes refused to find her.

Molly hadn't come. The Jetway reversed its suction. Anna was being pulled backward toward the plane. Then she saw him, leaning against a wall with angular grace, silky hair curling at his collar, glasses crooked on his fine long nose.

"Zach!" she cried and started to run to him. From behind her came the sound of static, and her legs went numb. "Zach!" She was screaming now.

He looked into her eyes. With his forefingers he traced a heart on his chest and let it fall into his cupped palms. He blew it to her like a kiss, then turned and walked away.

Again she screamed his name, but the static was so loud it drowned her out. He didn't look back.

Static. Scratching. A cry like that of a small animal being slaughtered.

Anna opened her eyes. She had broken her vow to stay awake. Crumpled, as if she'd collapsed midpace, she was on her side in the soft sand a yard from Kay's grave. The only hint of light was a faint oblong, slightly less black, on the floor of the jar, moonlight sifting through hundreds of thousands of miles of outer space to the earth's atmosphere, only to fall into inner space as dark as that from whence it had come.

Scratching.

Confused, Anna rolled onto her back. Her left arm fell from its resting place on her upthrust hip and sharpened her mind with a jolt of pain. Somebody was coming. Rocks were being moved, tiny pebbles, a stealthy coming, but erratic. Monster was coming. Anna tried to get to her feet, but the drug, like the dream, crippled her, and she floundered beetle-like on her back. Finally she made it to her knees. In the pose of a drunken penitent, she swayed and stared upward. If she tried to stand, she would fall. If she tried to struggle against whatever was coming, she'd lose. Thirst had undone her. Despite her promises, she had consumed more from the poisonous canteen than she should have. Unless it was in the second sandwich. It didn't matter. The monster was coming and she was helpless.

He—it—had already manipulated her body, carved WHORE on her thigh and very possibly done things she refused to let herself imagine, but he hadn't killed her.

Better to play dead than be dead. Anna rearranged herself into a fetal position on the sand and waited.

For a minute or so, no more sounds emanated from the upper realms, and she dared hope that she had been left to enjoy her personal Hades unmolested, at least for the night. Then the disturbance renewed, frenzied, as if the monster were scrabbling around, raking up gravel or rolling in something.

Fear loosened Anna's bowels, but she would not lose control of her bladder again. Now that she had clothes, it was unthinkable.

Now that she had clothes, the monster would take them away from her.

The thought terrified her more than the coming of her captor. Knowing it was irrational didn't ratchet

down the horror one notch. He would take her shorts
and bra, the belt sling.

He would take the watch.

Making so much noise she could no longer monitor
sounds from overhead, she squirmed out of the stolen
clothing, ripped the Velcro loose and kicked off the sandals, then lifted the belt and the bikini bra from around
her neck. The watch she put in the pocket of the denim
shorts where she had stowed Kay's anklet for safe-
keeping.

When she'd finished piling up her worldly goods,
she heaped sand over them. Without light she couldn't
tell if she'd buried them completely or not. Running
her hands over the sand, she checked for bits of exposed
fabric or leather. The motion gave her the sensation of
swimming through thick black waters so far beneath
the surface of the ocean that not a glimmer of sunlight
penetrated.

The monster would have a flashlight; Anna knew
that. Carving WHORE into her thigh had taken time
and a decent light to work by.

Scootching backward on her newly bare behind,
pushing with her heels and the palms of her hands, she
crossed the whisper of moonlight and reached the wall
of the jar. There she lay down on her right hip, the ques-
tionable left arm on the sand in front of her face. Pulling her knees up in the futile hope of protecting her
vulnerable belly and breasts, she waited.

The noise, light and irregular, was joined by the
sound of panting. Anna squeezed her eyes shut. A high-
pitched strangled cry jolted them open again. A small

black object, like the head of a doll—or a cat—fell into the crescent of waning light on the sand. It bounced into the impenetrable black of the datura patch near the grave.

Then nothing. Silence, so complete Anna could feel its weight on her skin, filled the solution hole. Staring up at the narrow mouth, she couldn't see anything but the prick of a single star.

Whatever was there was gone.

Whatever was here was here.

FOURTEEN

O pening the throttles, Regis reveled in the rush of speed as the powerful engine dug in and the hull climbed to the lake's surface. Three, four, five hundred feet below the keel were the rotting remains of dozens—if not hundreds—of boats. No one knew the precise number. Boats sunk too deep to be salvaged. In more wrecks than the NPS liked to admit, corpses, preserved by the cold, floated in dark cabins.

Lake Powell covered over two hundred fifty square miles of what had once been dry land. The ruins of ancient civilizations were drowned. Derelict machinery, trailer houses, sheep pens, watering troughs, windmills, broken-down vehicles, propane tanks, rubber tires—any junk that was not cost-effective to haul away was fed to the rising water.

The living danced, drank, partied, and water-skied over the dead.

As it should be, Regis thought. The pure joy of being one of the living caught him by surprise as it sometimes did when he was flying. Delicately he probed the phenomenon. Like a majority of the human race, he was accustomed to living in a psychic brownout: Barely There, walking dim pathways, hearing muted voices. The difference was, he was aware of the muffling. Others seemed contented with somnambulism. Whether he envied or scorned them depended on his mood.

Today, on this murderous playground of a lake, he was suddenly totally and completely alive. His veins and arteries hummed like high-voltage wires, electrifying every part of him. Maybe it was the speed of the boat cutting clean and fast through dark water. Speed sometimes affected him like a drug. No. This was new. This was speed and fear combined, a kind of wild, teetering high that pulled him from the shadows.

A single day of this high-octane life was worth years of reviewing seasonal applications, sitting through endless meetings, eating hash brown casseroles, and watching Bethy's bottom spread. A single day of this made going back wretched to consider. It wasn't that Regis had never felt good before. He'd thought he'd been happy enough, often enough. In early lust for Bethy he'd had his moments. Climbing with her up canyon walls so sheer even sunlight couldn't stay on them, he'd felt totally awake.

Risk. It came to him and he felt God's own fool. It hadn't been the young, and then nubile, Bethy who'd turned his life from black-and-white to living color those few months. It was risk, the risk of falling, being killed, of her falling, being killed or crippled. Risk and the promise of wealth; that was the combination that had him down on one knee, diamond solitaire in hand.

"Holy smoke." The wind snatched the words away

from his lips as they formed. Falling in love. Bethy was necessary, but it was the thrill of the fall he was in love with.

For the first time, he got why people chose to be firefighters, track down lions, arrest felons—type A's. Cops, rangers, sheriffs were always telling people to stand back, let the professionals handle it, call for help. They'd done a fabulous job of convincing the sheepish public that taking matters into their own hands would just make those matters worse.

They didn't care about the sheep; they wanted to keep the fun for themselves. Risk, that was what made the blood sing high and fine. Two hours ago he'd been afraid of the risk he'd taken calling in sick. Regis bleated, then smiled. When had the wool been pulled over his eyes? When had he donned sheep's clothing?

Cutting a sharp right into the mouth of Dangling Rope, head back, hair wild in the wind, he realized he was laughing.

"Slow down!" somebody yelled as he waked the marina, slamming boats into their bumpers. Regis waved. He wasn't going to slow down. He might not ever slow down again.

Unerringly, he speared the cigarette boat into the mooring slot nearest the marina store. The slot was reserved for NPS boats. Risk. Having leaped to the dock, he whipped his lines over the cleats. Mad dogs and Englishmen: In the noonday sun he jogged up the incline from the dock toward the gray duplexes hugging the square of green like elephants guarding an oasis. He'd resented spending the summer out here rather than in their house in Page. No more. Life was edgier at the Rope. People were more open. Gory memories of Kippa dulled. Sun blessed his bare head; the air was cut to fit his lungs. The desert was limned with gold and red, every dry blade of grass, every stone as clear-cut as a new diamond.

Sweat ran down his spine. Glen Canyon in July was so hot even Superman would sweat through his tights. Regis smiled at the thought and broke into a run for the last fifteen yards. Heart attack, heatstroke: risk.

Jenny would scream like a banshee when she found out he'd gotten her a new roommate and he was a person of the male persuasion. Jenny insisted her preference for women was not sexism but sanitation, citing the fact that women seldom, if ever, pissed on the floor and that, given her job, she should at least be allowed to eat in an environment free of human waste.

Barry Mack—aptly named "Mackerel" by his co-workers in honor of his body odor—the toilet scrubber, would be out to the Rope as soon as the paperwork to up-jump him from a GS-3 maintenance man to a GS-5 interpretive ranger was finished. Risk. Regis would definitely be on hand when Jenny was introduced to Barry and his grime-encrusted fingernails.

Panting, he let himself in through Jenny's battered screen door. He paused and looked back into a glare the honey locusts were too small to filter out. No one was watching him. Again he laughed. Risk bred paranoia. Who cared if anybody saw him entering Jenny's duplex? He was here on business, here to check the room the Mackerel was assigned. The room Anna Pigeon had occupied.

Bed stripped, closet doors partly open, window blind at a drunken angle in one window, air-conditioning unit in the other: The room was as he'd last seen it. Footsteps noiseless on the drab carpet, he crossed the room and turned on the swamp cooler. The fan thumped and clanked as if it were cutting carrots instead of air but, after a minute, blew cold.

He switched it off and stepped back into the hallway. The door to Jenny's room was closed, leaving the hall in semidarkness. What light there was leaked from the bathroom at the end of the hall. Feeling for the ghosts, Regis stood in silence and stillness. The Not There were not there for him in his present heightened state. He didn't miss their nonexistent emanations. No self-respecting ghost should be forced to haunt the likes of Barry the Mackerel.

Regis was turning to leave when the dim light from the bath caught his attention. On the bath mat in front of the sink cabinet somebody—Jenny, who else?—had arranged two lines of irregularly shaped objects. Backlit, they looked like men in a futuristic game of chess. Jenny Gorman was an interesting woman. Her sexual preferences never made her any more or less interesting to Regis. Playing peculiar games on the bathroom floor was another matter entirely.

Moving quietly out of habit, Regis closed the distance between Barry Mack's new room and whatever Jenny had set to guard her bathroom sink. At the door, he flipped the light switch. Along the ratty edge of a faded pink terry-cloth mat, Jenny had lined up two rows of feminine detritus, tampons, birth control pills, the usual stuff women keep in the bathroom. "Riddle me a riddle: Why did the lesbian line up her girl things?" he asked the ether as he squatted on his heels.

"To convince herself she is a girl."

That wouldn't fly. Jenny was all girl all the time, so much so she'd fallen in love with her own gender.

Hairbrush, Xanax . . . Jenny didn't strike Regis as the Xanax type. She loved the classics: nicotine and alcohol. Anna Pigeon, tranquilizers fit her.

"Damn it," Regis hissed and snatched open the door of the cupboard. Like items lined the top shelf. The shelf near floor level was bare. When Anna Pigeon's things were packed, these were forgotten.

Regis stood and switched the light off. People left things behind in the units all the time. Every fall, after the seasonal nomads moved on, maintenance collected the forgotten or abandoned bits and bites of them and tossed them in the trash.

These must have felt different than the usual leftovers to Jenny. Why else would she line them up as neat as soldiers on parade? Evidently, to her, these meaningless items had meaning. "When the Pigeon flies the coop, why does Jenny arrange her toiletries in two lines?" Regis muttered.

Playtex tampons, Secret deodorant—regular scent—Xanax, birth control pills in a flat round dispenser.

What they had in common was that these weren't things women could take or leave, these were things women needed. It was unlikely they would be forgotten or purposely left behind.

If they were not purposely left behind, it suggested Anna Pigeon did not leave on purpose either. She'd been planning to come back, shower, put on deodorant, maybe change a tampon, take a birth control pill and a Xanax and go to bed.

Fear welled up, curdling the exhilaration of risk. The downside of being fully alive was that even that which was bad was felt more keenly. Fear clenched Regis's stomach. Sweat broke out at his hairline.

What had Jenny Gorman done?

More to the point, what was she doing now?

He walked down the hall and let himself out into the sunlight. In three steps he crossed the barren ground between her porch and his own. Ignoring the heat and the glare, he collapsed into one of Bethy's pink-and-green Walmart lawn chairs. What, exactly, had he seen? Did Jenny leave Anna's things out knowing he would see them, knowing Anna's position needed to be filled and Regis would come check the room? That seemed a bit far-fetched. Yet there they were, basically on display.

Television—the movies—suggested some criminals, especially the serial murderers, wanted to get caught. The Zodiac and his letters. BTK and his hints. Until this moment on the porch, searing light making his shadow hard and black as it struggled to crawl from beneath his chair, Regis had thought that was absurd.

Anna Pigeon's belongings had been cleared out of her room. Everything except the things in that one cupboard. Regis wanted it to be simple oversight, but nothing was that simple, just like nothing was perfect. Maybe that was the catch with the perfect crime; it was impossible because the criminal would betray himself if nobody else did.

Feeble rattling trickled up from beneath the porch boards, faint as the ticking of a buried clock. Distracted from questions to which he had no answers, Regis rose from the chair and stomped once on the porch floor. Rattling came back stronger. He jumped off the porch and, in one fluid move, knelt on the dry earth. Palms on burning soil, he peered into the shadows beneath the duplex.

Pinky Winky, the midget faded rattlesnake, was pulled out to its full length. A nail behind its head and one at the base of the rattles pinned it to the ground where it was rattling out the last painful hours of its life.

FIFTEEN

As was beginning to be the norm, Anna woke with a drug hangover, a spotty memory, sand in every orifice, and thirst and pain her old familiars. Curled in a tight ball, spine against the reassuring curve of sandstone, she lay with her cheek pillowed on the sand. Night terrors, real or imagined, had settled to the bottom of the solution hole and weighed on her bare skin like chills following fever. Thirst was already clawing at her with scratchy panicked fingers. She knew she couldn't deny herself water long enough for the drug to clear from her system. Thirst was too cruel an adversary. She would drink and, always, the monster would find her helpless, hazy, unconscious, or nearly so. Drugged until she could die without even noticing.

For a time she lay unmoving, eyes closed, repositioning herself in the universe she had fallen into, much as Alice had fallen into the rabbit hole: the jar, the sounds of movement from above, the terror, the black thing thrown into the last whisper of moonlight.

Doll's head, she'd thought. Severed cat's head, she'd thought.

Tarantula, she thought now. Her eyes snapped open. Only in zoos and horror movies had Anna seen tarantulas. That had been sufficient. Though inferior in size to grizzly bears, muggers, vampires, and other assorted predators, they made up for it in sheer horridness.

Tarantulas were native to Glen Canyon. That, along with the fact that there were five separate species of rattlesnakes, had been divulged during orientation by the park naturalist with what Anna thought was an inappropriate amount of glee. He had gone on to say that certain kinds of the humongous bugs made wonderful pets. He assured the assembly that the immense hairy ugly spiders were not aggressive or particularly poisonous.

They had no need to be. One look and their prey dropped dead of a heart attack, to be dragged away at the creature's leisure.

The instant the thought scuttled into her mind on eight little feet, Anna was certain the fist-sized black fuzzy item tossed into her jar the previous night was a gigantic tarantula. Sitting up so suddenly her shoulder and head shrieked in protest, she quickly checked around her. In the meager colorless light of either dawn or dusk—depending on how long she'd been out this time—every ripple in the sand seemed the hunched back of a tarantula, ready to spring.

Hirsute insect legs tickled her lower back. Terror overrode the messages her sore tendons and bruised skull tried to send. Screaming, she thrashed, kicking and clawing to put as much distance between her and the spider as she could.

The thing came with her, running across her back where she could not see it. Still screaming, she twisted and bucked. It skittered up her spine to her neck, then over her shoulder onto her chest.

"God fucking damn it. God fucking damn it!" she wailed, wanting to cry but having neither the moisture nor the strength to do so.

It was the tail of her long braid that had tickled and clung and pursued her halfway across her sandpit. The waste of strength and the aftermath of fear burned down the channels of her brain to flicker out in the ashes of her mind.

Panting, tongue too dry to coax saliva from her cheeks or gums, Anna realized two things: One, she was naked again, and two, she was no longer afraid. The nakedness confused her. Had she imagined finding the body of a woman named Kay, stripping it, and reburying it? Had the monster come again while she lay drugged? The anti-Santa, the Satan, climbing down the chimney to steal from children and molest them as the sugarplums danced?

Day's light grew stronger. Sunrise, then, not sunset. Anna saw the hasty burial near the wall across from where she sat and remembered how she had tried to hide her purloined finery under the sand so Mr. Monster wouldn't take it. The belt was entirely exposed and one sandal only partially buried.

She remembered the cries and desperate scrabbling near the mouth of her lair. That memory should have engendered fear. She waited for it, but it didn't come creeping through her bowels and up her spine.

Freedom from fear. It had been a long time since Anna had been free.

Those long terrible weeks in the New York apartment alone, she'd been afraid to go to sleep, afraid to wake up, afraid to answer the phone, afraid not to. Sitting in a red plastic chair holding Zach's hand, she'd been scared to stay and terrified to leave. When Zach was truly gone, she was afraid of staying in the apartment they'd shared, afraid of leaving it and losing the last scents and relics of him. She'd been afraid of staying in New York, where every piece of concrete and steel reminded her of him, and afraid to leave the city they'd shared; afraid of forgetting and afraid of remembering.

Then here and this. WHORE on her thigh, thirst, drugs, pain.

Then now; fear gone as if it had been but smoke and a strong wind had blown it clear. It was as if she had been allotted enough fear to last a lifetime and she had squandered it all during three months in New York and three days in a sandstone jar. What remained in the cranial vault where decades of horror had been stored to be meted out as the slings and arrows of life demanded was a strange determination, grim and gray as slate. Determination to do what, Anna wasn't sure. Survive? Die as annoyingly as possible? Bite the hand that had forgotten to feed her?

Moving sluggishly, she reclaimed her treasures, the belt over her head to serve as a sling, the watch on her wrist, the bra as a token bib around her neck. As she shook the sand from these items and painstakingly put them on, she watched for the tarantula. Not afraid, but not particularly wishing to be surprised by the enormous arachnid.

It had either scuttled into the deadly nightshade patch or burrowed into the sand. She had a vague recollection of watching a PBS special with Zach where tarantulas dragged other bugs into holes in the ground, stung them, and then laid eggs in their comatose bodies so the kiddies could have a fresh snack when they hatched.

Dressed, she sat with her back to the wall and rested. The canteen was beside her. She picked it up and shook it. Not a lot of water was left, a quart or less. Enough to knock her out ten times over and never truly slake her thirst. Unable to stand the feel of her throat closing, the sides of her esophagus adhering to one another, she uncapped it and took a mouthful.

Since Mr. Monster apparently hadn't bothered to come down to torment her the previous night, maybe he was done with her, playing with her naked inert body and carving a rude word into her flesh the extent of his commitment to the relationship.

As she pondered the possibility that she had been left to die of unnatural causes, she saw the stem of one of the datura plants shift slightly. The tarantula. A black bead appeared a couple of inches above the ground. An eye. Or the tip of a feeler. Anna couldn't remember if tarantulas had feelers. She worked her way up onto her knees. Her left arm free of the sling, she held the canteen in front of her with both hands like a shield. Spiders could jump. Anna had seen the smallest of them jump several inches. For a being less than a quarter of an inch wide, including legs, that was a prodigious feat. A tarantula the size of the one she'd seen hit the sand the night before could probably jump five feet or more.

"I will squash you like a bug," she said to the black bead in the weeds and shook the canteen to show she meant it.

The plants quivered again, and a second black bead revealed itself.

Anna raised the canteen over her head.

The grasses moved, and a pointed black snout emerged between the beads. Both black eyes were fixed on her. Anna didn't move. She'd stopped breathing.

Cautiously, a tiny skunk kit poked its nose from the sere foliage, then dared a paw, then another. It was no bigger than Anna's hand, coal black with two white stripes originating above its eyes and streaming over the fur of its back to a plume of tail.

The cry in the night that Anna had thought sounded like a small animal must have been just that; the erratic scratching sounds, the paws of coyotes as they attacked and killed the mother skunk. The kit was too small to have been on his own. When the coyotes attacked, this little guy must have fled into the mouth of her jar for safety, then tumbled down. The kit couldn't weigh more than a pound, and he'd landed on soft sand. The impact must have been minimal. He didn't appear to be hurt, just frightened of the enormous bipedal beast whose den he found himself in.

No, Anna corrected herself, not frightened, more interested. Had he been frightened, she thought, he was supposed to turn away and point his bottom at her so he could spray. Chances were he'd never seen a person and was more curious than fearful.

"Hey, buddy," she said softly as she lowered the canteen and laid it gently on the sand. The little animal flinched but didn't run back behind the datura leaves. Stilling herself, she let her eyes wander, pretending she had little interest in him but sneaking glances. Watching the ball of fluff sniff around, exploring this new place with increasing confidence, she experienced a sensation she hadn't felt for so long it took her a moment to identify it.

Delight.

She was delighted. That an animal she could fit in a pocket, a wild creature, and a skunk to boot, could bring so much life into the jar that the air seemed brighter, the walls more cozy than forbidding, and her heart no longer too heavy to beat, amazed her.

Soon, she knew, she would worry about how to keep her new friend alive. How much drugged water would be too much and shut down his heart? Should she try to capture him and throw him up the neck of the jar into the real world before he perished from thirst? Or was he too young to survive in the world above without his mama? Like the writers of *Old Yeller* or *The Yearling,* had the fates given her this warm little soul only so the monster could take it away in some gruesome fashion?

Soon. Soon she would worry. For now she was content to sit, head resting against the stone, and revel in the tiny perfect creature toddling around on the sand.

Anna was no longer alone.

SIXTEEN

Anna's false sun moved through her sandstone universe, crawling down one side of the jar, creeping across the bottom, and lapping at the other side. On the surface of the earth the temperature was probably in the nineties; in the perpetual shade of the jar, Anna was not uncomfortable. No longer plagued by fear, and drifting on the low-level effects of sipping drugged water, it occurred to her that Nature wasn't as harsh as she'd thought when she'd come to Glen Canyon. It was Man's fighting against it that made it hard.

A woman—even a drugged and broken stage manager—who embraced it could find comforts. Solitude—something she'd dreaded since Zachary had gone—was, in truth, beautiful. Not loneliness, but freedom from people. How could she be lonely while Buddy delicately explored her toes with his snout and one wee paw?

The skunk kit wandered off to find something better than toes with which to play. A strange piece of music filtered through Anna's memory. Glenn Branca, she thought.

Running Through the World Like an Open Razor.

Human emotion was the razor: slights, sneers, mockery, love, hope, desire. All cut in their own way. Those wounds spawned their own cuts in actions taken, understandings and misunderstandings, then in the remembering.

Not so in solitude.

The prison of the jar she'd feared and loathed was simply stone. She was there uninvited. It neither hated nor loved nor cared. Today she found in it shelter from the sun; tonight, from the cold. Monsters and thirst and starvation were not part of the sandstone; they were of humanity, of the razors. The stone itself was pure, enduring. It had no ambition. It did not plot or pine, trap or torment. Rain deepened it, sand blew in, cold sheared flakes from its walls, torrents carved canyons, and forests poked roots into its crevices. Form changed without resentment, loss, or lust.

Bizarrely, given that she was probably going to die soon one way or another—and none of them pleasant—Anna was more at peace than she had been since she'd last lain in Zach's arms, oblivious to the fact that the end of her world was nigh.

The canteen was resting upright in a trench of sand she'd made. So far as she'd noticed, the cap didn't leak, but water—even poisoned water—was too precious a commodity to take chances with. Tipping the canteen, she filled the cap and poured it over her tongue. Using the cap as a measure, she found she could control her consumption to a certain extent. At least her parched innards had less of a chance to override her will and gulp it down.

Buddy turned at the sound—or maybe the smell. His tiny black nose had grayed. Part of it was dust from his explorations, but, Anna guessed, some was because his nose must be drying out. He took several steps in her direction, then stopped, gazing up at her, his nose twitching.

"I'm afraid to, Buddy. I don't know what's in it, what it would do to someone as small as you," she said miserably. "I would if I could. When I get us out, you shall have a mastiff-sized bowl in your room at all times. I promise."

When we get out.

Anna heard the words come into her ears. In this hole in the ground she had managed to undress and rebury a body, dress herself, stay moderately sane, make a sling for her arm, and acquire a pet skunk. Though drugged to the gills, she had made the attempt to hide her clothes when noises came from above. What she had not even considered was that she could get out. First, she'd hoped the rangers would come get her out, then she'd resigned herself to—to what? To living and dying in a buff-and-peach-colored bottle like a short-lived genie with a bra that didn't fit and no harem pants?

Could she get herself and Buddy out? Gathering the foggy tendrils of thought back from the drug marshes muddying her brain, she tried to focus. Moqui steps; that was what the park historian called the shallow toe- and fingerholds carved into the sides of some of the rock around the lake. The ancient peoples made them so they could travel to and from the river more easily.

The cap of the canteen was metal and had a small-linked metal chain that attached it to the mouth. Tin probably, a soft metal. Still, it might do to scrape away the soft sandstone.

Granules of sand hit her cheek and dragged her from her thoughts. Buddy was digging furiously. Since it was not right where the corpse was interred, Anna didn't stop him. For all she knew, skunks could be like cats and dig holes to use as latrines.

Lying back, the canteen pressed into service as a headrest, she studied the body of the jar—a space she had done nothing but study for days. It was shaped rather like a turnip, round and full at the bottom, then curving into a narrow point that veered off at an angle, before opening to the sky.

Moqui steps wouldn't work. A strong person, with two good arms, might be able to climb them on a ninety-degree vertical. No one but Count Dracula could climb them at ninety-five degrees. Gravity would not be defied. The inward curve of her jar was more pronounced than a mere ninety-five, closer to a hundred and fifteen.

The only way out was however the monster came and went. It would be easy enough to climb down a rope, but climbing up over the curve would require strength and agility.

Also, it would probably be better not to be drugged off one's ass.

Two good arms would help. Gingerly she shrugged

her left shoulder. Maybe it was her imagination, but she was sure she could feel the round bone end trying to push out of the socket. Whatever held her together—tendons, ligaments, muscles—was torn or stretched.

Sand scattered over her belly. "Buddy," she said as she struggled to a sitting position. "What are you doing?"

The skunk kit had dug up a moldy green snaky-looking thing. He had it in his teeth and, front paws braced, haunches bunched, was trying to pull the rest of it out of the dirt. It was a strap, Anna realized, army green and tightly woven like the belts with the flat buckles. Memory flashed and she saw the belt around Kay's hips as the boys abused her, saw the water bottle clipped to it with a carabiner.

"Let me help you, Buddy," she whispered and gently took hold of the strap between his jaws and the dirt. Buddy didn't run or let go. "We're a team," Anna assured him. With little effort she uncovered the rest of the belt. There was a small fanny pack she hadn't noticed before and the water bottle: one liter, clear plastic and three-quarters full. Pizarro looking on El Dorado, Ponce de Leon at the Fountain of Youth, Arthur and Excalibur: Anna was stunned by the glitter of the treasure Buddy had unearthed. Her hands shook so badly, she had to stop for a moment and rest them on her lap. The water bottle lay on its side. Sudden fear that it was leaking goaded her into movement. Carefully, as if it were delicate china, she set the bottle upright and banked sand around it.

The first capful should go to Buddy, she knew that.

Buddy was already onto the fanny pack, scratching and gnawing on the black dusty nylon. Anna pulled the zipper open for him.

"Granola bars with chocolate chips. That's what you were after all along, isn't it?" Using her teeth, she tore one of the two foil-wrapped packets open and bit off a corner of the bar. This she spat into her palm and offered to Buddy. Gingerly, one eye on the prize and one on the biped, he took it, then scurried away a few feet to eat it. The next bite Anna kept for herself. Hunger was with her these last hours or days, but thirst was a good appetite depressant and she hadn't suffered the pangs much. Chocolate awoke them.

Doling out the water as if it were the most precious commodity on earth—which, in fact, it was—Anna filled the cap from the plastic bottle with the good water and set it a foot or so from Buddy. The first swallow was his. The next was hers.

The urge to drink all of the water was almost too powerful to resist. Almost. Anna sipped and chewed. Once, she refilled Buddy's cap and gave him another chunk of the granola bar. It was his nose, after all, that had found the treasure. This time she picked out the chocolate chips first, then offered it to him. "Chocolate might not be good for little skunks," she said apologetically. Buddy, had he had any fear of her to begin with, had none now. He took the morsel from her fingers and ate it.

Anna returned the second granola bar to the fanny pack. Fortified with sips and bites, she was settled enough to see what else the pack contained. Sunscreen,

SPF 40—so shady was her jar, Anna hadn't much use for that, but she rubbed it on her face for the moisture. As the heavy cream soaked in, she felt her skin relax and expand to cover her bones. There was a ChapStick that she pounced on greedily, rubbing the oily wax into her cracked lips. The small sack was emptied. Having administered to herself, she replaced the lotion and lip balm inside and zipped it closed.

"I have a plan, Buddy," she announced to the baby skunk. "It's only partially baked. So it qualifies as a bona fide adventure." So saying, she wondered if the miracle of the bars and the water had made her giddy.

The first play she'd ever stage-managed was *Hello, Dolly!* The boys from Yonkers were off to New York City for an adventure. Barnaby, younger and having had no adventures, was afraid he wouldn't know when the adventure was happening and thus miss it. Cornelius, his older, wiser companion, promised he'd yell "pudding" when the adventure commenced so Barnaby would know it had begun.

"Pudding, Buddy," Anna whispered.

SEVENTEEN

Anna drank as much of the drugged water as she dared and slept the rest of the day. Buddy nosed her back into consciousness when the light was nearly gone from the sky and her circle of sand in deep shadow. She shared the last granola bar with him and opened the clean water from Kay's belt. Anna drank a good portion of what was left and gave Buddy his fill. If her half-baked plan fell flat, she doubted she'd need to ration the clean water. The drugged would be just fine; there would be little point in prolonging sanity.

The influx of fluid into her dehydrated body was nothing short of miraculous. As water seeped into her cells, she felt an opening inside, much as she imagined a flower feels when unfurling its petals. Strength, energy, hope: Those things that made life worthwhile flowed in with the moisture. Grabbing onto these sensations, Anna closed her mind to the possibility of failure.

Buddy watched while she put herself through deep breathing exercises, sit-ups, and rapid walks around the circle of their tiny arena, trying to shake off the effects of the drug.

Having achieved a modest level of alertness, she set about erasing all traces of herself from the bottom of the jar. The belt went into the loops to hold up her shorts. She would need both arms free. The fanny pack she wrapped around her waist, snapping the plastic buckle in place. The scraps of paper from her and the skunk's repast she shoved into the pockets of her shorts, then clipped the plastic water bottle to the strap of the fanny pack with the carabiner.

If the monster came, he must come down the throat of her jar. The angle dictated that, if he used a rope and didn't simply crawl down the sides like a blowfly, he would enter her world slightly off center. Beneath the angle where the throat widened into the body of the jar, and the stone overhung the farthest, was the least visible part of the bottom.

As the last of the light was going, she dug out a shallow trough six feet long and two feet wide in the exposed area where she could see the throat and the eye of sky. Sitting in it, legs straight, toes pointing toward where a rope thrown down the jar's gullet had to land, she buried the canvas-covered canteen next to her right knee and laid the strap along her thigh. That done, she swept sand over her feet and legs. When she was certain nothing of her extremities was visible, she lay down and, grateful that Kay had been so well endowed, arranged one triangle of the bra over her eyes and the other over her nose and mouth. Doing the best she could by feel, she buried her chest, neck, and head, leaving only a slit between the fabric of the bra and the bridge of her nose so she could see out. Moving as little as possible, lest she disturb her sandy shroud, she burrowed her right hand and arm under the sand till she felt the canteen strap and closed her fingers around it.

Buddy had watched her doings with interest and even found the courage to pounce on her foot when she moved it beneath the sand, much as a kitten might. It made Anna wonder if skunks hunted and, if so, what? Even through the sand banked around her head she thought she could hear him nosing around and several times felt him walking across parts of her anatomy.

Then he, too, was still. Night had come. The slit between bra and nose showed only black regardless of whether her eyes were shut or not.

Tonight it would be decided if she were to be, or not to be. A melancholic since Zach's abandonment, Anna knew the narcotic comfort in contemplating suicide. Molly would be amused that when the choice had been taken from her, and someone else could choose her "not to be," Death ceased to be a suitor and became the enemy. Sheer contrariness was an excellent motivator.

Anna opened her mind to the sand. For so long she had cursed its incursions into her crevices, its dust in her nose and eyes and ears, its grit between her teeth. Lying as one with it, she embraced the camouflage it afforded and tried to rethink herself as a trapdoor spider, hiding in her own controlled vortex of sand, waiting for her prey to come too near. She pictured the darkness overlaying the sand overlaying her, providing another layer of protection. Almost, she felt herself slipping into the stone surrounding her and wondered if it were the dregs of the drugged water, self-hypnosis, or incipient insanity. Regardless of the cause, for a moment she felt as at home as she did backstage in the dark; she knew where she was and was doing exactly what she should be.

She was waiting for the villain of the piece to enter.

EIGHTEEN

Time passed. Or not. Anna wanted to look at Kay's Timex but didn't dare move. Her carapace of sand was fragile. Itches she dared not scratch, thirst she dared not quench, cramping muscles she dared not stretch, chipped away at her sense of being at one with the jar. Thoughts of the kind embrace of the earth shifted to thoughts of hot baths, food, and clean sheets.

Mostly, though, she thought of the monster, willed him to come. It was opening night; the curtain was up, the audience waiting. That he hadn't come the previous night did not concern her overmuch. Even monsters, she supposed, had obligations they could not get out of. If he didn't come tonight, though, she would probably die in the bottom of this solution hole. If he didn't come tonight, maybe he was merely a murderer and not an even lower form of beast. Maybe he simply needed her dead because she'd seen Kay struck down. A plain old murderer would turn his back and walk away, satisfied she was no longer a problem.

She clung to the facts of the drugged water, the

sandwiches, the cuts in her thigh. Those had "monster" written all over them. A true monster would come back for her. A monster couldn't stay away two nights running, not with a captive so very captive and helpless as naked, incapacitated Anna Pigeon.

So she waited and her mind drifted. She did not give in to sleep. Instead she rehearsed: envisioning how her half-baked plan would be enacted, going over every move in her mind, cataloging her props and working out how best they could be used. In the impossible darkness, she toyed with dialogue. As a down-on-her-luck genie in a bottle, she had a right to the role of Scheherazade. Several scenes of charming the monster with words filtered through her mind as she lay in wait. Finally she decided a drugging, carving, murderous monster probably wouldn't be all that much into oral tradition. Besides, Anna had progressed beyond words. She wanted a pound of flesh.

She revisited the idea that more than one monster was involved. Should all three come together, or even two, she would not stand a chance. She put that thought aside.

Twenty minutes after her interment she was fighting sleep and losing. Then she heard someone walking overhead. Fatigue flared out in a gust of adrenaline.

Footsteps, louder, louder, were coming toward the opening of her jar. *Breathe two three, hold two three, out on a five count:* She calmed her twitchy muscles.

The footsteps stopped.

Anna forced herself to keep breathing, to listen past the rush of blood in her ears and the sigh of air from her nose. The exterior silence was solid as ice. Had she dreamed the footsteps? Imagined them?

Then they began again. This time they were walking away. Panic rose up from the adrenaline bath in which she lay. Someone had come, they'd come to look, maybe a lost tourist or a ranger on a camping trip, or Molly or Jenny or somebody looking for her, and they'd come and she hadn't called out, hadn't let them know she was alive and in this hole, and now they were walking away, leaving her.

Just when she couldn't bear it another second and was about to leap up shrieking, "It's me! It's me! I'm down here!" the sound of the feet hitting the gravel stopped. Whispers and thumps followed as if the walker were dragging something out of a sack or a hiding place.

Almost weak with relief that she hadn't destroyed her one chance before she'd had it, Anna gathered her scattered emotions and packed them back into her bones. One set of footsteps equaled one monster: so far, so good. Her wait had not been overly long. She was not too stiff. Legs and arms hadn't gone to sleep on her. Breath was coming too fast and too shallow. That, she adjusted.

The beam of a flashlight skittered across the throat of the jar. Slow erratic forays down into the throat. Anna imagined the monster holding it clamped between his arm and his rib cage as he arranged whatever it was he used to descend into, and ascend out of, the solution hole. With light she saw that the edge of the bikini bra over the bridge of her nose had settled, nar-

rowing her viewing slot to a scant quarter of an inch.
There was nothing she could do about that. After what
seemed a long time—and to have elapsed in less time
than it took to blink—came a loud scattering of pebbles followed by a slithering sound. The monster had
thrown a rope down the throat of the jar; it snaked
down the neck to the edge of the main body of the hole,
then fell in a hiss.

From her right came a tiny squeak. Anna hoped
Buddy was hiding, invisible in the patch of tattered
nightshade.

A grunt from above; the monster was lowering his
body down the angled neck of the jar. Dust motes
writhed in the flashlight's beam. From the angle and the
jerky movement, Anna guessed he had shoved the flashlight into his belt to free up his hands for the climb.

A rain of pebbles pattered on the sand as a form
wriggled feet first over the lip of sandstone. The light
played havoc with her limited vision, sending shadows
running and striking snatches of color as it glanced
across the ropes. Ropes plural. After thirty faithless
years, Anna believed in Santa Claus again.

What the anti-Santa was using to climb down the
chimney was a ladder of bright blue nylon rope with
plastic rungs, a style she'd seen on several houseboats.
The ladder could easily be pulled from the water and
stowed.

The monster got his feet on the second rung down
and righted himself from the belly-crawl required to
descend the throat. A beam of light shot up from his belt
as he pulled the flashlight free. Anna's vision blurred

with the intensity of her need to see: hiking boots covered in scratches and dust; socks, once white, now tiger-striped where dirt settled in the creases; one calf, muscular, no hair. Either he wore shorts or hiked naked.

Forcing discipline, she closed her eyes before the light could slip down the sides of the jar lest they shine, flash color, or catch the light. Red drowned her lids, strobing with black; the light passing over her face, flickering through the thin layer of fabric and sand.

A sharp intake of monster breath.

Nobody in the jar. Anna hoped that was what he thought.

A whirring sound. A thud.

He had slid down the ladder and landed on the floor. Again Anna was one with the sand and stone; she felt the boots strike, breathed the dust when they hit, cast back the light of the flashlight, felt the intrusion of his mass into her space.

Anna had buried herself not under the greater curve, where her shallow grave would be invisible from the throat of the jar, but on the exposed side. Years in the theater taught her the audience is less interested in the seen than in the unseen, in open doors than in those partly ajar. When the curtain rose on an empty stage, all eyes turned toward the entrance most likely to spew forth the expected players.

Watching those who watched also taught her that the mind fools the eye. The mind is too impatient to wait for a full report and makes snap decisions on what the eye has beheld. The curtain rises. No actors are standing onstage. The mind decrees it empty and orders the eyes to move on. Piles of silk begin to move; the audience gasps as thirty dancers flow up from the floor.

In choosing her burial spot, she had banked on the fact that what held true for New York theatergoers would also hold true for desert monsters; the man on the ladder would quickly scan the exposed area. No naked drugged woman. Ergo empty. His interest would then shift to beneath the overhang, to the unseen, his back to her, his light raking the alcove behind the ladder.

She waited, without thinking, for any sound of surprise or dismay. Thinking would destroy her nerve. A miserable, aching, eternal second ground by.

"Whuff?"

The grunt of a cartoon bear was her cue. Anna surged up from the sand, to one knee, to her feet, sand cascading from her body. Mouth wide, she roared, and in her mind the sound was a tide of fear and hope and determination and bloodred murder. From her dry lips and leathery tongue the sound was like that of an ancient coffin lid pried open with a crowbar.

Light hit her with the force of a fist, found her eyes, and blinded her. With strength born of desperation, she swung the half-filled metal canteen on its strap. Light leaped crazily around the circular walls. The canteen struck something solid, then banged back on its tether and cracked her shins. Pain opened her clenched fingers; strap and canteen fell away. Light steadied, drawing a perfect circle of bronze from the curving sandstone. The crests of the waves of sand streaked gold across the floor. By this faint illumination Anna stumbled for the ladder.

A black shape tottered from the deadly nightshade. Buddy. She couldn't leave Buddy. Snatching him up before he could startle and run, she slipped him into the hammock of a bra cup, then grasped the ladder. It moved like a living thing, the bottom step dancing away from her foot each time she tried to step on it, disappearing into the dark, then catching a scrap of light and reappearing.

"No, no, no," she murmured, her voice as high and frightened as a child's.

The monster groaned. He was coming to, waking up, hungry like an ogre is hungry. *Fee fie fo fum,* Anna heard from some long-ago fairy tale trapped in her mind. *I smell the blood—*

Her right foot was on the tread. The ladder steadied with her weight. Her left foot found the next tread up, and she came free of the sand. The ladder began to sway. She cried out but did not let go. Afraid to loose and regrasp the blue line lest it get away from her, she slid her closed fist up until it cracked against a higher tread. Gripping there, she lifted her right foot to meet with her left, then fumbled her left one rung higher. She was doing it. She was on the ladder. The prisoner was escaping.

Buddy's sharp claws scratched her chest as, panicked, he tried to fight free of the bikini cup. Her shoulder was failing. She let go of the line and closed the fingers of her left hand around her furry friend. One-handed now: another step, another slide of her fist.

Splinters of nylon jabbed into her palm. *Never mind. Don't care.*

"Uuhnn" from below and the susurration of feet dragging over sand, then light lancing up between her legs, over her shoulder to stab red from the stone where the ladder curled over into the canted neck of the bottle.

The ladder jerked sideways. Her left foot slid off the rung. The monster jerked it the other way, and her remaining foot fell free. She hung suspended, a spider on a single strand of web, held aloft only by the strength of the fingers of one hand. Below, the monster panted and grunted, a beast grasping at its meal. The head of her ulna twisted and came partially out of the socket. Pain scorched her will to hang on.

Buddy scrabbled, trying to free himself.

"Sorry," Anna whispered. Pinching one tiny paw tight between thumb and forefinger, she let her injured arm fall to her side, Buddy dangling in space.

In pain and terror Buddy fought back in the only way he knew how. Skunk spray filled the jar. The monster screamed. Anna heard him falling or staggering. The beam of the flashlight stilled into a single line across the floor. He'd dropped it.

In the enclosed space the stench was more than an evil smell; it stung Anna's eyes and burned the back of her throat. Gagging, the monster rolled in the dirt, oddly dismembered by the line of light across the sand. The little skunk's aim must have been true and hit him in the face.

She could see her feet and the ladder. Trying not to

breathe, she eased one foot back to the tread, then the other. The hand that had taken her full weight when she'd lost her footing did not want to open, then did not want to close. It felt as if muscle had turned to water and no longer had the power to move bone. Her left arm, swinging free, Buddy's little weight still suspended by her pincer grip on his forepaw, hurt so bad it was all she could do not to let the skunk kit fall, but she couldn't leave him. If Mr. Monster carved women who'd never done him any harm, what would he do to a baby animal who had effectively Maced him?

Rung by rung, she pushed up, sliding her rope-burned hand along the blue line stringing them together. The thrashing from below stopped—that or she could no longer hear it over the rasping of breath in her throat and the pounding of blood in her ears.

Then a rung was flush against stone, crushing her fingers as she clawed her way around the bulge. Pushing breast and belly over the next rungs in the sloping neck, she dragged herself toward the narrow eye of the world that had watched her for so many days. Afraid to let Buddy go, she pulled him along, her arm, half dislocated, bumping excruciatingly over rungs and rocks. The baby skunk had ceased to struggle, and Anna feared she had squeezed the life out of him or bashed him to death in her scramble to escape.

Head and shoulders cleared the neck of the jar. The world expanded around her, so startling in its immensity that she had the dizzying sensation she was expanding with it, her mind exploding toward the horizon in every direction.

Then she was well and truly out, belly down on the rocky ground, gasping for breath. A tickle at her thigh let her know Buddy was not dead. Relief at finding she had not killed her friend and savior rivaled that at having escaped the monster. "Run, Buddy," she whispered. "Run."

A breeze moved across the rocky plateau. After so long in the absolute stillness of her underground prison, wind felt like life itself. The moon had not yet set, and the desert glowed in stark blacks touched by silver, gentle washes of luminescence over smooth bulges of stone. Even the sharp gouge of rocks beneath her body felt good after an eternity of fine sand. To be free was so exquisite Anna was drunk with it.

Spread along the ground under the length of her body, the ladder twitched to life. Instantly sobered, she rolled off of it, onto her injured arm. Pain took her as she either relocated or totally dislocated her shoulder joint. Had she not been down already she would have collapsed.

The ropes between the rungs grew taut, lifting off the stone as the treads were set up on their edges by the tension.

The monster was climbing out.

It was too late to pull the ladder up. He was already on it and climbing fast. She staggered to her feet. If she ran he'd catch her, catch her and throw her back into the hole. She grabbed up a rock the size of a softball and threw it down the neck of the bottle. There was a grunt of surprise, but she didn't think she'd hit him. Without strength behind it, even if she did, it wouldn't stop him.

Bigger, she needed something bigger. "No, no, no," she sobbed, as she looked desperately around. Several feet from the hole was a roundish rock the size of a basketball. Too big; she would never find the strength to shift it.

The largest muscle in the human body is the gluteus maximus: She remembered that from somewhere. Falling more than sitting, she planted hers on the ground. Bracing the soles of her feet against the rock, she shoved with all the power of her thighs and butt. The stone came loose with a sound like ripping paper and rolled within a foot of the entrance to the jar. Scraping skin from her bare legs and elbows, Anna crab-walked after it and again shoved with both heels. The rock rolled to the edge of the hole, teetered, then, eerily silent, rolled out of sight.

A monster roar came from the depths, followed by the crash of rock and man at the bottom of the hole. Unless he'd been knocked senseless, he would be back at the ladder before she could drag it up. The ladder was not one but two boat ladders tied together, with wire wrapping the top rung of one tightly to the bottom rung of the other. The top ladder retained the two U-shaped metal hooks used to secure it the side of a boat. The monster had anchored it by laying a rusted metal fence post behind two boulders the size of Volkswagens, slipping the hooks over the post, and pulling the metal tight against the stones.

Crawling, Anna made it to where the hooks hooked over the post and jerked them free. The instant she did, they leaped like live things and ran scraping across the earth to follow the stone into the gullet of the jar. Silence followed, broken only by the gentle rain of sand trickling through the throat of sandstone that had swallowed so much so quickly.

Shaking and gasping for breath, Anna tried to stand. Her legs would not support her. On her knees, she stared at the black slit, expecting at every breath that it would suddenly spew forth life, that great angry hands and gnashing teeth would emerge to drag her screaming back down into darkness.

The trickle of sand ceased.

Anna's breathing evened out.

Buddy appeared from wherever he'd run to hide and watched her tentatively, ready to run if she began flailing and throwing things again.

The night grew so still, the moonlight fading, the stars achingly bright overhead, that Anna felt unreal, as if she had dreamed the whole thing, as if she were dreaming still.

Then came a voice into the world, soft and gentle.

"Anna? What have you done?"

NINETEEN

Jenny was thinking about snakes. Even as a child, she'd liked them. When other little girls were screaming and running from horrid little snake-wielding boys, Jenny had wanted to see and touch. An early lesson in life had been the gift of a snake-wielding boy—Carl Johnson. Jenny remembered him vividly; he'd been her first-grade crush. Carl had been pursuing her at the school picnic, yelling, "Snake! Snake!" Undoubtedly courtship as understood by six-year-olds. Jenny had run a few yards, then stopped to touch and see.

Carl had been chasing her with a crooked stick.

Probably why I'm gay, she thought idly as she sipped her coffee, then took a drag off the sorry-looking cigarette she'd rolled.

Jenny loved the way snakes looked, the way they felt—like the finest silver chain—as they slipped through her hands, the way they moved or lay sunning themselves. Pinky Winky, the faded midget rattler, had been beautiful in all the snaky ways. Until he wasn't.

Flies had let her know the pink-colored rattlesnake

needed burying. She'd seen them buzzing in a cloud near Regis's porch. The nails used to stretch the snake she'd left in the dirt. The snake she had interred, coiling the limp body as if it were preparing to strike, and marking the tiny grave with a rock that was almost exactly the hue of the snake's skin. Pinky's skull had been crushed. Jenny wanted to believe she had been killed before she was crucified, but the tearing around the nail holes and the amount of fluid told her otherwise.

The episode upset her more than she wanted to admit. This season on the lake—one of the few places in the world where she felt at peace, sure of her place, sure of her job, safe in the knowledge that here, at least, she knew what she needed to do and was the person most capable of doing it—had somehow gone awry.

Because she had backslid and begun to obsess about her housemate, a part of her wanted to lay the totality of her dis-ease at the feet of Ms. Pigeon. A woman who, for all intents and purposes, had vanished from the face of the earth. Silently, invisibly, little Ms. Pigeon packed up her clothes and keepsakes and disappeared to a place where women didn't need tampons, birth control pills, ChapStick, or Xanax.

Paradise, evidently.

Jenny shifted on the rough planking, folding one leg on top of the picnic table, canting herself west. The sun was nearly set. Perhaps, tonight, she could sleep free of weird dreams of the redheaded stage manager.

Tomorrow she would camp in the Panther Canyon grotto. There would be at least one other group and probably two or three. She would use the depredations of the party boaters as interpretive and educational opportunities for the newcomers.

Uncharacteristically, she was not looking forward to a night spent in the grotto, nor was she looking forward to a day on the water, visiting beaches, taking water samples, and greeting guests. That nasty snake business wouldn't let her alone. For reasons only a few old-line shrinks would think phallic, the fate of the snake and that of Anna Pigeon were related. Jenny couldn't say why, but it felt true.

She stubbed out her cigarette. As she field-stripped it, crumbling the last bit of tobacco and rolling the scorched end of the cigarette paper into a spit wad, she smelled the distinct odor of skunk. Wafting from a polite distance, the reek wasn't unpleasant. This was.

The stench heralded dragging footsteps.

Jenny stepped off the porch into the space between Regis's duplex and hers. Superstitious fear brushed her mind as she stared into the gloom beneath the cliffs. A skin walker, a Navajo creature half human, half animal, was shambling toward the duplexes.

She recovered in less time than it would have taken to speak the thought aloud. This was no coyote in human form; it was a woman, naked from the waist up, hair unbound, hanging witchlike past her hips, obscuring her face.

With her traveled the stink of skunk. Jenny did not move to meet her. As the apparition came nearer, she could see the woman's arms were crossed on her chest as if she cradled a baby.

The last ray of sunlight touched her, and the wild hair flashed dusty red. She shook it back, exposing a gaunt face, cheekbones prominent, eyes enormous. Blood had dried around her lips where they'd cracked and bled. She cradled not a baby but a skunk kit no more than seven or eight weeks old.

"Anna?" Jenny whispered. "Is it you?"

The woman stared at her with feral eyes. "Give me a drink of water," she croaked, "and maybe I'll tell you."

TWENTY

Anna gulped down a quart of water, then promptly vomited it up, as Jenny Gorman warned her she would. Anna didn't care. It had been worth it to drink as much and as fast as she wanted, a wild luxury she hadn't known before how to properly appreciate.

After Jenny promised to take care of Buddy, Anna showered, taking sips of water as it sprayed on her face, sticking her tongue out and wagging it so every part got its share. Dirt and blood sluiced from her body and hair. She felt the way a resurrection fern must in the first rain after a long dry spell, as if her leaves were greening and swelling, her hair becoming soft and fine, her skin supple and alive. Once clean, she poured two quart cans of tomato juice over herself and worked it into scalp and skin. Buddy had not sprayed her, but she reeked from lingering fumes.

When the last of the hot water was gone, and twenty minutes more of the cold, she put on the clothes Jenny laid out for her. Cotton was her armor, cloth a second skin to protect her from the elements, from exposure.

Anna wallowed in getting dressed in actual clothes. Beyond Jenny's bedroom door she heard forces being marshaled. Radios crackled as Jim Levitt radioed the chief ranger and whoever else had to know about laws broken in the park and rec area. Jim Levitt made his calls from the porch, kept from the apartment only by Jenny's insistence.

Soon law enforcement personnel would be descending on the Rope. Anna looked forward to it only slightly more than she'd looked forward to the monster descending into the jar. Knowing she would eventually have to face them Anna took her time, pulling on borrowed clothes: a soft white tank top, socks—despite the heat—and one of the finest gifts she'd ever been given, a pair of clean underpants. Dressed, covered, cloaked, her skin and her sins hidden, Anna thought she could find the courage to face them.

In long khaki pants and a long-sleeved cotton shirt, both three sizes too large for her, she emerged from the sanctuary of Jenny's room, sat at the Formica counter in the kitchen, and let Jenny serve her small bits of food.

From Anna's first vomiting to putting on clothes to the dessert of blueberry yogurt, Jenny pestered her with questions. "Where were you? What happened? Are you hurt? Why do you have a baby skunk? What happened to your things? How did you hurt your shoulder? Didn't you go back to New York? Why did you leave your birth control pills? Where have you been? Where have you been? What happened to you? Were you kidnapped? Did you fall into a ravine?"

Anna hadn't answered. Using exhaustion and dehydration and general pathos to put Jenny off, she had taken care of her body and let her mind idle, the decision of how much to tell, how to tell it, and to whom drifting in the background. The jar felt like a secret, one she wanted to keep.

As she lapped the last of the yogurt out of its plastic container much the way a mannerless child or a puppy might, Jenny let Jim Levitt in. The law enforcement rangers on Lake Powell were also emergency medical technicians. Jim had taken his education further and was a paramedic. He asked Anna to move from her solitary stool and sit on the dilapidated couch. Because she couldn't think of a logical reason to refuse, she did as she was bid.

She knew who Jim Levitt was. He lived in the other half of the Candors' duplex. Jenny's partner in training visitors in proper waste management protocols, he'd ridden with them a couple of times. Absorbed in miseries she'd bused in from New York, Anna hadn't given him much thought.

Now she was finding it hard not to leap off the sofa and run from the room as he unfolded a bright orange pack full of first aid supplies on the coffee table in front of her. Hard not to hit or push when he sat next to her. Hard not to jerk away as he prodded her arm and pinched her fingertips, asking where it hurt.

Understand the monster and live.

The thought startled her. Jim Levitt was not a monster—at least not that she knew of. He was a big, pleasant-looking man, no more than twenty-two at a guess, with dark close-cropped hair, dense as a knit cap, and wide-set brown eyes, kind and intelligent, under straight black brows. His shoulders were overmuscled and his neck thick. Probably he'd played a lot of football in high school and college. Crooked but very white teeth gave his smile character, as did the bump on the bridge of his nose from an old break.

Directors in New York would cast Jim Levitt as the small-town hero who went off to war and never came back, or the big brother who took care of the family when Dad was too drunk to.

Even as Anna made note of these reassuring characteristics, her stomach was clenching and her skin trying to shrink closer to her bones. She was not free of the jar. Men, all men, but powerful men in particular, were a threat to a small female with naught but a baby skunk for protection. The monster was faceless and so could be anyone. Could be everyone. The WHORE cut into her thigh felt as if it bled whenever Jim leaned too close, burned when he touched her.

As the paramedic palpated her head, seeking any residual damage from the bang to the skull she'd gotten, Anna dug her nails into her palms to keep from screaming. The blood pressure cuff felt like an iron manacle crushing her arm, the thermometer a blade beneath her tongue.

Either Jim sensed her fear, or had seen enough of it in his work to read it on her face. The examination finished, he closed the EMS kit and, moving slowly and deliberately, the way Anna did when she didn't want to frighten a skittish cat, stepped away and sat in the chair across from the couch. Anna liked him for that; it was easier to draw breath, easier to ignore the acid word on her thigh.

"The shoulder was dislocated?" Jim asked.

Anna nodded, afraid if she spoke her voice would quail. Back in the jar, a thousand years ago and yesterday, she'd thought she'd won free of fear. Evidently it was an ever renewable resource.

"What did it look like?"

Anna told him in as few words as possible. By clipping each one off with her teeth, she could keep the quaver out of her recitation.

"Sounds like a forward dislocation. That's when the upper arm bone moves forward and down out of its joint, tearing the labrum and joint capsule. Did it swell up?"

"Some," Anna said. Her voice wasn't strong enough to reach the orchestra pit in even a small theater.

"Did it feel numb or weak or anything?"

"Yes." Her throat was growing dry. Though the questions were well intended and for her welfare, they increased her anxiety. Knowing tougher questions were to come built on the anxiety until she felt made of wires strung to the breaking point.

"And you think it may have partially dislocated at a later time?"

Anna didn't answer.

"Any muscle spasms?"

"It's fine," she said more harshly than she'd meant to.

"Sounds like your dislocation diagnosis was right on the money. I can see it's still bruised. There'll be soreness for a week or so, depending on how badly you've strained or torn ligaments and tendons. You should get checked out at the hospital. An X-ray will be able to tell you if you've damaged the rotator cuff or the head of the ulna."

He stared at her, open, amiable, waiting for her to ask a question, state a desire, make a comment.

"No hospital," Anna said. In hospitals they took your clothes away, gave you drugs, and strange men came and did things that hurt you. Hospitals were jars. Even if a jar was for her own good, Anna had no intention of getting in it.

"You'll need to talk with Steve about that."

"No. I won't." Her voice was stronger; it might not reach the back of the house, but the first row of the balcony would hear her loud and clear.

Jim didn't argue. Leaning back in his chair, granting her another eighteen inches of space, he said, "Other than the sore shoulder, you're suffering from dehydration, exhaustion, and trauma. Your skin is warm to the touch—"

Anna flinched at the words the way she had when he'd laid hands on her.

"—so I don't think we need to worry about shock."

He waited, his big hands clasped loosely on his lap, his warm brown eyes full of kindness and understanding.

Law Enforcement Ranger Jim Levitt wanted her to talk. A hard mass of shame and fury clogged Anna's throat.

After a minute he stood. "I'm going to radio Steve.

Let him know you're more or less in one piece and see if he needs to come over tonight or if it can wait till morning. Jenny, you said something about Xanax?"

"She's got a prescription. She left it when she . . . she left it," Jenny said.

"I can't prescribe anything, but if it was me, I'd think now was a good time to take one. What do you say, Anna?"

Suddenly she was afraid he wanted her drugged, like the poison canteen, like the foggy nights and blurry days. She shook her head.

"Okay. Chill out. I'll be right back and let you know what Steve wants to do."

Leaving the medical pack on the table, he let himself out the screen door.

"You sure about that Xanax?" Jenny asked. "In your sandals, I'd take two or three and wash them down with red wine."

"After," Anna croaked and looked at the door to the deck.

Knowledge bloomed in Jenny's eyes. Her mouth thinned and her round cheeks went hard. "After," she agreed quietly.

Jim banged back in. For a large man, he was quiet and graceful. For a young man, he was sensitive and controlled. Still, large and young, he banged.

"Steve says to get your statement, then let you rest. He'll be over tomorrow, probably with Andrew, the chief ranger, to talk with you some more."

Dread curled around and settled in Anna's stomach. People wanted to get inside her, like the monster's knife, like the poisoned water. These were the good guys, she reminded herself. They only wanted to force themselves into her mind. Maybe there were no good guys.

Jim again sat in the far chair. She expected him to take out a pad and pencil to take notes, but he didn't. He sat as before, relaxed, hands folded. "You went missing four days ago. Want to tell me about that?"

"Four days?" The number surprised her. Surely it had been a year or a month. In less than a week she had been taken and changed as completely as anyone beamed up by aliens and subjected to medical procedures, their glands replaced by monkey glands or whatever the fashion of alien abduction was at the moment.

"Five, if you count today," Jenny said.

Five sounded more reasonable. Five months would have sounded more reasonable still. Jenny brought Anna a glass of orange juice. She took a sip, trying to find the words Jim Levitt needed. None came. Talking about it made it too real. Or too unreal, like a nightmare from which she'd awakened. To speak of her life in the jar felt like airing dirty laundry, made her vulnerable. Jim would picture her naked. In his mind he would see her posed, watch the monster cutting WHORE into her flesh. An echo of the horror she'd felt that the monster might take pictures of her after she was dead reverberated through her.

"I was hiking," she said finally. "I didn't bring enough water. I hit my head, I guess. I don't remember a lot." That was true. Also true was that she remembered too much. "I don't know why my things were gone from my room—or why my shampoo and other toiletries weren't," she offered. That, too, was the truth.

She did know where she'd been, that she'd roomed with a corpse, that she'd been drugged and stripped and molested, and that she'd come back to Dangling Rope in a dead woman's clothes. Soon—tomorrow— she would have to tell. Not telling Kay's family what had become of her was cruel. Anna's humiliation would eventually be made public. If the monster—or monsters—were caught, she'd have to testify in court.

Since, when her monster finally arrived, he was alone, she suspected two of the monster boys had run back to their real lives. Possibly they didn't know Anna had survived—that or they trusted thirst would do away with her in a day or two—and were unaware that the third monster was interfering with her demise.

"I'm tired," she said so pitifully it reminded her of the pain-in-the-ass little boy who'd starred in a production of *Oliver!* she stage-managed in college. "May I go to bed now?" *Please sir.*

Jim was either too nice or too inexperienced to say no. "Get some rest," he said. "This can wait till morning." He gathered up his medical paraphernalia and let himself out. Jenny crossed to the door and locked it.

"First time I've done that," she said as she turned back.

"Thank you," Anna said.

Jenny fetched her a Xanax. Dutifully, Anna swallowed it. She longed for sleep. Fear kept her from attempting it. What if she awoke in the jar, having only dreamed she'd escaped?

Jenny encouraged her to lie down on the sofa, then sat on the coffee table where Jim had put his EMS kit and took her hand. Anna let her. Waking up holding Kay's dead hand was added to the fear of waking up back in the hole. Anna snatched it back. Jenny's radio crackled, the hive of the park buzzing with the news of her miraculous return. Sounds of the living comforted Anna even as they rasped on nerves grown accustomed to the deep and abiding silence of sandstone. She would have to find that silence again, go back into the stone. But not until she knew how to come back out.

Exhaustion and tranquilizers finally dulled the dread. Anna allowed Jenny to put her to bed. She waited until Jenny's back was turned before slipping out of the borrowed trousers and between the sheets. She didn't want Jenny to see the cuts on her leg.

Buddy had been settled in her room, an old sweatshirt of Jenny's sacrificed to make him a bed in the bottom drawer of the dresser that had been emptied of Anna's clothes. Anna watched as her housemate put a teacup of water and a small salad of celery, bell pepper, and lettuce in his new home.

"Tomorrow we should take Buddy hunting for insects," Jenny said.

"Bug hunting, tomorrow," Anna promised her friend. Buddy sniffed at the celery.

"Want me to leave the light on?"

Light did not comfort Anna. Dark was safer. She could hide in the dark. "Could you just leave the door open an inch or so?" she asked.

"Your wish; my command," Jenny said and smiled.

She had a nice smile. The two front teeth were canted, the edges of the incisors crossing delicately like the feet of a dancer.

Still wearing underpants and the shirt, Anna lay between the worn flannel sheets Jenny had put on her bed and laid her head on the borrowed pillow. It smelled of Jenny, a beachy smell, hinting at coconut oil and salt and clean breezes.

The smell of good summertime things gave Anna a fragile sense of safety. She curled on her side to soak in the comfort. For tonight her own personal monster—she'd heard him call her name—was trapped in the jar. When she told the "good guys" where it was, they would take him out and she would never be safe again.

Had Kay's corpse not called to her to witness her death, Anna would have left the monster to die, as he undoubtedly would have left her to die once she ceased to amuse him.

TWENTY-ONE

Anna surprised herself by sleeping soundly. Not even the dream of Zach came to break her heart before the sun broke the night. Lying in bed, staring into the dove gray sky that ushered in the new day, she absorbed the strangeness of waking without that familiar pain. Unconsciously, she laid her right hand over her heart. Had the monster burned it out of her the way doctors once burned wounds with a hot iron to clean and seal them?

Scarcely had the strangeness receded when it was replaced by relief at not waking in the jar to find salvation was only a dream. Today she woke in a bed, free to come and go as she pleased. There was food to eat in the refrigerator and clothing to wear and water to drink. These were so precious, the part of her that stayed afraid feared to lose them. A lesson to be learned: For a woman with nothing, courage came cheap. The brave part of her, the fearlessness she'd found when tarantulas of the mind attacked her, wished she needed no more than a shell at the bottom of the ocean, loved no one, had no baby skunk to die, no sister to get lung cancer.

As she dressed, Anna concentrated on how pleasurable the slide of soft cotton over her skin was, how sturdy feet felt when encased in rubber and straps, how grand it was to run a brush through her hair, wash her face and hands, how glorious to have ChapStick and Jergens.

Focusing on these once mundane marvels helped keep dark thoughts at bay.

Having cleaned the drawer of Buddy's poop—piled neatly in a corner the way a tidy kitty-litter-less cat might have done—she took him into the relative cool of the predawn behind the apartments and turned over rocks for him. They found a grublike thing the little skunk thought delicious, a moth that was about to expire, and two vinegaroons. To Anna they looked as dangerous as the scorpions they so resembled, but Buddy seemed partial to them.

By the time she carried him back to the duplex, Jenny was up, sitting on her picnic table, a chipped mug with a bison's head enameled on it held between her hands. "Coffee's on the counter," Jenny said and, "Can I play with the skunk?"

"Buddy," Anna reminded her. "Don't let him fall."

When she returned with her coffee, she sat on the table next to Jenny. The Fecal Queen had folded her legs tailor fashion, forming a flesh-and-bone skunk pen. Buddy, full of breakfast bugs, didn't seem in any hurry to escape.

"Andrew Madden and Steve will be here in about

forty-five minutes," Jenny said. "You're going to have to tell them something."

She said this without looking up from where she dragged a bit of grass around her lap, trying to get Buddy to play with it as if he were a kitten. Anna noticed Jenny didn't say she'd have to tell them the truth, or what happened, or where she'd been for all those days. Only that she'd have to tell them something. Anna also noted the "them." Jenny said it in a tone that suggested there was Them and there was Us and she was part of Anna's Us.

"Yeah," Anna agreed, took a sip of coffee, and moaned softly. All things liquid were revelations of life.

"Is there anything you want to tell me first?" Jenny slid her eyes to check Anna's reaction to the question.

Anna did not react, not externally. She had the odd sensation that her ordeal had split her into two entities. The one with the fear burned from it housed a calculating mind figuring odds, assessing dangers, studying a situation from every angle. The other was like a puppy on a six-lane expressway, a tightrope walker watching the knots fray, a tasty morsel in a bikini treading water in a school of sharks.

As she considered Jenny's offer to listen, the fearless part of her schizoid self ruled, the seemingly sane self who conducted interactions with the outside world. The frightened puppy with nowhere to run curled tight around her breastbone, nose to tail, and tried to close out everything but the reassuring sound of her heartbeat.

Jenny was looking at her with a concerned frown.

By normal conversational standards Anna had been quiet too long. Silence was her new normal, Anna realized. In silence, as in solitude, there was a chance of peace.

Taking it for reticence, Jenny offered Anna the coin shared so readily among women and so rarely among men. She offered up her pain so Anna might not feel alone or fear judgment.

"When I was in college, I was raped," Jenny said quietly, her eyes back on Buddy, now sleeping in a perfect circle of black and white. "It was one of those weird *Lord of the Flies* things. You know, where the whole of the evil is greater than the sum of its parts."

Anna said nothing. Part of her wanted to hear Jenny's story, needed to. The part that knew she would have to pay in kind froze her tongue in her mouth.

"Some fraternity threw a beer bash at a lake. Usual story: girl drinks too much, the Lord of the Flies possesses boys, also drunk, gang rape on a picnic table becomes a sporting event."

The puppy curled around Anna's breastbone whimpered in its sleep. Anna wanted to speak, to commend Jenny's courage or offer a word of support in return. Not sympathy. With absolute certainty, she knew sympathy was wrong. Unable to sort out language for the situation, she sat mute, her coffee cup to her lips to hide their trembling.

"Aren't you going to ask me if that's why I became a lesbian?" Jenny asked with a trace of bitterness.

"No," Anna said. "The other girls didn't try to stop it. They were as culpable as anybody."

"They were afraid," Jenny said. It sounded as if she had said that more than once over the years.

"Not all of them." Anna sipped her coffee. It had cooled. Coffee was the only substance she knew of that could quickly cool to significantly below room temperature.

"No," Jenny said. "Not all of them."

"And they were supposed to be *us*, not *them*."

Jenny thought Anna had been raped. That's why she bared her own shame, so Anna's burden might be lessened by sharing. Anna wanted to insist she wasn't raped and not because, as far as she knew, she hadn't been.

Shared her own shame.

It was not Jenny's shame, Anna knew that. Had the monster of the jar raped her, it would not have been her shame. Even so, like Jenny, she would have had to carry it because neither monsters nor society—nor the legal system—would carry it for them. Anna wanted to separate herself from her housemate, from the girl who had been gang-raped, the girl who was not like her, not like lucky Anna, not like the unraped girls.

Anna pictured how these cowardly emotions would look onstage, how an actor might move her face or eyes, how she would shape her shoulders and spine to embody them for the audience. The image wasn't pretty.

Anna owed Jenny Gorman. She steeled herself to give what she could. Beginning her story, she creaked like the Tin Man croaking for oil. "I was knocked out and tossed into a solution hole. I don't know if I was raped or not," she said. "My clothes were taken. I woke up naked. The clothes I came back in I found on the corpse of a girl buried in the sand. It was one of those weird *Silence of the Lambs* things," she echoed Jenny's opening statement. The women exchanged wry smiles. Some humor was so black it had to be funny or tragic.

"I hiked out of here. Up there," she turned and pointed toward the escarpment, though, from the picnic table, neither of them could see it. "You said there was a trail." She didn't try to keep the accusation out of her voice, and, as expected, it won her a smile. The part about running out of water embarrassed her. Anna resisted the temptation to leave it out, to make herself seem more clever. When she told the story to the Bullfrog district ranger and the chief ranger, it would not be included in the recitation.

Anna told Jenny everything: how afraid she was, how hard it was to choose between drugged water and no water, about the sandwiches and digging a cat hole and finding it full of fine brown hair, about pulling Kay's clothes off and wearing them, about how important the watch was, how it anchored her in time as she was anchored in place. Then she told Jenny the other thing she would not tell the men coming on the boat, how WHORE had been carved deep in her thigh, how afraid she was that it would scar and every day she would see it there.

When she finished, they sat quietly for a while; then Jenny carefully scooped the sleeping Buddy out from the nest of her crossed legs. "Make a lap," she said to Anna. Anna obediently pressed her thighs together. The khaki of the borrowed trousers dragged over the healing wounds.

Gently, as if she were setting down a soap bubble, Jenny laid Buddy in the new-made lap. "Wait for me," Jenny said. She disappeared into the duplex and returned a few minutes later with a small glass bottle in hand. "Vitamin E oil," she said as she handed the bottle to Anna. "It's supposed to be good for diminishing scars."

Without further comment on Anna's story, she sat again and began rolling a cigarette.

"Do you want Buddy back?" Anna asked. It was the only way she could think of to say thank you.

"Secondhand smoke isn't good for skunk kits."

A week before, Anna might have retorted that it wasn't good for anyone. Now the halcyon days when secondhand smoke seemed a viable threat seemed decades behind her.

Jenny ran her tongue along the edge of the paper and rolled the cigarette between her fingers.

"It looks like the snake that swallowed the elephant," Anna said.

"I can't seem to get the knack of it," Jenny admitted as she lit the bigger end and inhaled.

"I can teach you if you like." Anna surprised herself by the offer.

"You used to smoke?"

"No," Anna said as a memory flooded back of a life that had happened long, long ago and far away in a different galaxy. Laughing over red wine, Andrew Lloyd Webber in the tape player, tobacco scattered over an old wooden table the size of a school desk in a kitchen so small the door could only be closed when both chairs were pushed in, and one could clear the dirty dishes from table to sink without getting up, running lines for a production of *Our Town* set in the Old West, Zach deciding to roll his smokes in keeping with the cowboy motif. Anna'd learned. Zach hadn't, and, since the show never opened due to financial disasters, it didn't much matter.

The growl of one of the ATVs used to carry supplies up the hill from the dock dragged her back into the still of the morning on Lake Powell.

"The guy is still in the hole?" Jenny asked. The admiration in her voice made Anna feel better than she had since she'd embarked on the telling and, so, the remembering of her days in the jar.

"I hope so," she said.

The ATV carried Chief Ranger Andrew Madden and Steve Gluck, Bullfrog Marina's district ranger. Steve was also acting district ranger for the Rope until funding came through to pay for another GS-11 permanent position.

Close behind them, Jim Levitt arrived in a second ATV.

"Jim is supposed to patrol with me today," Jenny said, "but there is no way in hell he would miss out on this."

Chief Ranger Madden was tall and lean and quiet. He wore the flat hat well and sported a lush mustache just starting to go gray. Had he not been black and spoken with a distinct Boston accent, Anna thought he would have given Tom Selleck a run for his money at the Marlboro Man auditions. There weren't a lot of black guys high up in the park service. Anna would have to tread carefully around Andrew Madden. He hadn't gotten as far as he had by being stupid—or nice. Steve Gluck Anna had met on several occasions, but she had never spoken more than a few words to him.

While the chief ranger leaned against the side of the duplex near the door, Gluck asked Jenny if she wouldn't mind making a fresh pot of coffee for "a broken-down old ranger." Gluck was nowhere near as pretty as Andrew Madden. He wasn't more than an inch or two taller than Jenny, five foot nine at best. Too many long sedentary winters had given him a sizable gut that rode hard and high above his belt. A life out of doors had weathered him. Anna, who was good at guessing people's ages, bet he was close to sixty.

Still and all, she doubted that he was a "broken-down old ranger," though she suspected he used the line with some frequency. Unoffended, Jenny went to fetch coffee. Steve Gluck turned a tired smile on Anna.

"Jim here says you've had quite an adventure."

He waited with his sleepy smile while Anna decided what she was going to tell him. All three law enforcement rangers bided in polite silence. A scholar of silences from years backstage, Anna could tell in a heartbeat whether an actor paused or forgot his line, whether an audience was asleep or in awe, whether the silence was active and tense or dead air, momentary confusion or smug prescience.

The three ranger silences radiating at her were as distinct as the men themselves. Levitt, young and fit and stony-faced, leaked the joyous excitement of a puppy ready to be taken on the best walk ever. Andrew Madden's silence was hungry and calculating. He needed information so he could start the political spin in his direction should Anna pony up anything in need of spinning. The Bullfrog district ranger—the only one of the three confident enough to allow the vulnerability of facial expression—was just a man waiting to get the details on one more hard dirty job he needed to do in a long line of hard dirty jobs he'd plowed through during his career.

Anna told her story again.

As she talked, her voice low and even, her sentences with beginnings, middles, and ends, her plotline sensical, her timeline as logical as a person drugged to the gills, in pain, and dehydrated could make it, she could tell she was not showing enough trauma to satisfy her audience. Not that she suspected for an instant any of them wished her ill. They wore varying degrees of the same look her sister the psychiatrist wore when she thought Anna was hiding some metaphorical boil that would heal better if lanced.

The lack of emotion surprised Anna as well. Trained in an era where a person couldn't cross Rockefeller Center without stepping on half a dozen psychotherapists, she worried she was bottling up, repressing, in denial, or one of the great many bad labels good old-fashioned stoicism had had heaped upon it.

When she began relating how she had found long brown hair as she dug a cat hole in the sand, she realized she was doing none of those things. She had not merely survived but won. Winning, and the fact that,

unlike for Jenny, there had been no witnesses cheering
and swilling beer as they watched her humiliation, allowed her a shred of dignity. Physical violation was the
tool men traditionally used to debase women. In wars
and feuds men debased women for the sole purpose of
humiliating the men to whom they belonged, reducing
the women to nothing more than vessels to carry man's
hatred for man.

Maybe that was why Anna left out the detail that she
had been cut with the casual mockery of a boy carving
his initials in his desktop.

She also did not tell them where the solution hole
was, insisting she'd have to take them there herself.
Had she done otherwise, she knew, as female, victim,
and non-law-enforcement personnel, she wouldn't be
allowed to accompany those who went to make the
arrest. Anna was determined to see what her monster
looked like by the light of day, how he looked beaten,
in handcuffs, outnumbered, outsmarted, outgunned.
She needed the monster, grown to enormous propor-
tions in her mind, cut down to size.

TWENTY-TWO

Anna's courage awed Jenny. The little Pigeon had snatched power from a psycho-rapist or psycho-rapists. Regardless of what she said, Jenny believed she was raped. The way her small, competent hands hovered protectively over her thighs, the way she kept plucking the khaki trouser leg away from her skin, her aversion to the three hulking males, suggested Anna's story had missing chapters. Anna's violation enraged Jenny. Anna's escape and trapping the rapist elated her.

Jenny was rapidly forgiving herself for falling into obsession over the woman from New York City. Who wouldn't? Gay or straight, anyone with a soul would have to be enamored of her. Even as Jenny laughed at herself, it amazed her that Andrew, Steve, and Jim weren't stumbling over each other to pay homage.

Buddy nestled in her arm, Anna was telling the law enforcement rangers about coming on a woman and three men of college age, of how one of the men was taking out his dick while another held the woman and the third watched.

The picture she painted jolted Jenny back to her sophomore year. At twenty she already knew her sexual orientation was firmly in the direction of the female of the species. She had known it since she could remember. As a tyke she'd loved dolls and girls and believed without reservation that boys had cooties. In middle school, when the other girls were proclaiming undying love for their favorite Beatle, Jenny was lusting after Linda Ronstadt. As a teen she'd had posters of Jane Fonda as Barbarella on the wall of her room. In college she'd taken her first lover, Adafaire Mason. Obsession with this first, long-imagined and magnificently forbidden, fruit overwhelmed everything else in her life.

Memories of her sexual assault were blessedly confused. As she'd confessed to Anna, she'd been drinking. She wasn't drunk, but close. She remembered the scrape of blunt fingernails and the sickening slip of nylon over her skin as her panties were dragged off. On bad days she could still feel the suffocation. A boy straddled her, his butt on the back of her head holding her down, mashing her nose and mouth into her own vomit. On really bad days she could feel the pounding as the rapists took turns. Alone, in a crowd of dead-eyed girls, and boys cringing with feral need, it had seemed to go on for eons. Looking back, she knew it had only been minutes. Two of the three rapists came in a thrust or two. The third Jenny didn't feel inside her at all, but the pounding of his pelvic bones was the most violent.

Much later she realized he had probably come before

he entered her and was putting on a show to cover his embarrassment at having prematurely ejaculated.

The memory that was clear as crystal and sharp as a razor was her cheek on the splintering planks, craning her neck, looking for Adafaire, finding her, tall and blond and confident, standing at the edge of the circle that had formed around the table. Jenny had screamed her name. Adafaire had a beer in her hand. As their eyes locked, she raised the bottle to her lips and took a drink. Then she turned her back and walked into the darkness beneath the trees.

Jenny came to know the major players, five "good boys," white, from upper-middle-class families. One was on the swim team, two others on the varsity wrestling team, the last hangers-on, soaking up what reflected glory they could. They were the ones who held her down on the rough planks, one sitting on her head, his knees on her upper arms, the other at her legs pulling them apart like a child breaking the wishbone of a chicken. Jenny knew this because she had researched them, dug for their secrets, watched and followed them.

Even before she'd been left to crawl off amid the splinters and spilled beer to put herself together as best she could, she knew she would not report the rape. There would be no justice for her—but, she had promised herself, there would be revenge.

The greatest revenge was saved for Adafaire. Cowardice and betrayal were sins greater even than the bestiality of the boys or the malice—or worse, pity—in the faces of the girls who had watched and done nothing.

Bony little Ms. Anna Pigeon was not a coward. For the first time in the decade since her sophomore year in college, Jenny thought she might again give into obsession, let it take her from lust maybe all the way to love.

Love and marriage. Jenny pushing a baby carriage, she mocked herself, her mind abruptly returning to the present.

Anna was speaking of Kay, the woman buried in the bottom of the solution hole. The Kays of the world hadn't the luxury of life and breath; for them there would be no satisfying dish served cold, only the cold of the grave.

As Anna detailed finding the body, Jim, fresh out of the six-week seasonal law enforcement training program in Santa Rosa, California, who'd practically had his tongue hanging out in anticipation of a grand adventure, lost his boyish glow. Jenny loved Jim Levitt like a warmhearted little brother or a very intelligent big-footed hound, despite the fact he was one of what the interpreters often referred to as "danger rangers," LE guys who were hooked on red lights and sirens, arrests and accidents and rescues. He'd graduated at the top of his class in whitewater rescue, self-defense, marksmanship, arrest techniques, search and seizure, pain compliance, and other macho things Jenny was fairly sure he couldn't spell.

He was an ideal lieutenant for her queenly rounds, dealing with the occasional harsh words and veiled threats, but this was Jim's first dead person.

The Bullfrog district ranger just looked older and sadder. Jenny had known Steve Gluck for years. He'd been a sheriff or trooper somewhere in Nevada before he'd joined the National Park Service. A lot of people in his position grew hard and slick so the day-to-day tragedies would slide off. A lot more drank to dull the sharp edges of memory and disappointment. Not Steve. Steve quietly carried every single lost sheep and broken body on his shoulders. The weight bowed his back so much he moved stiffly, like a much older man.

Andrew was clicking through scenarios so fast Jenny could almost see the shutter effect behind his heavy-lidded eyes: Accidents were bad, murder was really bad, deaths from NPS employee negligence were the worst, press was bad; bad press, no funding. That was disastrous.

Jenny smiled at the variables she invented. Perhaps one day, when she grew up, she should leave the no-madic life of a seasonal and become a park politician.

As the dust was settling from little Ms. Pigeon's announcement of finding the dead girl, she again sent the boys reeling with the news that not only had she escaped, she had left the bad guy caught in the trap he had laid for her.

Jenny was flat-out loving this.

After a moment's stunned silence Andrew Madden said, "We'd better get up there and get him out. Before you know it he'll be sticking his hands in Uncle Sam's deep pockets, suing the park for wrongful imprisonment."

"Can he do that?" Anna demanded with a fierceness that warmed Jenny's bones.

"Anybody can sue anybody for anything anytime—

and they do," Andrew Madden said with a bitterness that suggested he'd been ground slow and fine by the wheels of justice at some point in his career.

Then the wrangling began. Anna would not tell them where the solution hole was. She wanted to be there when the bad guy was hauled out. When she refused to be moved from that position by logic, threats, flattery, or wheedling, Glen Canyon Law Enforcement gave in. Had Jenny not already been deeply intoxicated by Ms. Pigeon, Anna's next words would have stolen her heart.

"I want another woman with me. I want Jenny."

TWENTY-THREE

The rangers crowded the narrow cabin of Steve Gluck's boat. "Cabin" was a misnomer; it was more of a roofed windbreak-cum-backrest. Like the front seat of a pickup truck, sans seat and doors. Steve piloted, the chief ranger to his right and Jim Levitt outside hanging onto the metal upright to his left.

Jenny and Anna sat shoulder to shoulder on a hard bench that ran the width of the abbreviated cabin, their backs against its outer shell, their heads a foot or so below the pilot's windscreen facing the bow. Anna was not sure she liked Jenny so close. Humanity, even a few humans, weighed on her like a summer thunderstorm rolling down the Hudson River toward Manhattan.

Utterly alone in the jar—at least while she was awake and before Buddy had dropped in—she'd craved company. So much so that she'd chatted with her sister, who was not there, and Kay, who was dead. Ensconced on the boat with Jenny and the rangers, she felt crowded, hemmed in.

The din of the engine noise made conversation difficult. She was glad of that. Telling—and not telling—parts of her story over and over again wearied her nearly as much as had living it.

No, she corrected herself. Little was more wearisome than waiting naked and thirsty for a miserable debasing death that never showed up. Her thoughts flashed to Zach, to his role in *Waiting for Godot*. Certain scholars were of the opinion that Godot was meant to be God.

Now Anna knew it was meant to be Death—or should have been even if Samuel Beckett didn't know it.

In the roar of enforced silence, Anna gave herself over to the miracle of wind on her face.

Because of her work, she was familiar with various brands of wind machines and audiotape manufacturers who specialized in wind sounds, from whisper to keening to battering gale. Much thought had been given to creating the illusion of wind, but she'd given none to wind itself.

When she'd escaped the sandstone-bottled air of the jar, and the desert night wind cooled her skin and ruffled the fine hairs around her face, fanning stale air to give life to curtains on windows that looked out to black-painted walls struck her as absurd as pretending an apricot was the sun.

The life she'd spent in the theater with Zach was gone as if it were a dream dreamed by someone else. It left her both too free and too alone. The life that would replace it remained to be seen.

Bullfrog Marina was bigger than Dangling Rope. There was covered docking for several hundred houseboats and yachts that stayed year-round, as well as a fueling station, pumping station, and small grocery store. Many of Glen Canyon's permanent rangers and their families lived in the tiny town of Bullfrog. They had a system for schooling the children, a medical clinic run by a nurse practitioner, a fire department of sorts, and an airstrip.

The airport was as tiny as the town, serving tiny little planes LaGuardia or Kennedy would use as doorstops or table decorations. It was also the reason the five of them were boating fifty miles from Dangling Rope to Bullfrog. The park owned a Cessna 180 and boasted a park pilot. With such a vast expanse of land and so few roads, flying was the only way to keep tabs on what was happening in the backcountry, to look for lost hikers, fires, floods, game animals, and poachers of deer, elk, reptiles, and artifacts.

Anna had flown on jets of various sizes, but she'd never been in a small plane. The wings looked fragile and stunted, the propeller about the size and effectiveness of a Popsicle stick, the skin of the fuselage and wings no better than the metal used to make beer cans. It looked as if it could be swatted down by any errant gust of wind as easily as Anna could swat a fly.

It did not reassure her when the pilot asked what she weighed.

"I don't know," she told him.

"Nothing," Jenny said.

He put her weight at a hundred ten pounds and told her to get in the rear seat. The chief ranger took the right front seat. Steve Gluck squeezed in beside Anna in the back.

"Hank will come back for Jim and Jenny," Steve told her. Anna had wondered but wasn't going to push the issue. She sensed it would take very little for the rangers to decide they could find the solution hole without her now that they had a general direction. They'd already made the transition from treating her like the star of the show to treating her like a walk-on who kept missing her cues.

Once over the shock of committing body and soul to a vehicle that felt no more substantial than a high-end kite, Anna found she loved flying in the small plane. It bore virtually no resemblance to flying on a commercial jetliner. The wings were high, and nothing obstructed the view. The Cessna flew slowly a thousand feet above the earth instead of at the speed of sound and five or six miles in the air. She could see everything: people on boats, water-skiers, Jet Skis throwing plumes. Her delight in the intimacy of peeking down on her fellows quickly gave way to pure awe at the staggering intricacy of Glen Canyon and Lake Powell.

Hundreds of zigzagging fingers of water reaching up jagged creek beds and drainages, snakes of blue curling around shattered rock piled as high as skyscrapers, cutting and poking into the desert, prying away secrets, creating more, hiding and revealing. Anna's head swam trying to grasp the immensity and complexity of this thing man had done and the foolish belief that he was running the show. Given this bird's-eye view of the world, she felt how very big it was and how infinitely tiny she was. She was both as indispensable and insignificant as any lizard.

"Aah," she murmured.

"What?" Steve's voice in her ear startled her. "Do you see the solution hole?" The four of them were wearing headsets with voice-activated mikes, and her exclamation turned everybody's attention to her.

"No," she said.

"That's Dangling Rope," came the pilot's voice. He dropped the left wing a little as if making the airplane point.

Laid out below, neat as any map, was the hopscotch pattern of the dock, the two squares of housing above, the sewage treatment pond above that, then the canyon wall she had scrambled up.

"There's where I came out." She pointed for Steve. He leaned across her, his shoulder hard against hers, the faint scent of his aftershave tickling her nose.

"I figured," Gluck said. "I doubt there's any other way to walk out of the Rope."

He stayed too close too long for Anna's liking. "Breathe on your own side," she commanded. Before the jar, she might have made room for him, might not have minded. She could have been polite or subtle. Maybe. She could hardly remember who she was back when she had her husband and not the monster as her constant companion.

Steve moved back, apparently unoffended. She didn't care either way as long as he did as he was told.

"A road!" Anna cried out in dismay. Male chuckles filled the space between her ears.

"Hole-in-the-Rock Road out of Escalante," Steve told her. "Look at the end there." He pointed his finger, poking past her nose. "That'll be the sheriff out of Kane County. Glen Canyon is in two states, several counties and an Indian reservation. You don't even want to know about jurisdictions. We called Sheriff Patterson last night. He's a good guy. You'll like him."

A car. A road. Anna felt betrayed. What had happened to her should not have happened anywhere near cars and roads. She comforted herself that the road scarcely deserved the name. From the air it looked like nothing more than a dirt track knifing away from the canyon to run parallel to the endless mesa that was Fiftymile Mountain.

The pilot flew beside the road for a while, then made a right-angle turn and another, until the airplane was lined up with the dirt track.

"Solution holes," Steve said and leaned into her to look out her window. She looked where he pointed. The plateau had great islands of stone bubbling up from it and forming smooth domes and humps polished by the elements until they shone. Pocked into these bubbles were deep, round, smooth-sided holes like the one that had held Anna captive.

"That's the biggest," Steve said, indicating a neat circular mouth over a white sand bottom. The hole was so big a good-sized oak tree had grown up inside of it, and so deep the crown of the tree would never reach ground level.

The pilot did something that made the plane slide sickeningly sideways, and Anna realized they were going to land the rickety little airplane on the dirt road, a road strewn with rocks and other unforgiving substances. At what seemed the last minute, the airplane stabilized and the wheels met the earth with surprising smoothness.

"Sorry about that," Hank said. "Bad crosswind."

They taxied to where the truck Steve had pointed out was parked. Literally, the end of the road. Beyond was canyon. An angular man in a cowboy hat unfolded from the cab as they deplaned. Frank Patterson, sheriff of Kane County.

Anna did like the sheriff, if for no other reason than he looked like Buddy Ebsen, and she was a big fan.

After introductions were dispensed with, the men talked among themselves, a soft rumble in Anna's ears. Sheriff Patterson took a pack of Marlboro Lights out of the pocket of his short-sleeved uniform shirt and lit one with a wooden match he struck on the sole of his cowboy boot. Chief Ranger Madden bummed a cigarette with the desperate relief of a man who had quit smoking and had been doing well until this. He struck the match on the side of the box. Two broke, the third one lit. His hands were shaking.

The wait while the pilot fetched Jenny and Jim was hard on Anna. She knew they waited for Jim with his muscle and the arsenal he carried on his belt. Andrew

Madden didn't look like he'd carried a gun in years. The sheriff was old—older than Steve—pushing seventy at a guess. Anna suspected all three were too canny to walk into anything that could turn out to be a fair fight. More firepower was undoubtedly wise; still, her monster was calling, and she needed to go to him, look on his face. With each passing minute her need to lay eyes on him grew more intense and more terrifying.

As did the thought that she would not be able to find him. Every rock and bulge in the landscape looked familiar and at the same time alien.

When she stumbled onto Kay and her attackers, Anna was exhausted and perishing of thirst—or so she believed until she was, indeed, perishing of thirst. She hadn't noticed scenery or noted landmarks. When she'd been taken to the jar, either she was already unconscious or quickly became so by striking her head on the way down. She had no memories between turning to run and waking up in the bottom of the hole. She hadn't a clue whether all three boys had stripped her and thrown her down along with Kay's body, or only two, or just one. She didn't know how many followed to bury Kay. She didn't know if all the men returned to leave her drugged water and snacks, or if only one returned without his pals to continue the game. It was possible all three took turns visiting, and the last had drawn the unlucky night and gotten his monstrous self caught.

Her escape had been at night. Drugs fogged her thinking; she was scared, dehydrated, malnourished, in pain, and carrying a skunk in her brassiere. She had no clear recollection of where she'd wandered during the hours prior to reaching the edge of Glen Canyon and accidentally turning in the right direction. It wasn't until she saw the housing compound that she'd known where she was.

Half a hundred times she told Steve and Chief Ranger Madden that she didn't know where, exactly, the jar was. She doubted they believed in her ignorance any more the fiftieth time than they had the first. If she did not find the hole, and the man she'd left in it, the chief ranger would probably be only too glad to write the whole adventure off as the deplorable—if understandable—histrionics of a city girl gone wacko under the pressure of the wide-open spaces.

That she had spent the last decade working in the theater didn't help her credibility. During the sixth or seventh rehash, Andrew had gotten the look of a man having an "aha" moment. Narrowing his eyes like a true-born gunslinger, he'd said pointedly, "You're an actress, isn't that right?"

The fact that she was not an actor but a stage manager had impressed him not in the least.

Sheriff Patterson, Steve, and Andrew seemed happy gossiping and ignoring her. Happy to be ignored, Anna took a water bottle from the cab of the truck, even though she had two full liters in her pack, and moved to the west side of the four-wheel drive to sit on the ground in the meager shade, her back against one of the big knobby tires.

The more she sat and sweated and thought, the more

certain she became that there was no way in hell she could find the jar.

The monster would shrivel up and die of exposure.

That was a cheerful train of thought, and she enjoyed riding it until it was derailed by the idea that if there were three monsters, monster-in-the-hole might have been fished out and be long gone or, worse, waiting for her behind a rock or a tree.

By the time the burr of the Cessna's engine returned, Anna's knees were drawn up and she was hugging the water bottle tightly to her chest. Before the Cessna rolled to a stop she was standing, shoulders squared. *Never let 'em see you sweat* was an old theater maxim. Or maybe it was *Never let them see your ass*. Either way, Anna had no intention of returning to the fetal position in public anytime soon. Not even when Jim Levitt and Jenny Gorman deplaned and ten eyeballs turned to her, demanding to know which way the jar was.

As the 180 taxied down the road for takeoff, the Bullfrog district ranger unfolded a map on the hood of the sheriff's truck.

"We're here." Steve tapped a blunt forefinger on the end of a broken black line that ran to the edge of a canyon. Hole-in-the-Rock Road, Anna guessed. "You crawled out of Glen Canyon here." He moved his finger an inch on the map. "So I figure your solution hole is somewhere in here." His finger drew a small circle on the map between the road and where Anna had come onto the mesa. "It's about a two-mile trip from where we're standing to where you came up the old trail. I figure what we'd best do—if it works for you, Frank—is to take the truck cross-country as far as we can. Get Anna to where she starts seeing familiar territory."

Relief washed over her. The rangers were helping; they were being *rangers* and arranging things. Anna's favorite colors shifted from black and black to green and gray as she began to recover her faith in her ability to lead them to the jar.

The truck had a double cab. Though Anna was the smallest, Jenny, Chief Ranger Madden, and Jim were condemned to the cramped rear seat. Sheriff Frank Patterson drove, Steve rode shotgun, and Anna sat uneasily between them trying to keep her knees out of the way of the gearshift knob.

As the truck jolted over rock and sand, trailing a plume of white dust, she scoured the land beyond the windshield trying to find a rock or bush she might have seen before. From a distance, the land along the rim appeared flat, nearly featureless. In reality, the weathered and broken chunks of sandstone were scattered like coins strewn across a floor: stones smaller than dimes, stones the size of basketball courts, of buildings, stones overlapping, piled up, falling down, scattered, clustered. They could hide ten thousand openings, ten thousand canted throats, ten thousand jars.

As she stared, they began to run together. Heat mirages melting the coins, melting the desert.

The truck lumbered up a slight incline, then down into a shallow swale on a low shining shoulder of stone. "Stop!" Anna cried.

Sheriff Patterson braked in a sudden cloud of dust, and everybody exited the truck. Patterson turned to

Steve. "You want any tracking done, better keep at least eight of these big feet off my ground."

Gluck said, "You heard the man."

No one got back in the truck, but neither did they follow Anna and the sheriff as they walked the small depression. It was not the swale where Anna had witnessed the murder of Kay. The shining rock was not the rock she had come gasping over.

The next time she yelled, "Stop!" it still wasn't.

As in all good fairy tales, the third time was the charm.

TWENTY-FOUR

When Anna found the bloodstained rock, Jenny suppressed a sigh of relief. The sheriff, the chief ranger, Steve, and even Jim, though she thought she'd trained him better, had begun to exude the unmistakable air that suggested they were about three manly breaths from writing little Ms. Pigeon off as a hysterical woman. If Jenny squinted her psychic inner eye, she could almost see "that time of month" and "rape fantasy" and "cry for attention" flickering behind their eyes. Jenny could tell Anna felt it, too, and, because this was Eve's Achilles' heel, was beginning to believe that maybe the men were right, maybe she was crazy, *maybe* . . .

The bloody rock changed all that. The guys went on point like good hunting dogs. Cameras came out, as did little orange flags; measurements were taken; radios were held up to mouths as the machinery of however many law enforcement officials of however many jurisdictions were called.

Anna, chastised for picking up the bloodstained rock, as well as for walking across the crime scene to do so—though, until she had, none of them had known it was a crime scene—stood at the right front fender of the sheriff's truck, clutching her plastic water bottle and looking stunned. More than anything, Jenny wanted to wrap her arms around the poor bewildered little person, cradle her and tell her everything was all right, that Jenny was here and she needn't ever be afraid of anything again. Instead, she wandered over and leaned against the hood next to her.

The metal was as hot as a branding iron. "Do you know where we are?" she asked gently.

Anna shook her head, one short jerk right, one short jerk left. She didn't look at Jenny.

"About three hundred yards that way"—Jenny pointed south—"is the head of Panther Canyon. We went there the first day we worked together, taking water samples at the grotto." Anna said nothing, gave no indication that she heard. Jenny wasn't an EMT. She had no idea whether a person could go into shock this long after the traumatic event had occurred. Anna had been held prisoner, starved and dehydrated, then had wandered lost for twelve or thirteen hours before finding her way home. That would have put Jenny in shock, but Anna had seemed to cope well enough, playing with Buddy, tending to personal hygiene, relating her story to Steve and Andrew.

Until now she'd seemed, if not a pillar of strength, at least a reed, bent by the wind but unbroken. "Anna?" Jenny dropped her voice to the place women use to communicate heart-to-heart with children, injured souls, and small animals. "Are you sure you want to go through with this? We could wait here while the rangers go get the bad guy. I bet Steve would even radio the pilot to come back if you'd feel safer at Bullfrog or the Rope."

Anna looked at her. The woman might be shocked into stillness and compliance with law enforcement, but her eyes were not blank and scared. They were determined and scared.

Unblinkingly she said, "What? And miss the eleven o'clock number?"

Jenny had no idea what that meant—something to do with the theatrical life, she guessed as she saw the ghost of a smile whisper over Anna's lips.

Sheriff Frank Patterson was a tracker of local renown. Jenny and Jim Levitt had been informed of this by the NPS pilot who spent his lieu days on a piece of land near Escalante where he was building a house. As the men were going all *Last of the Mohicans* and testosteroning up for the big tracking event, their efforts were made moot by what sounded like distant shouting.

The six of them went utterly still. Had the others not reacted, Jenny might have thought her ears were playing tricks on her. The canyons played havoc with sound, muting noise nearby, carrying a laugh a mile before letting it go. Echoes had echoes, yet silence reigned. No one moved. Shadows black as crude oil puddled between their feet.

"I think—" Jim began. The sheriff, ahead and slightly above the rest of them, hushed him with a raised hand. Quiet as a stalking cat, Patterson began following tracks in the dirt, his head cocked at an odd angle as if sound would drop into his ears more efficiently that way.

Thin and small, the shout came again. A faint dying "Heeeeeeeeeelp."

The eternal winds, breath of the canyons, sawed across the ears, and the voice sounded as if it emanated from the bottom of a well.

"Hello!" Steve Gluck shouted, hands around his mouth to form a megaphone.

Patterson pointed. "This way," he said. He'd found the tracks. "Stay off to the side. Don't foul the trail. It's got a story to tell."

Jenny was impressed with the display of woodsmanship until she topped the low rise where he stood. The trail wasn't exactly as challenging as tracking ducks across a pond. It was more of a scrimmage line where several heavy-footed individuals had stampeded across the desert's skin.

Anna started to trot. "Wait," the chief ranger shouted.

Steve Gluck yelled, "Hold up there."

Anna broke into a run.

"Damn the torpedoes," Jenny muttered and ran with her.

Anna came to an abrupt stop. "There," she said.

Jenny barreled into her and had to grab her lest the smaller woman fall to the ground. The feel of the bird-boned body and the clean smell of her sun-warmed hair robbed Jenny's apology of much of its sincerity. She steadied Anna, in no rush to take her hands off her.

Jenny would never, as the boys called it, "cop a feel," or force her attentions where they were not invited, but a gift was a gift and she enjoyed it.

"That's it." Anna pointed to a black hole gaping at the sky from a flat stretch of ground. The slit in the earth was no more than two feet wide at the center and about five feet long, both ends tapering to a point like the lids of a half-closed eye. Beyond it were two sentinel boulders, taller than Jenny, and squared off as if machined that way. Their shadows fell across the opening. Coupled with low scrub brush and a scattering of rocks, the twin shadows effectively camouflaged the opening of the solution hole.

"That's the mouth of my jar," Anna said. She sounded proprietary. Had Jenny been stuck in a jar like strawberry preserves put up for winter, she'd have wanted sticks of dynamite tossed in and her name severed from the ruin evermore. Anna sounded almost fond.

"Are you there?" The frantic cry warbled up from the opening.

Footfalls were thumping up from behind as the men caught up. Anna stepped closer to the hole.

"Stay back," Steve cautioned. He took hold of her arm. Anna shook him off.

"I hear you out there," came the voice. "For God's sake, get me out of here."

Jenny looked from Anna to Steve. Neither seemed to know what to do next.

"Talk to me," the voice begged.

Jenny walked past Anna, nearer the hole, and leaned down, hands on her knees.

"Regis?" she called down the stone throat of Anna's jar. "Regis, is that you?"

TWENTY-FIVE

Like great wings the sky flapped and the desert heaved beneath Anna's feet. Abruptly she sat, her butt smacking the ground hard as her knees gave way. Darkness gathered, the ghosts of crows flocking at the edges of her vision, until she saw only a long tunnel, at the end of which was the mouth of the jar. Jenny, Steve, Jim, Andrew, the sheriff, entered and exited from this circular stage, four actors talking at once; none making sense.

The jar interacted with the human cast, chattering as if it were the star, its voice rising hollow from beneath the ground. A rope was thrown. Brown gnarled hands flashed into the spotlight, and Anna watched the hemp snake down into its lair.

"Okay," the jar shouted. Anna heard scraping up the throat of sandstone, felt scratching in her own throat, a fishbone dragged up her gullet with a bit of thread as Sheriff Patterson pulled on the rope. Hooks of the boat ladder hobbled in jerks from the hole in the ground followed by bright blue line and plastic treads.

The hooks were whisked offstage; the ladder remained.

"We're set," Steve Gluck called and, "Come on up, Regis."

Regis, the neighbor guy, the personnel guy, the guy with the plump wife, the guy who sat with the others in the evening and drank beer from long-necked bottles, the guy who'd tried to lure her out of her shell, Regis crawled out of the ellipses, a worm from the eye socket of a skull.

"Water," he croaked like a desert rat in a cowboy film. Anna watched him gulp from a white plastic government-issue water bottle. The crows took flight; lights came up; the stage grew to encompass all the characters in this surrealist drama. A dun-colored set of Styrofoam rocks and artfully placed shrubs appeared against a scrim of deep blue sky.

Each and every one of the players was staring at her. It was opening night, and Anna didn't know her lines. Why would she? She was the stage manager. Zach was the star.

"Why did you attack me?" Regis demanded. "I nearly died in that hole."

Anna could not think of a single thing to say.

"Christ on a crutch, I should have you brought up on charges of attempted murder."

"Easy, Reg," Steve Gluck said.

"Leave her alone," Jenny snarled.

The chief ranger and the sheriff had no more to say than Anna. Jim Levitt radiated unasked questions.

"I was trying to save you, God damn it!" Regis sputtered—sputtered because he kept pouring water down his throat even while he was trying to talk.

"You're going to throw up." Anna's voice was flat and cold and sounded as if it came from some other place in time.

Like a good actor, Regis vomited on cue.

Behind him, Sheriff Patterson was backing into the mouth of the jar, using the plastic rungs on the slope to ease himself farther into the solution hole.

"Anna didn't know it was you," somebody said.

"I frigging told her it was me." Regis was wiping his mouth on a red rag, the kind car mechanics buy by the bushel. Someone must have brought it from the truck.

"I *fucking* told her it was me," Anna said. "'Frigging' is not a word." She wondered why she said this, why the cold flat voice came out of her mouth. *Anna, what have you done?* She remembered that.

"Back off," Jenny snapped at Regis. "Anna's been through a lot. She was stuck down there a whole lot longer than you were."

Regis blinked, seeming to consider her words. Anna watched him change: His shoulders relaxed, losing their proximity to his ears; his head rose up and settled on his spine.

"Yeah," he said. He pinched his nose and squinted past Anna. "Yeah. Okay. It was dark as the inside of a cow, Jesus." He shook his head and unclenched his hands from around the water bottle. "Sorry," he said to Anna. She watched his lips form the word. He smiled ruefully. "The damsel in distress isn't supposed to cold-conk and Mace the white knight."

"Not Mace," Anna said. "Buddy."

Without invitation, Jenny came over and lifted Anna to her feet by the arm, one hand on the bicep, the other cupping her elbow. Lifted, not helped up; Anna was amazed a woman could be so strong. Since Anna didn't care if she sat, stood, or was laid down on a slab in a butcher shop window, she didn't fight her housemate.

Jenny put her arm around Anna's shoulders and, still cupping her elbow, steered her away from the men, back in the direction they had come.

Walking away from a stage where the fourth wall had been summarily shattered and the make-believe world poured out into the real world, Anna began to gather herself together, reeling herself in as if she were a ball of string that had become unwound. At the pace of invalids, she let Jenny lead her over the broken ground. Mindful of tracks, they skirted the flagged area where Kay had fought for her life and lost.

Anna waited while Jenny opened the passenger door of the sheriff's truck and dumbly obeyed when she told her to get in. She watched Jenny walk around the hood of the truck and let herself in the driver's door, lower the sun flap, catch the keys the sheriff had put there, start the engine, and crank the air conditioner to high.

They sat facing front, not talking. An awkward date at the drive-in movies. Anna finished winding up the raveled string. When she could again speak, she said, "Well, that was an unforeseen turn of events," and was startled when Jenny laughed.

"Poor Regis," Jenny said when she'd recovered. "Clubbed and skunked and left in a pit."

"Yeah," Anna murmured. "The monsters got away, didn't they?"

"They'll get them," Jenny said. To Anna's ears it sounded as if she spoke without conviction.

"Your monsters got away," Anna said.

"Not from me, they didn't."

There was nothing to say after that until the men reappeared walking five abreast. Their faces set and grim, the sheriff with his cowboy hat pulled low over his eyes.

"The Earps," Anna said.

"The OK Corral," Jenny said.

If Anna remembered her film history correctly, that hadn't ended well for anybody.

Gluck carried the canteen Anna had become so familiar with during her time in the jar. Looped over one shoulder, Levitt carried the two boat ladders. Regis hugged a water bottle much as Anna was prone to do after suffering so much from thirst.

"That canteen the sheriff is carrying was the one with the drugged water in it," Anna commented with about as much emotion as she might have said, "That's the T-shirt with the stripes on it."

Because she felt vulnerable and marginalized sitting in the front seat of the cab as the men approached, Anna reached for the door handle.

"Wait?" Jenny cried, sounding alarmed. "Don't go out there."

"Why not?" Anna asked.

"I don't know," Jenny admitted. "I just had a weird bad feeling."

"A lot of that going around," Anna said and got out to stand on her own two feet. Regis saw her and waved and smiled.

"Hey, Anna," he said as he broke the line and moved rapidly toward her.

It took all of Anna's resolve to keep her face unreadable and resist the need to leap back into the truck and slam and lock the doors.

"I'm so sorry," he said. For a moment it looked as if he intended to give her a hug. Anna held up one hand, the way the Indians in those same Westerns had done while bizarrely uttering, "How."

Regis stopped. "I was just so blown away. I forgot how scared you must have been when I climbed down. You went through far worse than anything I did. I'm sorry I took my own fear out on you, that's all."

Anna said nothing. Bits of things she might have said skittered around in her skull, but making conversation was too pointless to bother dragging any one of them down to where her tongue could get around it. Lowering her hand was the best she could do. Unnerved, Regis looked over his shoulder at the other men. They had stopped several yards out from the truck and stood in a neat semicircle, a manly tableau against the canvas of the desert.

"You're lucky she didn't kill you," Steve said without a trace of humor. Broken by his words, the tableau came to life again.

"Where's Kay?" Anna asked Steve. He didn't answer

right away, and Anna was afraid there was no body, the body was gone or had never existed. "Did you find Kay?" she insisted, louder this time.

"We just dug enough to assure ourselves she was there," Steve said. He hadn't wanted to speak, Anna realized, because he knew it would be hard for her to hear. She didn't like him for the kindness. She didn't like or dislike any of them. She didn't care because they didn't care, not in any way it mattered. Not in any way that would ever make anything right.

"Frank's going to have the county coroner out here. They'll recover the body and take it back to Escalante. He's going to work with us to identify her. If we're lucky she's been reported missing."

They didn't know she was wearing nothing but underpants. Anna hadn't told that part of the story. It was ugly and it was hers and she would keep it. For now at least.

"We'll take good care of her," Sheriff Frank assured her.

"She's dead, and I didn't know her," Anna said, but she remembered how important it had been to her that Kay's hair be combed from the sand, not yanked, and she remembered sacrificing the tempting panties so Kay could retain a scrap of dignity.

Regis unscrewed the cap of his water bottle as the sheriff and Jim loaded the ladder and canteen into the bed of the pickup.

"I'll never take water for granted again," Regis said, offering a tentative smile to Anna. "I nearly thirsted to death."

"There was a canteen of water," she said.

"Empty," the sheriff told her as he dropped it onto the bed of the truck with a clang.

Anna said nothing. It had been over half full when she hit Regis in the head with it, heavy enough to stun. He couldn't have drunk it all. If he had, he'd be in a stupor. Instead he was hyperactive, the way a person is after a narrow escape. He could have dumped it, or, when it struck him, the cap might have come loose and the water drained out.

Anna saw no value in voicing these thoughts. She saw no value in speaking anymore.

Jenny and Jim were consigned to the bed of the pickup. Anna tried to follow. Steve cut her off and herded her back into the cab the way a good sheepdog would herd a stray lamb back to the fold.

The sheriff slid behind the wheel. Chief Ranger Madden started to climb into the front passenger side.

"Andrew, take the back again, if you wouldn't mind," Steve said. "Anna could probably use the air." Steve Gluck jammed himself in beside Madden and put Regis behind the driver, as far from Anna as he could be in the truck's cab. Anna didn't like him for that, either. "Air" was not what she needed. She needed her own planet.

With two people in the truck bed, the sheriff drove toward Hole-in-the-Rock Road more slowly than he had driven out. Regis couldn't stop talking.

An older man who wouldn't give his name had hailed him on the dock at Dangling Rope Marina, he told them as the cab jounced and swayed. The old man stank of beer, Regis said, and was none too steady on his feet. The guy told him a bizarre tale about a girl trapped in a solution hole up around Hole-in-the-Rock Road. He said he'd heard some kids bragging about it like they'd caught a bear cub or a cougar and were keeping it a secret from their parents. He wasn't clear as to how many kids there were, or how tall or short, and was pretty vague about where he had chanced to overhear the boasts.

Regis said he figured the guy imagined it, or half heard something in a drunken stupor and, when he sobered up somewhat, thought it was real and reported it to the first person in uniform he'd laid his bleary eyes on.

This had transpired around seven thirty or eight o'clock the evening before Anna attacked him, Regis said. Though he figured the guy was crazy, Regis had checked to see if anyone had gone missing. No one had but Anna. Since Anna'd packed up her things, he never thought it could be her, so he let it go.

Then, in the middle of the night, he woke up worrying about it. What if a woman were trapped, suffering in some way, crying for help? He couldn't stand it, he said, and got up and dressed and started up the unmaintained trail that scrambled and clawed up the escarpment behind the housing area, the only way he knew to get from the Rope to the area the drunk had mentioned.

He'd wandered around until nearly dawn and was about to give it up when he heard a woman crying. He'd found the hole where the weeping came from. Beside it, half hidden under the overhang of a rock, were the boat ladders.

All this poured out with no encouragement but the occasional grunt from law enforcement. As the sheriff turned the ignition off, the truck parked neatly parallel to the dirt track as if meter maids were watching, Regis finished his story.

Anna had not been weeping the night he came to the solution hole. She had been lying under the sand, waiting, like a trapdoor spider.

Anna said nothing.

TWENTY-SIX

There were two phones in Dangling Rope, one in the ranger station on the dock and the other in the small convenience store run by the park concessionaire. Since the Rope didn't have its own district ranger, as the senior NPS employee, Jenny had the key to the ranger station. Jim thought he should keep it because he was law enforcement.

When he grumbled about it Jenny had said sweetly, "Then next time *you* give Steve the blow job."

Anna had thought it funny. Gil, Dennis, Regis—the males—were not laughing. They were thinking maybe it was true. Jenny winked at Anna and rolled her eyes.

That was Anna's third or fourth day at the Rope. Cocooned in her grief, she hadn't put herself out to get to know her fellows, not even Jenny. That wink and eye roll surprised her. Jenny had seen her. Being unseen was one of Anna's skills. During rehearsals, stage managers were visible. During the running of the show, they were not. Anna dressed in black, as did the crew, so if the audience accidentally caught a glimpse of her it would make little impression. She cultivated a soft low voice so backstage noise wouldn't compete with the show onstage. She wore soft-soled shoes and moved quietly. She did not bump into things or set curtains moving as she passed through. She could see well in the dark.

Before she lost Zach, Anna used this learned invisibility only professionally. Jenny's wink let her know she had been trying to disappear during the light of day and it hadn't worked, at least not on Jenny.

That had been less than three weeks before. The jar had turned time on its end, and it seemed a story from when Anna was much younger.

As soon as the dock settled down for the evening, Anna got the ranger station key from Jenny and went down the hill to the lake. She needed her psychiatrist. More than that, she needed her sister. Molly had been so present during her days in the jar that, as she inserted the key and let herself into the cramped office, she reminded herself Molly had been present only in her mind. Her tale would be a shock to her.

Molly would go into one of her icy rages, the kind where her mind glittered like crystal and her eyes could slay at a glance. Anna needed that, too, needed someone to be furious for her, rage against the withering impotence of knowing life was very, very unfair, and there was not one goddamned thing you could do about it.

Having locked the door behind her, she slipped into the padded swivel chair in front of the desk, a narrow built-in behind a half-wall that kept visitors from wandering into the working portion of the office.

There was both an overhead light and a desk lamp.

Anna left them dark. Not only did she feel at home without light, she didn't want visitors trotting down to borrow a cup of sugar.

Finally alone, the last rays of the day making the dust motes sparkle and dance in the dim office, Anna realized how tired she was. After Regis had been rescued from the solution hole, Steve ordered her to the Bullfrog clinic. The nurse practitioner—a competent woman named Beatrice—wanted her to go to the hospital in Wahweap or, failing that, stay overnight in Bullfrog for observation. Anna refused, arguing her injuries were old news. If the bang on the head and dislocation of her shoulder were going to kill her, she'd already be dead.

Never again would she allow herself to be trapped and observed by strangers as she slept. After signing release forms, Beatrice let her go. The woman was so affronted by her refusal to see sense she'd actually said, "If you have problems with the concussion, let it be on your head."

By the time she'd gotten a boat ride back to Dangling Rope it had been after five. She had forgotten to eat. Now she was out of fuel, running on empty, and not running very fast. A few glasses of wine backed by a Xanax and sixteen hours in bed looked like her very own Eden. Still, she picked up the phone and dialed the many numbers needed to make a credit card call to New York.

"It's me, Anna," she said when she heard Molly's "hello." At the sound of her sister's voice, tears she had no idea were waiting gushed from her eyes. With an effort, Anna kept them from her voice.

"Well, well," her sister said. "Did you have to ride a yak to the nearest village where they had running water and AT&T?"

As was Molly's habit—both by training and inclination—she listened without interrupting while Anna told her tale of abduction, assault, and imprisonment. Trusting her sister absolutely, as she had done since she could remember and probably from the moment her mother brought her home from the hospital and laid her in six-year-old Molly's arms, Anna left nothing out: the drugged water, the carving on her thigh, being stripped, her nude body posed—all of it. Twice she heard the familiar metallic rasp followed by a short sharp intake of breath as her sister lit and smoked two Camel unfiltered cigarettes.

Anna was glad she could end the story with the odiferous heroics of Buddy. Neither she nor the little skunk knew the man in the dark was Regis Candor and not one of the young murderers and would-be rapists, so Buddy got full credit for saving her life.

That he had saved her in other ways she didn't bother to voice—not at twenty-five cents a minute. Molly would know. The healing power of friendship, the value of having someone to care for, to give and receive love, were things her sister often said she wished she could dole out in pill form.

The only part of the story Anna kept back was that not only had Molly's voice been with her in the jar, but it had pulled her back from the edge. Much as Anna loved and trusted her older sister, there was no sense giving her a big head. As a doctor and a New Yorker, Molly had sufficient arrogance to get her through the day.

Finishing her story, Anna brought Molly to the present moment: sitting in a small dusty ranger station, sun relinquishing its light to the first stars, absolute quiet a palpable thing. Over the phone line, from three stories above Seventy-seventh, off Fifth Avenue, Anna listened to the ululations of sirens, the sound track of cities.

For a long intake of breath Molly said nothing. Then she gave her professional summing up: "Yikes." Another long breath came and went. The slow response to a story full of danger and drama didn't offend Anna. This was how Molly designated levels of importance. Shallow thoughts brought quick rejoinders; serious matters deserved serious attention.

"This Regis guy stinks to high heaven," Molly said finally.

"Even without Buddy's ministrations," Anna agreed.

"But it was not he who struck the girl you unburied, or chased you and, presumably, knocked you unconscious, stripped you, and rolled you into the pit."

"Right," Anna said. "As far as I know, Regis wasn't within miles of me that afternoon."

"Easy enough to check," Molly said.

It was easy to check. Anna could find out. Until that moment, pursuing justice on her own behalf hadn't crossed her mind. There were professionals for that. Vigilante justice had struck Anna as an oxymoron. Until now.

"You're right," Anna said firmly.

"What? No you don't. I am most assuredly *not* right if you're thinking two of my rights are your permission to do a big fat wrong. What are you thinking, Anna?" Molly demanded. "Your voice has that terrifying 'fools rush in' ring to it."

"It's better than feeling helpless," Anna countered.

"It's not better than feeling dead," her sister snapped.

"Living, knowing the monster is out there, might not be better than dead," Anna said.

"Don't be such a melodramatic little ass," Molly said. "There are always monsters out there. Many of them in high places and respected professions. Do you think I just listen to bored housewives and neurotic rich people forty hours a week? I see monsters every day: men who batter wives, women who are cruel to their children, grown-up little boys who were used by fathers and uncles and cousins, grown-up little girls who were raped by their dentist or pastor or Daddy's best friend or Daddy himself. On Fridays, when I do pro bono work at Pelican Bay, I meet the batterers and child abusers and murderers. I know they are the tip of the iceberg, the small percentage that get caught and their lawyers don't get them a deal and the judge doesn't throw out their case on a technicality and the victim doesn't withdraw her accusation and the witnesses actually show up in court.

"Of course we're scared sometimes. Of course we sometimes feel helpless. Of course we all live knowing the monster is out there.

"You are not a monster hunter, Anna." Molly ran down, the heat leaking out of her tirade. "Leave this to the cops," she finished. "You are not John Wayne. You are just a stage manager."

Anna clenched the fingers of her left hand, making the tendons in her shoulder ache.

"John Wayne wasn't John Wayne," she said. "He was just an actor."

TWENTY-SEVEN

By gray-green fingernails dusk hung on to the edge of a star-studded sky. Chain-smoking and thinking and trying not to think, Jenny sat with her back against the wall of the duplex, legs stretched out on the picnic table, waiting for Anna.

Party boaters had defiled the grotto. She and Anna would need to sample the water there again, see if it was fit for human visitation. There was the beautiful little beach in Gunsight Bay, a prime spot for toilet paper blooms and graffiti, that she hadn't visited in a while. Interpretive opportunities would abound in Gunsight. It would be a good place to get Anna started on the higher education aspects of her job.

That was if Anna didn't bolt. Jenny wouldn't blame her if she did pack up her toiletries and head east on the first train, plane, or bus. Jenny hoped Anna would stay, figured she would run, and, in honesty, thought she probably should put as many miles between herself and the "jar," as she called it, as possible. Ms. Pigeon was incredibly ignorant of reality not created on stages in the Big Apple.

Too many questions about her abduction and imprisonment remained unanswered for her to feel safe anywhere near Lake Powell. Regis was not in jail. Anna wasn't pressing charges. Eyewitness to her own attack, Anna knew he had not been one of the three boys who dumped her in the hole. For tonight, Steve had asked Regis to remain in Wahweap so Andrew could take his statement at headquarters. Tomorrow night, he would be back at the Rope, sitting a few yards from Anna's bedroom window drinking beer.

Regis's intervention had rescued Anna from a very real hell. Anna didn't dispute that, but Jenny saw how she'd watched him, chin up, eyes hooded. Jenny'd seen an owlet looking at a snake that way once, waiting for it to strike. Come to think of it, Jenny had seen Bethy Candor looking at Anna that way. That her husband had left her bed to find another woman wasn't lost on Bethy. Before Anna disappeared, Regis's attentions to Anna hadn't been lost on anybody, with the exception, perhaps, of Anna herself.

The Rope was no longer going to enjoy the easy camaraderie it once had.

At the far end of the housing area, soundless as an apparition, Anna appeared.

Lost in thoughts of her, for an instant Jenny believed she had conjured her. Anna ghosted between the two duplexes forming the southwest corner of the square, walking as quietly as cats were supposed to. "Hey, Anna," Jenny said lest she startle her. "It's me."

"I saw you," Anna replied. She came down the concrete walk and sat on the bench, leaning her back against the table's edge, facing away from Jenny.

Jenny wondered if it was a rebuff. No, she decided, if Anna didn't want to be with her, she would have gone straight inside. "Did you get hold of your sister?" she asked.

"She thinks I should come back to New York."

"You probably should," Jenny said, proud of herself for putting Anna's well-being before her desire for her company.

"Yeah," Anna said. Then, "Do you know who took my things? My uniforms, clothes, all that?"

"Not a clue," Jenny said, "but that's why we didn't do a search. It looked like you'd cleared out."

"Do you think that's why they were taken? So nobody would come looking for me?"

"That's what I think." Jenny put added stress on the *I*. Steve Gluck and the chief ranger didn't buy that there was that much plot afoot. Kay's corpse and the mishmash of tracks on the plateau convinced them that there were three attackers, as Anna had said. They accepted her statement that they were college-age boys. These facts made sense. That three criminal opportunists were connected to the disappearance of Anna's belongings, miles away in distance and elevation, did not. Andrew Madden, at least, clung to the hope that Anna had cleared out her things, then coincidentally—or for personal reasons—met up with the men who'd killed Kay.

Jim Levitt—it was he who had carried the law enforcement gossip from Andrew's office to Jenny's ears—said there was some disagreement between Andrew and Steve as to whether Anna had been visited in the hole or merely been dumped there to die. The canteen she'd insisted contained drugged water was empty, and there was no evidence of any waxed paper, pudding containers, or paper bags to back up her story about the food.

Anna caught the emphasis on *I*. "You believe the monster took my things. Who doesn't?"

Jenny told her part of what Jim had said. "They aren't discounting the possibility that you knew Kay and went to meet her that day."

Anna was silent so long Jenny worried she'd dropped back into that fugue state she'd suffered when Regis popped out of her own personal rabbit hole and began berating her for skunking him.

"Want a beer?" Jenny asked helpfully.

Anna didn't reply. Jenny stubbed out her umpteenth cigarette, scooted off the table, and went inside. In less than three minutes she was back on the porch, two bottles of Tecate hanging by their necks from the fingers of her left hand. Buddy was tucked into the crook of her right arm.

"Medicinal restoratives," she said as she sat beside Anna on the bench and put the bottles between them.

As Jenny settled the sleepy skunk kit on Anna's lap, the back of her hand touched the other woman's thigh. Anna flinched as if she'd been poked with a hot iron.

Jenny didn't know if it was her touch, the fact of being touched, or the cuts. She didn't ask, just inched farther away on the bench as she pulled her hands back, in case Anna needed more space.

"Then they think I also knew the boys that were getting ready to rape Kay?"

Jenny didn't have ready words to answer this question. According to Jim it had been posited that either both Anna and Kay knew the boys and a day of fun had gone bad, or possibly only Anna knew the boys and they had turned on her when Kay was killed. As Jenny was searching for a way to say it that would not destroy the hearer, Ms. Pigeon figured it out.

"They think I killed Kay and made up the stuff about boys to cover up the murder?" The outrage in her voice was a balm to Jenny's ears. In anger was strength. She realized she'd been bracing herself for hopeless despair.

"They don't think that," Jenny said. "It's just something they have to consider, Jim says."

"I was alive, Kay was dead," Anna said after a time. "I hit Regis and left him—"

"And didn't mention that fact for quite some time," Jenny added.

"Right."

"For no apparent reason, you climbed a miserable dangerous trail in the heat of the day with no food or water to speak of."

"Right. Why would I do that if I wasn't expecting to meet someone?" Anna asked.

"Because you're a greenhorn, a citified, ignorant fool," Jenny suggested, a smile in her voice.

"Right," Anna agreed. "Start a list. We demand drinking fountains on backcountry trails. Any theories on how I ended up in the bottom of the hole with a dislocated shoulder and a ladder coiled up neatly beside the jar's mouth where I couldn't even see it?"

"Actually there are," Jenny admitted.

"You're kidding!" Anna exploded, rising half off the planks of the bench.

"Don't upset Buddy," Jenny cautioned. "I don't want to be washing in tomato juice for the next week."

Anna settled back. Night had come in earnest. Jenny could just see her housemate's outline. Lack of vision honed her other senses, and she breathed in the faint plumeria smell of shampoo and a hint of childhood innocence from the Jergens lotion Anna used. Cotton, washed and worn for so many years it was as soft as old flannel, whispered against the rough wood when Anna moved. The scents and sounds were familiar, comforting. Not surprising, given the fact that most of it belonged to Jenny. A trip to La Boutique Target would be necessary as soon as possible.

"And why, pray tell," Anna asked icily, "do the Powers That Be think I was in the jar and the ladder was not?"

Jenny took a breath to repeat what Jim had gleaned from the meeting in Andrew's office and conversations to and from Wahweap on Steve's boat.

"No, wait, let me," Anna said bitterly. "A life in the theater should make fiction my forte. Lying my second language. I kill Kay, bury her, climb out via the nifty boat ladders, coil the rope ladders up, and store them by the rock. Then I creep back to peek down the throat of the jar to admire my handiwork, slip, and fall in, banging my head and hurting my shoulder in the process."

Jenny was impressed. "In a nutshell," she said and, "Stranger things have happened."

"They sure as hell did," Anna grumbled.

"College-age boys," Jenny mused. "We've got Heckle and Jeckle on tap—Gil and Dennis, the maintenance seasonals," she added for Anna's benefit. "Three Hispanic guys about the right age work at the marina. There's more up and down the lake working seasonal for us or concessions. Then of course there are a zillion party boats vomiting über-rich teens and twenty-somethings onto the beaches daily."

"I don't suppose they bothered to wonder why I would choose a big flat rocky chunk of nowhere for a rendezvous with boys ten years my junior, or why any woman would agree to meet me there."

"Kay and or the boys might have driven out to Hole-in-the-Rock Road from Escalante. The quickest way for you would be up that trail. They're hoping to get an ID on Kay's body. That should clear up a lot of things—where she was from, why she was here, what vehicles she owned."

"If she drove out from Escalante, where was her car?" Anna asked.

"Maybe the rapist boys drove it away. Or maybe you hid it." Jenny said.

"This is a pretty pickle," Anna said.

Jenny laughed.

"Would you roll me a cigarette?" Anna asked suddenly.

"You don't smoke," Jenny said, oddly appalled by the request.

"I didn't think I did," Anna said, "but it's beginning to look like there's nothing I won't stoop to."

Jenny was stung. Because Anna was under a lot of stress, and because Jenny was enamored of her, she let it pass, but she didn't roll the cigarette.

"Somebody murdered Pinky," she said suddenly, having no idea why the thought popped into her head or out of her mouth.

"The little rattlesnake?" Anna asked.

"I found him under Regis and Bethy's porch. His body had been laid out in a line. A nail—big, maybe six-penny or ten-penny—was driven through each end of his snaky body and into the dirt."

"Somebody crucified a snake," Anna said flatly. "There is something I wouldn't stoop to after all."

"He was under Regis's porch," Jenny said.

"Regis found me in the solution hole."

"If what you told me is true, he lied about hearing you crying."

"What I said is true." Anna's voice was flat and cold.

Jenny shuddered inwardly. "Sorry," she said. Other than food and clothes the greatest gift she could give Anna was faith, utter and complete belief in her every word: If Anna said she saw pixies or skin walkers or flying saucers Jenny must believe.

"I know you're telling the truth," Jenny said.

"No you don't," Anna said. "Even I'm not sure what my truth is."

TWENTY-EIGHT

The pygmy rattlesnake was on Regis's mind. On his desk were background checks he needed to review and file. At present there were few job openings. Seasonals were in place. A full-time district ranger for Dangling Rope was the only job pending. Given that the federal bureaucracy ground slower than the wheels of justice, he didn't feel any urgency.

By choice Regis had never been hunting or fishing. Madison, Wisconsin, was not exactly Mecca for members of the NRA; still, hunting was seen as a noble tradition and bass fishing almost a devotional pastime. There had been plenty of invitations. None had tempted him, not even for the "bonding experience" with other males, or proving of himself in some outdated blood ritual.

Even as a kid he couldn't imagine a more miserable pastime than freezing in the snow, sputtering in the rain, or baking in the sun to acquire something that could be bought at Kroger's already gutted, butchered, filleted, and wrapped.

Some things did need killing. Pinky Winky the

snake had to be killed. What was Jenny's deal with naming the thing? It was a wild animal. Less than a wild animal, it was a venomous snake. Having a poisonous reptile under the porch wasn't cute, it was stupid. *Snow White*—the Disney animated version—had warped the minds of an entire generation of women. They thought the creatures of the forest would frolic on their skirts, dance with them. Forest creatures were more apt to spit and bite, in Regis's experience.

He did like the way snakes moved, water snakes through water, land snakes across land. No legs, no arms, not so much as a fin or a finger, yet they moved rapidly and with grace. The pygmy rattlesnake was a little thick and short for true gracefulness, but it moved well enough. Yet he killed it. Its death was such a nonevent. No more than wadding up a piece of paper and tossing it into the trash.

His mother and grandfather didn't value life, not this life anyway. They were devout, not just in church on Sunday, but Saturday night. As an only child and an only grandchild, Regis had gotten the full attention of their God. Not a particularly nice deity. He would never have dared say so, that was blasphemy. His grandfather's God, as manifest by his grandfather, was all about control. The old man had money, scads of it, and doled it out to his daughter-in-law and grandson only when he deemed them worthy in the eyes of the all-seeing.

There were the Rules. Abortion was murder. At eleven or twelve, he remembered a night foray to a liberal church and putting tiny white crosses all over the lawn to protest the fact they had a doctor as a member who worked with Family Planning. Regis told that story once to the horror of his college girlfriend and her roommate, but, in truth, it had been a hoot. They had even blacked their faces commando style. Black ops. He'd loved it.

When his dad died at forty of a massive coronary, family and friends stood in a half circle around the casket at the viewing. His mother in her ecru suit, his father laid out in gray pinstripe. He was so lifelike. Everybody said so. At least he was more lifelike than his mother, until she broke down and wept.

Regis didn't cry. Old Mrs. Burman, the pastor's wife, nearly smothered him in a great fat hug, crooning, "Let it out, let it out, there's no shame in crying for your poppa." Regis never did "let it out." For years he kept thinking that one day, boom, the dam would break and all that repressed emotion would flood the world. In his early twenties it dawned on him that wasn't going to happen. There was no repressed emotion. He'd liked his dad, but it just wasn't that big a deal. He was alive, then he was dead. So what?

He should have felt something.

He should have felt something—even just a glimmer of something—when he killed the damn snake. When his and Bethy's dog, Kippa, was killed he'd felt plenty. In a way it was good just to feel. He wished he could blow off the afternoon, take the Cub up and catch thermals or—and this would get him fired in a heartbeat— fly through Rainbow Arch.

Putting his heels on the edge of the open bottom drawer of his metal desk, he tilted back in his chair and stared out the window. Headquarters was surrounded by a narrow belt of greenery. In keeping with the park ethic, mostly indigenous plants had been used. Mostly: Whoever designed it could not resist a few nice patches of grass, real, suburban, green, watered grass.

The juxtaposition of this lush chlorophyll belt against hills that looked as bleached as bone left too long in the sun suited his mood. Rampant life smacked up against near death. He wished he dared leave the office and find that risk that had given him such a lovely illusion of life that day on the boat, the kid in the grotto. He had that rush when he dropped that ladder down the solution hole.

The rest of that incident was a bit of a buzz kill.

The midnight black ops up the cliff behind the Rope, the desert at night, everyone asleep in their beds, little red-haired Anna Pigeon in the hole—that part he would gladly do over again. He'd felt alive that night. After she'd knocked him down with the canteen, the flashlight beam chasing her, the way it cut across her bare legs, her cutoffs low and loose on her hips threatening to slide off.

The image of the writhing flailing rattlesnake recurred behind his eyes. Sunlight through the cracks in the porch floor, strobing as it thrashed. Fighting for life, both Anna and the snake were preternaturally vivid, as if they had walked and slithered through a black-and-white world in black-and-gray skins, then suddenly, suddenly were in full color, finally completely alive.

The snake nailed to the ground, Anna's bare legs on the ladder—

He brought his chair back onto four legs with a bump.

Anna Pigeon's legs were bare, her bottom was not. Anna had been wearing shorts.

"What's wrong with this picture?" Regis whispered. "Riddle me that."

TWENTY-NINE

Molly had begged Anna to come home. Knowing it would hurt her sister's feelings, Anna didn't say it: She had no home. Molly had the luxury of a twenty-eight-hundred-square-foot apartment and there was always a room there for Anna, but, without Zach, she couldn't face Manhattan, stages, theaters, or any of the places that were now only places where he wasn't—small, enclosed spaces where he wasn't. Small, enclosed, windowless spaces. Spaces like sandstone jars. Despite the heat and the monster, Anna had taken to sleeping with her windows open, bedroom door ajar, and was considering sleeping on the porch.

Besides, she had a monster to catch. Molly had been right about fools rushing in. Anna didn't know how she was going to go about this. What scraps of detective lore she had been exposed to—mostly through movies—only worked in cities. In the vast playground that was Lake Powell, cops couldn't very well check license plates. The vehicles were largely aquatic and/or rented and in constant movement. They couldn't question neighbors since they changed daily and came and went without identifying themselves. For all Anna knew, sandstone and rope wouldn't hold fingerprints. She doubted there was a local fence or informants. Catching a criminal in a wilderness recreation area would be like trying to catch a feather in a windstorm.

Crime in the park was a dark version of *Brigadoon*. The monster appears, does his song and dance, then vanishes into the fog for another hundred years.

Jenny banged out the front door of the duplex. In her NPS uniform short-sleeved shirt and shorts she looked more like an overgrown Girl Scout than a ranger. Anna had liked that at first—that rangers, even those bristling with weapons, looked gentle, like they were just pretending to be cops and were really only there to tell you the Latin names of plants. She still liked it on the interpreters. On the gun-toting rangers an edgier look would have been reassuring. Maybe an ensemble in black and red with tall boots like the Canadian Mounties wore.

"Smokey the Bear doesn't make a girl feel protected," Anna said, voicing her thoughts.

"That is because Smokey Bear—no middle name—is a Forest Service bear. A park bear, a grizzly or Kodiak or polar bear, would tear Smokey to pieces in a paw-to-paw match. Take Smokey's shovel away and he might as well check into the nearest petting zoo."

Anna smiled. "Wish I was going with you."

Jenny put on a ball cap, then slung her daypack over her shoulder. "This isn't one of your lieu days, is it?"

Anna didn't answer. She hadn't the faintest idea what day it was. She wasn't even sure what time it was. In the jar, Kay's watch was a gift, found treasure. Out of the jar, it was the ill-gotten gains of a grave robber, and Anna wouldn't use it. Along with her uniforms, Zach's picture, and everything else, the mysterious moving man—or woman—had taken her purse and wallet containing her driver's license, Visa, MasterCard, Equity card, library card, and ninety-seven dollars in cash. As soon as she got her new credit cards she would make a shopping trip to Page and buy shoes. Then Kay's sandals would be released from duty.

"Steve has some more questions. He didn't say if the chief ranger was coming or not. I figured I better hang around so he can arrest me for lying to federal officers, obstructing justice, and murder."

"Not to mention harassing the wildlife and keeping a pet in seasonal park housing." Jenny added. "It's an overnight in the grotto," she enticed. "Warm sand, pellucid waters, godlike pictographs, plenty of human waste, and soiled TP."

Out of doors. Away from any place the monster might think to look for her. "What about Buddy?" Anna asked. The baby skunk was nosing around on the square of grass captured within the phalanx of gray buildings.

"You can't keep him, you know," Jenny said gently.

"I know," Anna said.

"Even if you de-stink a skunk, they don't make good pets. They're wild animals."

"I know," Anna said.

"Even if you did de-stink him and he did make a great pet, you couldn't keep him in seasonal housing."

"I know," Anna said.

"Even if you didn't keep him in seasonal housing, you couldn't feed him. Feeding wild animals in parks and rec areas is verboten."

Anna knew that, too. "Buddy's too little to set free to fend for himself," she said.

Both women watched the toddling fluff of black and white investigating a fascinating leaf fallen from a honey locust.

"I'll talk to Steve—or you can," Jenny suggested. "He'll know if there are any groups that raise beasties and return them to their natural habitat when they're old enough. He grew up around here. His folks owned a trading post."

Anna thought trading posts became extinct when the Alamo fell. "I'll talk to him," she said, "and thanks."

"If they decide not to throw you in the hoosegow, radio me and I'll come get you when you're finished."

Anna nodded. The hoosegow was probably located at the nearest trading post.

After a while Regis's wife came out of their duplex and sat on the steps. She wore shorts and a tank top, both of which were snug, as if she'd recently put on weight. She carried a can of diet soda with her, which she set on the step beside her feet, then covered with a saucer.

"Yellow jackets," she said to Anna. "They crawl in, then sting you when you take a drink. I think it's the sugar that attracts them. I'm Bethy," she said, eyeing Anna narrowly. "Regis's wife."

Anna had not only met Bethy but shared a potluck picnic table with her more than once. Apparently Bethy thought decades had passed in the jar while only a handful of days passed on earth. Since Anna felt the same, she was kind. "I remember you, Bethy. You don't seem to have aged more than a few days since last we met."

Bethy giggled. "It's so weird," she said. "I'm, like, self-conscious to be talking to you. Like you became a big rock star or something."

That surprised Anna. Focused on shame, shame she struggled with and shame others would see as hers one way or another, she hadn't given a thought to the power of notoriety. Anna could star in a movie of the week about her exciting capture and escape. Except they'd never let Anna play the lead. The role of "Anna, Wilderness Sex Slave" would probably go to one of the *Baywatch* babes, an actor who had the talent to fill Kay's bikini bra.

"It's weird on this side of the lights, too," Anna admitted.

"Aren't you getting off on it just a little bit? I mean, one day you're just this nobody and then, presto! Everybody's All Anna All the Time," Bethy said.

Either Bethy was staggeringly insensitive or there was a stream of malice running through her. "You all thought I'd packed up and gone back to New York?" Anna asked.

"Yeah." Bethy removed the saucer from her soda can, took three neat little sips, then put the can down and replaced the saucer. "I mean, like, all your things were gone and you don't—you know—exactly fit in."

"Is that a fact?" The comment annoyed Anna, but it

was true. She had not fit in. She had not tried to fit in. She had not worked and played well with others. She had not come to Glen Canyon for what it had but for what it lacked: memories.

Anna hadn't left New York City, her job, and her sister to spend forty days and forty nights in the wilderness healing. She had come to suffer in silence, to wallow in grief where no one would pester her with good advice or helping hands. She had come to purgatory to work off her sins that the gods might relent and give Zach back.

Molly had hinted as much. Anna had chosen not to hear. Now she heard it in her own voice and knew, absurd and childish as it was, that was precisely what she'd been doing. Grief was not coin to purchase the beneficence of the gods, regardless of what self-flagellating hair-shirt-wearing religions might suggest.

Bereft of hope and free of despair, Anna tilted her head back and felt the clean desert heat on her skin.

"Regis said you'd gone," Bethy said in the tone of a woman quoting the ultimate authority. Off came the saucer, up came the can, three tiny little sips. Can back on the planking, saucer on top, she said, "We all said you cut and ran. I mean, why wouldn't you? All those stage-door Johnnys."

Anna laughed. The only place she'd ever heard those words uttered was in old movies. Even there the stage manager never got a single Johnny.

Her laughter seemed to bother Bethy. Sounding almost accusing, she said, "Regis kept going to your place like he could find out why you'd left. None of us would have bothered. Lucky that old drunk told him you were in a hole."

Saucer off, can up, three little sips; Bethy was getting on Anna's nerves. The plump little interpretive ranger had a bobblehead-doll quality about her, as if her words and movements were caused by outside forces rather than any inner logic. Anna checked her watch. Naked skin.

She wished Gluck would show up. With Bethy's help, she had come around to where she was actually looking forward to it.

"Lucky," Anna said.

It was lucky, freakishly, unbelievably lucky. An old drunk overhears boys talk of putting a woman in a solution hole. Old drunk actually knows what a solution hole is; drunk finds a ranger and tells the ranger not only what the boys said but where that one solution hole is—in a zillion acres of solution holes—where the woman was put.

The last ten years of her adult life, Anna had watched many of the finest actors in the country blow their lines. Remembering dialogue was hard enough for trained sober people. That a chemically impaired amateur could get it so right bordered on the miraculous. Miracle number two was that Regis believes old drunk, climbs a ruin of a trail by moonlight, no less, onto a mesa that's another zillion acres of holes and bumps and, in the dark, finds the very one that Anna is in the bottom of.

"Very lucky, indeed," Anna said. Had Regis invented the story of the vanishing inebriate? Anna hadn't heard he'd been turned up by any of the rangers. Not surprising on a vast lake crowded with inebriates of various ages. The only reason she could think of for making up a story like that was to protect the person who did tell him where Anna was.

Regis wasn't more than twenty-eight or thirty. He could have friends or brothers of college age. If he was covering for someone, then he knew more about the perpetrators than he was sharing, possibly even knew who they were.

He'd come alone and at night. All the better to tidy up any clues left by his murderous friends? Or his murderous brother's murderous friends? "Clues" was the wrong word. Miss Marple, Inspector Clouseau, Sam Spade, Lord Peter Wimsey: They looked for clues. Tree cops looked for tracks, spoor, fire rings, toilet paper, and graffiti.

"Does Regis have any brothers or sisters?" Anna asked abruptly. Bethy's head bobbled side to side as she reached for the saucer atop the soda can. Next time, Anna promised herself, she would try to be more subtle in her interrogation techniques.

Bethy concluded her beverage intake ritual, then said, "He's an only," with the air of admitting something she oughtn't.

Anna heard an ATV engine and retrieved Buddy. She couldn't keep him; it wouldn't be fair to him, but she didn't want Jim or Steve to take the decision away from her by snatching the little skunk. By the time she had him settled in his drawer, big feet were clomping up the porch steps.

"Jenny will take care of you if they haul me off to jail," Anna whispered to Buddy, then went out to see what the next act in this unexpected drama held.

To her surprise Steve was accompanied not by the chief ranger but by Regis and Jim. Letting herself out the screen door, rather than inviting them in, she heard Bethy whine, "I thought you had to work today."

"I am working," Regis informed his wife coldly.

Bethy picked up her drinking paraphernalia and disappeared into the gloom of their side of the duplex.

Regis was carrying a cardboard box three feet long and two feet high, a packing box sealed with clear tape and covered with black smudges, as if a cat had walked through soot, then tracked it all over the box.

Steve Gluck sat down on the picnic bench. Everything about him was heavy: the drooping belly, the jowls, the bags under his eyes. He looked as if he carried the sins of mankind on his back and they were dragging him down.

"Okay," he said, rubbing his eyes with thumb and forefinger, the brim of his NPS baseball-style cap pushed up like the flag on Opie and Aunt Bee's mailbox.

Regis set the cardboard box down on the table. He didn't sit down. Jim put one foot on the bench and folded his arms over his raised knee.

"Are you going to arrest me?" Anna asked and immediately wished she hadn't.

Steve's hand dropped to his lap, and he squinted up into her face. "Should we?" he asked.

"No. No. Not at all," Anna said lamely. "I was just asking to be polite."

"Mind if we go inside out of the sun?" Steve asked.

She did. Not because she was afraid Buddy would call attention to himself. They already knew she had the kit, and she was hoping Steve could find a good place for him to live and be a proper skunk. The thought of being inside, in a small dim living room with three large men—and without Jenny—gave her an unpleasant hollow feeling.

"Sure. Come in." *And that was how vampires got into the manor house,* she thought as Steve clomped in. Jim was behind him, and Regis followed, leaving the packing box outside.

Anna's New York instincts twitched. She ignored them. The box could probably sit out there for years and nobody would steal it.

Both windows behind the battered couch had the blinds drawn. Neither Anna nor Jenny spent much time inside, and when they did, they wanted their privacy. The single window in the side wall was blocked by a swamp cooler. Anna retreated behind the kitchen counter, wanting a barrier between herself and the men at least until her eyes adjusted and the giant killer butterflies in her stomach settled. Steve, Jim, and Regis hulked in the middle of the small living space, blinking.

"Sit," Anna said brusquely.

"Thanks. Good to take a load off." With a sigh, Steve lowered himself into the armchair matching the sofa in both hideousness and decrepitude. Jim perched on the edge of the couch, his belt bristling with too much law enforcement gear to allow him to sit back. Regis claimed one of the stools at the kitchen counter, crowding Anna's space.

"You don't happen to have any coffee on, do you?" Steve asked.

"No," Anna said.

"Okay, then. Okay." He took off his ball cap and arranged it neatly, using his knee as a hat stand. "Why did you think we were going to arrest you?" he asked amiably.

Anna didn't want to talk or answer or be in this shrinking space. Breathing deeply, she reminded herself it was only a dim crowded room, not a trap. Maybe not a trap.

"Jenny said you thought maybe I knew Kay before, that maybe I killed her. I didn't and I didn't."

"That did cross my mind," Steve said with what sounded like reluctance. "Professionally speaking, it's important to look at the ugly what-ifs. You didn't know her?"

"No. I didn't. I didn't push her into the hole. I didn't fall into the hole. Both of us were thrown down into it by three college-age men. I told you all this."

Anger was flaring. Anna welcomed it. Like cocaine, anger was a wonderful stimulant. She needed the boost.

"I know you did," Steve said. "I know. Frank—the sheriff you met—is a real good tracker. He said there were four sets of prints that he could find. Three big, probably the college boys, and a smaller set that might have been yours. By the way they were made, he's sure there was a chase and the little prints were the ones being chased. So you've got no cause to worry on that front." He was quiet for a minute, then asked plaintively, "You sure you don't have any coffee? Cold from this morning would be fine."

"No."

The district ranger sighed. "You're right," he said. "Nasty habit," as if Anna's main concern were for the health of his digestive tract. "Did you know any of the boys?" he asked in the same conversational way he'd asked for coffee.

"No."

"Ever seen them before?"

"No."

"Too bad," he said sincerely. "It would have made things easier."

Like the high of cocaine, the fierce energy of anger didn't last. It was hard to stay mad at Steve Gluck. Anna could feel the artificial heat draining from her belly, leaving cold dregs behind. The rangers had no idea who the monsters were. They were out and about enjoying their monstrous selves, and Anna was scared to be in the same room with three men she knew and worked with.

"Couldn't Frontiersman Frank track them back to where they came from?" she snapped.

Steve shook his head slowly, ignoring her slight of the sheriff. "If anybody could, Frank could, but, if you remember, where the three started chasing you was in a natural swale, wind-filled with sand. Around it is bare sandstone. Even Hole-in-the-Rock Road is difficult to follow over the harder rock. Frank could follow them most of the way to where you were in the solution hole, though.

"They turned back a couple times—that or there were more than three of them, but Frank doesn't think so. He got half a dozen fairly clear prints."

"They turned back because, after they took care of me, they went back, got Kay, then threw her down with me," Anna said.

"You say you buried her?" Steve asked.

"No, goddammit, I didn't say I buried her!" Anna shouted.

Gluck held up both hands in a gesture of peace. "Just asking," he said mildly.

On the edge of his chair, Jim watched like a devoted fan at a tennis match. Regis watched only Anna.

"I said I *re*buried her, and you weren't just fucking asking," she snarled. Snapping and snarling like a rabid dog, pacing behind the counter as if the kitchen were a cage and she the tiger: She forced herself to stop. Anna knew nothing about law enforcement and less about ranger enforcement, but she was fairly savvy when it came to the motivations and machinations of men in power. Lord knew she'd sat through *Macbeth*, *Coriolanus*, and *Richard III* enough times. Steve, Chief Ranger Andrew Madden, and even the sheriff of Dumbfuck County would find life a whole lot easier if it turned out she had brought this tragedy down on Kay and herself.

Because they were not evil or stupid men didn't mean they couldn't hurt her.

Stoicism: She would let in only as much as she could

tolerate and show only what emotions she couldn't mask.

"I'm sorry, Steve," she said politely. "Can I make you some coffee?"

Engaging in what actors called a "secondary activity," and normal people called keeping busy, calmed Anna. As she made coffee and got down cups, Steve asked her questions she'd already answered in various different ways. Though she disliked being made to repeat herself, and disliked the feeling of accusation, by the time the coffee was perked and the sugar spooned, she did remember a few more details.

The boy who merely watched was sandy-haired. He wore his hair long in front in what had once been termed a surfer cut. Acne ruined what might have been a handsome face. The kid whose face she'd never seen, the one stripping off his shorts, had a tattoo on the back of his right shoulder, a round shape like a planet or a tortoise. His hair was dark and curled at the nape of his neck. The third boy—the one who killed Kay—was big, tall and big.

Steve ran out of questions. For a moment he sat staring into his coffee cup. Then he heaved a great sigh and pushed himself up off the couch. "I think you're in the clear on this," he said.

"Thanks," Anna said acidly. "Can I go back to being a victim now?"

The district ranger put his ball cap on, tugging the brim down low over his eyes. "Never go back to being a victim," he said. He stood staring at the floor, thinking. "Skunk and box," he said as if retrieving a mental list. "Come out and take a look at the box we brought, if you would."

Obediently Anna followed the men out onto the porch. The instant largesse of space and light allowed her to expand her lungs. Muscles she hadn't been aware she was tensing relaxed. Her shoulders squared, her spine straightened, and her chin came up. For a second she wondered how she could ever have felt at home and safe in the dark confines of a stage manager's booth.

"This is it," Gluck said unnecessarily. The packing box dominated the picnic table.

Because he wanted her to look at it, Anna became afraid of it. A startling image of folding back the flaps to a mass of tarantulas flashed behind her eyes, and momentarily she felt the panic that had overtaken her in the pit when she'd believed the tickle of her braid had been one of the hairy-legged things. Bugs shouldn't have hair.

"What of it?" Anna asked warily.

"We were hoping you could tell us," the district ranger said.

Anna took a couple of steps closer to the box but didn't touch it.

"Why is it covered with black smudges?" she asked. Another ludicrous vision darted past her mind's eye, Wile E. Coyote, black with smudges of blasting powder.

"Fingerprint powder," Gluck said. When he didn't volunteer any more, irritation overcame caution. Grabbing the box, she pulled it to the edge of the table. It was heavy, but she could have lifted it by herself. The tape had been cut. The box had been opened, then closed again by folding the flaps together.

Bracing herself for the eight-legged hordes, Anna curled her fingers around the edges of the flaps and yanked them open. On one, hidden before she'd unfolded it, was an address, typed on plain white paper and taped down with clear tape.

Anna recognized the address. "This was being sent to my sister, Molly?"

"It turned up in the outgoing mail at Wahweap," Steve said. Jim Levitt hovered at the opposite end of the table, noticing everything and saying nothing. Anna suspected he might be in the doghouse for relaying to Jenny—and so to her—the information that Anna was considered a suspect. Regis had retreated to his own porch and leaned against the wall in the shade, an audience of one watching the play.

Anna looked in the box: NPS uniform shirts and shorts, bedding, underwear, black Levi's, black Reeboks, a picture of Zach on the beach at Cape Cod. "These are my belongings," she said. Confusion boiled out of the box in the place of tarantulas. "The stuff from my room. Somebody was mailing it to my sister?"

"Looks that way," Steve said.

He was waiting for her to say she didn't send the box or admit she did. Instead she said, "You dusted it for fingerprints. Whose were on it?"

"There were a lot of prints. Mail here gets picked up and hauled down to Wahweap sometimes in one boat, sometimes handed off to two, even three. Loaded and unloaded, then, finally, Wahweap. There are a lot of prints."

"Are mine on it?" Anna asked, afraid that in this surreal place, where Disney and Dali and T. S. Eliot fought over landscape design, the whorls and ridges of her fingers had made it to the cardboard.

"They are now," Steve said. He took an efficient-looking folding knife from his belt and cut off one of the flaps she had handled. "Yours aren't on record," he explained. "We had nothing to compare. I ought to be able to lift them off this. If not, Jim here can use you for practice taking prints. It's not as easy as it looks on TV."

Anna felt as though Steve Gluck had stolen something from her. He could have asked. Was the tricky business to throw her off balance? "I wasn't on balance," she said waspishly.

Ignoring the apparent non sequitur, Steve said, "Give me a half hour or so, then meet me on the dock. Bring the skunk. I found him a home. Skunk paradise."

With that he left. Jim gave Anna what she assumed was supposed to be an encouraging smile and trailed after his boss. Regis looked as if he were going to say something. Then Bethy called, and he went inside without speaking.

Buddy had a home. Sadness welled up, pricking Anna's eyes with tears. Of course Buddy had to go. She knew that. She just wasn't ready now, not today. Putting the thought from her, she lifted the smudged packing box and carried it into the duplex. In her bedroom, she set it on the floor.

Buddy stood on his hind legs, his tiny forepaws not quite reaching the edge of the drawer. "I'm sure going to miss you," Anna told him. "Skunk paradise," she told Buddy, "Ranger's Honor. That's got to be a step above Scout's Honor."

With the skunk kit as her sole companion, she removed the items from the box. Sheets went on the shelf in the closet. They were the cheapest kind Walmart carried and held no comfort. For a few more nights, Anna would sleep on the worn flannel Jenny had lent her. Towels she hung in the bathroom, uniform shirts in the closet. Socks she put into the top drawer of Buddy's condo.

Next she pulled out the pair of black jeans, beneath which were a black T-shirt and her Reeboks. It was then that it registered.

They were the clothes she had worn the day she climbed up to the plateau. The day she disappeared. A jolt of panic twitched her as if a mad puppeteer had been entrusted with her strings. Muscles jerking, she flung the trousers from her.

"Uh, uh," she heard herself grunting, the sounds of disgust she made when finding a revolting substance on her flesh.

Panting as if she'd run the quarter mile uphill from the dock, she crabbed around the box and the foot of the bed until her back was wedged in the corner of the room opposite the door where no one could come up behind her.

"You're okay," she told herself. "It's okay, Buddy," she said when she heard alarmed skritching from the bottom drawer. Two bead-black eyes appeared over the edge. "Don't get scared and stink up anything, and I won't either."

Seeing and talking to her tiny friend centered Anna in a way nothing else could have. "What will I do without you, Buddy?" she whispered.

The Levi's lay between them, crumpled like the legs of a person shot down while running. They repulsed Anna the way seeing her own skin flayed from her body, or her scalp hanging from a stranger's belt, would have.

Shame drenched her. She didn't want anyone to see them, ever. No one knew she'd been wearing them, that they had been stripped from her body. Even so, she wanted them hidden or gone, destroyed. Still with her back to the wall, her eyes moved to the items remaining in the box: black T-shirt, Reeboks. Panties. Panties peeked from beneath the running shoes, the bright candy colors she wore under her uniform.

Pushing away from the wall, she fell to her knees, looked beneath the bed, sprang up again and rolled open the closet door. Crazy as it was to be looking for the boogeyman, she didn't care. Hidden places were threats. She needed to be able to see what was coming for her.

Satisfied she was alone, she stepped warily around the discarded trousers, leaned down, and, with thumb and forefinger, pinched up a corner of the neatly folded T-shirt and flung it over by the jeans. Using the same fingers, to keep the taint at a minimum, she plucked out first one Reebok, then the other.

The panties had been carefully displayed, fanned out like the petals of a flower, making a colorful circle on the bottom of the box. The center of the flower was a tangerine lace pair folded in a careful square. Anna wished she didn't remember which pair she'd had on, didn't remember pulling the soft nylon up her legs, zipping the black jeans over the bright lace, but she did.

This box had been prepared as carefully as a stage is dressed. The panties were the centerpiece. A joke, a mockery of Anna, being mailed to her sister, and Molly would never have known what it meant. Anna could almost see the monster's self-satisfied smirk as he pictured Anna's only living relative handling the last things her sister had worn when she was alive and, maybe, silently thanking whoever had been so kind as to take such pains in packing her things.

She was rubbing the palms of her hands compulsively on the thighs of her borrowed khakis. "All the perfumes of Arabia," she murmured, forcing herself to stop.

The monster had stripped her, packed the clothes she'd been wearing with those stolen from her room, then addressed the carton to Molly Pigeon in New York. This was very creepy; creepy, but not life-threatening. Yet Anna felt a sense of dread as deep as if her life—or something very like—could be snatched from her by scraps of cotton, leather, and latex.

The monster—or monsters—had touched everything in the box with scaly clawed fingers. Cleared out Anna's room so it would look like she'd moved out, gone home. Monster claws touching her things was creepy, but those he had actually stripped from her body freaked her out, and the tangerine-colored panties terrified her.

The pants and underpants, could they tell her, in fact, that she had been raped? That she wasn't lucky Anna, the girl who hadn't been raped, but one of those "rape victims"? Fluids or bloodstains or tears that would indicate she had been penetrated by the monster or a stick or fingers or—"Stop it!" she commanded herself. "Just fucking stop it!"

Shame pooled cold and low in her abdomen, shame for wanting to distance herself—even if only mentally—from women who had suffered this special brand of degradation, from Jenny.

What if she had been sexually assaulted? Was that worse than having WHORE cut into her skin? Worse than days and nights of drugged nightmare? Worse than a dislocated shoulder and a battered skull? Than hunger and thirst and finding a dead body?

It was not. The shame attached to rape was men's shame, shame they were too weak to carry: that their gender could do this, that they could do it, that they wanted to do it, that they could not protect their wives and sisters and daughters from it, that they could not stop it. That a thing they believed to be solely theirs could be taken by another man. That, should a child be born, the cuckold would be left to raise another man's bastard.

Snatching up the tangerine panties, Anna brought them to her nose, determined to know if there was a scent, a signifier of anything.

They smelled of laundry detergent. Kneeling, she examined the shirt and jeans, sniffing and running her hands over the fabric. They, too, had been washed. The running shoes were wiped clean; even the soles were free of dirt.

Of course they had been washed. Anna sat back on her heels, a Reebok in her hand. Mr. Monster would wash them to get rid of any trace evidence. Now Anna had pawed and sniffed every item, rubbing them around on a carpet that undoubtedly had trace evidence from seasonal rangers that went back ten years.

She should have watched more *NYPD Blue* and less Molière.

THIRTY

Steve Gluck stood in the doorway to her bedroom, thumbs hooked in his belt, a pained expression on his face, as Anna explained about the black clothes, the shoes, and the panties.

When she'd finished, the district ranger said nothing. Pushing back his ball cap with a forefinger, he scratched his head. Anna wondered if he intentionally embodied the cliché or if his scalp itched.

"Okay," he said finally, settling the cap firmly. "Jim and Jenny said when you came in you were wearing cutoff jeans, sandals, and a bathing suit top. We bagged everything but the shoes for possible trace evidence. Now you're telling me you were wearing these." He pointed accusingly at the pile Anna'd made as she'd tossed the offending items from her.

Guilt lapped around her ankles. She hadn't told them the clothes she'd come back in didn't belong to her, that she'd been stripped, and in turn stripped the corpse. What difference would it make? She gave them the clothes. Telling would have made her feel dirty, violated in their eyes; more men taking mental snapshots of her naked and helpless.

"I didn't think it mattered," she said truthfully. The words sounded lame. They sounded like a lie.

Gluck looked at her, a hard piercing stare. "Now you know it matters. You want to fill me in?"

Anna told him then of waking naked, of taking the dead woman's things. Speaking of it made the wounds on her thigh burn. Still, she didn't tell him about the cuts. He would ask to see. He would want to take pictures. That's what they did with evidence. Even the thought was intolerable. It was personal, a secret that was hers to keep, it didn't matter—at least not to anyone but her and the monster.

Steve let out an explosive sigh and shook his head the way a teacher might at an impossible child. "So the anklet you 'found,' did you find that in the sand or on the dead woman's ankle?"

"It was on her right ankle."

"The watch?"

"Left wrist."

"Is there anything else you haven't bothered to tell me?" he asked.

Guilt rose to knee level. Anna had been attacked and nearly killed, and yet it was she suffering the suspicions and accusations of law enforcement. It was she they interrogated. Fury rose. Guilt boiled away.

"No."

Steve Gluck put the black trousers, T-shirt, sneakers, and the tangerine panties in a paper bag, leaving the rest of the box's contents in Anna's room. He didn't give her any hope that these laundered artifacts would yield useful information. Not only because they had been sanitized but because testing for trace evidence was expensive and took time. The park didn't have enough of either resource to throw down what appeared to be a rat hole.

Since there was no federal law against homicide, Kay's murder fell under the jurisdiction of the state of Utah. Kane County had significantly less money and manpower than the park. Kay's clothes would probably either rot in an evidence locker or be returned to her relatives when the corpse was identified.

Along with the clothes, Buddy was to go. Putting it off as long as possible, Anna took him insect hunting one last time, then made a wonderful nest for him in the bottom of the emptied packing box. For his water bowl, she cut a foam coffee cup in half and secured it to the side with duct tape borrowed from the maintenance barn. Finally there was nothing else to be done. She whispered her good-byes and gratitude. Buddy allowed her to kiss him on his little skunk head; then she carried him across the square of lawn to Jim Levitt's porch, where Steve was drinking coffee.

Steve politely ignored her sniffling as he told her he was longtime friends with an old Navajo who ran a filling station outside of Fry Canyon on 95. Lawrence Yazzi had kept a pet skunk for eight years. A year or so back it died. He'd been on the lookout for another. Buddy would be de-stunk, Steve warned her. There was no help for that. He was too little to be let go on his own. "Lawrence is good people," he finished as he took the box and Buddy from Anna's arms. "Your pal here has got it made skunkwise."

Anna nodded. She didn't walk with them down to the dock but waited in the duplex until she was sure Steve would be headed back toward Bullfrog. A little after noon, she went down, bought a Dangling Dog, chips, and a Coke, and sat at one of the picnic tables wondering what to do with herself, where to go, who to be, what to feel, what to think.

It was a relief when Jenny's Almar putted into the harbor, its blunt nose plowing through the blue-green water. Whoever Anna was, and whatever she felt, she suddenly knew what she wanted to do: work. Not with her mind but with her body: to walk, chop wood, dig ditches, lift heavy objects and carry them up steep hills, clean Westminster Cathedral with a toothbrush, load all the human manure on Lake Powell's beaches into five-gallon cans.

She rose and went to meet Jenny as she leaped to the dock and began winding the bow line around a cleat.

By day's end, Anna's shoulder was killing her and she was so tired she could barely think. Other than the aching of her knitting flesh, this was ideal. Taking pity on her, Jenny let her sit and sip red wine poured from a red fuel jar dedicated to that purpose, while Jenny set up camp.

They were spending the night in the grotto at the end of Panther Canyon. Two adults and two children under the age of ten had pitched their tents beneath the curving wall to the lake side. Their boat, scarcely powerful enough to tow the two Jet Skis tethered to it, was beached nearby. To give them their space, Jenny had chosen to make camp at the opposite end of the crescent.

"Maybe I shouldn't tell you this," she said as she shook out the collapsing tent poles and began snapping them together on the elastic rope that joined them, "but we are camping five yards from where an army of party boaters relieved themselves for two days. They'd actually marked off that part of the grotto with empty beer bottles and jury-rigged a privacy screen for those few individuals who remained sober enough to appreciate such an amenity. Would you believe I hauled fifty-four *pounds* of human waste out of here? Four five-gallon cans."

Anna pulled her feet up, her knees to her chest. "Did you get it all?"

"Ah, that is the question I ask myself as I dig and burrow in the beaches of Lake Powell."

"Maybe the park should replace the sand with clumping litter," Anna suggested.

Jenny laughed. "I'll mention that to the superintendent next time he asks a GS-5 seasonal for her opinion."

The tent was orange and dome shaped and sat lightly on the sand like half a melon on a plate. Human waste or not, Anna would leave the tent to Jenny. The space inside was too small and the color too much like sandstone at sunset for Anna to allow herself to be enclosed within. The day had been ninety-two and cloudless.

The night would be warm. The tent was for privacy and to keep out the bugs and the sand.

"I'm going to go introduce myself to the neighbors and see if I can't strike up an elucidating conversation about poop," Jenny said as she tossed the stuff sack containing her sleeping bag into the tent.

"The little kids ought to love that," Anna said. The wine was good. She stretched out her legs and felt the muscles begin to relax.

"Kids are great audiences for poop talks," Jenny said. "These are a little young. Boys eight to twelve are the best. Want to come?"

"I'll pass." It was after six, suppertime for campers. Anna had yet to let go of the schedule she'd kept for so many years; lunch around three, supper at midnight after the curtain came down.

Though the sun still shone on much of the lake, it had long since set in the narrow tongue of Panther Canyon. Twilight would last several more hours. Anna leaned back into one of the "chairs" Jenny had brought up from the boat. They were clever things, two thin pads with a fabric hinge between that could be locked into an L shape by snapping straps that extended from the four corners. Camping had changed from the heavy canvas and cots Anna remembered from when she was very small.

She watched Jenny cross the sand to the visitors' camp. Jenny was wide hipped with long strong legs. Muscles in her calves bunched as she stepped over the uneven ground. Her shoulders were square and her arms brown from working in the sun, biceps well defined.

Jenny moved with the ease and grace of a warrior who had vanquished the invaders and returned to tend the land.

Physical strength had never been high on Anna's priority list. Her work had demanded the ability to organize and focus. A stage manager's greatest asset was the gift of paying attention at all times and to all things so none of the thousands of threads that must be woven together to create the director's vision was lost, late, or broken.

Zachary, her husband, tall as he was, was not a strong man. He was willowy, slender, and supple, with long fingers that could speak as eloquently as most men's tongues.

Smiling, Anna remembered a crew member asking Zach to pick up the other end of a massive oak refectory table that needed moving. Zach had been unable to so much as disturb the wood. Sweeping a gracious bow to the other man, he had said, "Alas, all I have to offer is my civility."

A day spent fetching tools and carrying buckets and the case containing Jenny's water-sampling paraphernalia had worn Anna out, while Jenny remained unfazed. The ill-fated trek up to the plateau had exhausted her to the point that her muscles were quivering and she could scarcely breathe. Unearthing Kay had been a Herculean task. Carrying a fifteen-ounce skunk up a twenty-foot ladder taxed her strength. The hours she'd been lost, looking for the trail back down to Dangling Rope, she had almost given up because she was so weak and tired.

Had she been stronger, maybe the boys would not have caught her. Maybe she could have fought them off long enough to get away.

Anna resolved to eat more and get strong. Everybody died. Cars killed, microbes, viruses, cancers, plaque, bullets, knives, gravity: Death came in one form or another in the end. Death would come for Anna, she knew that. She swore when it came it would find her strong.

Never again would she go down without a fight.

THIRTY-ONE

Jenny was in excellent form. She charmed the adults, entertained the children, and left their camp feeling she had enlisted four more people in her campaign to free Lake Powell's beaches from the rising tide of toxic waste.

As the campers headed toward their Jet Skis for an evening ride, she turned and went back toward her own campsite. Her feet felt light, her heart soared, and she laughed out loud. She was young, living in the most amazing place on earth, doing important work for reasonable remuneration, and she was in love.

The exhilarating alignment of the heavens was sufficiently rare that she recognized her moment of joy, thus making the joy that much more potent. That her darling little pigeon was probably woefully heterosexual, and their union might never be consummated, didn't dampen her enthusiasm by any noteworthy amount.

"Statistically insignificant," she called to her beloved, not caring that she got nothing but mild confusion in return. Infrequently—but nonetheless deliciously—loving pure and chaste from afar was a grand thing.

Then, too, sometimes a girl got lucky.

Flopping down on the sand next to Anna, she asked, "Is there any more wine?"

Anna handed her the red fuel bottle. This wasn't Jenny's cheap *vin ordinaire* but a twenty-seven-dollar bottle of Chateau Ste. Michelle Merlot that had been reserved for a special occasion. Two more bottles of her usual waited on the boat as backup. Not to inebriate for the purpose of seduction—such acts were beneath an enchantress of Jenny's stature—but to ensure a mellow evening.

At the moment Jenny felt anything but mellow. Had there been tall buildings, she would have leaped them, dragons, she would have slain them, if it would have enhanced the pleasure of her new mistress.

"You look like the cat that ate the canary," Anna said.

Would that it were a pigeon, Jenny thought wickedly and smiled. "I feel positively grand," she said. "We've hours of light left. Where can I take you? What can I show you? Your wish, my command."

"You can show me who shoved me into the jar," Anna said flatly.

With that jab of reality, Jenny's elation deflated somewhat. "Ugly thoughts for such a beautiful evening," she said gently.

"I know. Sorry," Anna apologized. "My solution hole isn't all that far from here, is it? Not as the frog hops?"

Anna must have been looking at maps. A week ago Jenny would have bet she neither knew nor cared about the geography of the lake and its environs.

"The end of Hole-in-the-Rock Road is maybe a quarter of a mile from the head of this canyon," Jenny told her. In saying the words she realized not only was that true but— "Those college kids," she said suddenly, sitting up straight. "They didn't have to come up from the Rope or down Hole-in-the-Rock from Escalante. They could have climbed out of Panther."

Now Ms. Pigeon was interested. She looked out over the skinny lick of water that fronted the grotto. "Sheer cliffs," Anna said. "What? Sixty, eighty feet up to the plateau? They would have had to be bitten by a radioactive spider to pull that off."

"Come with me," Jenny said, delighted she had found a gift for her new friend. "Be prepared to strip to your underwear—or skin, if you prefer the classics."

Watching how stiffly Anna got to her feet, Jenny felt a pang of remorse. The poor little thing had seemed determined to do the work of ten men regardless of the fact her shoulder hadn't fully healed and she should have been on bed rest after the trauma she'd suffered.

"We don't have to go," Jenny said earnestly. "I was just going to show you the slot canyon that forms the end of Panther. It's been there since Zeus was in knee pants. It will still be there tomorrow. You should rest. Let me fix you some dinner."

"No," Anna replied, evidently determined to push herself until she dropped in her tracks. "I want to see it. I like the idea they could have come up from here. It makes more sense than the road or the trail. Show me how."

Jenny looked at her for a second, watching her

gather her little strength around her great heart, and silently mocked herself for describing it as such. Despite the mockery she was so proud of Anna tears stung her eyes.

"I am so very completely and totally an idiot," she said softly.

Anna had ducked into the tent to get her boating shoes. If she heard Jenny's brief autobiography she gave no sign.

Beyond the grotto, the long skinny finger of lake snaking its way along the bottom of Panther Canyon narrowed precipitously. The gunwales of Jenny's boat were scarcely a foot from the eighty-foot-high cliffs forming the sides of the slot canyon. Running at idle, she nosed the boat forward until both sides of the Almar's bow touched the sandstone, then scraped, then the boat stuck like a cork in a bottle. Having shut down the engines, Jenny joined Anna where she knelt on the bow looking, to Jenny's eye, like one of Arthur Rackham's fairies.

Three feet from where the bow was wedged, giant stone steps, with an almost man-made symmetry, rose thirty feet above the lake level. Like a calving glacier, great rectangles of rock had sheared from the sides of the slot and fallen in a neat pile, completely blocking the canyon. To either side of the giant's staircase another sixty feet of cliff cut upward before the earth gave way to the ribbon of sky. With the sun gone from them, and the sky turning pearl, the rock appeared dove gray and soft as velvet. The water ran dark, a blue that is only the blink of an eye from black.

"Pretty amazing, huh?" she asked when Anna didn't speak.

Anna was shaking her head. The end of her long braid twitched across the back of Jenny's hand. She stifled the urge to catch it as she might a cat's tail.

"It's too steep. It's too high. Nobody could get out." Anna's voice, usually an alto, smooth as warm honey, had risen an octave and was all sharps and flats. Her eyes were too wide. Around the dark hazel irises Jenny could see white.

As a gift to her beloved, Jenny had effectively put the poor thing back into the jar. "Oh, honey," she cried. "I am so sorry. I should have known. I'm such a blockhead. Come on. Let's go back to camp, forget we ever came here."

Anna didn't move. She was shaking her head again.

"No," she said, her voice still unnaturally high. "I can stay. I will stay. This is just a crack full of water. It won't slam shut."

Anna's last word finished on a high note. Not quite a question, but clearly a plea for reassurance.

"The walls will not slam shut," Jenny said firmly and waited as Anna breathed slowly in through her nose and out through her mouth. Meditation, Jenny knew from her years of shrinkage. Three breaths and Anna said, "Tell me how they could have gotten to the plateau from here."

"Not here," Jenny said. "Past this pile of sandstone."

"What happens past the rocks?"

"The slot starts to get seriously narrow."

Anna groaned. "You're kidding?"

"Cross my heart and hope to die," Jenny said. Then, because she couldn't help it, she added, "It's really beautiful."

"In a strangled creepy kind of way?" Anna asked. She was using humor to cover her fear. Jenny admired that and laughed to reward her courage.

"Coming here wasn't that great an idea. Let's go back and finish off the wine. Besides, wait till you see what I brought for supper." She laid her hand on Anna's arm. The gesture had been meant to reassure but it had sent a jolt of pure lust right up the center of Jenny. Pure and chaste from afar, she reminded herself.

Staring at the immense steps rising out of the lake, Anna hadn't noticed Jenny's brief internal battle between good and evil.

"I don't see how anybody could possibly climb out of here without those things climbers nail into the walls and the ropes and pulleys or whatever they use," Anna said.

Focus had taken the glaze from Anna's eyes and the edge from her voice. Seeing her somewhat recovered, Jenny said, "Come on. I'll show you." The bow of the snub-nosed boat was sufficiently wedged—and this far from the washing-machine action of the main body of the lake, it wasn't going anywhere. Still, Jenny jumped the yard of water between the boat and the sandstone stair and secured the bow line around a big friendly rock. Little was more embarrassing for a boat ranger than to lose her boat. Fortunately Jenny was an exceptionally strong swimmer. Both times she'd let her boat escape she'd been able to reclaim it without hopping pathetically around on shore begging kindly visitors to take their boat out and retrieve it for her.

"We're set," she said. "Feel free to disembark."

Anna leaped gracefully onto the natural step. "Lay on, Macduff," she said.

Jenny started up the pile of stones, thirty feet an easy scramble, Anna was mastering the climb, but she was sweating and breathing hard. Jenny reminded herself to quit showing off and take it easier on her companion. Women as fragile as her darling didn't belong between a rock and a hard place.

"You okay with this?" she asked solicitously. "I'm a tough old thing. I'm used to it."

"I'm getting used to it," Anna said grimly.

When Anna reached the summit, Jenny gestured toward the sculpted slot canyon beyond and said, "Tada! Beautiful in a strangled creepy kind of way."

"My gosh," Anna breathed, and Jenny was gratified. They stood ten yards above an ever-narrowing waterway that had been cut off from the larger part of Panther Canyon by the rock fall. At the base of the obstruction the waterway was twelve feet wide, an almost square pool surrounded by sheer cliffs rising perpendicularly sixty or eighty feet.

"It's like a quarry," Anna said. "Like the granite quarries near where I grew up, but in miniature. Molly used to dive in them. Seventy feet. Not me. Too scared."

It looked not only like a quarry but like a square sandstone jar with water in the bottom. Short staccato sentences: Jenny guessed Anna was afraid longer ones would betray her fear. She opened her mouth to again offer to go back to camp, but knew she was doing it because she felt guilty. Anna would leave when she needed to. At present, she seemed to need to stay and endure.

"A quarry with a tail." Jenny pointed to the far end of the rectangular pool where a crack opened in the cliffs and the water slipped into a dark and twisting channel. "Runoff carved that slot down from the plateau. Of course, there wasn't a lake here for most of the millions of years of cutting. That's what makes the slot canyons here unique. The lake inhabits them. Look how sinuous the walls are. Nowhere near straight up and down. Eons on eons of water carved that S shape into the plateau on its way down from Fiftymile Mountain to the Colorado River. I love the way the wall on your left curves away, like it's shying from the other's touch, then, up higher, see how it sways back till it almost meets the opposite wall? Now close as lovers, now falling back. They always look to me like they're in the middle of a sensuous dance to music timed to a millennium beat," Jenny finished. "When you're in the slot you can't see the sky because of the curves in the cliffs above you."

"It reminds me of ribbon candy. The kind we used to get at Christmas," Anna said, sounding determinedly cheerful.

Jenny added her own nonthreatening image, hoping it would help. "Or taffy the way they'd pull it at the county fair, the colors stretching and twisting all through it." It also resembled the elongated cousin to the canted neck of Anna's jar. "That's it," Jenny said. "The goddess's own sculpture. Had enough?"

In answer, Anna started down the three giant steps to where the rock sheared off in an eight-foot drop to the water. "Does the slot eventually lead up to the plateau?" Anna asked. "Run uphill getting shallower and shallower and then there you are?"

"Nope." Jenny joined her on the edge of the drop. "The slot stays between sixty and a hundred feet deep and, for the most part, no more than a few feet wide. Often less than that. It runs back into the sandstone another two hundred yards or so, then ends in a chimney that goes vertically up to the plateau. Or almost all the way up. The last fifteen feet or so you need a rope to traverse. It's too wide to shimmy up and too smooth to free-climb."

"Can you swim to the end?"

"No. The water's still there, but sometimes the walls of the canyon are only six or eight inches apart. Great place to wedge a foot."

"There must be a beautiful waterfall back there when it rains."

"I suppose you could enjoy it for a minute or two before it killed you," Jenny said. "Everything washes down. Traversing the last fifty yards of the slot is an obstacle course the Navy SEALs would appreciate, but it's definitely doable. Canyoneers do it a couple times during a season.

"Kay and the men who attacked you could have gotten up to the plateau. They would have come out north of Hole-in-the-Rock Road, about a quarter of a mile from where Frank Patterson parked his truck." Jenny was enjoying herself. She loved being able to tell Anna of wonders, introduce her to stunning mysterious slots. *Stop it,* she chided herself without rancor. Obsession was a bad thing. Feeling sixteen with clear skin and no curfew was delicious.

Jenny sat down on the edge of the drop, feet over the water below, and made herself comfortable. "Have you ever heard of canyoneering?" she asked.

Anna eased down beside her, groaning softly. When she noticed the sympathetic look on Jenny's face, she stopped abruptly and finished her move without showing fatigue or pain. What a woman.

"I haven't," Anna said. "I have lived only in the canyons of steel. New York's skinniest alleys are six-lane highways compared to this. This isn't a canyon, it's a crevice, a crack."

"Cracks are growing in popularity. When I started here nobody much paid attention to anything too narrow to drive a Jet Ski up. The whole Escalante region is full of winding, wandering, narrow canyons. More and more we have people come for the purpose of climbing them. Sandstone is too soft for any true technical climbing, but get a good crack, not too wide, and you can sort of wriggle and worm your way to the top. Of course, if it widens out you're screwed, and if it gets very, very skinny at the bottom, and you fall, you can get wedged."

"Like this one does?" Anna asked.

"Pretty much."

"Sounds like a nightmare," Anna said.

"Actually, it's satisfying. You use your whole body like you did when you played as a kid. Grown-up amusements don't allow for crawling and wriggling, getting good and muddy, and tearing the knees of your pants."

"True," Anna said. "Why doesn't the water fill up behind this dam?"

"Only the top forty feet or so is solid. Below it's boulders and rubble. The water can flow through."

"Ah."

For a minute they sat shoulder to shoulder, feet dangling like children, and soaked in the utter silence of the canyon. Not even the sound of water lapping against stone disturbed it. Lest they forget they were in a recreation area, the thin roar of an approaching engine made its way up from the direction of the grotto.

"Campers returning on their Jet Skis," Jenny said.

"How would Kay and those guys get a rope to the top if they were climbing up from here?" Anna asked.

"You're a single-minded wench, aren't you," Jenny teased.

"How could they?" Anna asked.

"Lookie there." Jenny pointed at a frayed old climbing rope anchored around a boulder on the right side of the step where they sat. The rope snaked over the edge and down the sheer rock face into the dark water below.

"Canyoneering types don't use fancy new climbing gear for this grubby sport. Often, if they've found a way, or gotten somebody to drop a rope so they can make the impossible spots, they'll leave it behind for the next guy. This rope's been here a couple of years. If somebody left a rope down that last fifteen or so feet from the plateau you could make it out."

"Is there a rope?" Anna asked.

"There was the last time I was there," Jenny said, "but that was a couple of seasons ago. It's possible it's still there. If it is . . ."

"The murderers could have climbed out," Anna finished. "How far down the slot can we wade before it turns into an obstacle course?" she asked.

"Not wade, dear heart. The water here is over thirty feet deep."

Anna drew her feet up and tucked her heels next to her butt, her arms wrapped around her knees.

Jenny laughed. Knowing a vast lake was hundreds of feet deep was entirely different from looking on a body of water scarcely more than a few yards wide and knowing that beneath were fathoms of water. It brought on the sense of perching on the edge of an abyss, a pit so bottomless as to create its own mysteries. After years on the lake, Jenny could still feel the pull.

For a moment they sat, Jenny savoring the stripe of gold thirty yards above, where the last ray of sun struck color from the stone, the impossible depths below, and the warmth radiating from Anna's shoulder.

Anna was fixated on something else. "What's that?" she demanded suddenly.

Jenny dragged her attention from the glories of nature. Obviously Anna was not sharing in the exalted experience. "What's what?" Jenny asked.

"There." Anna stood and pointed toward the end of the pool to where the slot began.

Getting to her feet, Jenny tried to see in the growing gloom.

"Under the water. A shape," Anna insisted, still pointing.

It was easy to get spooked by the twisted earth and sinister darkness of the water; easy to imagine leviathans of the deep—albeit skinny leviathans—reaching up with skeletal claws or fins or whatever leviathans reached with. Jenny's mouth was full of warm reassuring words. She swallowed them. There was a shape beneath the mirror-still water. A pale rectangle with a dark oval in the middle of it. Unless monsters of the deep wore T-shirts with logos on them, it was either lost laundry or a dead body.

Jenny stripped off shirt, shorts, and sandals. Just in case, she had forgone her old-lady panties that protected her skin from her uniform shorts and tossed aside her workmanlike brassiere. For Anna—just in case—she'd donned matching red bikini and bra with oodles of lace and industrial-strength underwire. She hoped Anna was appreciating the view.

"I'm going to check it out," she said. "Wait here." She didn't inform her that this might turn into a body recovery. The poor thing had enough grisly images, without her adding to them. Maybe it was just a T-shirt or a plastic bag.

Catching up the rope near the frayed knots where it was tied around the boulder, Jenny lowered herself the few yards down the sheer rock face and into the water.

"Yikes," she squeaked, hanging on to the rope.

"What?" Hands on knees, pigtail swinging, Anna looked over the edge.

"I forgot how cold the water can be in these slot canyons," she admitted. "It's so deep and gets zero sunlight."

Needing to generate body heat, she let go of the rope and swam toward the unidentified floating object. From where she'd entered the water to the body—and it was a body—was no more than forty feet, not enough to get the blood flowing. Six inches beneath the surface of the water was a back and a head covered in dark hair long enough to halo out around the skull like seaweed. The drowned man added to Jenny's chill.

Kicking powerfully with her legs and sculling with her right arm, Jenny grasped a handful of T-shirt. The wet cloth rucked up and her knuckles brushed bare skin. She emitted a horrid little gulping sound she hoped Anna didn't hear. What the backs of her fingers brushed didn't feel like skin. Eight seasons on the lake, Jenny had seen her share of drowned people; two were little kids. This was the first time she had ever touched one. She didn't know what she'd expected a dead body would feel like, rubber maybe, or cold skin, maybe like a chicken breast out of the refrigerator. She hadn't expected it would feel exactly like a dead body, a body a thousand times deader than a cold dead chicken.

"Someone's drowned," she called to Anna. "A man, I think. The water is so cold I'm afraid to leave him. He might sink or something." Holding the corpse out to one side, she swam back toward Anna with a one-armed frog stroke. Jenny had her lifeguard's license. High school summers were spent on a white wooden tower blowing a silver whistle at obnoxious children. She knew how to rescue a swimmer: arm under the shoulder, backstroke, the swimmer towed along, nose and mouth clear of the water, but there was no way in hell she was going to hug a dead body snuggled up to her best red lingerie.

The corpse tugged back. Again Jenny squeaked. Above, the light had gone gray; below was liquid darkness. The air in between was thick with permanent shadows. Given the setting, the cold, and the corpse, Jenny was beginning to believe in things she would have mocked when she was high and dry with Anna. It was in her mind to leave the dead to care for the dead and let go when Anna called, "Are you okay?"

Jenny looked to where she stood, rope in one hand, all one hundred and ten pounds of her ready to come to the rescue.

"I'm okay," Jenny assured her quickly, hoping the fact she was becoming less okay by the minute didn't bleed into her tone. "I think the—it—got caught on something."

"What could it possibly catch on?" Anna asked. "This is a slither slot in a rock."

Pointy bones, Jenny thought, lake zombies wanting to feed on warm human flesh, soggy vampires. What she said was "Could be anything. Flash floods wash entire trees down. Rusted-out truck bodies, shed roofs. You name it."

Kicking and tugging jostled the corpse a foot or two

farther. Something from below touched her foot. The corpse began a slow roll; a shoulder, an ear, the bloated face came free of the water, gray eyes open and glassy, followed by an arm that slid across the chest to flop in the water, splashing like a fish. The second arm loomed up from the dark and a hand drifted palm up and jellyfish-like. Then a third arm floated up beside it.

"God damn!" Jenny yelled, let go of the body, and put a couple of yards between herself and it.

"Holy moly," Anna called from her elevated vantage point. "It's two people stuck together. Maybe one was trying to save the other and they both drowned."

More likely one was trying to climb out over the other and they both drowned, Jenny thought. There came a splash. Jenny turned back to see Anna, fully clothed, in long pants and long-sleeved shirt, disappear under the water at the base of the sheer wall that blocked this side of the canyon from where the boat was moored. The rope was still swinging when Anna resurfaced, sputtering, and began swimming toward her and the corpses.

"The water's too cold," Jenny cried. "Go back. I can do this."

"Many hands make light work," Anna said as she stopped to tread water near Jenny.

Despite the cold and the dead, Jenny laughed. Or, more likely, because of the cold and the dead she needed to laugh. "One day you must introduce me to whoever taught you to talk." Before she could lose her courage in front of Anna, she said, "Grab a handful of something on your corpse and I'll grab mine. They're too heavy to try to hoist out of here, and it's not like they're going to get any deader. We can tow them back and slip the rope through their belts or whatever. That should keep them afloat until the rangers get here. Law enforcement gets all the good assignments: domestic violence, knife fights, body recoveries."

Anna maneuvered through the water with a dexterity and confidence that encouraged Jenny. The woman could swim. Her long braid seemed to swim as well, coiling like a copperhead snake beneath the water. Near the corpses' heads, Anna stopped, treading water. Jenny watched her lips firm up and her eyes narrow. Then she quickly reached out and took a handful of hair in her left hand.

"Bravo!" Jenny said. Grabbing "her" corpse by the wrist—the part of its anatomy that was closest—she said, "Take it slow. We don't want to get tangled up with one of these unfortunate citizens and pulled under."

Anna said nothing but swam behind and to the left of Jenny, combining the sidestroke and frog stroke so she could pull her burden and stay afloat.

Jenny arrived at the sandstone wall first. Though she hadn't exerted herself unduly, cold water and the touch of the dead sapped her strength. She turned to grab the rope they'd descended to hang on to until Anna reached her.

There was no rope.

THIRTY-TWO

Jenny pushed back from the wall, treading water. It had to be there. The rope must have caught on something when Anna let go of it. Sheer, clean, the rock face kept no secrets, no cracks where a rope could hide, no knobs where it could hang up, no fingernail grip for hope. The rope had been there and now the rope was gone.

Old, worn, the knots frayed: They must have given way. The rope fell into the water and sank.

Anna gasped up beside her. Pushing the corpse, she wrangled it past Jenny toward where its companion bobbed just below the water surface at the base of the wall.

"The rope's gone," Jenny said evenly, her arms making pale fishy sweeps as she stayed afloat. In the seconds it had taken to search the rock face, the seriousness of their situation settled into her brain. If they did not find a way to get out of the water, hypothermia would set in. Their bodies would start to shut down from the cold. Soon, they would be unable to swim.

That must have been how the two men had died.

Probably they had braced themselves up in the rocks until they were too exhausted to maintain the necessary tension. Then they fell into the water, the cold shut them down, and they drowned.

"No rope? Well, that's a drag," Anna said. She was exerting too much energy keeping her head above water. Using mostly her right arm to scull.

"Did your shoulder go out again?" Jenny asked.

"No. It just hurts," Anna replied.

For a moment, both of them looked up the sheer rock to the top of the sandstone block, gray now against the fading light.

"We are in a world of hurt, aren't we?" Anna asked.

"Help," they yelled in unison.

The slot sent back a muffled echo that struck Jenny's ears as mocking. The canyon walls were smooth and vertical or, worse, leaned in, affording not even the smallest ledge on which they could perch in the warm night air, not a fingerhold they could cling to to keep their heads out of the water. Not that a handhold mattered. Stopping movement would only hasten hypothermia. Their fingers would slip off and they would drown.

"You said there was a rope at the far end of the slot. The one left behind so people can climb out after the canyon gets too wide for shimmying," Anna suggested. "We'll climb out that way."

"I said there was a rope there last season," Jenny amended.

"It'll still be there."

"We'd be out, but we'd be nowhere. No food, no water, no shoes, and me in my underpants." Jenny's teeth were beginning to chatter, and, despite Anna's bravado, the hollow pitch of her voice let Jenny know with what horror she contemplated a return to a place that had very nearly claimed her life.

"We'll be warm," Anna said firmly.

Anna had never done the slot canyons of Utah and Arizona. This one was not the easiest by a long shot. Jenny had her doubts whether Anna could make it during the daylight with a healed shoulder. She knew at night, without protective gear, it would be suicide for them to attempt it.

"We really can't get out the slot," Jenny said gently. "If we stay here the rangers will find us." Anna made a noise that sounded a lot like "Hah!"

"Come on, I can get us out of the water until the cavalry arrives with hot beverages and thermal blankets." Jenny struck out for the far end of the rectangular pool to where the slot made a black line from the water up sixty feet to the rim. There, she waited for Anna to catch up. By the way Anna moved through the water it looked as if not only were pain and cold sapping her strength, but the long pants were dragging her down.

"Here's what we have to do," Jenny said when Anna was beside her. "I'm going to show you. Do what I do, okay?"

Anna nodded.

Jenny paddled into the knife cut. The canyon walls were a little over three feet apart. Turning, she faced Anna. "Okay," she said. "You kind of wedge yourself between the two walls." She pushed a hand out to each side, palm on the sandstone. "Put your hands like this and push as if you're trying to shove the walls farther apart. Okay?"

Anna nodded and spread her arms out, palms on opposite sides of the narrow channel.

"Now do the same thing with your feet under the water. Put the ball of one foot on one wall, the ball of the other on the opposite wall. It's awkward, but you can do it. Okay? My feet are pretty much doing the same thing as my hands. Now I'm going to lift myself out of the water by pushing up with my feet and inching up my hands. Here goes."

It was harder than Jenny had thought it would be, and she had swimmer's shoulders and legs made strong by years of holding herself upright as her boat pounded over rough water. In a couple of minutes she was free of the ribbon of lake, her body forming an upright X between the cliffs, toes and fingers splayed like a tree frog's.

Immediately, the desert heat began taking the feel of death from her skin. Given enough time it would warm her blood from reptilian levels to that of a mammal. "See? Out and warm. Nothing to it. Now you try."

"Have you ever done this before?" Anna asked.

"I've seen it done," Jenny said, trying to make it sound as if Anna were in good hands.

"In a cartoon?" Anna asked.

"In a video," Jenny admitted.

"My sister and I used to do it. We'd climb up the door frame between the kitchen and the living room."

"Then you're going to be an ace," Jenny said.

"I was four," Anna said. "My technique is bound to be rusty."

The water had gone black with evening. Anna's face and arms showed a fish-belly gray. Jenny doubted the latter was a trick of the light. Anna's blood was probably withdrawing from her extremities to keep the all-important internal organs alive and functioning. "We don't have to get way up," Jenny said encouragingly, "just out of the water."

A gentle plinking, the sound gravel makes when falling into water, caught Jenny's ear. "Shh!" she hissed at Anna. Beneath her the smaller woman ceased to splash, seeming to understand implicitly when shushed not to say "What?" at the top of her voice. Jenny listened with such hope she could picture every pore in her skin opening, every ganglion gangling after the illusive spatter. When the silence grew so deep she could hear the rocks aging, she gave it up. "Thought I heard something," she told Anna. "Aural hallucination."

Anna put a hand on each of the walls. Slender long fingers, small palms, and delicate wrists: Anna was too fragile for this. Jenny wished she could reach down and pluck her bodily up, but there was no way she could help without falling back into the water.

"That's my girl," she said encouragingly. "Are your feet wedged out?"

"Yes," Anna said.

"Okay, scooch up." It was almost physically painful watching the woman she adored inching up the stone, left arm not extended as far as the right and left shoulder lower as she tried to protect the ball joint. This soon after the injury there was a danger of the shoulder dislocating again. Jenny would not think about that.

In the time it took Anna to clear the water, Jenny cursed herself for ever having brought Anna to the slot, ever having gotten into the water to show off, ever having lured Anna to follow with the enticement of genuine corpses.

"Atta girl!" she said when Anna made it.

Both of them spraddled out, face-to-face, dripping, in a crack, would have made Jenny laugh at another time. Now the only positive emotion in her breast was gratitude that Anna was clear of the heat-sapping water. The pants she wore were heavy with water, and her long braid dripped a steady stream back into the lake.

"You'd be warmer with your clothes off," Jenny blurted out, her recent ulterior motives making her awkward.

"I'll take off my pants if you'll unbutton them for me," Anna said.

Jenny did laugh then. "Point taken."

"Behind me, the walls get too close together to make this work," Jenny said. "The slot has to be narrow enough we can brace our backs against one side and our feet against the other. Any narrower than this and we'd lose our leverage. Watch me. Most of my weight is on my hands and right foot. Now, I bring my left over to where my right foot is. A twist and a prayer and bingo, I've made myself into a flesh-and-bone bridge between the walls. See, wedged in with the muscles of my thighs, feet pushing that side, my back pushing this side. Hands free." Shaking blood and feeling back into her arms and hands, she said, "Think you can do that?"

Anna made no reply but began her contortions. She

was forcing herself to use her left shoulder. Barely aware she was doing so, Jenny strained her arms toward Anna trying to help. Then Anna was within her reach. Braced tightly in the crack by the soles of her feet and the small of her back, Jenny was secure enough to catch hold of Anna's right bicep. "Let me take the weight. You're almost there. Back to the wall. I got you. Both feet on the other side." It surprised Jenny how supple Anna was. What she lacked in strength she made up for in agility. With less of a struggle than it had caused Jenny, Anna unkinked the leg beneath her and moved her right foot to the opposite wall alongside her left.

Both hands on one wall, both feet on the other, Anna twisted until she could slam her back flat against the wall. There was a wet sucking sound. Anna shrieked and started to slide. Grabbing the collar of her shirt, Jenny held her in place. "Straighten your legs," she said with a degree of calmness she would congratulate herself on should they survive. "Push out. I've got you. Shoulders back. Steady."

Anna got herself wedged tight again, soles of her feet on one cliff, shoulders and back on the other. Her legs were not as long as Jenny's. It would be harder for her to keep up the tension. Jenny wished she'd pushed farther, gotten Anna to a place where the walls were a little closer. That was water under the knees now, crying over spilt blood.

Anna's face was sheened with sweat and her lips a thin gray line.

"Shoulder went out? Did your shoulder pop out?" Jenny demanded.

"No. I think it started to," Anna managed. "I could feel the bone slide, but I'm pretty sure it went back." Gingerly, she raised her left arm. Her face was bleak with remembered pain. The arm rotated. There was no new onslaught of trauma to her already pale cheeks. "Yeah. It went back," she said. "I feel like a puppet that wasn't put together very well."

Jenny managed a nod and looked away to hide the panic in her eyes.

For a minute there was no sound but the dripping of Anna's trousers into the lake.

"What next?" Anna asked finally.

"I'm thinking," Jenny said. "Are you getting warm?"

"Are you kidding? I'm sweating."

Jenny turned her head to look down the ever-narrowing slot. Night was drawing on, and, this far from the sky, it was already difficult to tell rock from water. A few yards from where they sat in thin air, the cliffs came so close together a person would have to turn sideways to squeeze in, the water beneath so pinched a slip could get one's foot jammed in too tight to pull free. Debris, naked limbs, sharp, dry, and honed to needle points, would be stuck in places; various bits of desert skewered on branches, maybe a long-dead rabbit, rat nests of spiny plants, things washed down in flash floods.

For a few minutes Jenny considered trying to make it out that way. There was no way she could do it before dark. With luck, maybe she could scale the chimney by feel. It was a crevice. It wasn't like she could wander off-trail. Without boots, helmet, or any other protective gear, she'd be skinned alive, but in four or five or six hours, she could be on the plateau. Maybe. She could light a fire. That would bring the rangers quicker than anything.

A memory of sitting with her sisters in a circle in their grandparents' backyard, all five of them diligently rubbing two sticks together because their granddad said that was how men made fire before matches were invented, quenched the signal fire idea. None of the sisters' sticks got warm, let alone burst into flame. By the time Jenny got help—if she didn't die of exposure after crippling herself on spiny pointy things—Anna would be drowned.

"Damn," Jenny said to no one in particular.

Anna broke into her thoughts. "The dead person you gave me? I might know who it is—was. The back of his—its—head looked familiar. Or maybe it's the T-shirt. I don't know, but it could be the guy who had his back to me and was undoing his pants. If he doesn't sink we can check his back. He had a tattoo. A turtle, I think."

"Do you think the other guy was one of the other attackers? The one who held Kay or the one who watched?"

"Could be."

A beat passed.

"Do you figure there's a third dead person floating around that we missed?" Anna asked.

"The joint seems full of corpses tonight," Jenny said. "It's a regular dead zone."

"Do you think they got caught in here like us? Then drowned?" Anna asked.

That was exactly what Jenny thought, that they became too exhausted to maintain the muscle tension that was keeping her and Anna high and dry, they fell into the lake, became too hypothermic to stay afloat, and death flowed into their lungs.

"No," Jenny lied. "They could have fallen, or maybe the third kid—the one you said had dishwater blond hair and acne—killed them and rolled the bodies over the rim of the slot." Jenny thought it more likely the third bad guy had done to his pals precisely what somebody— maybe the third bad guy himself—did to her and Anna; pulled up the rope so they couldn't get out, so Anna couldn't identify him.

After a moment Anna said, "I see a star."

Jenny tilted her head back and looked up. Night was upon them. The dark at the bottom of the earth was absolute, the water beneath them invisible ink in midnight. In comparison, the slender scrap of sky was translucent and rich with life. The star was the brightest Jenny had ever seen.

"There is no 'what next,' is there?" Anna's voice was soft beside her.

"I actually did have a plan," Jenny defended herself, though there was no accusation in Anna's tone. "You really can chimney up out of here at the end of the slot. Unless the rope has been taken or rotted, you can climb out. I hadn't realized how late it was," Jenny finished. "I think we'd be worse off trying it in the dark than we are here."

"You could make it without me," Anna said.

"No I couldn't," Jenny said.

"It's stupid to stay here. Go for help. I'll wait. I waited for days in a jar, didn't I? And there I only had one corpse to keep me company."

"You had Buddy. Besides, I don't think I could make it. Trying that slot in the dark without protective gear, I'd end up getting slashed or impaled or wedged and die screaming in pain," Jenny said honestly.

Anna didn't reply to that. Instead, she rested her hand on Jenny's thigh. Jenny took it, entwined her fingers with Anna's. There wasn't a lascivious twitch in all of Jenny Gorman's many cells. When it came to dying, she found she wanted a friend more than a lover. She turned her face in Anna's direction but could see nothing. The darkness in the slot had become an absolute. Without visual verification, Jenny had the sense they were wedged not a few feet above water level but over a chasm ten thousand feet deep.

Soon they must fall. Anna's grip communicated the fatigue in her body. Jenny's own thigh muscles were beginning to tremble the way they did before they cramped or failed.

Anna gasped.

"Slipped," she explained.

Jenny drew Anna's arm around her neck. "Move your right leg over mine and put your foot between mine. Stay strong. I can take some of your weight. We'll keep each other warm."

"Warm" was a metaphor for "brave." The night hadn't cooled much below ninety degrees, and the effort of keeping herself from sliding into the cold water had sweat running between Jenny's breasts and down her back, making the canyon wall even more slippery.

Anna's foot nudged hers. "I'm afraid to take it off the wall," she said. "I'll take us both down."

"I've got you," Jenny assured her.

"Your legs are shaking." Anna didn't sound alarmed so much as sympathetic. During all of this—the cold, the dead, the pain, the whole mess Jenny had gotten them into—Anna had not complained. Not once. Self-pity was a pool into which Jenny dove deep on occasion. Wee little Ms. Pigeon seemed to have none.

"How come you're so brave?" Jenny asked; death and the dark making intimate communication possible, even necessary.

"I'm not," Anna said quietly, her voice deeper than one might expect from so slight a source. "I'm afraid of everything; waking up, going to sleep, living alone, living with someone new. I'm afraid of whoever put me in the jar and cut me. I'm afraid of disappointing my sister. I guess the only thing I'm not afraid of is dying."

"What made you so afraid of living?" Jenny asked. Her right calf was trying to cramp. Pushing her heel hard into the rock face, she drew her toes back as far as she dared and felt the cramp pull out.

"I killed my husband," Anna said.

The words stuck in the slot like the echo of a thunderclap. Jenny jerked and the back of her head rapped against the sandstone.

"Like what?" she managed after a moment. "You shot him or knifed him? Like that kind of killed him?"

"No. Zach was coming down Ninth Avenue. I was coming home from D'Agostino's. He saw me and started across. A cab hit him. He died a couple hours later."

"And you think you killed him?"

Anna didn't answer. Jenny took silence as an affirmative.

"A cab killed him. You get no credit for that. Us poor mortals live under the 'shit happens' rule of nature. Life doesn't make sense. Unearned guilt is hubris, a claim to powers you don't have. I understand the temptation. It's less scary than admitting shit happens, because if shit does just *happen,* it can happen again and tomorrow your sister or your dog gets run over by a cab." Jenny wasn't lecturing Anna but herself, for the guilt she'd carried; guilt that she had done something, been something that brought on the gang rape at the beer bash.

"Shit happens," she repeated and closed her mouth.

For what seemed like an eternity Anna made no reply. Twice more the cramp twisted in Jenny's calf. Twice more she pulled it out by stretching her toes. The soles of her feet and the small of her back were simultaneously numb and on fire. Her spine was a line of liquid agony from coccyx to skull. She could no longer tell where the quivering and twitching of her muscles left off and Anna's began.

Finally her companion spoke.

"I did not kill Zach. He was hit by a cab."

"There you go," Jenny said.

"Thanks a heap," Anna replied. "Now I am afraid to die." With that she fell, and Jenny with her.

THIRTY-THREE

Anna expected to fall a long way. Forever. When she immediately struck the water it startled a squawk from her. Then she went under and there was no way to know up from down. Weight crashed onto her, plunging her deeper. Jenny. She must have dragged Jenny down when her feet slipped from the wall. Anna's hip struck something solid, and she curled into a ball. She was afraid to try to swim. She might be swimming toward the bottom. A heel or an elbow struck her on the side of the head, not enough to stun, but enough to shock and hurt. Then a painful jerk and she realized she was being reeled in, like a fish on a line, her braid being the line.

"Breathe," she heard Jenny command, and so she did.

"Thanks," she gasped. "I didn't know if I was still underwater or not." She couldn't see Jenny, or the walls, or the water. All that remained to let her know she was not blind, and was more or less right side up, was the single star allotted to this graveyard. Astronomy was not one of Anna's strengths. Living in the city, working a night job, was not conducive to stargazing. Still, she knew stars moved across the sky at night and was surprised to see this one had yet to rotate from view. In her previous incarnation, Anna's internal clock was trained to register time to the minute. How long the first act was, how many seconds for Juliet to change backstage, one minute of blackout, the length of time it took for the night-blind lead to fumble his way down the stairs. Reborn to die in a ditch, Anna's internal clock insisted the star had come into view hours before and should have been halfway to setting by now.

"Anna! I asked if you were okay." Jenny twitched the pigtail she held. Given the situation, to answer "daydreaming" didn't seem a logical choice. That's what Anna had been doing, and, being called back to reality, she realized why.

"This feels so good," she said, then laughed at the relief and wonder in her voice. The water was heaven; it cooled her burning muscles, refreshed her parched skin, supported her weight. She felt as if she'd fallen from the gallows into loving arms.

"It does," Jenny admitted.

Anna was grateful she didn't say more. At this blissful moment she didn't want to hear the rest of the story; how the cold would sap their body heat, extremities would cease to function, lethargy and disorientation would follow, and they would drown. For this moment, tragedy could wait, as it waited in the second act of *Romeo and Juliet,* when the lovers were so beautiful and young the audience chose to forget they die horribly in the end.

"Can you get up out of the water again? After we've rested a minute?"

Movement felt grand after holding Scylla and Charybdis at bay for however long it had been, but treading water was difficult. Muscles, quick to uncramp and feel blood flowing again, were just as quickly complaining of fatigue. "I can try," Anna said.

"If you put your hands on my shoulders, I could help hold you up for a bit, give your arms a break."

"No," Anna said, then, feeling she'd been an ingrate, added, "Thanks all the same." Water flowed into her mouth. Who would have thought it would be so difficult to know how deep one was in the soup? In the black-on-black universe it wasn't only muscle failure that could pull one under. Anna swallowed so she wouldn't choke. Not a time to consider how many parts per million of human waste this part of the lake contained.

"Do you still have the end of my braid?" she asked the darkness.

"I do."

"Don't let go of it, okay?"

"I will cling to it as long as there's breath in my body," Jenny said. "I wish you could see me crossing my heart. Let me know when you're rested enough to try the wall routine again. We don't want to get too cold or we will never make it."

"Why don't you go back up now? I'll try in a minute."

"No," Jenny said. "Thanks all the same. Do you want to swim back toward the sandstone where we came in? It's wider there, and you could see the sky. That's where they'll look for us."

"Unless they've gone to the bottom, our dead guys are floating around there," Anna said.

Anna felt Jenny tug her braid gently. "Pretty scary stuff," Jenny said.

The bodies didn't scare Anna. When had she become so comfortable with corpses? When Kay had turned out to be such good company? The dead required nothing from the living, and there was nothing the living could offer the dead. All in all, it was a relaxed and amiable relationship.

Jenny must have mistaken her silence for fear.

"It's not far to the mouth of the big pool. Let's at least go that far. It will be easier to tread water with a bit more room. I, for one, am tired of skinning my knuckles and knees every other stroke. When you're ready to try to get out again, we'll pop back in the slot."

Anna felt her braid move, Jenny leading her like a puppy on a leash. That was good. Otherwise she would have had only a fifty-fifty chance of swimming in the right direction.

In seconds the unutterable blackout of the slot was relieved by a slender line of, not light, but a less complete darkness. There was sufficient sky to house more than one meager star, and the canyon's rim showed a silver sheen of moonlight. Across the water, the rock face they had descended caught the faint light—enough that Anna could discern it from the water.

"Do you feel like we're being watched?" she asked suddenly.

"We are," Jenny replied. "Can you see him there, near the blockage but way on the left?"

One of the dead men floated barely above water, eyes open, the iridescence of the moon caught in the whites.

"That must be it," Anna said. It was not what she'd meant. This was reminiscent of when she was in the jar, naked, and felt eyes crawling over her skin like phantom cockroaches.

"What should we do?" Anna asked. "Sorry," she apologized. Putting the onus of their survival onto Jenny wasn't fair. Anna had been doing it, not because she'd abdicated responsibility for herself, but because Jenny had superior knowledge. Jenny had gotten them out of the cold water for a while.

"Do you know what the water temperature is?" Anna asked to change the subject. The bliss of chill weightlessness was becoming cold misery.

"Forty, fifty degrees, maybe a little more," Jenny said. "The surface of the main part of the lake can get up to eighty degrees this time of year, but only the first ten feet or so where the sun warms it. The deeper you go, the lower the temperature. Are you getting cold?"

The concern in her housemate's voice was so sincere Anna said, "No. You?"

"No," Jenny replied. Both were lying, both knew it, yet it helped marginally.

"How long does it take for the hypothermia to get serious in forty-fifty-degree water?" Anna asked. Not that it mattered. After so many years practicing the intricate timing of cues and effects required of a stage manager, Anna couldn't break the habit.

Stage-managing my own demise. Too bad life didn't

have a better playwright, she thought. Sam Shepard, that's who she would have chosen to write her final scene. The man knew how to keep the action moving, yet never at the cost of language or emotional content.

"I don't know much about hypothermia," Jenny said. "Lake Powell's a heatstroke kind of park. Are you ready to try getting out of the water now?"

"I can't." Anna was ashamed of her weakness but knew she hadn't the strength to spider up the wall and wedge herself again. Jenny might as well have asked her to smash the sandstone separating them from the boat and safety with one blow of her fist. "You go."

"I don't think I can either," Jenny admitted, "and I'm not just dying to be nice here. Climb twice, with the cold . . . I've lost my strength of ten men."

Talking was too much work, and they stopped. Anna tried to think of warm things, but thinking was too much work as well. Rumor would have it that dying people saw their lives flash before their eyes. Anna saw a hundred plays enacted in a single heartbeat. "I have a variation on the climbing thing," she said as the last image faded. Her jaw ached with the effort it took to keep her teeth from chattering as she spoke. "Want to try it?"

"Got to try something," Jenny said. Holding Anna's pigtail, she followed as Anna swam the few strokes into the slot.

"Like you were before—wedged—feet on one side and back against the other, but in the water," Anna instructed. Blind, she waited until Jenny grunted, "Okay."

"You're all wedged in? Not treading water? Just braced?"

"Ten-four."

"Be ready. I'm going to crawl on you, if I can find you," Anna said. She felt a tug on her braid and followed it until she ran into her housemate's legs where they were braced across the narrow water channel. "Here I come," Anna said. She fitted herself into Jenny's arms, her back against her housemate's breasts, and braced the soles of her feet against the stone between Jenny's. Jenny wrapped her arms around Anna's, and in turn Anna hugged Jenny's arms to her chest, sharing as much body heat with one another as possible.

"Am I squashing you?" Anna asked.

"Not yet," Jenny said. "This is an aquatic variation of getting naked with friends in a sleeping bag, isn't it? Where did you learn it?"

"*Terra Nova,* a play about Scott and Amundsen's race to the pole. There was no sleeping bag scene, but the crew got a lot of mileage out of the image."

Out of the water Anna's plan wouldn't have worked. The pressure she would have to exert to stay in place would have been too painful for Jenny. With the buoyancy of the water helping, they were able to raise heads and shoulders above water level, exposing a few more square inches of skin to the kindness of the July night.

"I definitely think it's warmer," Jenny said after a minute.

"Definitely," Anna said. *Marginally,* she thought.

"Mmm," Jenny murmured in her ear. For a time they didn't speak. Braced as they were, sharing heat, partially supported by the water, they might last a while.

Not forever, not till daylight. Not even until midnight, Anna guessed.

Since Zach died, and Anna'd given her mind to the Grim Reaper, she'd almost come to believe in his corporeal existence the way children believe Santa comes down the chimney, eats the cookies, puts the gifts under the tree, then leaves the way he came.

Trapped in the jar, she'd realized the Grim Reaper wasn't the guy for her, unless the monster was planning a fate worse than death. Embraced in stone and Jenny's arms, Anna knew there was no "worse than death." There was only life and the cessation thereof. Zach had not left her, he had died. Anna was not abandoned, she was widowed. God was not punishing her or testing her; he, like Zach, was simply dead.

"We are probably going to die in the next few hours," Anna said, to see what it was like to state a truth such as that.

"Probably," Jenny said, her breath warm on Anna's cheek.

"I can live with that," Anna replied in all seriousness.

The cold leached the life from them. Anna lost feeling in her feet, then her hands. Jenny was losing strength as well. The arms that held Anna trembled. The two of them slipped a few inches deeper.

For bits of time, seconds, or perhaps years, Anna forgot where she was, why it was so cold, when she had been rendered sightless. She was glad not to be alone. A sharp pain in her ear shocked her back from a mind drift where she raced, soaring over a cloudless landscape.

"You bit me!" she said.

"You were going to sleep," said a voice so close she wasn't entirely sure it wasn't in her head.

"Jenny?"

"If we go to sleep, we won't wake up," Jenny said.

Anna remembered that from somewhere. A production she'd crewed in college, she thought.

"Savage Mountain," she said. "K2, second highest in the world."

A tiny whisper of a groan let her know Jenny thought she wasn't making sense. Anna hadn't the energy to assure her she was perfectly sane. *Perfectly, perfectly sane. Perfectly perfect.* Again the gentle wafting threatened to carry her away.

"Tell me a story," Anna pleaded.

"What kind of a story?" asked the warm sweet breeze in her left ear.

"One with lots of explosions and sirens and slamming doors," Anna replied. "I think I might be falling asleep sometimes."

"Okay." Jenny was silent long enough Anna had to fight the drift by biting her tongue and the insides of her cheeks. Digging her nails into her palms was an impossibility. Her hands were either curled into fists or clamped on Jenny's. They wouldn't open or close. Dark was so dark she didn't know when her eyes closed, and she couldn't lift her hands to find out.

"Once upon a time," began the whisper in her head, "there was a beautiful princess named Adafaire. God, was she a princess! Right out of a fairy tale. Her hair was blond, honest blond, and straight and fine. The princess wore it long and knew how to toss her head so it shone. That hair was as expressive as a cat's tail. Adafaire would twitch it, and disdain filled the air, toss it, and hearts pounded.

"The princess was rich as well as beautiful and lived with other princesses in the sorority house. Delta Gamma or Theta Tau, I can't remember. Let's call it Kappa Kappa Damn. Picture a place the likes of me would be allowed in only as the hired help.

"I was seventeen. Since I'd skipped a grade, I went to college a year early."

"Smart cookie," Anna said with difficulty. Her brain did not seem to be in earnest about sending messages to her lips. That or her lips had become anarchists and no longer took orders from her brain.

"Book smart, life stupid," Jenny said. "I grew up in a podunk town, one of five daughters of parents who went out to a movie one night and didn't come home for years. Grandma was strict because, without order, there was no way she could have kept all of us fed and clothed. Not mean, though. We all worked. Little jobs when we were little, bigger jobs as we got bigger.

"Socially my sisters and I were functionally illiterate. No time for that sort of thing in our formative years.

"So I get to college in the big city and lay eyes on Adafaire. She was wearing tennis whites, can you believe that? Talk about a cliché. I loved her instantly, madly, passionately."

Memory ticked at the edges of Anna's hibernating mind. "The girl at the rape, one of the ones who watched."

"One and the same. Adafaire had taken me to the frat party; Kappa Kappa Damn girls were the frat boys' "little sisters." A misnomer if there ever was one."

"Did she want you to be raped?" Stringing seven words together took an effort, but Anna needed to know the answer for some reason.

"I've thought about that a lot," Jenny said. "I don't think she did, consciously. Unconsciously? Maybe. Adafaire hated me because I was the one who made her realize she was gay. Lesbian. Once she knew why she had all those feelings all those years, she couldn't unknow it and go on pretending."

"Sad story," Anna managed.

"Ah, but it has a happy ending," Jenny murmured. The breeze in Anna's ear felt as if it blew from the north this time. "Revenge."

"*Count of Monte Cristo,*" Anna put the words together carefully. Still, they more spilled from her tongue than were spoken. She wasn't cold anymore.

"I didn't drop out of college," Jenny said, "though I think anybody who was there that night expected me to. I wanted them to have to see me every day, look me in the eye and see my hatred. That worked for about a day and a half. Then it was like collective amnesia, like nobody but me remembered."

"P'leece?" Anna asked.

"I didn't report it to the police," Jenny said, and Anna marveled that her words were so neat and well formed. One day, she promised herself, if I'm not dead, I will be as strong as Jenny Gorman.

"I had a plan, and I didn't want to be the prime suspect. I knew two of the frat boys who'd benched me by sight. The others . . . I think two but I don't really know how many. The two I'd seen were seniors, roommates, BMOC. One had been accepted to Stanford for law and one to Cornell. I can't remember in what, but I knew then. I made it my business to know. Adafaire, Leo, and Phillip never saw me after those first two days. I saw them constantly, learned everything, watched and timed everything."

"Kill them all?" Anna pushed out the question.

"No. But there were a lot of thefts after the incident at the frat picnic. Jewelry from the sororities, watches and cash from four frat houses. Three professors' cars were broken into, the stereos stolen. Handheld calculators were taken—and in the eighties, a Hewlett-Packard ran four hundred dollars. A regular crime spree. Thousands and thousands of dollars' worth. Acting on an anonymous tip, the police found the bulk of it in Leo and Phillip's storage area in the basement of their frat house. The police also found stolen items in their apartment and cars, along with a very expensive Rolex that had gone missing from the home of the president of the university.

"Leo and Phillip were rich; their daddies got them off with community service. Cornell and Stanford were not that forgiving. They unaccepted them. Not what they deserved, but the best I could do short of killing them."

Anna didn't know if she'd asked about what happened to Adafaire out loud, or if Jenny chose to go on with the story without urging.

"Adafaire never admitted she was a lesbian, though she was one of the most enthusiastic and passionate 'experimenters' I have ever known. Beautiful and sexual and vain, Adafaire loved posing for pictures. For three or four years, every time Adafaire got close to a longed-for goal—marriage, a job, a membership—darned if one of those old pictures didn't show up in the wrong person's mailbox. Petty, but satisfying.

"Until it wasn't. Now even the memory isn't satisfying. More like the taste of ashes. She knew it was me. I wanted her to know it was me. Finally, she took me to court. Since she didn't want publicity, I got off easy. A restraining order and court-ordered therapy."

"Did you fall in love again?" Anna asked or thought she did. She must have, because Jenny answered softly.

"I did. Shall I tell you about her?"

Anna did her best to nod. Jenny's arm had fallen from her curled fingers, and Jenny's words were slurring much as Anna's.

"She had hair the color of an autumn leaf," Jenny's love story began. "She wandered in one day reminding me of a scared, starving, stray kitten."

The words might have gone on, Anna wasn't sure. The next thing she was sure of was the water closing over her and she couldn't raise her arms to swim.

THIRTY-FOUR

God damn that woman.

When Anna Pigeon had first slunk, catlike and all in black, from the shadows of Jenny's duplex to sit as a shadow in the evenings, the long dusky red hair roped down her back in a sailor's queue, Regis had thought she might prove a pleasant diversion, an entertainment to get him through the summer exiled in Dangling Rope with the ever-clinging Bethy. Bethy, who was too insecure to trust him alone for five days a week in their perfectly respectable house in Page.

Anna Pigeon had proven more than an entertainment; she had turned into a nightmare.

"God damn that woman!" Regis shouted as he pulled back on the throttles. The red speedboat sloshed around the final curve and waked the beach of the grotto where Jenny was camping. Two tents were pitched, one at either end of the grotto. The visitors were out on the lake, Regis knew that. Riding Jet Skis with the kiddies.

Anna and Jenny were bobbing around like icebergs in the slot canyon beyond the rock fall. If they were still bobbing and not yet drifting lifelessly toward the bottom. Adjusting the spotlight to the left of the boat's windscreen, he idled past the grotto and into the narrowing crack. Jenny's boat, its fat gray stern reminding him of his wife in sweatpants, was moored at the bottom of the rock fall. He cut the engines, shoved a six-cell battery in his belt, snatched up two personal flotation devices, and draped two coils of yellow nylon line over his shoulder.

Having thrown out a bumper, he jumped agilely from the bow of his boat to the Almar and rafted the red cigarette boat of the NPS patrol boat. In seconds he was climbing the rock fall. Seconds after that, he was on the top of the rock pile.

The flashlight yanked free of his belt, he played the beam over the water. Beneath the blockage, the rectangular pool was flat and black. From the far end, where the narrowest portion of the slot cut up in a blacker shadow toward the plateau, crescents of silver were fanning out, ripples catching the last of the moonlight. Movement.

Damn that woman, he thought again.

"Hey." The voice was so close it made Regis twitch. Had he not spent years controlling his body and face, he would have jumped a foot in the air.

"You need help? We were behind you. There's a gray boat. Is somebody in trouble?"

Rudely, Regis trained his flashlight beam into the face of the intruder. An Asian man, thirties maybe, tall and leanly muscled, had scaled the rocks behind him and was standing helpfully at his heels in wildly pink-and-turquoise print swim trunks.

A witness.

"I got a call someone may be in trouble here. There's no time to explain." He pulled the park radio from its holder on his belt, keyed the mike, and said Jim Levitt's call number. When Jim's voice crackled back, he said, "It's Regis. I think Jenny and Anna are in trouble in the slot at the end of Panther. I'm going in. I got a visitor here—"

"Martin," the young man said.

"Martin. I'm leaving the radio with him." Regis shoved the radio and the flashlight into Martin's hands. "See if you can locate bodies in the water," he said sharply, uncoiling the rope. When he had a line looped over a rock that wasn't going anywhere in the next fifteen thousand years, he kicked off his deck shoes and dove off the rock, the yellow line, held in his right hand, trailing after him.

When he surfaced the water was alive with reflections. The Asian guy methodically sweeping the waves with the flashlight. "Anna!" he yelled. "Can you hear me? Anna! Jenny! Answer me!"

THIRTY-FIVE

Jenny's feet had cramped, the insteps curling in on themselves. When she'd tried to pull her toes back toward her knees, she'd lost her grip on the wall. It wasn't like before, when they plunged; this time she and Anna, held together by muscles too cold to move, sank gently. Anna Pigeon and the warmth she shared floated away into a lightless universe.

In Jenny's fist was the front of Anna's shirt. When Anna had drawn her arms around her, Jenny took a fistful of cotton to fortify an embrace she knew was going to get more difficult to maintain as the minutes clicked by. It wasn't strength or courage that kept her holding tightly to her friend but the inability to unclench her fingers.

Too confused to know which way was up, Jenny waited, unafraid, in limbo. The air she'd drawn in as they sank carried her back to the surface. Her lungs sucked in the oxygen greedily. Jenny was oddly indifferent, as if the bellows pumped in a body not her own.

She had thought Anna was completely submerged. She wasn't. Her chest was rising and falling under Jenny's knuckles. Had she been able, she would have wrapped the smaller woman in her arms. When she could no longer move her legs sufficiently to keep them afloat, she promised herself, that's what she would do.

Wild and racing, lasers slashed the slot walls, cutting out ribbons of darkness that fell into the darker waters. Hypothermia was disorienting, Jenny knew that. Hallucinations hadn't been mentioned. Not that it meant anything. Not that Jenny could hold on to the thought or care.

A deep, ragged voice jangled through the stillness. "Anna! Can you hear me? Anna! Jenny! Answer me!"

The shouting seemed part of the death Jenny and Anna were sharing. When it penetrated the area of her brain still operable, and she realized the cavalry had finally arrived, Jenny tried to call out. Her jaws would not open, not at all, not one millimeter.

A splash. The cavalry had dived in.

Hope generated enough strength that Jenny kicked, keeping them above water a few more seconds. A blow landed on her upturned face. Bone and muscles, paralyzed with cold, clanged a death knell and she sank like a stone, Anna's shirt still caught in her fingers.

Her hair snagged on something; there was no pain, just pressure as she was dragged. Jenny's face came clear of the water. Her head rested on something warm; above her were stars. Slow as a dream, she began drifting on her back. An arm was across her chest. A lifeguard had jumped into the pool. Rescue had come. *Salvation,* she wanted to tell Anna.

Though her mind did not remember the lifesaving

moves, her body did. From a source not her own, strength flowed into her arm, enough so that she could draw Anna onto her breast. She hoped Anna's nose and mouth were above water, and that there were not now three dead children in the deep end.

Stars slowed, then stopped. No. She had slowed, then stopped.

"Okay, Jenny, this is going to be a bit crude, but you're about one angle from an ice cube. I'm putting a rope around you."

A light shone down from above. A beam like from the star to the baby Jesus in his cradle. In its vague glow she watched a bright yellow rope in dark brown hands pass under her arms and across her back.

"I'm going to tie this off, okay? When it's tied, I'll take Anna. Don't you worry. Hey, guy! Throw me down the PFD."

"Martin."

"Yeah, Martin. There's two there by the rock. Throw one down." Warm hands threaded the rope over her rib cage, pushing it between her and Anna. Jenny tried to take it and make it go around both of them, but the hand that wasn't clenched in Anna's shirtfront was of no more use than a club.

The lifeguard who was saving them kept on talking. The words were too quick to catch, but the tone was comforting. Then he began pulling at Anna, digging at Jenny's fingers to free them from the shirt. Anna was being taken from her arms. Jenny fought in her mind, screamed in her mind. Her hands let go without her permission, her arms fell away, traitors.

"It's okay, Jenny. Don't fight me." It was wrong to fight the lifeguard. Jenny used to know that. She watched him buckle Anna into an orange Mae West. Then the lifeguard went away and left them in the cold water. Anna bobbed gently out of the erratic circle of light. Jenny waited to slide under. The rope didn't let it happen.

"Jim. Hallelujah," burbled up from somewhere. "Tie off that second line and throw it to me."

Time passed. Jenny's eyes closed, her mind went away. Grunting, like that of a pig in labor, enticed her to open them again. Nothing remained of her but eyes and mind. Her body was a quiet invisible thing she could not feel. Perhaps she was dead and watched, as spirits are said to, hovering above the operating table while the body dies, only to swoop back down when the body is shocked back to life.

Anna, clownish in the orange life vest and white face, bobbed back into the spotlight. *Send in the clowns . . .* Jenny heard Joni singing. No. Not Joni. It was from a Broadway musical.

Anna would like that.

As if Jenny's thought were her cue, Anna floated across the watery stage until she bumped up against the rock. There she struggled, not like a woman, but like a fish on a line, then up she went. *Like Lazarus from the tomb,* Jenny's mind said. Like an unlucky trout from a pool, like a woman lynched by a mob. And up. And gone.

Now only she and two corpses remained in the deep end, said the mind that had been Jenny's, herself and the dead men who had tricked them into going for a swim in Ted Bundy's backyard pool.

The sow in labor increased her grunting.

Jenny's old body sent a message that the world was changing, and not for the better. The lungs she'd been using were squeezed so tightly air had little space for going in or coming out. Her head fell forward until she could see the faint light of the night sky on her breasts. They'd bobbed up out of the inky briny deeps. *Good breasts. Buoyant boobs.*

In a scattering of male voices, grunting redoubled. Jenny watched with disinterest as her belly and thighs, knees and feet rose out of the black water.

Hands closed on her upper arms, "Gently, gently," someone was saying. "Very gently. We don't want to shock her into a worse state. Easy does it. Got her? Okay, on three. One, two, three." Jenny levitated, flying upward like magic; then strong arms were supporting her and hard light was striping across the rock, illuminating three pairs of feet, one in boat shoes, one bare, one in flip-flops.

"Jim?" Jenny asked.

"It's Jim. I'm here. Let's get you warm, okay? Don't you worry about anything, Jenny. We're going to warm you right up."

"Anna." Jenny tried to look around. Jim's arms not only supported but imprisoned her.

"Anna's fine," Jim said. "That burrito over there is her." He turned his body so Jenny could see what he was talking about.

Anna Pigeon was wrapped up in silver blankets. Nothing showed but her face. Jenny took comfort in the face. Had Anna been dead, the face would have been covered.

"Let's get you out of those wet clothes," Jim said.

"What clothes?" another man asked.

Regis. It was Regis. "Hey," Jenny whispered.

"Martin, thanks a million. We're going to need to get the boats out of here . . ."

"No problem, man. I'm moving the Jet Ski. Let me know how they do, okay?" The flip-flops flip-flopped out of the light.

Strong, warm, flesh-and-blood arms and warm night air restored Jenny sufficiently that she progressed from feeling nothing to shivering violently. Jim sat her down on a rock, unhooked her bra, and slid it off her arms. With a pair of scissors from his orange emergency medical pack he cut off her panties.

"A shame," said Regis. "Nice outfit, Jenny." She tried for a smile. Chattering teeth turned it into a grimace. Handling her as if she were made of glass, Jim wrapped her in a silver blanket designed to maximize body heat, then sat her on his lap, his arms around her while Regis lifted Anna and carried her to his speedboat.

"Hot drinks to come," Jim promised. "Can you walk? I won't let go of you."

Jenny found she could walk, after a fashion, and with the support of Jim's beefy left arm around her waist. Moving slowly, trailing silver like a fairy—or a snail— they got to the bottom of the giant steps, across her boat, still nosed in at the blockage, and into Regis's red-red cigarette boat rafted off its stern. Jim's patrol boat was third in line.

Anna, in her cocoon, was lying on the padded bench that spanned the stern of Regis's boat. Jim settled Jenny next to her. Carefully lifting Anna's head, he pillowed it on Jenny's thigh. "Keep each other warm," he said and, "Gently, gently."

The trip back to Dangling Rope was a blur. Jenny held Anna, trying her best to protect her from jarring and wind. As Regis slowed at the NO WAKE sign marking the Rope's docking area, Anna struggled to a sitting position, fighting to free herself from the bundling of the heat blanket. Jenny helped her up but pulled the blanket back around her bare shoulders. "Your skin is still cold to the touch," she said.

"I'm hot," Anna said.

"No, you're not. You just feel hot."

For a wonder Anna didn't fight her. Jim Levitt pulled his boat in beside the red speedboat. Between him and Regis, the women were handed to the dock. Anna was buckled into the first ATV, and Regis drove it down the quay. Jim helped Jenny into the passenger side of the second and slid behind the wheel.

The ten feet from the ATVs to the duplex Anna managed on her own two feet, though Regis helped her keep her balance. Anna had progressed from numb to shivering, and both she and Jenny tottered like fragile crones afraid of slipping and falling.

Regis argued they should be taken to the hospital in Wahweap. Jim said no, the long boat ride would do more harm than the hospital would do good. He left the swamp cooler off and opened the door to the porch so warm night air could come into the duplex. Jenny knew she should be helping but couldn't remember what she was supposed to do, so she held on to Anna as Jim escorted them to her room.

While Jenny sat on the edge of her bed watching, he helped Anna into a long-sleeved flannel shirt, a pair of her soft sweatpants, and socks. A man stripping her, a man manipulating her naked body: Jenny wanted to tell her it was okay, it wasn't like the jar. Anna kept her eyes on Jenny's face. "He's taking the thorn out of my paw," she said, and Jenny relaxed.

The cuts on Anna's thigh were drained of color, the cold and blood aging them into scars at least until the blood returned. Jim saw them and looked over at Jenny, brows raised in a question.

She pretended she didn't notice. Once Jim had settled Anna beneath the covers, sitting, back against the wall, he helped Jenny to put on her flannel pajamas and socks, then tucked her in beside Anna.

It was then Jenny remembered. "Jim, there are dead bodies where we were. Two. That's why I went in. Men."

"Men. Two. Dead," Anna whispered a confirmation.

"You sure they were dead?" Jim asked Jenny, his voice low and pleasant. *Gently, gently.*

"Dead. Drowned probably, but way dead," she said.

"I'll deal with it. You just work on getting warm."

Regis was standing in the door to the room holding mugs of warm weak tea with sugar. His face twitched at the news of the bodies. Tea slopped onto the floor.

"What's this about bodies?" he asked in a strangled voice.

"Later," Jim said warningly and left the room. Jenny heard him calling someone on the radio. A few minutes later he returned with four chemical heat packs and tucked them to either side of her and Anna's stomachs.

They were finishing their second mugs of tea when a decidedly disgruntled Bethy arrived to insist Regis come home. He looked at his wet-hen spouse with shark eyes, carp eyes, eyes flat and dead.

Jenny shook off the mood that brought those images to mind. Anna was nodding off. Jenny yawned widely. Jim tucked the covers around them as if they were children, turned off the light, and left. Anna, no longer shivering, pressed close. Jenny curled around her back, spooning her with living, healing warmth.

Anna fell asleep first snoring softly, a sound as amiable as the purr of a cat.

For a while Jenny lay awake, just existing in the warmth and the flannel sheets.

As first dates went, this wasn't the worst she'd had.

THIRTY-SIX

A sound, a shift of the light, or the pressure of another mind awakened Anna. Someone was in the room. When she'd been with Zach she had slept the sleep of the innocent—or the dead. Sirens, subway trains, shrieking couples in the next-door apartment: Nothing woke her. Being able to sleep through anything had been a standing joke. "Was there war?" "Yes, you must have slept through it." "Thanksgiving Day parade?" "Slept through it."

In her new incarnation, if a tree fell in the forest, and there was no one there to hear it, it woke her. If God saw every little sparrow that fell, the thump of their tiny bodies on the earth woke her.

Jenny had risen early. Though she'd tried to be quiet, it woke Anna. The shower, the toilet flushing, the screen door opening and closing, woke her. Someone alien was in the room. It woke her.

On her side, covers thrown off, knees pulled up, arms hugging the pillow, Anna lay with her face to the wall, her back to the door. Another thing she would move to the category of things she used to do.

"Who is in here?" she asked without moving. Rolling over in the tangle of tossed covers would expose her soft white underbelly. A foot shifted on the dingy worn carpet. Quick as a cat, Anna sat up, back against the wall, hands up to ward off a blow.

Bethy was standing next to the bed, leaning over slightly as if she'd been interrupted in the act of kissing a child good night. She was dressed for work in NPS uniform shorts and short-sleeved shirt. Fabric pulled across her breasts, and the tailored shirt gapped between the buttons. Her face was one no child should see before going to sleep, suffused with blood and anger.

"What do you want?" Anna asked.

"Stay. Away. From. *My*. Husband." She made each word separate and distinct, like commands to a bad dog.

"I don't have designs on Regis," Anna said truthfully. As alarming as this woman-scorned apparition was, it simply could not compete with the closet full of horrors Anna'd accrued since leaving New York for Page, Arizona. She felt no fear, merely confusion and annoyance.

"Oh. Right. You're queer now. I forgot." Bethy's voice dipped and rose in a parody of high-school-girl sarcasm. "This is Jenny's room, isn't it? You're one of those lesbo dykes like Jenny Gorman. A carpet sweeper."

Anna was growing more annoyed but no less confused.

"A carpet sweeper?" she asked. Then it came to her. In her desire to wound, Bethy thought she'd pulled out all the stops. "Carpet *muncher,*" Anna said. Bethy's mouth formed a little *o*. Giggles bubbled through Anna's lips, then full-blown laughter, the kind that brings tears and skips along the slippery slopes of hysteria. Hilarity was not soothing to her caller, and the more upset Bethy grew, the more Anna's control slipped away.

When Bethy's face began to look like a tomato about to burst, Anna laughed so hard her stomach hurt. Sitting up straight was more than she could manage. Literally doubled over with laughter, she fell off of the bed. This was funnier still. Fear that she could not stop laughing, not ever, that she would die laughing, finally sobered her. Gasping and hiccuping, she pulled herself up and leaned her back against Jenny's bed.

Bethy was gone.

"What in the hell was that about?" Anna whispered. The habit of talking to herself aloud had been born of isolation and fear while in the jar. In the real world it was a habit she was going to have to break. People would think she was insane. Worse, people might hear what she was thinking when she preferred to keep her thoughts to herself.

Having showered and washed her hair, Anna returned to her own room. This was where she would sleep tonight. Without hypothermia demanding body heat, she would sleep alone as she had every night since Zach died.

Wrapped in a towel, on the edge of the bed, she sat and stared at the open bottom drawer of her dresser.

She missed Buddy. Zach was gone. Molly was two thousand miles away. Anna guessed she was like a lot of people in the world, just one baby skunk away from lonely.

For a cowardly moment she wondered if Jenny would let her sleep with her a few more nights. It was reassuring to hear another person breathing when one woke up in the creepy hours between midnight and 4:00 A.M.

Would Bethy's accusations hurt Jenny? Were there still people in the world whose best friend *wasn't* gay? Not in the theater. Homophobia might live on in the hinterlands. Anna infinitely preferred to be thought gay than to be known a coward. Compromising Jenny Gorman to save herself a few bad nights would be the act of a craven.

Given Bethy's preposterous rage—and Anna's less than soothing reaction—she was undoubtedly broadcasting to anyone who would listen that her neighbors were carpet sweepers.

Carpet sweepers. Giggles started to rise in a frothy tide. Anna quashed them. The line between mentally stable and not had been worn too thin to take chances. Of course, with Bethy "outing" them, there was no point in worrying whether hiding out in Jenny's room a few more nights would damage their reputations.

She examined the wounds on her thigh. The cuts had been deep, and those first days she'd had no way of cleaning them. It was pure luck—or the sterility of the desert air—that they hadn't gotten infected.

The night she staggered back to Dangling Rope in Kay's cutoffs, Jenny had cleaned the cuts and used but-

terfly bandages to pull the edges closed. They looked to
be healing okay. The scabs were mostly off, and, though
the wounds were still dark red, there was no proud
flesh. She'd been using Jenny's vitamin E oil. Maybe it
was helping, maybe not. There was no way to tell, lack-
ing anything with which to compare the progress.
WHORE was still clear and angry. One day it would
fade to thin white lines. If Anna were fortunate, there
might even come a time it could be seen only with her
mind and not her eyes. Until then—or until she grew a
skin as thick as that of an armadillo—she would es-
chew bikinis.

Dressing herself in her green uniform shorts—
summer weight and feeling like there was not a single
natural fiber in their makeup—and the gray NPS shirt,
Anna replayed her wake-up call.

Bethy thought she was after her husband. Twice Regis had rescued Anna; was that what set Bethy off?
After Regis saved her from the jar, Anna occasionally
felt he was either looking after her or watching her, depending on her mood. It wouldn't be unusual if he was
concerned for her well-being. Saving someone's life
could up one's interest in that individual. The Chinese
went so far as to say it made one responsible for the life
saved.

Regis was Johnny-on-the-spot at her interviews with
law enforcement. Boredom? Wanting to get out of the
office? Gathering information he could barter for star-
dom at the next cocktail party? Or whatever passed for
a cocktail party in Rangerland. A potluck, probably.

Bethy must have seen this as romantic interest. Anna

was older than she was, older than Regis by a few years, but Anna was thin and Bethy was not. Sometimes that was enough.

Anna threaded the cordovan-colored belt through the belt loops of her shorts and buckled the brass buckle. There was such a thing as too thin, and she was it. Two Dangling Dogs with chips for lunch, she told herself.

Grabbing her ball cap, the traditional NPS Stetson being impractical on a boat, she shoved thoughts of Bethy's morning speech from her mind. A life observing great drama, both on- and offstage, had taught her that there was no way out of an imagined love triangle. If it was a comedy, all was revealed in act three; if a tragedy, everybody died in act four. Trying to talk to Bethy or Regis would only prolong the action.

Anna had consumed a minimum of six hundred calories in hot dogs and chips, and was nearly to the bottom of her sixteen-ounce Pepsi, when Jenny finally made it back to the marina to collect her.

She rejoiced at the sight of the woman and the boat. Though a night's rest hadn't cleared out the fatigue of a long day's work followed by treading water in the cold, Anna was anxious to be put to work, the harder the better.

THIRTY-SEVEN

For the next three days Anna worked and ate and slept. Along with Jenny, she cleaned two beaches. A grand haul of sixty-two pounds of human waste gathered and sealed into five-gallon cans. Under Jenny's tutelage, she learned to pilot the twenty-eight-foot Almar cuddy and to anchor in the water and to land. The second day Jim rode with them. Anna was impressed with how he dealt with those who, in Jenny's vernacular, "failed to see the light."

Inexperienced as he was, Jim was a natural when it came to handling difficult people. Though her interactions with him as an EMT had been pleasant enough, given his youth and macho good looks, Anna had expected a hard-line swagger.

Apparently for Jim, law enforcement was as much about education as enforcement. Park rangers—if Jim Levitt was any indication—were a lot more lenient when it came to "ignorance of the law is no excuse." If the ignorance was sincere, often it earned the miscreant a second chance.

On occasion, Anna helped by sensing who was sincere and who was not. Anyone who sat through thousands of auditions got to where she could spot a bad actor before he opened his mouth. Anna could often tell if they lacked sincerity within seconds of the lie's commencement.

There was an old theater joke, attributed to everyone from Jean Giraudoux to Groucho Marx, that said sincerity was the single most important thing for an actor, because once you can fake that you've got it made.

Both nights she and Jenny camped on beaches. Their first camp was on a willow-fringed white sand beach in Warm Creek Bay. A piece of land, round as a coin and smaller than a Lower East Side block—less than an acre, according to Jenny—snuggled into a crescent of high sandstone cliffs that were slightly undercut, forming a natural shelter. A cave, not natural, but made by native peoples long before Columbus talked Isabella out of her jewels, burrowed twenty feet into the stone at the northernmost point of the arc.

A favorite place of the Anasazi, the beach was rich with potsherds, scraps of dusty history that fascinated Anna. Warm Creek Bay's beach, also favored by modern humans, had subsequently been turned into an open-air latrine. Willows screened a wealth of toilet paper blooms. The small cave was as full as a week-old cat box, and the walls sported as much graffiti as a subway car on the 7 train to Queens.

While Jenny and Anna separated the ancient garbage from the modern, leaving the former and canning the latter, Jenny fumed and sparked. Anna was more baffled than anything. Poop, she could understand. Options were limited and people unprepared. What she couldn't understand was the graffiti vandals had painted and scraped into the stone. In the city it made a twisted kind of sense. People who had nothing in their lives wanting to be seen, to leave a mark. *Kilroy was here.* Teenagers, who'd never known beauty, unaware they were destroying it, or enraged because they didn't understand it. Kids who were never heard expressing themselves the only way they knew how. Gangbangers marking territory by spraying like tomcats leaving their sign.

In a playground for the wealthy, people destroying the beauty they'd come to enjoy mystified her. During orientation they'd stressed the parks-and-recreation ethic of preserving the natural and historical area to be enjoyed by future generations. On man-made surfaces graffiti could be painted over. Not so in a park. Paint had to be removed from rock. Scraping it off left scars that would not heal for many hundreds of years.

Anna argued for leaving the ancient cave in all its squalor and degradation. She tried to talk Jenny into posting a sign in front of it reading: IF THIS IS THE PARK YOU WANT, KEEP ON DOING WHAT YOU ARE DOING.

Not the NPS way, Jenny told her.

They cleaned and hauled.

By day's end, Anna was tired and sore, her hands beginning to blister and her back and legs aching. It was pain she welcomed. The approval and concern in Jenny's eyes dulled the worst of it, and, not now, not this week, or maybe even this month, but soon, it would make her stronger. Already she could work harder and longer than when she'd first arrived at Lake Powell.

Dinners were sacred events for her and her housemate. Hunger was indeed the finest spice. The Almar cuddy was well stocked with red wine and a cooler with cheese, bread, tomatoes, avocados, cold chicken, and candy bars. Anna ate more than she ever had before. The food made her stronger, she could feel it.

At the close of the third day, they returned to the Rope. The next two days were Anna's lieu days.

Though Jenny insisted she didn't have to, work, food, and nights in the open gave Anna courage, and she moved back into her own room. "Don't want to compromise your sterling reputation," she kidded Jenny.

Unsmilingly, Jenny replied, "What about your reputation?"

Having nothing to say to that, Anna went to bed. Guilt nudged her as she slid between the borrowed flannel sheets. In a few days she'd launder and return them, she decided. It would be foolish to go cold turkey on the whole comfort thing.

Without Buddy in his drawer and Jenny at her back, she slept restlessly. Dreams of being chased by unseen malice haunted her. The stuff of nightmares—inability to move her legs and arms, inability to see clearly or cry out—had come true in the jar and the slot canyon. Dreams that came true were not necessarily a thing to be wished for.

Unrefreshed, she woke dreading a day with nothing to do to keep body and mind occupied. Buddy was gone. Jenny was working. Anna didn't have a boat or

Jet Ski and was not the least bit tempted to hike the trail out of Dangling Rope again. Effectively marooned, she could read or write letters, but that required thinking, and thinking was an activity she no longer trusted herself to do without supervision. She wanted to *do*. She needed to armor herself with muscle and purpose.

Over coffee she decided she would get in shape for the big fight or joust or whatever was coming. *Rocky, Karate Kid,* and half a dozen other movies that showed the hero doing the pre-hero warm-ups in a montage of scenes made her laugh at herself. Jogging had come into fashion her first year in college. Anna had never seen any point in running unless late for a train or being pursued by slavering Doberman pinschers. Still, she put on her shorts and Reeboks and went running.

The only trail in the limited navigable land around the Rope went down a long sloping gravel road that ended at the shore of a small finger of the lake. Heavy machinery and supplies required by maintenance were off-loaded there so they could be more easily transported to the maintenance building behind the housing area.

Thirty yards before the boat ramp, a sketchy trail veered to the left, leading up through dirt, rock, and scrub to the top of a knoll. From there it descended to an upthrust thumb of earth and rock over a hundred feet high. The only access to the thumb was a narrow land bridge. When that eroded away, the thumb would be an island. The trail wound around its base. Jim Levitt, who ran most evenings, said the circuit from housing around the rock and back was close to a mile.

Before Anna reached the point where the trail left the road, she was panting. By the time she'd run the little distance to the land bridge, she had a stitch in her side. Forced to walk a ways, eyes on her feet so she wouldn't stumble, she began to notice that what she had spurned as sterile desert was nothing of the sort. Just as the brochure had promised, Glen Canyon boasted a rich and varied plant life. Unlike the east, where plants were grand and green and rushed into spring and summer with a blaze of color, the plants of Glen Canyon were spread out, careful to claim sufficient space so they could collect water enough to survive. Fierce and independent, they protected themselves with spines or tiny fine hairs that prickled out from the fleshier leaves. In place of the infinite palette of greens Anna'd seen in the eastern forests, here the palette was in subtle hues of sage and gray. Leaves that looked more blue than green and leaves that turned silver in the sunlight.

It surprised her to see flowers. Deep in the arid heat of summer, their defiant blues and hot pinks struck her as courageous. They did not clump together in gay profusion. She had to look for their small insistent glory and was inordinately pleased when she found it. Next time she ran, she promised herself, she would bring the brochure so she could introduce herself properly, name for name.

Breath recovered, she began to run again. Twice more she stopped and walked, but by the time she made it back up the incline to the duplexes, she guessed she'd run easily a third of the one-mile circuit.

Bethy was sitting in a lawn chair on her porch when

Anna came puffing into the square. Anna didn't know whether it would be better to ignore her or greet her as if nothing had passed between them. Either way, she figured she was going to get a black eye out of the deal.

Bethy spared her the choice.

"Your face is the color of Rudolph's nose," she said, looking up from the magazine opened across her knees. The comment wasn't particularly complimentary, but the tone of voice didn't seem malicious. Not that Anna could discern.

"I'm not used to the altitude," Anna said, having no idea what the altitude of Glen Canyon was.

"I saw you go running," Bethy said and pointed at the side of her duplex. "Through the kitchen window. I've been waiting for you to come back."

Anna looked at her warily. "Okay," she said, carefully neutral. "I'm back."

"I wanted to talk to you." Anna couldn't tell if the slight reticence in Bethy's voice was from shyness or because she was about to launch a particularly nasty verbal assault and was saving her strength.

"Okay," Anna said again. "So talk." Turning her back on the other woman, she went to her and Jenny's porch. Putting her left heel on the raised platform, she began stretching the way she'd seen dancers do after rehearsal.

"I guess I kind of wanted to say I was sorry for, you know, like, waking you up the other morning."

"Sorry I laughed," Anna said in payment for the apology, though she wasn't in the least sorry.

"I know you aren't after my husband," Bethy said.

She said "husband" as if it were a unique and grand acquisition.

Anna lifted the other heel and stretched down over her leg, her hands folded around the instep of her foot. The black leather of the Reebok was hot both inside and out. The thin soles wouldn't last long in country as rough as she'd traversed today.

To Bethy's comment, she said nothing. There was no response to it that wouldn't be more damaging than silence. It was clear Bethy thought her husband irresistible to women. If Anna said he was, Bethy would assume she was after him. If she said he wasn't, they'd be back into carpet sweeper territory.

"I mean, you're a lesbian. Lesbians don't like men."

The silence that followed was as tense as a mousetrap waiting to be sprung.

Anna straightened up and, hands on hips, turned to face Regis's wife. "My sexual orientation is not up for public discussion," she said evenly.

"So you are?"

Anna just looked at her.

"I mean, I don't care. I'm not like a lot of these people. It's not like a man being gay or anything. You don't have to stick anything anyplace or anything. Ugh! Anyway." Bethy gusted out the last word. "That's not what I wanted to talk to you about."

"Well, that's a relief," Anna said acidly.

Bethy didn't feel the sting or, if she did, hid it admirably. "What I wanted to talk about was that other thing. What I said. I was jealous. But only because you're so pretty and small and delicate and I was like that, but now I'm not and Regis loved me like that. I mean, like, I had bigger tits than you. I always did even when I was thin, way bigger, and he didn't mind that, but now the rest of me is like, you know, *porky* and you're still thin and that long hair. Regis really needs me, but, I don't know," Bethy ran down. "You know what I mean."

Anna had a few vague notions of what Bethy Candor might mean, but she was not fool enough to put voice to them.

"Anyway, could I work out with you? You know, run, and there's some machines maintenance has, like a kind of weight room, and we could do that."

"Sure," Anna said because it was the only thing she could say. The fact that Bethy probably wouldn't follow up for a single run made it almost easy.

"Want to go now?" Bethy asked, surprising her. "Or are you all tired out from running?"

That pricked Anna's ego. "Now would be fine," she said.

The weight room was tucked behind a row of generators in the long low-roofed maintenance building. It was built on a concrete slab and had thick cinder-block walls. Anna guessed it had been designed to house some volatile piece of electricity-generating machinery that was never installed. The space was small, eight by eight feet, and dim. The only light coming from a high slit of a window made for ventilation. The weight-room gear was as basic as its housing: a bench with a weight rack, round weights of various sizes scattered near the bar, and a metal unit holding barbells.

"Do you want me to spot you first?" Bethy asked.

Anna didn't know what that was and didn't want to admit it.

"Back when I was me, I used to work out with my housemate. She was really into it. Here, I'll show you like she showed me."

Back when I was me. The phrase unsettled Anna. She must remember to ask Molly about it when next they talked. Pleased that Bethy had chosen not to notice her ignorance, Anna followed her instructions and lay down on the bench.

"Okay." Bethy picked a silver bar off the floor and fitted it into the two Y-shaped holders. "Lift it off the stand." Anna pushed it up. "Now bring it down to your chest." The bar felt heavy, but it triggered no new pain in her healing shoulder, so she lowered it to her chest. Bethy put her hands to either side of Anna's and pressed down; the bar slid from chest to neck, the weight on Anna's throat.

Panic ripped up from her gut. *Rocky* and *The Karate Kid* were a dim future. Running in the heat had sapped her strength. Insects pinned to corkboard were more powerful than she. The shoulder had not healed. Hypothermia had weakened her in ways she wasn't aware of. Helplessness flowed like poison through her body. Tears filled the corners of her eyes. The room wavered and shrank until finally all that remained was Bethy's round face floating above her like a birthday balloon.

She would not cry. She would not beg. She would not.

THIRTY-EIGHT

Absurd as it was, Jenny missed Anna, and she'd only been out on the lake without her for three hours. Before Anna Pigeon flapped her little bird body into Jenny's nest, Jenny loved her hours alone on the water, loved having to please no one but herself, loved being alone with the world and her thoughts.

Being solo for less than a half a day, she was beside herself with joy at having been given even such a grim excuse to go back to Dangling Rope before lunch. Having docked the Almar, she climbed the hill toward housing. Because of the steep grade, she walked on metal grid steps built alongside the reinforced concrete of the road.

Maybe they should have a picnic. Jenny wished she had something worth eating in her refrigerator to offer Anna. During the summer, Jenny pretty much lived on beer, wine, and peanut butter. Anna deserved better. Day after tomorrow, Jenny promised herself, when she was off duty she'd make a shopping trip to Page. Not that the little town had anything in the way of gourmet delicatessens. Still, it would suffice.

Flinging open the door to the duplex, Jenny had an urge to call, "Honey, I'm home!" Whimsy died a sudden death. The swamp cooler was off and the front room empty. "Anna?" she said.

No response. She poked her head into Anna's room, then the bathroom, then her own room. No Anna. Jenny was so crushingly disappointed she frightened herself. Sure she was besotted with Ms. Pigeon. Sure she kidded herself she was "young and in love." If it turned out she genuinely was *in love,* that would be truly scary. Playing with the idea of pure and chaste from afar, flirting with possibilities—even trying them on for size—was one thing. Breaking her heart against a heterosexual rock was something else altogether. That could seriously scar a girl.

Jenny stepped out onto the deck. There weren't a lot of places Anna could be. She didn't have access to a boat. Jenny knew for a fact neither Steve nor Jim had given her a lift anywhere. Regis was supposed to be at his office at headquarters between Wahweap and Page. Was supposed to be. Lately Regis had been turning up mysteriously in unexpected places and in the nick of time, sort of like the Green Lantern.

Would Anna try the climb out of the Rope a second time? After the hard work the woman had put in, Jenny would have thought she'd want a day off to do whatever passed for lying on the sofa, eating bon-bons, and watching the soaps in Anna's hierarchy of relaxation, but she was a freakishly determined little creature. Returning to the scene of the crime and facing her fears might appeal to her.

Jenny didn't like that at all. Certain fears needed to be faced. The majority needed to be run away from. That's why feet and denial had been invented.

She went inside, took the binoculars from her day-pack, and ventured back out into the hard-baked glare of afternoon. Ninety-six degrees, virtually no humidity, stiff breeze out of the southwest; Jenny doubted Anna had the strength to carry enough water for a sentimental journey to the jar. In the high desert there were days that sucked the moisture from a human body almost faster than it could be replaced.

Having walked a ways up the gentle rise behind the housing area, she put the binoculars to her eyes and scanned the faint tracking of the trail up the rubble in the side canyon and back across the broken cliff.

No Anna. She couldn't have made it to the top in the three hours Jenny had been gone.

Gil and Dennis in dust-covered green-and-gray uniforms—good camouflage for this part of the country—walked into her line of sight from the direction of the sewage treatment plant.

"You guys see Anna around?" Jenny asked when they were within hailing distance.

"What's it worth to you?" Dennis grinned and waggled his eyebrows.

Jenny was not in the mood. "Have you?" she demanded.

"Guess you don't rate, Dennis," Gil said and whacked his pal's shoulder with his ball cap.

Jenny waited, and not patiently.

"Yeah," Dennis said, "a while back. She and Bethy

were headed into the maintenance barn. If they're not still there, I don't know where they are."

"Thanks," Jenny said and brushed by them.

"Whoo!" she heard Gil stage-whisper, "wonder what blew up her skirt?"

Though it was bright and sunny with no dark alleys in sight, dread built as Jenny headed to the maintenance building. She had never felt fear on the lake. Physical fear, yes, of a near miss with a boat or a hostile drunk, but not haunted-house-graveyard-fog-goose-prickles-down-the-spine dread. Of course, nothing more malevolent than snotty über-rich kids had crossed her path until this summer. This summer there were redheads carved with the word WHORE, crucified pink pygmy rattlesnakes, ropes that vanished, and water that killed.

The maintenance building was seldom quiet. Four big generators gutted the silence most of the time. Today was no exception. Jenny walked in the open garage-like front and stopped. There was only one reason for Anna to come here; the old weight room. No one but Jim ever used it. Threading her way behind the generators, she stepped into the concrete doorway.

Bethy was hunched over Anna like a Kewpie doll intent on drinking human blood. Pale and looking scared, Anna lay on the weight bench, the bar pressing down on the soft flesh of her neck. Her braid fell to the floor and coiled like a line waiting to be tied off.

Bethy lifted the bar.

"That's what a spotter is for," she said matter-of-factly. "You get to doing reps and the point is to push yourself to muscle exhaustion, but then, like, well, your muscles are *exhausted*, and somebody's got to be there so the weight bar doesn't strangle you to death."

The bar settled back into the metal stand with a clank, and Jenny's heart began beating again. Relief made her dizzy. Slouching a shoulder against the concrete, she gathered herself together. For a moment she had thought Bethy Candor was choking the life out of Anna. Love was said to make one blind, but paranoid? That was a bit beyond the pale. Jenny never trusted herself to travel beyond the pale, not by herself.

Anna and Bethy were so wrapped up in what they were doing, neither noticed her. "Wanna try it with five pounds on it?" Bethy asked. "That'd be ten, five on each side. The bar I think is thirty-five or maybe forty-five. I don't really remember."

Anna didn't look like she wanted to try it again. She looked as if her organs and viscera were still quivering from having the bar pressed on her trachea. Or maybe Jenny was projecting and it was her own innards still aquiver.

"Okay," Anna said. "Five pounds."

Jenny shook her head and smiled. Got to love a woman with pluck.

Anna managed to lift the bar six times with Bethy helping a little on the final one.

"Pathetic," Anna murmured disgustedly as she sat up.

"Sort of," Bethy said.

"Yeah," Anna said and laughed. "I coulda been a contender."

The laugh jarred Jenny. An unpleasant tentacle coiled around her esophagus. The green-eyed monster, she thought and poured self-mockery on it to loosen its grip.

"Marlon Brando, *On the Waterfront*," she said and stepped into the room.

Anna's face lit up with pleasure. So very good.

Bethy's did not. That, too, was good.

"Both bodies were recovered," Jenny said. "Steve wants me to take you over to Bullfrog and see if you can positively identify them before they're flown out to the morgue."

THIRTY-NINE

Are you freaked at having to look at the bodies?" Jenny asked.

Anna and Jenny were perched on the high white vinyl cabin chairs in Jenny's gunmetal gray boat. Jenny let Anna drive. Anna tried to resist the impulse to yell "Whee!" when the little boat came up on plane.

"Nope," Anna answered. "Not to seem callous or anything, but once you've had the opportunity to really get to know some dead people, you find out they're not half bad."

"That night in the slot canyon they did prove to be quiet and well behaved, particularly for men of that age," Jenny concurred.

"What do you think it will mean if I can identify one or both of them as the guys who attacked Kay and me?" Anna asked.

"I guess just that the slot at the end of Panther was how they got onto the plateau. It's two more chances to get an ID. Maybe somebody reported one of them missing."

"I don't get why nobody has reported Kay missing

yet," Anna said. "She had good teeth, hair, Tevas, the stuff of a well-raised girl with a family that loved her."

"If she was on vacation, maybe the vacation isn't up yet and nobody knows she's missing," Jenny suggested.

"Maybe."

Anna and Jenny talked a lot about what the bodies had to do with the jar, if anything, and what the bodies meant to the two of them specifically. Had the third man killed his two companions? More importantly, had the third man tried to do the same to them? Were these just two unlucky, inexperienced guys who got hypothermia and drowned?

Jim and Steve had gone back in the daylight and tried to find what happened to the missing rope. So had Jenny and Anna. It was simply gone. There was no way to know if it had been pulled up and carried away or had fallen into the water and sunk.

The divers who recovered the bodies said they didn't see it. They said the corpses were only twenty-seven feet below the surface. Below that, the canyon walls pinched in too close together for anything as large as a full-grown man to pass. A rope could have slithered down without a hitch.

Anna leaned back in her seat. By Lake Powell's agitated standards the water was smooth. Aside from the psychotic predator stuff, Glen Canyon was the perfect park to take her virginity, she decided as they sped toward Bullfrog. The part of her soul that would always belong in the theater gloried in the sheer bodacious unnaturalness of it. Putting a great blue-green water park smack down in a red desert complete with cactus, trading posts, genuine Navajo Indians, and five kinds of rattlesnakes was theater of the absurd at its most outrageous.

The dam and the lake did everything a good piece of art should: provoked, evoked, inspired, incensed, amazed. Lake Powell made visitors question their relationship to the earth. Was it a toy to be played with, broken, and cast off? Was it a tool to be used as Man saw fit? Could it be destroyed? Could it be remade?

Desert formations rearing defiantly out of the water were so staggeringly out of place as to appear manmade or out of context, the way a stuffed grizzly bear in a glass case in a bank foyer is out of context. Anna could easily picture how the formations would look backstage, the supporting two-by-fours, and the unpainted backs of the papier-mâché rocks.

When she was six and Molly twelve, their mother had gone to Southern California to visit her only sister. While there, Uncle Clarence had taken the children to Disneyland. They'd gone on a ride that was in a mine cart through Old West gold country. To Anna's childeyes the landscape seemed far more authentic than that of Lake Powell.

Even the recreation area's names had a theme park feel: Rainbow Bridge, Twilight Canyon, Anteater Arch, Pollywog Bench. The juxtaposition of this lighthearted romp of imagination with the stark and beautiful reality of the drowned river canyons moved Anna the way the finest offerings of the theater once had.

One of the many differences between this grand play of Nature against Man and the plays she stage-managed

was that, in this world, she was not running the show.
She enjoyed watching a drama unfold never knowing if
she would be part of the story or not. Should she be
given a part, she did not enjoy never knowing if she was
to be the windshield or the bug, but then no one in New
York knew that either. One day you were the front end
of the Yellow Cab. The next you were the jaywalker.

Steve Gluck was on Bullfrog's dock waiting for them.
Arms crossed over his chest, he leaned against the side
of the convenience store in a scrap of shade.

"Nice job docking that pig-nosed little boat," he said
to Anna. The compliment delighted her. The slight to
Jenny's boat did not.

"Meeting us in person. To what do we owe this
honor?" Jenny asked.

"Needed to air myself off," Steve said. He fell in step
as they walked up from the docks toward the employee
housing area and the town of Bullfrog.

"Where's your vehicle?" Jenny asked. "Why walk
when you can ride?"

Steve patted his gut. "Need the exercise." Then, "We
got company. Andrew flew out this noon. The assistant
superintendent is with him and, believe it or not, a state
senator."

"That's what drove you down here; the BS got too
deep," Jenny said.

An audience. Anna didn't like that and had to fight a
wave of shame for what she'd suffered. Circumstances
made her into a spectacle to be gawked at. *Rock star,*
Bethy Candor had said. Bethy was an idiot. This was a
small, cringing, nasty little fame. A physical sensation

of shrinking crept through her, as if she could make herself smaller, more of a child. Small children were supposed to be protected from the ugly truths.

Disgusted by her cowardice, Anna stacked her bones one on top of the other until she stood tall. Pulling back her shoulders, she shook the tension out of her hands. Anthony Heald did that every night before he went onstage. She'd watched it from her perch as assistant stage manager during the Off-Broadway revival of *The Glass Menagerie.*

Thinking of actors, she thought of Sir John Gielgud. Once upon a time she told him to pick up his cues. Facing NPS and state bureaucrats couldn't be nearly as intimidating as facing a legend with a knighthood.

Bullfrog's clinic was a small white prefab building with a flat roof. Inside, it was spare but well appointed. There was a room for overnight patients and a small operating room—for sewing up gashes and cutting out fishhooks, Steve said. Anna hadn't thought they did much open heart surgery in Bullfrog but was impressed nonetheless. The last room before a locked closet that Steve told them was the pharmacy was the examining room. The door was closed. From behind it came a low murmur of voices.

"Holy smoke," Steve muttered. "They're all still in there. We're probably going to have four more cases of hypothermia to deal with."

He pulled open the door and a blast of frigid air rolled out to meet them. "No morgue," Steve said. "Just AC."

The district ranger stepped back to allow the women to precede him.

"SRO," Anna commented sourly. When Jenny looked a question, she added, "Standing room only."

There were two hospital beds in the room, each with a sheet-covered occupant. Beatrice, the nurse practitioner, stood by the head of the bed nearer the window, hands folded over her stomach as if her intestines might spill out if she let them.

The assistant superintendent, who put Anna in mind of a jolly Boy Scout on steroids, loomed large and green and gray at the head of the nearer bed. Grinning amiably down the shrouded length he said, "Hey, Jenny," and, "You must be Anna Pigeon."

He didn't remember her from his brief visit to her orientation.

"Yes," Anna admitted.

"This is State Senator Billy Wilson."

The senator, a lean handsome man with a whiff of Iago about him, and dressed down for the event in gray linen trousers and a pale pink Izod shirt, stepped out from the wall, hand extended, canvassing for votes over the dead.

Anna nodded politely but pretended not to notice the outstretched hand. Nothing in his behavior offended her; she just didn't want to touch the man.

"Let me see the corpses," she said.

"Are you sure you are okay with this?" Nurse Beatrice asked solicitously. The presence of important men evidently improved her bedside manner.

"If it's not, be it on my head," Anna returned, remembering the phrase from when she'd refused to let the nurse ship her off to Page because she'd had a concussion. To her surprise Beatrice laughed.

"I guess it's not just your head that's hard as a rock," the nurse said good-naturedly. Reaching across the lump on the bed, she delicately pinched the top edge of the sheet between her thumbs and forefingers. Before she unveiled the dead man's face she looked at Jenny. "Steve, Jenny doesn't need to see this, does she?"

"No. You want to wait outside, Jenny? Beats freezing to death."

Jenny shook her head, her eyes on Anna's face. Anna appreciated the support.

"Okay," the nurse said and peeled back the sheet. A puffy, white, but surprisingly unaltered face was exposed. Fine, curling dark brown hair framed eyebrows that darted toward the aquiline nose like seabirds going into a wave. The eyes were closed.

"I recognize him as one of the bodies we found in the slot canyon," Anna said. "I don't recognize him from the assault up on the plateau. Could I see his back?" She stepped closer and leaned in. Her braid fell against the sheet. She snatched it back and tucked it through her belt where it wouldn't get tainted.

None of the men stepped in to help Beatrice roll the corpse. Anna doubted she would have welcomed the assistance. Expertly, she rearranged the body without ever endangering the dignity of the dead man, if the dead had dignity, then tipped it up onto its side.

On the back of the right shoulder was a tattoo of a

sea turtle about six inches long from head to tail and five inches wide.

"I recognize the tattoo from the attack," Anna said. "The shape and placement of it anyway. I was right. It was a turtle."

"Tortoise," Jenny corrected her automatically. "Sorry. Hazard of the profession."

"Show me the other guy," Anna said.

While Beatrice redraped the tattooed corpse, Steve stepped up and efficiently folded the sheet back from the face of the second body.

The hair was the right color, and, judging by the form under the sheet, he was big enough to be the man who hit Kay. "Sorry," Anna said. "I don't know for sure that I've seen him before."

"I have," Jenny said.

FORTY

The bodies in Panther Canyon's end were recovered by the dive team, sans Jenny Gorman. Jenny was Lake Powell's best diver, but Steve hadn't wanted her back in the cold water after her bout with hypothermia. Regis guessed there were psychological reasons as well. Steve hadn't said as much. Since anything that smacked of psychotherapy got Gorman's hackles up, he wouldn't have.

Regis spun his office chair in a full circle just to feel he was moving. He'd played every angle he could think of to be in Panther during the recovery. He wasn't law enforcement, or a diver, or high enough in the pecking order to stick his nose anywhere he wanted, so he'd failed. Pushing harder—or simply going AWOL from headquarters and showing up—would have looked peculiar. Since he and Bethy had stayed in Page on their lieu days, it was more difficult to keep abreast of things without calling attention to himself.

Best scenario, they'd think he was a ghoul with poor work habits. Worst scenario? He didn't want to think about that. The brief high he'd gotten from playing cat-and-mouse was burning out. Would they find tell-tale marks on the bodies? God, he hoped not.

"It was an accident," he said firmly. Not firmly enough. It sounded like he was trying to convince himself. Trying again, he said, "It was an accident." Better. Accidents did happen. People died. It wasn't that far-fetched. Canyoneering was a dangerous sport. Inexperienced—even experienced—climbers died every year. These two could very well have died by accident.

The logic of this argument lowered his blood pressure a few points. In the parks, deaths were nearly always accidental. During the six years he'd been at Lake Powell he couldn't remember a single homicide.

"It was an accident," he said for the third time. Perfect. It sounded true.

God damn, but he hadn't bargained for this. The thrill of feeling alive, of knowing he was fully in the world, that his life was not being measured away in meetings and memos and conversations that never changed, had gone into overdrive. Nerves accelerated from charged to jangling. Excitement became fear. He felt like a man flayed alive. Every word spoken, every movement made, crashing against raw flesh.

Regis hadn't been able to worm his way into the viewing of the bodies either. He knew Anna identified one of the bodies, more or less. Not as anybody specific but as one of the attack boys. Jenny'd recognized the other as a partier on the houseboat that defiled Panther's grotto. College-age men accidentally dying in the slot canyon that led up to the plateau where, a few days before, college-age men had assaulted a woman was not a coincidence anybody would swallow. Poetic justice was even more rare than the ordinary prosaic justice occasionally available in the courts.

Even the dullest law enforcement type—and neither Steve nor Jim was a dullard—would know these men had been murdered.

Regis rose from his desk and closed his office door so he could pace without being observed. Three steps, turn, three steps, turn. The office was cramped, but pacing was better than sitting.

He sensed killing could become an addiction. Having once taken a living creature that was There and changed it into a chunk of meat, rendering it Not There by an act of will, if one was not horrified by the act—or perhaps even if one was—the power of the act would eventually draw the killer back. A need to kill again would build, to see if it was the same, see if it was different, got better, harder, or easier.

What had never crossed his mind, in all of the hours he'd spent thinking of Anna and the jar, Kay and the assault, was that killing could become an act of indifference. Taking a life should be a passionate interaction, not a whim or a matter of convenience. It chilled him to think death and life were no different, that There and Not There were equally insignificant, equally banal.

The perfect crime.

He remembered thinking of the ultimate seduction of a life without consequences. There was no such thing. Webs were woven and flies were caught in them. Threads snapped until everything was in ruins. A need to confess, pour everything out in a putrid flood before a priest or a ranger, was building. The need was so great, membranes in his mind grew thin with the desire to burst, let secrets spew like pus from a suppurating wound.

Shaking his head, he paced three steps, turned, paced three, and turned.

He was in too deep for confession. Prison would kill him. Not neatly or cleanly or quickly. It would kill him with ten thousand days of gray, each taking a bite of his sanity until all that remained was huddled terror with the body of a man wrapped around it.

Too late for confession.

Maybe not too late to end it.

FORTY-ONE

Steve and the chief ranger wasted no time. The senator was abandoned to amuse himself as best he could until Hank and the plane had time to come back for him. Chief Ranger Madden debated whether it should be he or Steve flying back to Wahweap with Anna and Jenny. The need to be in charge vied with the need to do what was best. At least that's what Jenny thought as she watched inner shadows flit across his face while Hank walked around the plane doing a preflight check. Regardless of the fact he'd flown in only a few hours earlier, Hank erred on the side of caution. Once he'd told Jenny his goal in life was to die a very old pilot.

Madden chose to stay in Bullfrog. It had been a decade or more since he had practiced hands-on law enforcement, and Steve did it every day. Jenny was impressed by the decision. She'd thought his vanity greater than his intelligence.

Steve took the right seat. Anna and Jenny buckled themselves in back.

Nearly a week had passed since Jenny saw the man now cooling his heels—and the rest of his anatomy—in

Beatrice's examining room. Houseboats were allotted two weeks on the water with any given group. If she'd met up with the partiers during their second week, by now they would have dispersed, back to wherever home was. Conceivably, the boat could be cleaned and back on the lake with another group, but Jenny didn't think so. From Anna's description of Kay, someone, somewhere, was waiting for her to come home, and as yet there'd been no alarm raised. So, instead of enjoying the beauty of the landscape as seen from the air, Jenny searched the surface of the lake for the old-model houseboat. Judging by the cant of their heads and the concentration on their faces, Anna and Steve were doing the same.

At a quarter of five they landed on the small strip the NPS maintained on the outskirts of Page. Awaiting them was a 1979 Jeep Cherokee, painted Park Service green, with the bison badge on its doors and the Wahweap district ranger behind the wheel. Doug Schneider was in his early fifties, well muscled, his iron gray hair worn in a brush cut that had been fashionable when Jenny was in grade school. The soothing gray and green of the NPS uniform did nothing to soften the military look he cultivated. Jenny was willing to bet his wife had to iron all his permanent-press uniform shirts. Simply plucking them from the dryer in a timely manner couldn't create the crispness of Doug's pleats and creases.

As they climbed into the Jeep, Steve made introductions. Again Anna and Jenny took the rear seat. The moment the doors were closed the two rangers began to talk.

"I think we've found your boat," Doug said as he

backed out of the gravel lot behind the hangar. "According to Dream Vacations—the outfit that rents it out—their last day on the lake is tomorrow. They have to be back in Wahweap by nine A.M. I sent out an APB. A boat that fit the description was spotted in Padre Bay around two thirty. With luck, it is headed in and will moor at Wahweap tonight. By now they've got to be running low on beer."

Doug Schneider smiled grimly. Doug Schneider always smiled grimly. Jenny guessed it was probably the same smile he used when watching lambs play or Donald Duck cartoons.

"We'll need to do a stakeout," Schneider said.

"Sure," Steve replied easily. "Let's stake out in the fancy dining room overlooking the bay and get something to eat."

Doug Schneider's smile grew grimmer. When he raised his eyes and caught Jenny watching his reflection in the rearview mirror, she winked at him. He blinked as if she'd spit in his eye. Anna elbowed her in the ribs but didn't look at her. Not good to be giggling girls at the district ranger's expense.

"Who's the boat rented to?" Steve asked.

"The guy that signed the check was a Trey Benton out of Fort Collins, Colorado. I got hold of his mother. She said he and a bunch of his buddies from a paintball club sold tickets on campus to raise the money for the boat. Kids could buy in either for one week or both. Other than her son and his best friend, an engineering student named Leo Sackamoto, she didn't know who had bought into the deal."

"That's just nifty," Steve said. "The third man could have cleared out by now. We got a dead girl on the plateau. We got the two boys dead in the slot. Pretty little line of corpses from point A to point B. The third kid, the one we assume stayed alive long enough to mess with Anna, is unaccounted for."

"Unsub three looks good for it," Doug said.

The cop-speak sounded silly to Jenny. It was just wrong to hear park rangers say "the perp" or "scenario" or "unsub." It was like hearing small boys practicing saying "fuck," like they were pretending to be bigger or tougher or more experienced than they were.

"I guess he'd look good for it if we could see him," Steve said.

At the end of hour two at the restaurant, the rangers ran out of speculation and small talk. In their capacity as potential witnesses, females, seasonals, and subordinates, neither Jenny nor Anna had the energy to speak. At least Jenny hadn't. Anna might have been keeping quiet for her own reasons. It was Jenny who broke the last dragging silence in over an hour of dragging silences.

"There it is," she said, pointing out the window toward Wahweap's mooring area. A majority of the boats on the lake did not dock but tied up to buoys and used smaller runabouts or skiffs to get to shore.

The houseboat was silhouetted against water turned silver with evening. The stone-and-sand landscape beyond had the dull glow of antique gold. Square-bowed and riding low, the houseboat drove a wide vee through the molten water.

"Vamos," Steve said. "We don't want anybody scattering before you girls get a chance to look at their shining faces."

From another source Jenny might have taken umbrage at the "girls." From Steve Gluck, she didn't. He was an equal-opportunity kind of guy and often called visiting mucky-mucks he was shepherding around "you boys." Jenny sensed that, in some indefinable way, Steve felt older than all other living humans.

Doug Schneider pulled up next to the houseboat as Steve threw the bumpers over the side to cushion the hulls from one another. Jenny leaped neatly over the gunwale onto the party boat and began lashing the NPS boat to the houseboat's cleats.

Music played loud. Their arrival didn't even make a dent in the chatter and laughter of the kids on board.

"Hey, man, it's Smokey the Bear," someone called down from the upper deck. "Where's your Smokey Bear hat, Ranger Rick?"

Jenny stepped back to see who was doing the talking, caught her heel on a battered boogie board, and fell on her ass in an undignified fashion. Pratfalls were clearly considered high comedy by this stratum of society. The entire upper deck burst into raucous laughter. Someone shouted, "Not Ranger Rick, Ranger Rita!" and "Ranger Grace," and more hilarity was enjoyed by all.

Having washed aboard on the gale of laughter, Anna held out her hand to help Jenny to her feet. Pretending not to see it, Jenny rose in one smooth motion. It was bad enough to make a fool of herself in front of people whose shit she had hauled. To make a fool of herself in front of Anna made her want to send each and every über-rich spoiled kid to sleep with the fishes. Instead of giving in to this tempting tide of pique, she made herself laugh. Helpless adult anger would delight the drunken little sots. She refused to give them that pleasure.

Doug and Steve followed them on board, and the partiers crowded back into the cabin to make room. The Wahweap district ranger gave Jenny an irritated scowl as he stepped around her. Probably feeling she'd shamed the entire Park Service by landing on her rump.

Schneider stepped to the center of the small deck in the stern and held his hands up for quiet. "No one is to leave this boat," he ordered in a voice that had been born to shout orders to the troops from horseback.

For a second the gabble faded to a dull roar, and Jenny thought Doug had the buggers cowed. She was wrong.

"Oooh," came a taunt. "Hey, we better not leave town or the sheriff will shoot us!"

"Who shot the sheriff?" several girls sang and leaned over the rail from the upper deck, breasts spilling from tiny bikini tops.

"He's kinda cute."

Doug Schneider's hard-boned face was getting harder, his thin-line lips thinner. If he could have gotten away with it, Jenny didn't doubt that he would have pulled his gun and fired it into the air to get their attention.

Steve ambled into the space where Schneider was affixed like a land mine waiting to be stepped on. He put his hands on his hips and surveyed the box of drunken kids wearily. Scratching his head the way Jenny'd seen him do so many times over the years, pushing his ball cap back, exposing a slightly receding hairline, he said quietly, "We got us a couple of dead bodies. We think they might be friends of yours."

Those in the front lines who heard Steve's words passed them back. Quiet and attention flowed out from the stern until it had snuffed the jeering and the drunken fun from the entire boat.

When the transformation was complete, Steve fumbled in the left breast pocket of his shirt, saying, "We'd sure appreciate if you guys could give us a hand with identifying them so we can get hold of their folks." He fished out a packet of Polaroid snapshots.

"These were taken postmortem and they're going to be pretty hard for some of you to look at, but I'm asking you to try."

A girl in her very early twenties, if that, stepped out from the wall of flesh that had formed outside the sliding patio doors to the cabin.

"How do you want us to do this, Officer?" she asked with complete sobriety.

"He's good, isn't he?" Jenny murmured to Anna.

Anna nodded. "Twenty years and twenty pounds ago he'd have been a great Marc Antony."

"Ouch," Jenny said.

"What?" Anna looked mildly confused. "Marc Antony wasn't old and fat," she said matter-of-factly.

Theater people were more pragmatic than Jenny would have thought. Maybe one had to see oneself realistically before she could know what had to be done to play someone else with any insight. As good an actor as he was, Brian Dennehy would probably be wasting his time auditioning for the part of Tinker Bell.

"Are you okay with this?" Jenny asked Anna.

"Yup."

"Are you scared?"

"Nope."

"Am I annoying you?"

"Is that a trick question?"

Jenny smiled both to herself and her housemate.

"Shall we?" Jenny asked. She and Anna moved apart and began amiably circulating through the boaters as they'd been instructed to during the ride out, making no challenges, asking no questions, just searching faces. Anna was looking for the third man who'd been present during the assault on Kay. Jenny was just looking, hoping something she saw—or something she failed to see—would trigger a flash of brilliance. At this point, even a spark would be reassuring.

The high spirits, or imitation thereof, leached from the gathering by Steve Gluck's plea for assistance, the milling kids looked more like kids, tired sunburned kids who'd eaten too much, drunk too much, and secretly wanted someone to order them to go to bed early. Their densely packed bodies mumbled and shifted or asked questions Jenny pretended not to know the answers to as she swam through the human pond. She saw kids fondling each other in a desultory way. She saw kids smoking dope and shooting her challenging glances as if she were DEA and not NPS. She saw one kid puking over the rail. She saw kids who looked vaguely familiar. She didn't see anything that helped sort out the quagmire that had culminated in the deaths of three young people and the scarring of Anna Pigeon.

Having stared into every bleary-eyed face she could find, she stopped mingling at the stern end of the upper deck and rested her forearms on the rail, looking over the now dark water to the lights of Wahweap. Jim and Steve were no longer in sight. Undoubtedly working their way through the crowded cabin and foredeck.

After a few minutes, Anna came and leaned beside her. "Anything?" Jenny asked.

"No. You?"

"No."

For a moment they stood without speaking. With what sounded like a contented sigh Anna said, "Dark is very dark out in the wilds. Dark is safe here. In the city, at night, if you find yourself alone in the dark—on an empty street or in the hall of a building—that's when your antennae are out. There's safety in light and crowds in a city. Out here, it's just the opposite. Dark is good. Alone is safest."

"Unless you're in a solution hole," Jenny said and immediately wished she'd bitten her tongue off. Why on earth had she felt the need to drag out Anna's nightmare and shove it in her face? It was Anna saying, "Alone is safest," she realized. The words had shut Jenny out.

Fortunately Anna seemed unfazed by her lack of sensitivity.

"Even in the jar. I was trapped, sure, but alone was safest. Darkness was my friend."

Jenny bumped shoulders with Anna to let her know, safest or not, she was not alone. Anna returned the pressure, and they stood in the velvety night in companionable silence, looking over the water until Steve stepped out on the stern deck and waved them down.

Doug was in his boat by the time they squeezed and excused their way down the narrow stairs and through the main cabin.

"Any luck?" Steve asked as they came aft to meet him.

"Nothing," Anna said.

"Nada," Jenny added. "How'd you guys do?"

"Three positive I.Ds," Steve said. "Not bad for an hour's work. Get the lines, would you?" he asked, then stepped over the space between the two boats and jumped heavily on deck. Jenny made short work of loosing the bow and stern lines from where she'd secured them. This done she followed him, then turned to make sure Anna was coming.

She wasn't. She was standing in the houseboat's stern staring at the deck, a look of concern on her face.

Jenny held the boats together while Steve stowed the lines. "Anna?"

Anna shook her head as if answering a question she asked herself, then stepped over the gunwales and into the district ranger's boat. He chugged away at little better than idle speed. Jenny pulled up the bumpers. Anna seemed distracted. Jenny fought down the desire to pester her with any more uninvited concern. Still, she watched her from the corners of her eyes, worried that the visit to the houseboat had upset her more than she was willing to admit.

Doug piloted the boat up and docked with military

precision. A feat anyone could perform on still water, Jenny observed, but she kept her petty observation to herself. Anna was first off the boat. She didn't stay to tie lines to cleats or even say where she was going. She trotted to the shore end of the NPS dock and stopped. Hand on hips, she appeared to be searching the beach. The grounds of the hotel and marina were well lit— tastefully, Jenny admitted, but up to OSHA standards.

Anna jumped from the end of the dock and jogged away from the marina toward the dark of a ravine that cut up from the lake toward the employee housing near the road.

"Where's she running off to?" Steve asked.

"Beats me," Jenny said, "but I'm going to find out."

Jenny traversed the dock and was partway down the beach. Anna had stopped at the ravine. Hearing Jenny's approach, she looked up.

"Jenny," she called. "Come take a look at this."

Hoping it wasn't anything too grisly, Jenny broke into a jog. Anna was staring into a clump of sage bushes. As Jenny reached her she pointed into the shadows beneath.

"Is that the boogie board that caused the comic interlude during our entrance?" she asked.

It was—and there were tracks leading away from it up the ravine toward the highway.

"Damn," Jenny whispered.

Unsub three had jumped ship.

FORTY-TWO

The boy who escaped the houseboat on the boogie board was found two days later smashed at the bottom of an escarpment below Glen Canyon Dam. There were no signs of violence on the body that couldn't be accounted for by a sixty-foot dive onto rocks.

Anna and Jenny were again called to look at a corpse. Anna recognized the boy as the sandy-haired kid with acne who had been watching the other two as they assaulted Kay. Jenny recognized him from the grotto when the party boat was anchored there. His death was ruled a suicide.

"Kay" was Katherine Nelson from Durango, Colorado, a sophomore at Colorado State University at Fort Collins. The tattooed boy was Caleb Fieldhouse. The body Jenny recognized from the slot canyon belonged to Adam Toleodano. The suicide was Jason Mannings. Fieldhouse and Mannings were juniors at Colorado State. Toleodano was a high school friend of Fieldhouse.

According to Steve, Kay and the suicide had not known the other two prior to the trip to Lake Powell.

Fieldhouse and Toleodano had a history of being bad boys and getting away with it because they were college students, white boys from decent families.

Katherine Nelson died from blunt trauma to the head. Bruising suggested she was alive when she'd been tumbled into the solution hole and died shortly thereafter. Caleb and Adam died of drowning, probably brought on by hypothermia. There were no marks of violence on either of the bodies.

As all three of the perpetrators were dead, no charges were filed.

The predominant belief regarding the suicide was that, after participating in the murder of Katherine Nelson, and possibly the deaths of the other two boys, fear of exposure, guilt, or fear of prison had driven Jason Mannings to take his own life.

Radio traffic had alerted Regis and he had met them at the dock the night they'd visited the party boat in Wahweap. At the viewing of the suicide, he backed up Jenny's statement that the dead boy was in the grotto and with the party on the houseboat. After overhearing Jason Mannings making vicious remarks to two of the college girls when the houseboat was tied up at Dangling Rope, Regis had followed the boat back to the grotto in Panther Canyon and spoken to the kid.

Anna had admitted to reburying Kay. It was suggested that perhaps it was she who buried her first in a state of confusion and thus knew precisely where the body was. As for the drugged water, there was no proof of that. No trace of the sandwiches was found. The clothes boxed and addressed to Molly? Well, everyone knew Anna had not been happy. Perhaps she had decided to go home, then changed her mind, and due to the ensuing trauma forgotten. Anna had never told law enforcement about the word WHORE carved on her thigh and was glad she hadn't. It probably would have been passed off as the self-cutting of a neurotic woman.

There was a collective sigh of relief when the nasty little mysteries were put in the box labeled THINGS DONE WHILE ANNA WAS NOT IN HER RIGHT MIND.

Everything tied up neatly. Crime didn't pay. There was no honor among thieves. God was back in his heaven and all was again right in the world.

The questions bothered Anna, as they did Jenny, but the need for answers was subsumed by relief that the bad guys were dead and the desire to put the horror in the past. Anna's view of life, the shattered kaleidoscope with cutting edges and chasing colors, that had formed after Zach's death, and re-formed as the fragile nature of her physical self was repeatedly challenged, began to change yet again.

Each day she rose early and ran the mile circuit around the upthrust of rock. To her amazement, most mornings Bethy Candor ran with her. Evenings she was not on the lake with Jenny, she worked out on the weights in the maintenance shed. When Jim wasn't on duty, he worked with her. As often as not, Bethy joined them.

Within a couple of weeks, despite the temperature having ratcheted up from a cool ninety-two in July to a hundred degrees in the heat of August, if she took it at a slow jog, Anna could run the circuit twice without stopping to walk. Her arms built strength and muscle.

A day of pounding over rough water or hauling heavy cans of human dung no longer left her exhausted.

Bethy began to lose weight. It melted away as if she were made of butter and dared run in the sunlight. Anna took pleasure and pride in that as well, though she knew it was not her doing.

As she grew thinner, Bethy grew bolder. When Anna first arrived at Dangling Rope, Bethy had seemed little more than a scuttling waitress, painfully shy, afraid of her own shadow and terrified of the two maintenance seasonals, Gil and Dennis. Anna guessed she'd been neither; she'd been ashamed of how she looked. Regis had exacerbated the situation with barbed remarks about the size of her derriere.

Anna'd forgotten that. Her first weeks at Lake Powell she'd been self-involved to the point of being deaf, dumb, and blind. Compared to her personal drama, those around her seemed staggeringly unimportant. With food, strength, and freedom from the fear a monster waited around the next bend, Anna came out of her self-imposed isolation.

A newness highlighted the people she watched and the landscape she traveled through. There were times Jenny glittered as much as the wind-scattered lake surface. Even Bethy was growing on her. The woman's butchery of the English language grated on ears trained to the Bard, but Bethy had mettle. Beneath her vague babbling exterior was a vein of something strong. Anna'd seen flashes of it when she'd pushed her maximum weight up from the bench into Anna's waiting hands and, once, when Regis had made a deprecatory remark that managed to simultaneously flatter Anna and disparage his wife.

It seemed to both Anna and Jenny that the more Bethy slimmed down and firmed up, the more cutting Regis's remarks became. Sly and cutting, the kind that are tricky to confront, but felt all the more sharply for being served with that spice of helplessness. It was almost as if he hated seeing his wife becoming what she thought he wanted.

Disturbingly, Regis became Anna's cheerleader in the fitness game, remarking—always politely and never with an underlying leer that either Anna or Jenny could detect—on how much stronger she looked, how much faster she ran. It was annoying to the point Anna avoided him when she could. If he had the itch to be a personal trainer, he should scratch it with his wife. Even Gil and Dennis, as obtuse as they seemed to be, noticed how Bethy hungered for Regis's approval. They would flirt with her a little after a rebuff, their inherent good natures wanting to bolster her up.

The night Regis offered to teach Anna canyoneering, Anna thought Bethy was going to burst into tears. Instead she'd stood up for herself for the first time in Anna's acquaintance with her.

"I taught you," she'd snapped at Regis. "If Anna wants to learn, she'd be better off coming to me." The half-hangdog, half-hoping look she'd shot Anna was painful to see.

"I'd like that," Anna replied firmly. Regis didn't let the matter drop with any grace. His demeanor turned so cold Anna half expected icicles to form on the eaves of the duplexes. Shortly thereafter, he left the picnic benches for their apartment and didn't return.

Since then, Bethy had taken Anna on two tiny canyoneering adventures in an old Zodiac she brought out from Page.

In the slot canyons, Anna suffered mentally. The sense that the walls were closing in and trapping her never entirely went away. Physically, she did herself proud, enjoying the playground-jungle-gym way she worked her body. Moving like a child awakened the spirit of a child in her as she bent and twisted, crawled and wriggled.

On their first adventure, Jenny was with them; on the second, Jim. The third time it was just Bethy and Anna. The canyon Bethy chose was off Rock Creek Bay, half an hour's ride in the Zodiac from the Rope. The afternoon was still and hot, and after a day of trying to talk a string of uniquely unpleasant individuals into being better stewards of the land, Anna was glad to lounge in the bow of the puffy little boat and watch the unfailingly awesome grandeur of Glen Canyon fold into the secret jewels of the smaller side canyons.

"This is an easy one," Bethy said as she expertly herded the fat little craft up a snaking waterway, dyed deep turquoise by the shadows. "A walk in the park," she said and laughed.

Anna laughed with her. Bethy's sense of humor was woefully undeveloped, and Anna felt duty bound to reward even the smallest glimmer of it. After years around actors, Anna had come to believe that people in general were witty and entertaining. That this was not so had been dawning on her over the past months. In general, people were plodding creatures. Occasionally, she missed the brighter-colored social butterflies, but only occasionally. Lack of repartee was conducive to honesty and solitude. Both of which she was coming to crave.

Bethy beached the Zodiac on a spill of sand on a flat stone outcropping no wider than the boat was long. Anna climbed out of the bow and, line in hand, walked the few feet to the only anchorage, a dead tree wedged tightly between a rock and a hard place.

The sand apron that formed their landing area had been washed down from a slot canyon, a mere crack in the sandstone cliffs, carved and smoothed by the runoff from a million years of rain on the plateau and Fiftymile Mountain. A gold-and-gray pathway beckoned them into the heart of the rock. Straighter and shallower than many slot canyons Anna had seen in previous weeks, it was not dark and did not fill her with the mix of excitement and foreboding she'd grown accustomed to.

While Anna tied off the line, Bethy unloaded the gear. "This one's not a technical thing. We're not going to need ropes and stuff. I'm not even going to wear a helmet," she said as she sorted through the plastic laundry basket that served as her gear chest. "You want one?"

Anna knew she should—safety first and all that—but it was hot and she hated wearing the things. "I guess not."

"We won't need ropes either, but I'm going to carry this one. Just in case."

"Just in case what?" Anna asked, resisting the impulse to offer to carry the coiled line with a carabiner affixed to either end. Once she had eschewed the helmet, the idea of scrambling totally unencumbered took precedence over good manners.

Bethy looked nonplussed. "I don't know. Just in case, I guess, you know, we need to tie something to something or something."

"Be prepared," Anna said and raised her hand in the three-fingered Boy Scout salute.

Bethy wrinkled up her nose and forehead like a little kid trying too hard to think. Finally she gave it up. "You're so weird," she said. "Is everybody in New York as weird as you?"

"In New York the people are as gods," Anna said as she followed Bethy down the yellow sand road. "Spider-Man: a New Yorker. Batman, the same. Gotham was just an alias. King Kong immigrated to New York. In New York I am considered to be the most banal of beings." There was a quality about Bethy Candor that allowed Anna the peculiar freedom of chatter, or, when feeling wildly audacious, of babble. Only with Zach had she given herself permission to free-associate. With her husband, it was their shared joy of whimsy, wordplay, and language that lowered the inhibitions and opened the mental floodgates.

With Bethy, Anna suspected it was because, cruel as it was to think—let alone put into words—it was rather like talking to the family cocker spaniel. Not being understood, how could one be judged in any meaningful way? Once in a while Bethy surprised her by responding intelligently, but not often enough that Anna worried about it.

Anna paid as little attention to, and understood as little of, Bethy's monologues as Bethy did hers. Friendships had been built on less camaraderie than that, Anna supposed.

The canyon, half again as wide as Anna's shoulders, had a flat sandy bottom and the lazy curves of a snake's trail. Sunset wasn't for a couple of hours, but it had long since finished its brief visit to the bottom of the forty-foot slot. The air was cooler between the walls, and a pleasant breeze blew down-canyon, as it often did at this time of day. Light was clear but didn't have the glare it did on the water. For the first time in a closed-in space Anna felt relaxed. She must tell Jenny. Jenny was the kind of girlfriend Anna hadn't had since she was in grade school and spent most of her free time with Sylvia Gonzales; the kind of girlfriend for whom one saved up successes and failures along with foolish remarks and astute observations, like treasures to carry back and share. Jenny would be pleased Anna had entered this benign bit of Mother Earth with fearlessness.

Jenny. Anna had accepted her with ease, as if such friendships came along every day or sprang fully formed like Venus from the sea. She supposed it was shared trauma. Emotions became accessible in times of stress or high drama. One of the dangers of the theater was that actors could so easily fall in love with one another in the same way people thrown together on a great adventure often did. When the final curtain came down, it was anybody's guess as to whether the romance would survive the daunting ordinariness of day-to-day life.

The canyon narrowed but didn't squeeze, and there was no water in which to fall and die of cold. Happily, Anna scrambled along in Bethy's wake as she climbed upward through crevices and rock chimneys that reminded Anna of the children's board game Chutes and Ladders.

Bethy chattered breathily as she climbed. "I can't wait until Regis turns thirty. It's not even two whole years and then we're going to go to Europe and see stuff. He promised me. And I'm going to get all new clothes and we'll cruise. Have you ever been on a cruise? I haven't, but I'm probably supposed to have a baby pretty soon and cruises are supposed to be, you know, all romantic and everything . . ."

Anna's ears pricked up at this. Whether Bethy was telling the truth or spinning a fantasy, Anna couldn't guess. Either way it was a bit of gossip to share with her housemate. The wicked glee at such a human foible was untarnished by guilt. Needing to catch her breath, Anna stopped for a moment, her butt on a slanting four-inch shelf, feet and hands on the two sides of the triangular chimney they clambered up. Gossip, unless aimed or honed sharp like a weapon, was natural to human beings. It showed interest in one's fellows, interest in the well-being of the tribe. Gossip was a way to learn taboos, pass on warnings, share the burden of being human among many so the onus of bearing it alone would fall on no one person. At least that's what Molly always said, and who would know better than she?

"Rock!" Bethy shouted.

Anna pressed her head back against the chimney

wall and covered her face with her forearm. A stone the size of a softball grazed her right knee as it fell between her legs to clatter down the chute beneath her.

"You okay?" Bethy called.

"Yeah," Anna said.

"Sorry about that. My fault. I shoulda poked it before I stepped on it," Bethy said.

Looking up, Anna could see the other woman about twenty feet above her looking down through her wide-set feet, head and fanny in alignment with the forced perspective.

"No harm done," Anna said and then checked her knee, locked to keep the pressure that wedged her in the chimney. Her trousers hadn't torn, and no blood was seeping through. That was all she would know until she tried to bend it. Settling her other limbs and digits more firmly, she put her foot on a nice little outcropping. The joint was in good working order.

"Almost there," Bethy called. "Don't be such a slow-poke." She vanished from Anna's line of sight. Anna followed. Feet, hands, knees, back, and brain occupied with the business of ascent, she moved quickly. When she reached the point where she'd last seen Bethy, a vertical crack, two feet wide, with a lovely smooth rock bottom led off to the right. Anna levered herself into it and stood upright. After the chimney, the going was as easy as a stroll down a sidewalk in Central Park. Within less than a minute the crack ended. Anna stepped from the sandstone's embrace onto a natural balcony the size of the stage's apron in a small theater. Tumbled rock and blown sand created enough earth that a few hardy plants had taken root and were surviving, if just barely. Bethy was sitting on a rectangular boulder, sides so straight and size so perfect it would be easy to believe it was man-made.

"Cool, huh?" Bethy said, as Anna took in the vista.

The balcony was sixty or more feet above a finger of the lake, as close to an aerie as anything without wings was likely to get.

"This is amazing," Anna said and laughed because, in this place, language failed her. The depth and beauty of evening's muted palette on a canvas too immense for man's imagining was enough to strike a poet dumb and a painter blind.

"Cool, huh?" Bethy repeated.

"Exceedingly cool," Anna replied. Crossing to the stone, she sat down next to Bethy and let her soul drink in the intricacy of the view. The climb had taken less than an hour, and, though in the morning there would be new aches in heretofore unchallenged muscles, for the moment she felt pleasantly tired and inexplicably moved by this gift Bethy Candor had given her.

She doubted they were the first white women ever to set foot in this tiny Eden, a suspicion borne out by the dull round of a beer bottle cap pocking the dirt at the base of a small but dedicated cactus. Yet it was new and fresh for Anna, and she was grateful for having been led there.

"Thanks, Bethy," she said earnestly. "This is a real treat." She turned to smile at her companion just as Bethy Candor lunged for her.

FORTY-THREE

Regis was in a foul mood. Jenny was half sorry she'd bummed a ride with him back from her shopping trip in Wahweap. For the first time in years shopping was a pleasure. Commuting to town once a week to hit the grocery store for peanut butter and booze, and the Walmart for paper and plastic items that had become necessities for a modern household, was usually a tedious waste of a perfectly good lieu day.

Shopping for treats to share with Anna filled Jenny's head with delicious plots and plans for camp suppers and lunch picnics. Now that Anna had taken on the task of turning herself into Superwoman, she was a most appreciative audience for Jenny's culinary surprises.

"Bethy's sure looking good," Jenny said, thoughts of Anna reminding her of Regis's wife.

Regis grunted. Rather than enjoying the lush bucket seats, he was standing behind the wheel of his sexy red boat as if by so doing he could urge greater speed from it. Lounging in the left-hand seat, Jenny had to admit he was visually compelling: good jaw, good chin and nose, hair wild in the wind, dark and wavy. Such a good-looking man, yet he'd always struck her as a non-event, a bit of a cipher. Not that she didn't like him, he just didn't seem vital enough to waste much attention on. This season that had changed. Somebody or something had turned the lights on in his haunted house.

Rescuing her and Anna from drowning had been positively heroic. Even when they'd been wearing the tights and cape and rescuing him from the jar, he'd been more engaged than she'd ever seen him. Sniping at his wife, once done in an offhand desultory manner, was now done with a keen edge and an eye to her weak points. Regis Candor's wattage had definitely been amped up. The anger he radiated as he pushed the cigarette boat to its limit was almost as tangible as the late afternoon sun on her skin.

Was it possible the someone who lit all her candles this season was the same one who turned on the lights for Regis? Jenny pondered that for a moment. Love of—or lust for—Anna Pigeon was not an area where she could be objective. Her heart insisted that, of course, every sighted intelligent creature on the planet must be head over heels for the little redhead. Intellectually, she knew that was nonsense. The rose-colored glasses had been given to her alone. Like Joseph Smith's God-given golden spectacles, her glasses for translating the tablets of Anna Pigeon were not shared by the hoi polloi.

But Regis? It was possible. Clearly he admired Anna. From admiration it was but a small step to the desire for acquisition.

Jenny waited for jealousy to raise its little green head. It didn't. It was Regis's wife Jenny was jealous of: jealous of the time she spent with Anna on their shared lieu days, jealous of the mornings and evenings she stole for runs and working out on weights, jealous of the places she showed Anna and the knowledge of can-yoneering she gave away, jealous of the temptations of the Zodiac and borrowed gear.

"Why are you staring at me?" Regis demanded.

Caught out, Jenny said the first thing that came to mind. "Didn't you and Bethy used to stay in town on your days off?"

"We did. Why?" Her conversation distracted him from whatever was ruining his day. The white left his knuckles as he loosened his grip on the wheel.

"You seem to be more at the Rope this summer."

Regis's eyes darted to her face, to the windscreen, and back to her face. Not the double take of a comedian; the frightened look of a rabbit that can't decide which way to run.

"Not complaining, mind you. I appreciate the ride and the company." The last wasn't entirely true. Jenny felt it was best to work and play well with others when-ever possible.

Regis returned his gaze to the bow cutting through the waves, the boat's steady pounding against the rough water echoing in the slight spring of his knees.

"We are spending more weekends at the Rope, I guess," he said in an oddly confessional tone. "Used to be we'd go in every week to spend time with Kippa."

Kippa, Jenny knew, was a French bulldog, a caramel-colored bowling ball eight parts energy and two parts unadulterated joy. Meeting Kippa was akin to wrestling with a manic dwarf Santa.

"She a year old now?" Jenny asked to be saying something.

"Died this winter," he said and smiled at her, more a baring of teeth than a show of camaraderie. Jenny didn't know whether he hid deep emotion or a heart of obsidian.

Either was too much to delve into. She let the conversation drop. Judging by the set of his mouth, she doubted Regis wanted to pursue the subject any more than she did.

Lost in their own thoughts, Jenny's mostly pleasant, Regis's, she guessed, not so much so, they rode with nothing but the whine of the engine for company until they rounded Gooseneck Point, a long knuckly finger of land poking into the main body of the lake.

"Isn't it wonderful that Bethy and Anna are becoming best friends?" Regis asked, looking at her from the corner of his eye, a slight curl to his lips, virtually a smirk.

This was not an innocent question. That unmistakable fishhook-in-the-sternum bite and pull let Jenny know it was on a par with asking Barbie if it wasn't wonderful that Ken was all over Skipper.

"They sure are getting in shape," Jenny said carefully, more or less the same remark she'd made an hour earlier that had elicited nothing but a grunt.

"You and I are gym widows. They seem totally engrossed in life without us." He shot her a smile that she didn't like one bit. Regis was fishing. For what? Secrets of the lesbian sisterhood? Regis had figured out her sexual orientation years ago, Jenny knew that. Straight men who also happened to be idiots thought woman-on-woman was the bee's knees. As if the lesbian couple was going to spot them lurking in the hall and yell, "Come on in, the sex is fine!" According to Jenny's totally unscientific research, that had happened exactly never. Besides, Regis wasn't an idiot and he'd never come across as lascivious.

"I do miss the hash brown casseroles," Jenny said neutrally. "Green salads with lo-cal dressing just aren't the same. Why? Does their friendship bother you?"

He seemed to give the question serious thought. "I guess it does," he said after a few seconds. "Don't get me wrong, I like Anna well enough, but I think she's a bad influence on Bethy. Since Anna's been hanging around, Bethy is . . . it's hard to put into words."

Jenny crimped her lips together as if she held straight pins in her mouth. Had Regis been trying, she doubted he could have been more insulting. Anna was not "hanging around" Bethy. If anything, the opposite was true. As for his "liking Anna well enough," the way he fawned over her put the lie to that. Jenny suspected the "bad influence" Anna exerted was the self-confidence Bethy had begun to exhibit on rare occasions.

Not trusting herself to speak, she said nothing. Flying to Anna's defense would expose more about her than she cared to make public.

Jenny wasn't rising to the bait. Regis could tell his disparagement of Anna upset her, yet she'd chosen to

shut him out rather than side with him. Fear coiled
through his insides, loosening everything in its path.
What had started out as a fine adventure was now officially a horror show.

Ecru, he thought to himself and smiled sourly. His
mother's favorite color. After all these years he finally
saw its charm. A period of bland nothing would be
restful. Having discovered the darkness he'd long suspected all people carried within, he doubted he could
go back to ecru anytime soon.

"I don't like them spending so much time together,"
he said, trying another tack.

"So you've said," Jenny replied.

No softening there. Tough bitch.

"I don't think it's fair to you." Regis pitched his
voice to the tune of concerned empathy, no mean feat
over the engine racket.

Jenny glanced at him sharply. He held her gaze until
he was sure she knew he knew she was gay and infatu-
ated with the woman from New York. That no one else
noticed Jenny Gorman was gay and in love he put down
to mass hypnosis. People believed what they wanted to
believe and saw—or didn't see—whatever they needed
to in order to ratify their beliefs: angels, aliens, ghosts,
the Virgin Mary, demons, the Loch Ness Monster, Big
Foot, leprechauns, or Jesus's face on a grilled cheese
sandwich. Those who wanted to believe the earth was
only six thousand years old did not see history, archae-
ology, paleontology, geology, or astronomy.

The Park Service did not see lesbians. The fact that
Jenny was wearing her hair down more often, buying

more expensive wine, shaving her legs with regularity, and sparkling every time her housemate appeared went unnoticed.

"What do you mean it's not fair to me?" Jenny asked after a minute or so.

"Don't play games," Regis said coolly, keeping the smile from his lips. The hook was set. With luck it would prod her into a territorial mood and she'd insert herself between Anna and Bethy, keep them from spending their lieu days together.

A woman alone was easier to kill.

FORTY-FOUR

Despite mental gymnastics, Jenny couldn't eradicate the seeds of uncertainty—jealousy—that Regis planted. For the remainder of the trip she didn't see desert varnish or intricate sculptures of stone; she saw Anna and Bethy enacting all the boisterous joyous fantasy scenes in which Jenny would have liked to star.

The sort of betrayal Regis suggested, that his *wife,* for heaven's sake, and Jenny's housemate were supposedly laying the groundwork for, was not new to Jenny. Mostly she'd been named the betrayer. She never saw herself in that light. Where neither promises nor commitments were made, she felt no promises could be broken nor commitments go unmet. That's what she told herself when the proverbial shoe had been laced to her own slender foot. Now that the shoe was on the other foot, it felt like a knife between the shoulder blades.

As she and Regis pulled into Dangling Rope she saw Jim, out of uniform, sipping a beer, and chatting up Libby Perez, this season's lone female concessions worker. Libby was twenty years older than Jim and had the lush velvet beauty of a full-blown rose when the petals are loose and lazy and the reds grown deeper at their edges.

"Jim!" Jenny called before Regis had shut down the engine. "Do you know if Anna's around?"

Afraid of seeing a smirk on Regis's face, she didn't look at him as she jumped ship.

"Is Anna up at housing?" she asked.

"Why? Something happen?" Despite the sandals, Dos Equis, and Libby, Jim came into law enforcement focus so quickly he almost shimmered badge-gold.

Jenny realized she sounded anxious. Damn Regis. Emotional balance was difficult enough to maintain without louts with hidden agendas tipping the scales.

"Regis is worried Ms. Pigeon has eloped with his wife," she said and was rewarded by a look of annoyance as Regis came up beside her.

Jim laughed. "I think that's the case," he said easily. "As I was coming off duty, I passed them in the Zodiac. Bethy said they were headed for Lover's Leap to do a couple hours in the slot."

Lover's Leap. Jenny was crushed. That was a place she'd been saving to show Anna.

"What do you say, Jenny? Shall we go surprise them?" Regis asked.

To her shame, she immediately said yes.

The boat ride to the little canyon with its here-today-and-gone-tomorrow beach was less than half an hour. Neither Jenny nor Regis spoke. Both seemed to have dropped the pretense that this was spur-of-the-moment fun.

The closer they got to their destination, the worse Jenny felt. In acquiescing, she had shown disrespect for Anna, herself, and their friendship. Even in the sanctity of her own mind, she didn't call it a relationship. The societal connotations of that word were too fraught.

More than once she thought to tell Regis she'd changed her mind, that she needed to get back to the Rope, but a cruel aspect had shut down his face. He looked much as she imagined a soldier would before battle or a cowboy before he shot his crippled horse, so she'd said nothing.

Jenny knew Regis had maneuvered her into this so misery would have company. He wanted to break up Anna and Bethy's outing and thought he could use Jenny as an ally or at least an excuse. Jenny didn't picture him as the jealous husband, rushing out to catch his bisexual wife in flagrante delicto. More likely he didn't like his wife monopolizing a woman he was interested in. Didn't want them becoming friends, swapping notes.

The whole thing was sick. Jenny was sick of her part in the soap opera. "Regis!" she called over the engine noise. "This is a bad idea. We need to turn back."

"We're almost there," he said determinedly. Less than a minute later, when he throttled back to turn the boat into the side canyon, Jenny tried again.

"Regis, take me back. The sun is nearly down. It will be too dark to make the climb up and back."

"So we meet them halfway."

He was set on making this particular mistake, and Jenny was along for the ride. She gave up.

Anna didn't know she was in love with her, Jenny reasoned. Anna wouldn't know that she'd agreed to "surprise" her and Bethy from base motives. No one would know except Regis and herself. That Regis now knew she was an easily manipulated lovesick fool didn't much bother her.

That she was one did.

Regis nosed the speedboat in beside the Zodiac on the minuscule beach, nimbly walked over the pointed bow, and began tying up to the same deadwood to which the Zodiac was moored.

Before he finished, Bethy came stalking out of the opening in the sandstone. Suffused with blood, her face lent her the aspect of an exceedingly angry beet. Her hair, pulled back in a high ponytail, fifties cheerleader style, had partially escaped its rubber band and made inharmonious lumps on the side of her head.

"Bethy, is everything okay?" Regis asked cautiously at the same moment Jenny demanded, "Where's Anna?"

"I want to go home," Bethy said as she clambered over the side of the speedboat. "She can take the Zodiac." She turned cold eyes on Jenny and said, "You can wait for her, for all the good it will do you." Bethy dug the key to the Zodiac out of her shorts pocket and was about to heave it over the bow onto the sand.

"I'll take it," Jenny said quickly, grabbed the key, and climbed awkwardly out of the boat.

"Regis, I want to go home *now*," Bethy hissed at her husband.

"Anna—" he began.

"Now!"

Emotion left Regis's face with the suddenness of a shade being drawn over a window. Without another word, he untied the boat, shoved it back from the sand, then leaped over the gunwale. In thirty seconds all that remained of the Candors was a wake lapping fiercely at the beach.

Key clutched in her hand, Jenny turned toward the neat vertical crack in the cliff.

"Anna?" she called timidly. Then, with rising panic, "Anna!"

Before Jenny could rush headlong into the slot, her housemate stepped from the dark of the crevice into the shadowless gray light of the evening. Her shoulders were slumped with weariness, a bruise was forming around her right eye, and a thin trail of blood from her nose had been smeared into a fan across her cheek.

"Jenny!" Anna said with a start.

"I came to surprise you," Jenny said lamely.

"Everybody seems bent on surprising me today," Anna said.

FORTY-FIVE

For the first time since Anna had arrived at Dangling Rope, she and Jenny spent the evening in the dim cool rattle of the swamp cooler's realm. Anna was in no mood for social intercourse with their next-door neighbors. One on either side of the kitchen counter, she and Jenny sat on stools picking over the carcass of a frozen chicken-and-pineapple pizza.

"So she just hurled herself at you?" Jenny asked.

"I sat down next to her, prepared to be awed by natural beauty, and she went in for the kill. Our foreheads banged together and her chin hit me so hard it made my nose bleed. If we were still in high school, I swear our braces would have gotten locked. I haven't been kissed like that since I was in fifth grade and George Cramer kissed me on a dare."

"Is Bethy gay?" Jenny sounded more shocked than questioning.

"Beats the hell out of me," Anna said. "If she is, she's not very good at it." Carrying her wine in the jelly glasses Jenny kept for that purpose, Anna slid off the stool and spread herself more comfortably on the couch, feet up on the scarred coffee table. The entire doomed affair was ridiculous. Anna doubted Bethy was now, or ever had been, homosexual. She dove in for the kiss with all the romance of somebody bobbing for apples.

"Regis was acting like he was afraid she was," Jenny said. "He seemed jealous. That's why we so conveniently turned up. Regis, checking on his wife."

That surprised Anna. That he cared enough to be jealous of Bethy surprised her as much as the idea that he thought he might be married to a follower of Lesbos. Then, again, jealousy was not about caring, it was about fear of loss: loss of love, loss of power, or loss of security.

"So he thought Bethy took me out to the overlook for, well . . . for exactly what she did take me out to the overlook for?"

"To deflower you," Jenny said wickedly.

"Compromise me," Anna added.

"Take advantage of you."

"Ruin me." They laughed together easily. "If he thought Bethy was up to something, she had to have been dropping clues," Anna said. "It's not like anybody watching us together would get the wrong idea. Unless, of course, they were prurient bastards."

"I don't know," Jenny said teasingly. "Pumping iron. Running bras and sweat."

Anna scooped a none-too-clean sock up from the floor and flung it at her housemate.

Jenny snatched it out of the air and lofted it expertly into the wastepaper basket on the far side of the room. "What are you going to do?" Jenny asked. "Tell Regis he's got nothing to worry about? Tell Bethy she's straight?"

"Nothing," Anna said. "I'm going to do exactly nothing. This is the sort of situation in which not taking any action whatsoever is the safest course. In fact, I'm going to pretend it never happened. Maybe that will let Bethy save face."

"Maybe she's been locked tight in the closet and this was her attempt to kick down the door," Jenny suggested as she settled on the opposite end of the couch and propped her feet next to Anna's. Between them was a triangle of sofa cushion fenced in by their legs, precisely the right size for a little skunk to safely play in.

"Wish Buddy was still here," Anna sighed.

"Me, too," Jenny replied.

They shared a moment of remembrance before Anna said, "I don't think this was a closet thing. Have you ever felt one shred of heat from Bethy? I sure haven't."

"Me neither," Jenny admitted.

"Sexual beings exude pheromones, esters, vibes," Anna said. "If Bethy is gay, she is flying so far under the radar I doubt she'll ever know why she cried more at the end of *Thelma and Louise* than her girlfriends did. Does she have girlfriends?"

Jenny thought about it for a moment. Anna waited. Whatever else Bethy had done today, she had certainly given her and Jenny endless grist for the gossip mill. It wasn't often that anyone took Anna as off guard as she'd been at Lover's Leap.

"No, now that you mention it," Jenny said. "At least I don't think so. I don't know what her social life is like in Page, but on the lake it's always been about Regis. Her first season she had a female housemate. They occasionally did things together—lift weights mostly, I think. They had different lieu days. After Regis started paying attention to her, that was that. No more time for the girlfriend. Regis loved his fast boat; Bethy loved fast boats. Regis loved to fly; Bethy loved to fly. I think she even soloed. If Regis had loved rolling in bat guano, you can bet that would have suddenly become Bethy's favorite pastime."

Holding a tangy swallow of wine in her mouth, Anna closed her eyes and returned to the unfortunately named Lover's Leap. Bethy hadn't reached for her, touched her, or taken her hand; she'd just gone for Anna's lips like a pelican going for a fish.

When Anna had fallen off her end of the natural stone bench, half stunned and cursing, Bethy looked affronted. Propped up on her elbows, her nose hurting and her eyes watering, Anna'd asked, "What did you do that for?"

"I thought that's what you wanted," Bethy had said coldly.

"Not even close," Anna replied.

With that, Bethy stood up, dusted off the seat of her shorts, and left Anna there in the dirt.

Anna swallowed the wine. "I had to hustle down after her so she wouldn't putter off in the Zodiac and maroon me," she said.

"She was probably mortified," Jenny said, and Anna heard genuine sympathy in her voice. "God knows I would have been."

"Me, too. I'd want to dye my hair, change my name, and leave town for a while. I don't think it was a sex thing at all. I think she wants to be a part of something. Maybe a part of our friendship and she thought those were the dues she had to pay," Anna mused.

"That's about the saddest thing I ever heard," Jenny said.

"I don't think Bethy thinks about too much more than Bethy. That wouldn't make for a particularly happy life."

Jenny levered herself off the couch, crossed to the kitchen counter, and brought back the wine bottle. She held it up to Anna. Anna shook her head. The congenial beverage had a way of turning on her if she didn't watch it. Having sat down, Jenny poured herself a generous amount, then took a long swallow. Elbows on knees, eyes on the scratched surface of the coffee table, she looked to be making a serious decision. Anna stayed quiet, letting her think.

At length, Jenny set her jelly glass on the table, faced Anna squarely, and said, "I'm gay."

"A lot of people are," Anna said and waited for her to get to her point.

Jenny seemed to be waiting as well, her eyes on Anna's face.

"And . . ." Anna offered to help her move past whatever had gotten her stuck.

Jenny relaxed. She shook her wild hair until it coiled Medusa-like in gravity-defying ways. Shrugging sheepishly, she said, "And you're not."

There was the barest hint of a question in Jenny's

tone. Anna considered her post-Zach sexuality for the first time. Many truths she held about herself and others—her ability to read people, her understanding of herself—had been uprooted as life repeatedly bulldozed its way through her preconceptions.

"I don't think so," she said finally, "but then I guess a lot depends on who you fall in love with."

FORTY-SIX

A scream, cut off in its infancy, brought Jenny out of a sound sleep. In T-shirt and panties, she stumbled to the door and flipped on the light.

"Anna?"

"Here." Anna's bedroom light came on, backlighting her. She wore a lime green tank top and men's plain white boxer shorts.

"You?" Jenny asked.

"No. Outside." Anna trotted down the hall. Jenny ran after her. The scream concerned but didn't frighten her. There was nothing to be afraid of at Dangling Rope other than sunburn and bad dreams. Three seasons before, she'd been awakened by just such a noise and had to ferry a seasonal interpreter with acute appendicitis to Bullfrog to be medevacked out. Banging through the screen door, she nearly bowled Anna over.

Without a word, Anna made room for her, and they waited in the hot darkness, listening.

"What time is it?" Anna whispered.

Jenny pushed one of the buttons on her diver's watch,

and the screen lit ghostly green. "Quarter to one," she whispered back.

No lights showed in Jim's duplex. The alien gray from a television screen glowed in Gil and Dennis's place. The reception couldn't be all that great. Jenny wondered why they bothered.

"Maybe somebody saw a mouse," Anna said in a more normal voice.

"Maybe Heckle and Jeckle are watching old horror movies," Jenny suggested.

The faint ticking of insects and the hush of dry wind over arid soil went uninterrupted. Jenny's stomach began to unclench. "Cougars sometimes scream. They can sound just like a woman," she said to Anna, still and alert at her side.

Anna shook her head, a movement that caught the trickle of light from her bedroom window. It occurred to Jenny that Anna might have heard a lot of screams in her life, screams produced by actors and, in the dense hive of apartments that made up New York City, the screams of whichever of a multitude of neighbors happened to be feuding at any given moment.

The barely audible sound track of the desert night ticked away another minute, then two. "I guess whatever it was is either all the way dead or gone," Jenny said. Then a short sharp cry, followed by the sound of a heavy object striking a solid surface, shattered the calm.

"The Candors," Anna said and ran down the two steps of their porch, over and up the two to their duplex.

"Wait," Jenny called, but Anna was already banging

on the screen door. As Jenny ran the short distance in her bare feet to stand by her diminutive noisy housemate, she wondered where Jim was. Probably with Libby. Even in the national parks you could never find a cop when you needed one.

"Regis! Bethy! Are you all right?" Anna called, pounded again. Silence seeped from behind the closed door. The desert music had ceased.

Trying not to be obvious, Jenny insinuated herself between Anna and the door. "Let me," she said and raised her fist to knock.

The porch light came on, blinding in its sudden assault on their eyes. From the door came the unmistakable sound of a dead bolt being thrown. Jenny's duplex had only the key lock in the doorknob. The dead bolt must have been either Regis's or Bethy's innovation.

Behind the screen the door opened halfway. Regis, shirtless but wearing shorts with cargo pockets, stared out at them.

"Hey, Regis," Jenny said, feeling both foolish and righteous. "We thought we heard something."

Regis said nothing. His face was devoid of emotion. In Jenny's psyche, foolishness was beginning to get the upper hand. It easily could have been a cougar or the death throes of an unfortunate rabbit in a fortunate fox's jaws.

Anna stepped up next to her. A show of solidarity. Though she didn't think it necessary, Jenny was honored. "Regis, we heard two screams. They came from your place," Anna said. "Are you both okay?"

There wasn't a tremor in her voice. It was as solid as granite and as implacable. Given that voice, Anna Pigeon organizing groups of artists—a skill Jenny equated with herding cats—seemed suddenly plausible.

"We're fine," Regis said coldly. "Thanks for checking." He started to close the door.

"Is Bethy okay?" Anna demanded.

"Bethy is fine. Good night."

Before he could make his escape Anna said, "Let me see her."

Regis went very still. "She slipped on the rug by the kitchen sink and hit her head on the corner of the table. She's embarrassed because she's such a klutz, but she's fine." His voice had warmed significantly. He smiled ruefully and shrugged. The understanding husband.

"I want to see her," Anna insisted.

Discomfort boiled inside Jenny, acute, but hard to define, containing as it did elements of insecurity, bad manners, guilt, and genuine concern for both Anna and Bethy. The curse of girls who've been raised right. For a second Jenny thought Regis was going to slam the door in their faces. Then what would they do?

Try to track down Jim Levitt.

Blowing out a gust of air so vehemently Jenny felt it through the wire mesh, Regis gave in. "Bethy!" he called over his shoulder. "Get out here so the Misses Marple can see I haven't murdered you."

Snuffling and shuffling heralded the woman's arrival. Regis stepped away from the door and guided Bethy into the place he'd been standing. Light from the porch did more to illuminate Anna and Jenny than the person behind the screen, but Bethy was moving easily and on her own; that was to the good.

"Bethy," Anna said. "What happened?"

"I'm such a klutz," Bethy apologized. "I slipped on the bathroom rug and hit my head." She smiled and raised two fingers to her right cheekbone. "Smack in the eye. I'm gonna have a big ol' shiner for sure."

"We'll be twins," Anna said. Jenny was startled at the depth of kindness in her voice, especially considering Anna's black eye had been given her by Bethy's aborted pass on Lover's Leap.

"Do you want to come over? Have a glass of wine and a bag of ice?" Anna had taken on a coaxing tone Jenny'd never heard before. How Bethy resisted it was a mystery.

"Regis will get me some ice," Bethy said. Awkwardly, she smiled. "I'm okay. Really. I'm just such a klutz."

It was clear she wasn't coming out.

"Holler if you need anything," Anna said. "We'll be listening for you."

Jenny expected this last was said as much for Regis's benefit as Bethy's.

The door snicked shut. The porch light winked out. "Well," Anna said after a moment of standing in the dark.

"Yeah," Jenny agreed. "I guess that's that." Together they turned and trailed back to their own duplex.

Without turning on a light or speaking a word, they flopped on their respective ends of the couch, feet up on the coffee table.

"Slipped on the kitchen rug," Anna said flatly.

"Slipped on the bathroom rug," Jenny said. Deeply disappointed in Regis, she added, "I can't believe it. He was smacking her around!"

"Is this the first time?" Anna asked doubtfully.

"First time I've ever gotten wind of it," Jenny said. "I'll tell Jim, of course. I have to, but I doubt it will do any good. It's not like Bethy called for help or we saw anything."

"Bethy the klutz slipped on a rug and hit her head on the way down," Anna said in the tone one might use reading a headstone.

"I'm afraid so."

"Do you think she told him about trying to kiss me?"

"Maybe she did. Maybe she wanted to make him jealous. Or turn him on," Jenny added acidly.

"I guess we should try to be nicer to her."

"I think we are plenty nice to her already," Jenny said.

FORTY-SEVEN

Anna and Jenny spent the next three days and nights on the lake, where they neither saw nor heard from their neighbors. For that, Anna was glad. The Candors exuded what, in her college days, had been referred to as bad vibes, an underlying sickness or misery that oozed out around the edges of conversations and interactions.

Apart, they were less toxic than they were together. When Anna and Bethy exercised, and the times they had gone canyoneering with Jim and then Jenny, Bethy seemed almost free of whatever darkness the two of them spawned at home. Since finding out Regis beat Bethy at least once—and battered wives were seldom beaten but once—Anna had made the decision to be available to Bethy Candor. Not to befriend her. Friendship built on pity had a tendency to go sour. The balance of power was too out of whack.

Being available sidestepped that pitfall. Being available was simply a matter of putting aside one's own considerations for a time. When her lieu days came around, and Jenny headed out with Jim to potty-train the masses, Anna decided if Bethy approached her to work out she would be open-minded, if not open-hearted.

Anna didn't have to make good on her best intentions. Bethy and Regis evidently decided Dangling Rope wasn't the heaven it had once been. They stayed at their house in Page, not only on their weekends but during the week as well, Bethy making the long commute to Rainbow Bridge from the Wahweap Marina, Anna assumed.

Having them gone was more of a relief than Anna would have expected. As she ran and worked out on weights with Jim, joked with Gil, Dennis, and Jenny as they shared their cocktail hour at the picnic tables on their porches, she sensed the others were relieved as well. No one said anything; it was the subtle relief of a constant noise finally going silent or a small splinter finally working itself out of the ball of one's thumb.

When, three weeks after Bethy had been screaming, Anna stepped out onto her porch on her day off, with her first cup of coffee, and found Bethy waiting, the surprise wasn't entirely pleasant. Any bruising resulting from Regis punching her was gone. She looked calm and rested, her soft brown hair framing her face in a pixie cut that was more becoming than the thin ponytail into which she'd formerly dragged her hair.

Bethy wasn't in uniform. She wore old, threadbare canvas trousers, sneakers without socks, and a red tank top. Her bare arms were well muscled, and she had lost more weight since Anna had last seen her.

"What are you doing here? Wednesday isn't your

lieu day," Anna said ungraciously before she recovered from the shock of seeing her. Hurt shadowed Bethy's eyes and was as quickly gone.

"I didn't mean that the way it sounded," Anna apologized. "I love your hair," she added as she took her accustomed place on the picnic table, feet on the bench in unconscious imitation of Jenny.

"Regis always liked it better short," Bethy said, sounding almost shy. "I don't know why I got the bug to grow it out."

"You look great," Anna said honestly. "Cross my heart and hope to die."

Bethy looked away, squinting her eyes against the early light cresting the canyon rim to the east. She nibbled on her lower lip with child-sized teeth. Anna hadn't noticed the small teeth before. Perhaps because Bethy seldom smiled.

"Are you still mad at me?" Bethy asked without looking at Anna. "You know, because I . . . well, you know."

"I was never mad," Anna said truthfully. "Just confused. Then, when I figured out Regis was beating you, worried."

Bethy's eyes flashed. She looked away quickly, but not before Anna felt the white-hot glare of anger. Whether it was at Regis for doing it, or her for noticing, she couldn't decide.

"I don't know where you got that idea," Bethy said carefully, still not looking at her. "I fell down. People do, you know. Regis would never hurt me. We love each other too much."

Rehearsed, Anna thought. "Okay," she said. There was nothing she or anyone could do until Bethy reported it. Or Regis finally killed her.

"Anyway," Bethy said, heaving a great sigh of relief at leaving the topic of domestic violence behind, "I didn't come here to talk about that. I came here because I'm leaving Page tomorrow and will be gone for a while. I wanted to tell you I was sorry I did that thing on Lover's Leap." She looked at Anna shyly. "I just wanted you to like me is all."

This last was said in the voice of a wistful child. Anna couldn't help but be affected.

"I like you, Bethy," Anna told her. "You don't need to try so hard. Why are you leaving Glen Canyon? Your season isn't up until the end of September."

"I quit three weeks ago. Regis comes from money. His grandfather is, like, real rich. Regis can't have it till he's thirty or worse and jumps through hoops and stuff, but he gets some now, and I've always wanted to study cooking, you know, like a real chef school? Like in Paris? Regis wants me to have that, so . . . off I go to do it," she finished with a shrug. "Regis is like that, you know, with me? He's always doing things just to make me happy."

And a bright, bright smile. Anna didn't even have to work at it to see the brittle edges.

Bethy's smile slipped, then vanished. The dream vacation smacked more of an exile. Maybe Regis had thrown her out. Maybe he was sending her off to rehab for one addiction or another. Maybe he "needed space" and Bethy was going home to Mom until he came to his senses. Whatever it was, Anna doubted the Parisians would be introduced to hash brown casserole anytime soon.

"I brought some food and gear and stuff," Bethy said. Anna was relieved she'd returned to real-world subjects. "I was hoping we could do another canyon together so you'd remember me different, not like the total spaz I was last time?" Her voice went up at the end in a question. The look on her face was so beseeching it reminded Anna of a ham actor—but a very fine singer—in a production of *My Fair Lady* she'd stagemanaged. When he sang "On the Street Where You Live," his mugging made him resemble a particularly needy dog.

That same look was all over Bethy's face.

Anna caved without even a token struggle. "Sounds like fun. Let me get my shoes."

Hugging the canyon walls, Bethy piloted the Zodiac uplake, then turned into the mouth of Panther Canyon. There were several good slot canyons in Panther. It surprised Anna when Bethy passed them up to nose the Zodiac into the blocked slot where Anna and Jenny nearly lost their lives, and the college boys did.

"Isn't this a little macabre?" Anna asked as Bethy sprang to the sandstone step at the base of the obstruction and began looping the bow line around a rock.

"What's 'macabre'?" Bethy asked as she finished and started up the giant's stairsteps.

Nothing else to do, Anna followed her. "Creepy. Gruesome. Grim. Horrible. Ghastly."

"Why is it all those things?" Bethy asked, stopping on the top, hands on hips.

Anna joined her, not in the least winded, and remembered how short of breath the climb left her the last time. "Believe it or not, Bethy, some people think corpses and near-death experiences are off-putting," she said.

In the morning light, the rectangle of water and the narrow slot beyond—grown terrifying in Anna's memory—didn't look all that sinister.

"I guess," Bethy said, sounding unconvinced, "but that was just then and this is a real cool climb. I thought you'd like to, you know, do it because last time . . . you know. Like you're supposed to get back on the horse? Come on," Bethy said, maybe realizing choosing this particular canyon wasn't in the best of taste. "I got another idea. Way easier and prettier. We can do it in a couple of hours." She started down the steps, sitting down on the lip of each and then hopping to the next.

Anna stayed where she was.

The water, black as squid ink, cold, and bottomless in her mind, was turquoise in the sunlight and unbelievably clear. Gold sandstone walls shimmered beneath the surface, water acting as a magnifying glass, until the drowned canyon seemed more real and inviting than that above the lake. Canyon walls, leaning, waiting to snap shut like the jaws of a hungry alligator on the edge of her dreams, soared in the varied hues of a sepia rainbow to a ribbon of achingly blue sky. At the far end of the crystalline pool, the crooked narrow slot Anna remembered as a torture chamber worthy of the

Spanish Inquisition was a shadowed lane of water that drifted from turquoise to teal as it meandered deeper into the rock.

It was morning, not evening. They had the entire day before them. Anna's shoulder was healed, and she was stronger than she'd ever been.

"I do want to get back on the horse," she said to Bethy, who was standing below, near the bow of the Zodiac.

"Goody," Bethy said. "It'll be cool. You'll see." She snatched a bulky daypack and a coil of climbing rope with carabiners affixed to either end out of the inflatable boat and brought them along with Anna's pack to the top of the sandstone blocks.

A rope had been looped over the stone to replace the one that had gone missing the night Anna and Jenny were stranded. It was new and the knot properly tied. Anna checked it anyway. Butterflies the size of bats were fluttering madly in her stomach. Fear, yes, but mostly excitement. This slot, this climb: It was what she needed to do. One day, someday, maybe even this day, she would go back to the jar and exorcise the demons that remained there.

Bethy pulled a green garbage bag from her pack, then put the pack and rope inside it. "Anything you wanna keep dry?" she asked. Anna put her daypack in with Bethy's. The water bottle on her belt wouldn't suffer from a dunking. Bethy closed the sack by tying a knot in its neck. That done, she attached the awkward bundle to a belt loop on the waistband of her shorts with another carabiner.

As Bethy descended the sheer eight feet of sandstone to the water, Anna again inspected the rope and
the knot. Nothing short of human intervention would
loosen it, and the men responsible for Kay's death were
dead. Anna had seen them. She reminded herself of this
fact when the stomach butterflies threatened to rush up
her esophagus along with coffee and a raisin cinnamon
bagel.

"Don't be such a slowpoke!" Bethy called back as
she frog-stroked across the rectangular pool toward the
slit in the stone.

Taking a deep breath, and bracing herself for the
cold, Anna climbed down. In her mind this rock wall
was a thousand feet high. In reality, by the time she
was an arm's length from the top, her toes were in
the water.

The water wasn't as cold as she remembered, nor the
swim to the slot as long. Reality was going to go a long
way toward defanging her nightmares. As they were
passing through—as opposed to trying to defy gravity
by suspending themselves between—the canyon walls,
they made short work of the twenty yards of sinuous
swimming to where the canyon closed down tightly.

At water level the crack was no more than six inches
wide. Four feet up it opened to where a human being of
average size could fit in sideways. Fifteen feet higher
and the walls bulged away from the crevice as if an
enormous balloon had pushed them out. High in the
shadows, they flowed back together, leaning in like
dancers and shutting out the thread of blue sky.

Bethy tossed the line with the carabiners over an

anchor of bleached driftwood a couple of yards above water level and began climbing.

"This isn't the best for climbing," Bethy said, "but use the rope and be sure and test every hand- or foothold, like, twice before you trust it. Some stuff is stuck real tight and that's okay. Some tries to get you." She made it up, the dead tree, her feet out of sight beyond the branch. Braced against the east wall of the crevice, she began unclipping the garbage bag with their daypacks from her waistband.

Anna climbed up easily.

"Looks pretty bitey, huh?" Bethy asked happily, glancing over her shoulder into the gloom.

"Exceedingly bitey," Anna agreed. In the surreal passage debris had collected, some half submerged in the water-filled six-inch crack at the bottom, others wedged at varying levels: entire trees, mangled and dry as bone; rocks; what appeared to be part of an ancient rusted cookstove; the bones of a raccoon or bobcat scattered like caltrops. The crack was not full, not like a junkyard or a garbage can. It was like a gauntlet devised by a particularly malicious child. It was not a place a barefoot woman in bra and panties would want to travel alone in the dark, even if she could have attained the crack without a rope.

Since their bonding in the cold water and colder prospects, Anna had suffered a sneaking suspicion that Jenny could have climbed out but stayed because of her. Knowing Jenny told the truth when she insisted she couldn't freed Anna of a load of gratitude too heavy to comfortably bear.

Bethy gave Anna her pack, shouldered her own, and led off down the crevice. Following, Anna marveled at the human body, at her own body, the way ankles and feet moved to catch an angled stone, knees braced against walls, hands and fingers clutched and spread catching the weight of an ever-changing center of gravity. In a more sedentary life it had been easy to forget a body's miraculous engineering and notice only its small uncomfortable failures.

Within two hours they had traversed the slot with no more mishaps than a bit of flesh peeled off the inside of Anna's ankle by a deer antler wedged with a single prong above the strangled line of water.

For several yards near the end, the slot opened up to the width of two midsized sedans parked side by side, then dead-ended. In that dead end was a three-sided cavity running straight up for fifty or sixty feet. The wide area where they stood was dry and littered with stones and broken branches smashed when the rains carried them over the fall to shatter at the bottom.

The three-sided cavity, a chimney twenty yards high, and the circumference of a phone booth, had formed when a vein of weaker stone broke from the rest of the rock face.

"It's good to see the sky," Anna said, tilting her head back to admire the patch of blue the wider section allowed.

"You wanna eat lunch down here or up there?" Bethy asked.

"Up there," Anna said immediately. Much as she had enjoyed the journey through the center of the earth, she was looking forward to having room to fill her lungs completely and focus her eyes more than a foot or two from the tip of her nose.

"This chimney is super high, like, one of the longest ones here," Bethy told her, "but it's pretty easy. It's easier than the first one we did. That one was just shorter. Once you get going there'll be lots of good places for your feet and hands to be at." She pointed nearly straight up. "See that poke-outance there at the top where the chimney becomes like a weensy crack?"

Anna followed where Bethy pointed and saw a thin blue line on the rock. From where they stood it looked no more substantial than a thread.

"That rope is tied on the top and falls into where the chimney ends there. See? That's how we go the last ten feet. Last one up is a sore loser," Bethy said and, stepping into the bottom of the chimney like Clark Kent into a phone booth, began to ascend rapidly.

For several minutes Anna just watched. To watch anyone perform with such confidence and grace was a pleasure. In these narrow stone canyons Bethy was at her best. A vision of hippopotamuses, lumbering on land, rotund ballerinas beneath the water, made Anna smile.

When Bethy was about halfway up, Anna stepped in the chute and began to climb, albeit more slowly. As Bethy had promised, there were lots of good foot- and handholds and the regularity of the chimney's size and shape lent a sense of security, which, climbing sixty feet with no belay, Anna deeply appreciated.

As she ascended, the view of the slot canyon changed.

By the time she neared the top of the chimney she was looking down on the torturous route they'd just traversed: A dark crack in the pale stone that snaked, curling almost back on itself in one place, slithered out, then ended abruptly in hard blue sky. That would be the top of the rectangular pool, Anna guessed, where the true skinny slot began. Beyond, hidden from view, would be the block of stone that dammed the canyon and nearly damned Anna and Jenny.

From above, the distances appeared paltry, Panther Canyon, with its beautiful grotto, so close it was hard to imagine how two people had died and two more had almost died, so near civilization.

"I'm going to eat your half of the potato chips if you don't hurry up," Bethy called.

Anna looked up. Bethy had vanished from sight over the rim of the plateau. The rope was still twitching like a cat's tail. As Anna watched, it began to snake upward, the end of it flipping as it was hauled up. "Very funny," Anna shouted. A shiver welled up from the depths of the jar that still existed within her. It wasn't funny, not at all. Anna climbed, fear giving her tired muscles added power.

"Just kidding," Bethy laughed. The rope dropped again. Within seconds Anna had grabbed it, relief palpable in the tremor that took her when her fist closed around it.

Some kindly soul had knotted it every foot or so to make climbing it less hazardous. Deciding that looking down would be foolhardy, Anna turned her back on the void and grasped the first knot.

From above she heard the unmistakable rattle of a bag of potato chips being torn open; then came Bethy's voice. "I'm eating 'em!"

Bethy sounded like a little kid. "Don't you dare," Anna called back. Hands moving from knot to knot, feet scrabbling on the last of the chimney, she began the short ascent. Once she'd cleared the rectangular chimney she used feet and thighs on the rope as well. The distance wasn't great, no more than a few yards. Within minutes she'd reached the rim.

"That was quick," Bethy said and smiled. "You got to kind of kick and crawl over the edge on your elbows. Here, lemme help." She dropped to her knees and took a firm grip on Anna's wrist.

Before Anna could say, "Thank you," Bethy's free hand flipped a clink of glittering silver metal from the backpack at her side. Handcuffs. In less time than it took Anna to realize what they were, Bethy had snapped them on her wrists.

"What are you doing?" Anna asked, dumbfounded. Fear followed on the heels of shock, and Anna pulled hard on the rope, dragging one elbow over the sharp lip of stone topping the cliff. Bethy, face intent, movements sure, snatched the rope with the carabiners tied to either end from beside her, threaded it between Anna's cuffed wrists, and clicked the carabiners together, making a loop. That done, she removed herself from Anna's limited field of vision.

Saving her breath for the work, Anna pushed on a knot with her feet and got her other elbow over the top. With a strength that surprised her, she closed her manacled hands around the next knot and yanked hard enough that she landed herself like a fish, belly-down on the plateau.

"God damn it, Bethy," she grunted as she pushed herself to her knees.

She looked up in time to see Bethy's foot coming at her face. Her nose exploded in pain and blood and she toppled backward.

Her hands slipped on the knots and she couldn't close them tightly enough to stop the rope from paying out through her hands.

Then the rope was gone and she was falling.

FORTY-EIGHT

Anna shouted what she believed was her last soliloquy on earth: "Shiiiit!" Not even fit to carve on a tombstone. Scarcely had the word passed her lips than her fall was stopped with bone-snapping abruptness. Again Anna screamed, wordlessly this time, as pain seared from her broken nose and shoulder sockets through every cellular matrix in her body.

She thought she'd surely die of it, but, like a whack to the crazy bone or a little toe jammed into a table leg, intense as it was, the agony passed through her and was gone. More or less gone. Her nose still throbbed, blood dripped salty onto her lips, and her wrists ached furiously where the handcuffs cut into them.

Deadweight, her body bumped gently against the sandstone, breasts, belly, and knees, as gravity settled her. Tilting her head back, she tried to make sense of the last few seconds. Her wrists were cuffed, a rope looped through them that ran in two lines toward the lip of the canyon, no more than five feet from the tips of her fingers. Bethy had made a loop of the rope with the carabiners and thrown it over a rock to anchor it before she kicked Anna back into the void.

Hung out to dry, Anna thought idiotically.

Bethy's face popped over the horizon of Anna's world, round and peering down, giving Anna the view babies in bassinet have of their mothers.

"You're stupid," Bethy said cheerfully. "You think you're so smart, but you're stupid. Stupider than stupid."

Anna looked down past her toes, dangling fifty feet above a litter of shattered wood and stone. "I can't disagree with you there," she said.

The worst of the shock passed. The worst of the pain, Anna suspected, yet to come, fear and fury and confusion had space to explode through her with such force she jerked on the line like a landed fish. Bethy giggled.

The Perils of Pauline, Anna thought, and for a moment sheer embarrassment at her predicament stopped the avalanche of more logical miseries.

She breathed in through her nose slowly and out through her mouth more slowly still, trying to quiet the shrieking in her skull. A pathetic semblance of calm regained, she tried to think of her options.

"Are you passed out or something?" Bethy asked from above. She sounded annoyed and, maybe, a little concerned.

Anna ignored her and began her list. She could beg. Begging never worked in the movies, but in real life it was occasionally efficacious.

"Hey!" Bethy snapped. "Talk to me. No naps! No naps!"

Anna gave no sign she heard. Playing possum was an option, but only if the possum wasn't strung over a chasm by her little possum paws.

"Stop it," Bethy shouted and plucked the rope looped through the chain between Anna's handcuffs. "You better not've had a heart attack and died." Bethy's voice was graveled with fury.

Anna could try talking Bethy into letting her go. Given Bethy's rope was all that kept her from death by falling, being "let go" didn't sound as appealing as it might have. Anna slid her eyes to the left. Nothing inspirational. To the right, a couple of feet away, was the knotted rope. If she could reach it with her foot, there was a chance she could pull it over far enough to get her fingers on it. She might be able to work her way up. Even just to the first knot would relieve the pressure on her wrists.

As she watched, the knotted rope began to twitch and dance against the cliff. From overhead came Bethy's singsong voice: "I know what you're thinking." The rope twitched and danced up past Anna's eyes, then flipped over the rim. First the gravelly anger, now the childish singsong. The change was jarring.

A last option came to mind. Anna doubted it was any more promising than the others, but she could try to reason with Bethy. Letting her head fall back, she looked into the gloating eyes of her erstwhile pal. "Why are you doing this?" she asked.

Bethy's eyes narrowed slightly as if she suspected this was a trick question. Anna tried to look open and nonjudgmental. In case Bethy could see the repressed fury burning behind her eyes, Anna focused a few inches above the floating head.

"I know what you are," Bethy said as if that explained her actions. "You lied. You told me you were a dyke and hated men."

"I did not!" Anna exclaimed. Of all the reasons Bethy might have listed for dangling Anna over a chasm, that hadn't been one she'd thought of.

Bethy's bizarrely childlike expression turned mean. "Yes. You. Did."

Anna knew she hadn't. She also knew it mattered not one whit. Because she and Jenny were close, and because she didn't vehemently deny being homosexual, in Bethy's mind it was the same as saying she was.

"Maybe it wasn't a lie," Anna tried. "Maybe I was telling the truth." To be or not to be gay, that was the question. Which answer might save her life?

"Nope. You lied. I tried to kiss you and you wouldn't let me," Bethy said.

"Gay or straight, you're the last person on earth I'd want to kiss," Anna snapped.

That was the wrong thing to say.

Bethy spit in Anna's upturned face and withdrew her head from view.

A sigh was ordered up by Anna's brain to express the utter futility of trying to communicate with the Bethys of the world. Her lungs did not follow through. Suspended with her arms over her head was making breathing difficult. Circulation cut off by the cuffs, her hands were growing numb. Soon she would not be able to climb up even if Bethy threw her the rope.

"Do you think I was trying to steal your husband?" Anna asked. That was the only misapprehension she could think of that might have triggered Bethy's psychosis. Not for a second did she doubt that Bethy Candor was in the midst of a full-blown psychotic episode.

Bethy didn't reappear. Anna strained to hear her. Paper crackled. Bethy hadn't left.

"What are you doing?" Anna called.

"I'm eating your potato chips," Bethy yelled back, her voice full of malice. "I'm going to eat your whole lunch."

"Then what?" Anna asked.

"Then we wait for my husband," Bethy said, her words slightly garbled as if she spoke around a mouthful of food.

What then? Anna wondered but did not ask.

Bethy fell silent. Impotent rage drained from Anna. Its place was filled by helpless confusion. Years of listening to her sister had taught Anna that mental illness was more widespread than one might think. Those with sociopathic tendencies or narcissistic leanings were often presidents, superstars, business moguls. Powerful men with destructive sex addictions were in the news every other week. Lots of people were crazy in lots of ways, most of them damaging but still socially acceptable—or at least not illegal. Mental illness was as common as the cold, but full-blown homicidal maniacs were rare.

The boys who'd assaulted and killed Katherine—Kay—Nelson wouldn't be considered insane. Brutish, certainly, but rape was a constant the world over. From what Anna'd seen, the murder wasn't intentional, merely a by-product of anger. Rotten as shoving her and Kay into the solution hole was, it made sense in the pseudo-sanity of human existence: a crime covered up, a witness silenced, a consequence avoided.

Stripping a woman naked, drugging her, and carving WHORE into her flesh should definitely be considered serious symptoms of major psychosis. Letting two college boys die of drowning and hypothermia was also a tad too far from the norm to be considered sane.

Along with everyone else, Anna had laid the blame at the feet of the conveniently suicidal unsub three, Jason Mannings, the boy with the acne.

That was one psychopath.

Bethy made two.

Two, both bent on tormenting Anna, was too much, too many, the audience wouldn't buy it. Anna didn't buy it.

An anomaly that had been tacitly ignored flared in her maelstrom of thought: the box of her belongings, packed and sealed and addressed to her sister in New York. Due to the jangle of jurisdictions, the paucity of investigators, and a general wish of all concerned to put the tragic incident behind them, the mystery of who had cleared out Anna's room had been mostly ignored. The fact that it didn't make a whole lot of sense had been glossed over.

Bethy could easily have done it.

Bethy or Regis.

"You're the reason Regis hit me," Bethy said, breaking into Anna's distractions.

"I am?" Anna called back to keep the conversation going. Bethy's chatter might be enough to cover the noises she was about to make.

"Yeah. He didn't like that I was spending time with you. He hates you. He said you're ugly as dog shit on the side of a new shoe."

Anna was swinging gently, pumping her legs to propel her body back and forth across the cliff face like a metronome. Despite weeks of physical training, she would need momentum. She only had the strength for one good try. Gravity was a lot higher in the real world than it was in the weight room.

"And you're the reason Regis is sending me away. He thinks I shouldn't be around you. Regis hates your guts."

"Sure sounds like it," Anna said and hoped Bethy didn't hear the effort in her voice. At the top of her truncated swing, Anna bent in half, throwing her legs upward above her hands. One heel missed. The other went between the two lines tethering her to the cliff top. Before her strength failed, Anna managed to bend her knee, catching the rope behind it.

Now she hung by her wrists and one knee. The relief to her blood-starved hands was immediate. Inch by inch she pulled her upper body skyward with her manacled hands and the muscles of her stomach and back. Sweating, smothering lungs that wanted to gasp for breath, she got herself upright, straddling the rope, her hands clamped at eye level around one of the lines. Stable, she let herself rest and tried to remember what Bethy had done.

She'd linked the carabiners, then thrown the looped rope over a rock the size and shape of a big television set. If Anna tried to climb one rope, it was possible that the loop would slip and Anna would be in much the same situation as a hamster running on a wheel.

"Regis thinks you're a whore," Bethy gloated. Food still factored into her diction, but a packed lunch could only last so long.

Forcing herself to move, Anna dragged one foot up, knee under her chin, and pressed the sole of her sneaker against the line, heel in her crotch, toe pointed out. "I figured as much," she called up to Bethy. WHORE, Regis had cut it into her flesh. He hadn't come to rescue her; he'd come *back* either to harm her further or finish her off.

"W-H-O-R-E. All capital letters so's everybody would know what you were."

Despite the heat and exertion, suddenly Anna felt chilled. The healing cuts had not been reported, nor had Anna worn anything short or sheer enough that they could be seen.

"Regis tell you that?" she asked, then sucked in a breath of air, held it, and pushed up with every aching ounce of strength in her butt and thigh. Pressure on the rope through the sole of her foot, she dared pull up harder with her hands and arms without the fear of shifting the rope loop and warning Bethy that she was moving. That or it would spill her out of her single-thread hammock and leave her again dangling like a trout on a line. She would not have the strength to perform this mutant high-wire act a second time.

"No, stupid, I told Regis you were a whore." Bethy laughed. Paper was being crumpled, wadded up. Lunch must be at an end.

Anna was upright, her leg trembling. She jammed her other foot in the rope stirrup and looked up. The top of her head was only a few inches beneath the sharp stone lip where the plateau fell away into the canyon. Her toes and knees pressed hard against the rock, she leaned into the cliff, letting it steady and support her. Her wrists were slightly above her head, one on either side of the looped rope. Anna wondered if Bethy had packed two lunches and eaten them both, or if she guessed Anna would opt to dine above the slot canyon. Then she wondered why the human brain would wonder over trivia when it might be smashed like a melon in the next few minutes.

"It was me that cut you. It was me Pizza Face ratted out his buddies to, it was me. All me. You should've seen yourself. Pathetic!" It sounded like Bethy was standing up.

"Did you bury Kay?" Anna asked, afraid no response would bring Bethy back to the cliff edge.

"Shut up," Bethy said. "I gotta pee." Anna heard her footsteps walking away, the need to hide behind a rock or bush for the private act apparently unabated by the fact there was no one to see her for miles in any direction.

This was it. This was the chance gamblers bet on. Mentally walking with Bethy, Anna pictured her stopping as the faint crackle of her shoes on the sand ceased, pictured her undoing her belt, unbuttoning her shorts, unzipping, pulling shorts and panties down, and squatting. She would get no more vulnerable than that.

Anna shoved her cuffed hands over the lip of the canyon, forcing the chain to move under the taut rope. Skin was scraped from her forearms; she didn't feel it, just noted the red streaking the dirt.

Closing her fists around the rope as far as she could reach, she levered herself up by her forearms, her feet scrabbling for purchase. The loop of rope, no longer stretched and held by her weight, whipped around her legs. Then her chest was on solid ground. Sweat blinded her, and dirt was scoured into her mouth as she grunted and gasped for breath. Her belly was on the plateau. Only her legs and feet still hung over the sixty-foot drop.

"What're you doing?" she heard Bethy call. "Are you doing something?"

No breath to spare for an answer, Anna dragged herself a few more inches and twisted. One foot, one knee, a leg, jackknifed on the tableland.

"No!" she heard Bethy yell. Anna didn't dare pause to look up. With an effort that wrenched a scream from her as muscles in the small of her back tore, she got her other leg up on the plateau and began to belly-crawl from the edge of the ravine, her manacled hands scraping across the broken landscape. The earth, mere inches from her eyes, unrolled with agonizing slowness, inches only as Bethy's furious shriek, guttural, then high like the war cry of a banshee, pulled the oxygen from her lungs and the blood from her heart.

FORTY-NINE

At one thirty Regis realized he'd forgotten to eat lunch. He'd been on the phone interviewing a fascinating woman in Olympic National Park for the district ranger position at Dangling Rope. The woman was eminently qualified but hadn't a snowball's chance in hell of getting the job. Three veterans were blocking the register. Vietnam had dumped an endless supply of vets into the federal system, and they got preferential treatment. If they all dropped dead, he still doubted she'd get it. He didn't think Glen Canyon had ever had a female district ranger and doubted Andrew Madden was chomping at the bit to change that during his tenure.

At one thirty-two Regis was unrolling the top of a paper bag, soft from being reused a number of times, to see what his wife packed him for lunch.

At one thirty-four he was running from his office, ignoring startled looks from the people he passed.

At the small municipal airport on the outskirts of Page he untied his Super Cub, started the engine, and cleared for taxi, without pausing for a preflight check, a flight plan, or even to close the clamshell doors.

Folded on top of his tuna sandwich had been a note: "Hi Baby! Meet me at the head of Panther. I got a surprise for you! xxxooo Bethy." He thought he would faint or vomit as he'd raced to the airport, but the fear solidified into a column of ice that ran from rectum to sternum.

Takeoffs and landings were a point of pride with him. An airship was most at risk when moving from one element to the other, from earth to sky and back again. The rest was easy. This time he didn't so much take off as jerk the airplane off the runway and stagger into the sky. In the superheated air of the desert there was little lift. Fear of wrecking the Cub shoved aside the panic of Bethy's upcoming "surprise" for a tense thirty seconds until he got enough air under the wings to stabilize the plane.

He was already late. Usually he ate lunch around twelve thirty. Bethy knew that. Bethy might have waited for him. He hung on to that thought as he climbed free of the traffic pattern and leveled off at seventy-five hundred feet on a north-by-northeasterly heading. Once across the bottom of the reservoir, he turned right, flying along the jagged northern shoreline. Winds over the lake were unpredictable. Besides, he didn't particularly want anyone to recognize his plane and wonder what he was up to in the middle of a workday.

The Piper Cub, built in the fifties, wasn't a fast plane. Her top speed was around seventy miles per hour, slower than most cars on the road. Push the throttle as much as he might, the flight to Hole-in-the-Rock Road, and the head of Panther Canyon, took the better part of an hour. Hot wind and engine noise buffeted Regis through the open doors, sucking the moisture from his lungs and fanning the flames of a vicious headache, but he couldn't focus long enough to wrestle them closed.

Forcing calm, he made himself execute a neat pattern over Hole-in-the-Rock Road. The prevailing wind was from the north. He touched down near the canyon rim and slowed. Chafing, he turned and taxied back toward Glen Canyon. When he ran out of dirt road, he jumped from the Cub and chocked the wheels as best he could with rocks.

Hands on a wing strut, he ceased his frantic movement for a moment, staring at the ecru sand between his feet, trying to make room in his mind for thought.

His head jerked, and his hands fell from the aluminum wing support. Moving deliberately he opened a small baggage compartment behind the rear seat and lifted out his desert survival pack, a precaution most small-plane pilots took in rugged country.

Having ripped open the Velcro straps, he folded back the flap and removed the hunting knife in its leather sheath. He didn't thread his belt through the loop on the sheath. He unbuttoned a shirt button and pushed the knife in where it could ride between belt and belly.

After closing and restowing the survival kit, Regis headed toward the head of the slot canyon that eventually widened out into Panther.

He did not run but walked, swift and sure.

FIFTY

Enraged, Bethy descended on Anna like a hoard of furies, kicking dirt in her face, kicking her head and ribs and back. Reflexively, Anna curled into a ball to protect her belly, her hands closed over her skull, forearms over her face, letting her daypack absorb the worst of the blows.

For a fraction of time the kicks ceased; then a jack-hammer blow hit her shoulders. Half stunned, Anna felt herself shoved nearer the precipice. Another blow and another few inches. Until she'd hit Regis with the canteen and rolled rocks down on him, Anna had never struck out at anyone in anger, at least not since she was three and beaned Jimmy Newton with a dirt clod. The beast instinct had not atrophied. Time to fight or die.

Rolling to elbows and knees, she sustained another shattering blow that nearly knocked her back to her side. Refusing to let the shock nullify her mind, Anna forced herself out of her defensive position. The instant her head came up she could see what Bethy was doing. She'd dropped to the ground and, propped on elbows and back, was using the powerful muscles in her legs to drive Anna over the edge.

Thrusting out with her toes, Anna lunged forward, sprawling on her attacker. Bethy's bunched legs pistoned into Anna's midsection. Gasping for breath, Anna fell to the side, her shoulder slamming into Bethy's. Before the other woman could recover, Anna slipped her manacled hands over Bethy's head, trapping her in a mockery of a lover's embrace.

"If I go over, I'm not going over alone," she promised in a voice more akin to an animal's growl than a human utterance.

Thrashing and bucking, Bethy tried to head-butt, tried to force her knees between their bodies. Chin tucked protectively into her shoulder, Anna hung on, hugging Bethy more tightly. Screaming, Bethy turned in Anna's arms and tried to crawl away.

Quick as a cat, Anna was on her back, her legs wrapped around Bethy's waist, the chain between the handcuffs jerked tightly across her throat. As Bethy ran out of oxygen, the fight went out of her. Finally, she collapsed, facedown in the dirt, Anna riding her like a demented jockey. Muscles spent, throat dry and raw, it was all Anna could do not to collapse on top of her. The battle had lasted less than sixty seconds, yet both women were utterly spent. Fleetingly, Anna thought to mention this fact to the fight choreographer.

"Uncle," Bethy muttered, a puff of dust rising with the word.

"Uncle" was what children cried when they lost a wrestling match. Fury, smothered until now by fear and exhaustion, roared up from the paltry reserves of Anna's strength. Tightening the chain across Bethy's throat, she croaked, "Uncle, my ass. You tried to kill me."

"I didn't, though," Bethy managed. "So you can't strangle me to death."

Anna wasn't sure of the legalities of that argument and at the moment didn't care. During the brawl they'd tumbled up against the TV-shaped boulder Bethy had looped the rope around. Grunting, Anna rolled herself and an inert but conscious Bethy Candor over and sat up. Wriggling back against the rock, Anna used her daypack—effectively locked onto her when her hands were cuffed—as a cushion. She dragged Bethy with her, squeezing until the other woman was sitting between her legs, Anna's still locked around her middle, the cuff chain hard against her throat.

Slowly, their breathing returned to normal. Twice Bethy struggled, and twice Anna tightened the chain around her neck until she became docile.

With air and rest came thought. Anna's first was: Like a dog chasing a car. She'd caught Bethy. Now what? If she let loose of her, she didn't doubt Bethy would try to kill her again. Anna was strong now, but Bethy was bigger and heavier and younger. In a fair fight Bethy would win. So fighting fair was out. Anna'd always thought it was silly anyway, like the rules of war. War was war; the point was to kill and prevail via the use of force. Pretending to do it in a civilized manner was a sop to the conscience of killers.

Continuing to sit stalemated indefinitely, they would die of thirst before anybody came upon them. Already

Anna felt she was dying of thirst, though she knew she had many hours of torture to look forward to before she would actually expire.

The rope running between her cuffed wrists inspired her. Gathering a length of it, she began pulling it through her hands, dragging the loop around the rock they leaned against, moving the circle of rope.

"What're you doing?" Bethy asked.

"Making us more comfortable," Anna lied.

"You better let me go," Bethy warned, but she made no effort to escape. "Regis is coming, and he's going to make you let me go."

"That so?" Anna wondered if it was true. More rope paid out between her hands. She felt her senses split, the hands working toward one goal, the rest of her alert to any change in her prisoner that might signify imminent danger.

"Yup. It sure is," Bethy said with a smugness Anna found alarming. "He's going to kill you," she announced with satisfaction. "That's why I didn't just kill you right away. I was saving you so he could do it."

"That was nice of you," Anna said. A clink of metal let her know the carabiners affixed to the ends of the rope were moving closer.

"I'm a nice person," Bethy said with what sounded like absolute sincerity.

The carabiners were in sight. Bethy reached out and grabbed them.

"Let go." Anna tightened the chain.

"Bitch," Bethy gasped and let the interlocked carabiners drop.

Two more pulls and Anna had them in her hands. Fingers thick with dust and aching from dragging the rope, she fumbled the carabiners open with difficulty and broke the loop. Before Bethy could get any ideas, Anna whipped one end of the rope around her neck and clicked the carabiner back on to it. An effective noose created, she jerked it tight.

"What are you doing?" Bethy screeched and reached up to claw at the rope around her neck.

"Shut up," Anna said. "Hands down."

Bethy did as she was told. Despite the fact Anna had her in a stranglehold, and had a slip knot around her windpipe, the lack of fight was worrying. Maybe Bethy hadn't been bluffing, and Regis was coming to murder her. A couple's bonding experience. Shared interests were important in a marriage.

Shoving that thought aside, Anna lifted her manacled wrists and arms from around Bethy. Too long held above the level of her heart, the hands were beginning to numb. Needles of feeling prickled as blood flowed back in. With the heels of her hands she shoved Bethy off her chest, jackknifing her nose toward her knees while keeping the slip knot around her neck tight.

"Give me the key to the handcuffs," Anna demanded.

"I don't—"

Anna jerked on the slip knot she'd made with the carabiner. She hated doing it, hated choking Bethy. The temptation to pull the rope tight enough to kill the horrid woman was too great. Each time Bethy forced her to do it, it was a little harder to back off the pressure when Bethy became compliant. The need to kill wasn't fueled merely by anger but by exhaustion. Anna wasn't sure how much longer she could maintain the upper hand.

"Key," Anna demanded.

Bethy reached into her trouser pocket, contorting her upper body since Anna had no intention of allowing her to sit up straight or lean back against her. As Bethy's hand began to pull free, Anna tweaked the rope enough to get her attention. "If you even look like you're thinking of tossing that key into the canyon I will kill you without a qualm."

"You don't need a qualm, you've got a *rope*," Bethy grumbled.

The key was out; pinched between her fingers, she lifted it toward her shoulder. The instant Anna reached for it Bethy turned her head and popped the tiny silver key into her mouth. Any shred of conscience that remained to Anna burned off like sulfur off a match. Bracing her knuckles against Bethy's neck, she pulled the rope so hard the other woman's flesh popped through the carabiner next to her spine.

"Spit it out," Anna said; venom through clenched teeth.

Bethy spat it out.

"Give it to me."

Bethy gave it to her. Anna unlocked the cuffs carefully. The lock was easy but the mechanics of the handcuffs unfamiliar. When they were off, she dropped them over Bethy's shoulder into her lap.

"Put them on."

Bethy put them on.

Working as quickly as she could, Anna wrapped the long rope around and around her prisoner, trussed her up the way people in cartoons were trussed, with coil after coil pinning her arms to her body. When she was nearly out of rope she wove the other end, with the mate to the carabiner serving as a noose, through several coils on Bethy's back and clipped it to the rope still circling her throat.

"If you struggle you will slowly strangle yourself," Anna said. She didn't know if that was true or not, but Bethy apparently believed her. As Anna backed away on shaking legs, Bethy sat perfectly still.

With a thump, Anna sat in the dirt and shrugged out of her daypack. Hands finally free, she took her water bottle from its canvas pouch on her belt and, never taking her eyes from Bethy, drained it. She had another in her pack.

Immediately a modicum of strength and sanity flowed back. In grade school she'd learned the human body was 60 percent water. Until she'd known extreme thirst she'd never really appreciated that fact.

"Can I have a drink?" Bethy begged.

"Maybe." Anna eyed her coldly. "If you tell me what is going on with you and Regis."

"We're in love," Bethy said smugly.

Very deliberately Anna rose, crossed to where Bethy's pack lay, took out her water bottle, uncapped it and took a long swallow.

"Bitch," Bethy cried. Anna took another.

"You were doing everything you could to make my *husband* pay attention to you. You were acting like the whore you are," Bethy snapped. "Then this pimply-faced creep told me that him and his pals threw you guys in that hole. I knew it was you. All that skanky red hair and nasty black clothes."

"Why would he tell you?" Anna asked suspiciously.

"Because I was the first uniform he saw, stupid. Visitors don't know law enforcement from interp," Bethy told her with scorn.

"And you told Regis."

Bethy smiled a perceptive close-lipped smile. "That's right, and he hated you and he went to kill you. Now can I have a drink of water?"

The smile bothered Anna, though why, of all the alarming upsetting things about the bad-seed-child in a woman's body, one sneaky little smile should set off alarm bells, she was unsure.

"In a minute," Anna said.

"Now!" Bethy screamed.

Anna just watched her. After a few minutes, she rose, walked to the bound woman, and poured a bottle's cap full of water. Bethy tilted back her head and opened her mouth wide like a baby bird waiting for a bug.

"Don't choke," Anna said and tipped the teaspoon of water in.

"More," Bethy demanded.

Anna ignored her. Sitting down again, sun like molten lead on her head and shoulders, earth nearly as hot beneath her, she studied Bethy. The sneaky smile was what poker players called a "tell." Anna'd seen it before. Bethy did it before she lied.

"You didn't tell Regis, did you?" Anna asked.

"I did, too," Bethy insisted.

No sneaky smile.

"But not right away."

"You won't give me water and I'll die."

For a second Anna thought she was going to burst into tears of self-pity, but she didn't. "You came to the jar first, to make sure the kid was telling the truth, didn't you?" Anna asked.

Bethy's eyes narrowed to reptilian slits in her heat-reddened face.

"If you tell me I'll let you have a real drink," Anna offered. Bethy glared at her, hatred burning in her eyes. "Why not tell me?" Anna asked conversationally. "If Regis really is coming, and really will kill me, it won't make any difference, will it?"

Bethy tried to spit at Anna, but her mouth was too dry.

"Regis likes me," Anna goaded. "He didn't come to the solution hole to kill me. He came because he loves me. Regis brought me water and food. We picnicked and made love."

The struggle in Bethy's face was almost comical in its intensity. Muscles bunched and brow furrowed, lips twisted until it looked as if several personalities were fighting for the same body. Fascinated and repelled, Anna watched. This was something she had to tell Molly.

Careful Bethy lost to Vicious Bethy. "You did not. *I* took your clothes. *I* cut WHORE in you. *I* made you drink shit water. *I* spit in your sandwiches. *I* said when you were supposed to die."

The pure vitriol smacked into Anna's mind. For a minute, she could do nothing but stare at Bethy in revulsion. In all her years watching the best in the business play every villain from Lady Macbeth to Cruella de Vil, Anna had never seen evil. She'd seen actresses playing evil, some of them brilliantly. The real thing wasn't merely something seen; it was a tangible wave felt on exposed skin, on the retinas and the lining of the throat.

Mental illness and evil were not the same. Molly, who dealt with all manner of nutcases on a daily basis, and knew mental illnesses for the diseases they were, also believed in evil, a darkness that transcended the malfunctioning of human brain chemistry. Crazy people, Molly insisted, were only dangerous the way abused dogs and frightened horses were dangerous. In their struggle for what they perceived as necessary for survival, other people occasionally got trampled or bitten.

Evil people hunted and hurt because they hated. Truly evil people did it because it was fun.

Poison washing over her, Anna felt a need to return to the pragmatic.

"How did you find me?" she asked. In the broken pocked landscape, riddled with basins and stones, Anna, with the help of a tracker and two rangers, had had a tough time finding the jar.

"Pizza Face said he didn't know where you were dumped. I made him take me to his guy friends and they showed me," Bethy said with satisfaction. "They couldn't wait for me to see. Then they stripped you naked and raped you a bunch and I did it to you with a stick." She smacked her lips as if the vile words tasted good to her.

Though Anna was about ninety-nine percent sure those things had not been done to her, the shame she'd worked so hard to overcome returned with a vengeance. She breathed through it. When all but the stink of it was gone, she said, "They. You said 'they.' All three of the boys came back with you?"

"Don't you listen? I told you Jason Pizza Face said he hadn't been with the other guys. He was like this big innocent, you know? Just watching and stuff."

The rope wrapped around Bethy was loosening, not because Bethy struggled but because Anna hadn't done a good job of tying her up. Like many other things, tying a person securely was a lot harder than it looked. Before Bethy got free, Anna was going to have to act. In a minute, she promised herself, too tired and hot and freaked out to move.

"Let me get this straight," Anna said with a sigh. "These guys kill a woman and throw the dead and the living women in a hole and they're all Johnny-on-the-spot, gung ho to tell the ranger all about it and lead her to the scene of the crime." Anna pushed herself to her feet, picked up her daypack, and shoved Bethy's half-full water bottle inside. "You're so full of shit I can't stand to be around you. When I get back to the Rope I'll tell Jim Levitt where you are. If I happen to remember." Shrugging into the pack, Anna started southwest toward where the trail led down to Dangling Rope Marina. It was longer and much farther than going by way of the slot canyon and Panther, but she had had her fill of hanging by a thread from high places.

"No!" Bethy shouted, finally sounding afraid. "No. I'll tell you stuff. Real stuff. True and everything."

The note of genuine panic—the first honest emotion Bethy had evinced other than fury and smugness—stopped Anna. She looked back at the filthy woman, trussed up like a cannibal's catch, her skin beginning to burn thought the dust and the sunscreen, and felt a tickling of pity. Not for Bethy. In Anna's opinion she deserved whatever came, as long as it was unpleasant. Pity for the person she would be if she allowed Bethy to die of thirst knowing firsthand what torture it was.

"Tell you what," Anna relented. "I'll split the water with you. You'll be able to wriggle out of your ropes before you die and can drink it then. It will keep you going until somebody comes to get you." She started to fulfill the promise by retrieving her own empty water bottle so she could share what she had.

"No! No," Bethy cried. "Don't leave me alone." Her eyes, beseeching, held Anna's. No sneaky smile. She genuinely was afraid of Anna leaving.

Anna stopped what she was doing, too rattled and weary to think and move simultaneously. Her previous adventures had taught her a little something. She'd left a note telling Jenny she was going canyoneering with Bethy Candor. Of course she hadn't said where because she hadn't known at the time.

Bethy's Zodiac was moored at the sandstone blocks separating Panther from the slot. Jenny was working,

due back at the Rope around six thirty. If she patrolled
Panther today she might even see the Zodiac.

Anna also carried a few more practical things with
her when she was going away from civilization. Besides the additional water, she had matches, a compass,
a Swiss Army knife, a Maglite, granola bars, sunscreen,
a ball cap, ChapStick, and a paperback book—*The
Tenant of Wildfell Hall*. Since last time she'd found
herself on this plateau in the company of persons who
meant her no good, she had become much stronger and
more savvy in survival skills.

Still, unless she ignited a piñon tree with the matches
and Anne Brontë's work, she had no way to let anyone
know where she was. Where they were.

"If I don't leave you, nobody will come find you,"
Anna said reasonably, "and I'm sure as hell not taking
you with me."

"Just stay a little longer," Bethy begged. "Please?
Please? Pretty please with a cherry on top?"

It was quarter past two. There would be enough light
to hike out for another six hours. This time it would not
take Anna twelve hours. Knowing the way, and being
hydrated and fed, she could do it in four. Maybe less.

Bethy's fear and pleading didn't factor into her decision. Bethy's willingness to tell her "real stuff, true and
everything" did. It wasn't in Anna's nature to walk away
before the final scene played out.

Feeling more saintly than she had a right to, Anna
gave Bethy a good long drink of water before she sat
down to finish interrogating her. She opened with "If
I even think you're lying to me, I'm gone." With a

small plane's engine droning in the distance like the buzz of a bluebottle fly, she said, "Start with why those guys agreed to show you my jar."

Had Molly not insisted there was no such thing as multiple personality disorder, Anna would have sworn Bethy Candor suffered from it. The childish talk stopped. The slyness abated. The smugness went into remission. She began to speak as if she sat in the witness box and the truth, the whole truth, and nothing but the truth was the key to her salvation.

"Jason, the boy with the pimples, told me what he and the other two—Caleb and Adam—had done. He wanted me to be sure he hadn't done anything wrong, only watched. He didn't go with the other guys to dump you and that girl in the hole, he said. He didn't know where it was or if you were dead, only that Caleb and Adam said both you and the girl were alive.

"I told Jason I would make things okay because he was a good kid, what with telling me all, and he hadn't done anything wrong and he shouldn't say anything to anybody because not all rangers were as nice as me. So he's a happy camper. I wanted to see, so I made him bring me to his buddies.

"I told them I was a law enforcement ranger and I had got a statement from Jason What's-his-name and they were in a lot of trouble. A *lot* of trouble. Then I said I knew it was an accident and they shouldn't have to go to jail or anything, and if they would show me where you were, I could probably get them off with just a warning or something because they were helping and that showed they were good guys. So they showed me.

Kay was dead and I made them help me bury her, and you were unconscious but sorta started to wake up, so I bonked you with a big rock and took the rock with me when we left. I took your clothes, too."

Boys, scared, guilty, wanting to believe they were going to get off lightly; Anna could see it working the way Bethy said. Right up to the burying and bonking and stripping. "Didn't your little buddies think it kind of un-rangerly when you made them hide the evidence? Lie to me and I'm gone," Anna reminded her.

"I told 'em it would keep the body from rotting and the FBI could see their hitting her was a mistake." Bethy was clearly proud of her abilities to manipulate and prevaricate.

"How about hitting and stripping me? Did you tell them that was standard operating procedure as well?"

"I didn't tell 'em anything. They were stupid, but they kinda knew something was hinky. They just wanted it to be okay, so they pretended it was okay and I pretended it was okay, and we left."

"How did they end up dead in the water?" Anna asked.

"By the time we got out of the slot it was dark. They—Caleb and Adam—were worn out. Doing the slot twice, killing that girl, and chasing you and everything. I knew they couldn't go back up or anything. They were strong, but they didn't know much about the canyoneering stuff.

"I got to thinking they were gonna talk. First time they got drunk they would blabber out everything. Weenies. That couldn't happen. So when I climbed up the sandstone block there at the end, I took up the rope after.

"You found 'em frozen and drowned. I didn't do anything to them. I wasn't even there when they died."

Anna was amazed at Bethy's belief in her own innocence. The phrase "she had no shame" fit the bill. Bethy had no conscience. She did what she did because it was best for her, or she wanted to, or to avoid repercussions. Bethy had reasons for each and every horrific act. Since to Bethy, only Bethy was real, no one else factored into her rationale.

"Yeah," Anna said. "We found them. Was it you who took up the rope and left Jenny and me to die the same way?"

"I'm not responsible for every stupid thing you and *Ms.* Gorman do," she said, suddenly haughty.

In the distance the buzz of the small aircraft, one of the sightseeing concessions, Anna guessed, coughed and went silent. Another day, another time, she might have been concerned that it was going to crash. With her plate already full she didn't give it a second's thought.

"So you left the—Adam and Caleb to die, and the next night you came back up to the plateau and cut me?"

"Yup," Bethy said.

"That's a lot of up and down. Nobody can do the slot in the dark. That leaves four and a half miles from the Rope. Nine miles round-trip. I don't believe you," Anna said.

"Well, I did. Maybe I didn't do your stupid nine miles. Maybe I flew up like Tinker Bell."

Tinker Bell. Bethy was a pathological liar. Anna

would get no answers she could trust, and the swift transitions from vicious to begging to sanity to snobbery had her mind reeling. Realizing her curiosity was tethering her to a person so toxic she poisoned the very air around her, Anna rose again.

"Got to go," she said. "I'll send somebody."

Bethy startled her with a giggle. "Too late," she singsonged.

FIFTY-ONE

Anna whipped around to see what Bethy was looking at with such unholy glee.

Regis Candor stood no more than fifty paces away, his face a mask of hatred, his eyes desperate. His hands, hanging limply by his thighs, twitched as if they yearned to be rending something—someone—into small gobbets of flesh.

The growl of the small-plane engine.

The engine cutting off.

The abrupt change in Bethy from cooperating to gloating.

Regis came from money. He owned a tiny airplane.

He'd landed on Hole-in-the-Rock Road the way Hank had.

What had Jenny said? That Bethy Candor had learned to fly—soloed—but never got her license.

Bethy had flown to the plateau to torment Anna in her jar. Just like Tinker Bell.

The thoughts crashed through Anna's skull with the force of bricks knocked from a fifth-floor balcony.

Options dwindled. She didn't have the reserves left

to outrun or outfight Regis. He was fit, fresh, and forty pounds heavier than she was. Her only hope was to disable—or kill—him.

"Hey, Regis," she said, those being the only words available to her at the moment. She hadn't yet shouldered her pack. Clutching it over her stomach, she unzipped the side pocket surreptitiously when Regis looked away from her to where his wife, looking like a giant larva, wriggled in her rope chrysalis.

Bethy fell over on her side and glared at him. "Regis! Help me get out of this," she whined.

His glance came back to Anna. Her fingers closed around the pathetically small Swiss Army knife.

"You didn't tie her up all that well," he said in a cold flat voice.

"Sorry," Anna said. "It's my first time."

He crossed to kneel beside his wife. Anna let the pack fall away and quickly pried out the knife's longest blade. Four inches. It wouldn't cut him much. Not so deep as a well, nor so wide as a church door, Anna thought, but it might serve.

Regis was unclipping the carabiner that held the rope noose around Bethy's throat. His back was to Anna. Moving quietly and quickly she traversed the few yards between them, drawing the knife into striking position—or what she assumed, from watching Anthony Perkins in *Psycho,* was striking position—as she came.

"Are you all right, Anna?" Regis asked without looking back. "I've been worried sick about you."

Anna stopped in her tracks. Would it be worse to be murdered or to murder an innocent man?

The ends of the rope loosed from her throat, Bethy began squirming out of the coils. "Make her give you the handcuff key, baby. She *handcuffed* me!"

Anna reached in the front pocket of her shorts, pinched up the handcuff key, and, with a flick of her wrist, snapped it over the cliff. From the corner of his eye, Regis saw her do it and smiled.

"In a minute," he told his wife. "Let's get you some water first. You just sit still, I mean it."

Bethy kicked away the last bit of the rope and relaxed back against the rock, her legs straight out in front of her like a little girl or a doll. "It's in Anna's pack. Anna stole it. Anna tried to kill me," she told her husband. Her voice quavered with shock and fear, but her lips smirked at Anna and her eyes danced.

Regis returned with the water and blocked Anna's view of Bethy while he gave her a drink.

Regis was here to kill Anna.

Regis was worried sick about Anna.

Bethy had saved Anna for Regis to kill.

Colors got too bright. Rocks shifted and slid. Sunlight hot and hard as a shovel in a coal furnace pressed on the back of her neck. The glare of the sky met the glare of the sandstone, breaking the desert into prisms. Anna staggered.

Too close to the cliff. She turned back.

Bethy, still cuffed, was up and running toward her, a hunting knife clutched in her two raised fists.

She, too, had seen *Psycho*.

Anna was slow. Her mind was slow, her body heavy; she couldn't even draw breath to scream.

"No!" she heard Regis cry. Her peripheral vision blurred. Regis. Flying low to the ground, his shoulder crashing into his wife's hip, a look of shock on her face, the knife falling from her hands as she flew backward, her feet not touching the ground as her body hurtled over the canyon rim, a sound like a watermelon dropped from a sixty-foot tower hitting the sidewalk.

Squatting, Anna put her head down in an attempt to postpone passing out. Giving in to gravity, she allowed herself to fall back on her rump, still hugging her knees.

Regis stood at the edge of the precipice looking down on what was left of his wife. Anna considered shoving him off just to be on the safe side. Given he'd saved her life twice, she decided not to.

He wasn't an innocent man. She sensed that with every nerve in her body. Then again, who was? She'd worked in a scene shop one summer. The foreman believed in hiring ex-cons. "At least you know what they're guilty of," he'd said. "With everybody else you have to guess."

Anna didn't doubt for a second that Bethy Candor intended to stab her to death with that knife, or that Regis Candor had saved her life at the cost of his wife's.

She also didn't doubt that Regis gave Bethy the hunting knife. In the forced intimacy of their struggle, Anna would not have missed a lump of that size, nor would Bethy have hesitated to use it.

Regis turned away from the cliff edge.

"She killed Jenny's snake," he said distantly. "She nailed it to the ground while it was still alive." Jenny had told Anna about that. Wanton cruelty to an animal sickened her more deeply than murder, more deeply than the scars Bethy left in her skin.

"And Kippa," Regis said. "She killed Kippa. Kippa was just a puppy." His eyes shone in the harsh sunlight as they teared up. "She never would have stopped," he said. "It never would have stopped."

Anna nodded, not knowing how thin the ice was or if, indeed, there was any ice at all.

"She left me a note," Regis said. "I flew up. I'll take you to Bullfrog if you want, or back to Wahweap."

His voice sounded mechanical. Anna suspected hers sounded much the same when she said, "I'll walk, thanks."

"Sure," he said. "Sure." He left her sitting in the dirt. When he was out of sight she shoved herself to her feet and began the long walk home.

FIFTY-TWO

Two weeks had passed since Anna watched Regis shove his wife to her death at the bottom of the slot canyon. The same canyon Bethy had used to murder the boys and for the attempted murder of Anna and Jenny Gorman.

Where others expected Anna to be curious, wanting to know every twist and turn of the tale, Anna was indifferent. The indifference wasn't for show. Inside she was indifferent as well. Molly thought it a form of self-preservation. Molly and occasionally Jenny were the only people Anna could discuss the issue with. Law enforcement got the facts that she'd witnessed but nothing more. Joe Friday would have been impressed. At least that's what Steve Gluck told her.

Both she and Jenny were happy to return to the good clean world of excrement and heavy lifting.

Molly postulated that Bethy Candor had a history of psychotic behavior that probably predated killing Kippa and the snake. From the rapid weight loss and other symptoms, she suggested that Bethy might have gone off medication, possibly lithium, any number of tranquilizers, and/or other antipsychotics. Both Anna and Molly suspected a cocktail of these medications had been thrown haphazardly into the canteen Bethy left in the jar for Anna. As to Regis's motivation for rescuing those his wife endangered without resorting to the simple expedient of telling the chief ranger and getting the woman locked up—or at least in for a psych evaluation—they could come up with no cohesive explanation. Love didn't seem to cut it. From what Anna and Jenny had witnessed of the Candors' relationship, Regis didn't even like his wife much.

Anna hadn't seen Regis to ask him since he'd walked away from her on the plateau the day he killed his wife. Given the chance, she doubted she would ask. Molly's job was to figure out why people exhibited insane destructive behaviors. As a lover of the theater, Anna had been fascinated by what drove the human heart to self-destruct. That was over. Now all she cared about was that they be stopped.

Sitting in Steve Gluck's cramped office in Bullfrog, she let these thoughts drift through her mind while she waited for Steve to open the conversation. Jenny was in the barely padded chair next to hers, the space so cramped they couldn't stretch their legs without smacking their toes against the metal desk. The small space was made smaller by detritus and memorabilia collected over forty years in law enforcement and stacked untidily on metal shelves along with manuals on the Park Service way of doing everything from high-angle rescue to cleaning backcountry toilets. In pride of place on top of a scarred beige metal filing cabinet was a battered tan ball cap with OLD SCHOOL embroidered on it, Steve proclaiming where his value system was formed.

Finally Steve spoke. "Here's how things stand. The kid, Jason Mannings, probably didn't jump off the cliff below the dam. It's a good guess Bethy heard all the radio chatter, came to see what was happening, and ran across Jason when he was trying to get away from us. Wrong place, wrong time. He's a link to her; he gets a free ride to a long drop. I told his folks what we suspected. It meant a lot to them that he most likely didn't kill himself, but, as the primary suspect suffered death in the same manner as their son, they may not push it. If they don't, it'll lay around in law enforcement limbo. Anyway, it didn't happen in our jurisdiction. That part of the shore is on the Navajo reservation.

"Regis is no longer with the Park Service. No charges are being filed against him. Anna, by your own admission, Bethy was attacking you with a knife when Regis knocked her into the canyon. You also stated you weren't one hundred percent sure Bethy didn't have the knife on her.

"Andrew and I and Frank from up Escalante way talked about obstruction of justice, failure to report a felony, and a handful of other charges, but the long and short of it is, Regis saved you two and it's possible he didn't know anything about his wife's extracurricular activities until moments before he ran out to see if he could save the day.

"He had provided her with psychiatric care at his own expense earlier in the year. That was verified. And he had booked her into a facility in Virginia. She was

supposed to go in the day after she died. So . . . that's
pretty much that. We did manage to track down her
folks. They hadn't seen her in ten years. They 'emanci-
pated' her when she was fourteen. They wouldn't tell
me why, but my guess is too many of the neighborhood
pets went missing. If anything, they seemed relieved
she was dead."

Anna nodded. This was all blood under the bridge.
Regis had set his wife's murder up by giving her the
knife, but Bethy Candor needed to be killed. In Anna's
conscience it was a wash.

"Wanting to keep it quiet that your wife's crazy isn't
against the law," Steve said, sounding tired and a little
defensive.

"Wasn't there a money thing?" Jenny asked. She had
not been as sanguine as Anna about letting over be over.
The tale of Anna's cliff-top adventures had thrown her
into a fit of growling and hissing that lasted a couple of
days.

"Yeah. We talked with Regis's grandfather and his
mom. The dad is dead, heart attack at forty-one. Granddad didn't give numbers, but it sounded like there was
a lot of money in a trust fund. Regis was to come into it
at thirty, but only if he had a job and a solid marriage.
The old man is big on proving responsibility, gave me
quite a lecture on earning money before you're allowed
to spend it. Regis had the job; he needed the solid marriage. Not exactly a motive for killing his wife."

"Better a heroic widower than the husband of a mur-
dering psychopath," Jenny grumbled.

"Anywho," Steve sighed, putting an end to the discussion of all the bad things he could do nothing about, "I've got the two of you scheduled for critical incident stress counseling—"

"No!" Jenny and Anna said simultaneously.

"Hey, don't bite my head off. New regulations. Something bad goes down, we all have to go in for group hugs," Steve said.

"Have to?" Anna asked. Molly was all the psychiatrist she needed. The thought of telling some fool who didn't know her from Adam, knew nothing of where she'd been or what she'd done, exhausted and annoyed her.

"I won't do it," Jenny said flatly.

Steve leaned back in his chair, the spring groaning pathetically. "I'd recommend it," he said. "It's free, and you bottle this stuff up, you'll be old and fat and tired like me in a few years."

"Are you going?' Anna asked him.

There was a moment of silence. Steve creaked forward and rested his forearms on the desk. "I've got firearms qualifications all that week," he said.

"Bummer," Anna said with a smile. "I've got to wash my hair."

"I've got to help her," Jenny said. "Anna has a lot of hair." Reaching up, she snagged Steve's—OLD SCHOOL cap from the filing cabinet and put it on.

"Suit yourselves," he said. "Can't say I didn't try. Anna, you've had a hell of a season so far, and you've got four more weeks before it's officially over. No one would think less of you if you wanted to leave before that. If you want to come back here—or any other park, for that matter—as a seasonal interpreter I'll make sure it won't count against you. That's a promise."

Anna thought about the offer.

"I don't want to come back as a seasonal interpreter," Anna said finally. Jenny looked crestfallen.

"I don't blame you for that," Steve said. "Let me know when you'd like your last day to be and I'll get to work on the paperwork."

"No, I'm staying," Anna said. "I want to come back in law enforcement. I believe more women should carry guns. I believe armed women will make the world a better place. Women need to come to think of themselves not as victims but as dangerous." Realizing she was speaking too vehemently, she forced herself to smile, to lean back.

Steve looked at her for a long moment, his face unreadable. At length, his eyes crinkled at the corners as he said, "Anna Pigeon, you scare the hell out of me just the way you are."